The Code Hunters

A Nicholas Foxe Adventure

Jackson Coppley

Contour Press

The Code Hunters
A Nicholas Foxe Adventure
Second Edition

ISBN: 9798644003198

Published by

Contour Press

Chevy Chase, Maryland

www.ContourPress.com / / (301) 587-4343

To Ellen

The Code Hunters

A Nicholas Foxe Adventure

Chapter 1

Afghanistan

THEY PITCHED THEMSELVES INTO THE DARK, COLD NIGHT, 20,000 feet above the earth.

It was a high altitude, low opening descent, HALO for short. The acronym sounds ethereal, but at odds with a free fall dropping thousands of feet, the air rushing by at gale force. Their mother ship, the C-160 aircraft provided by the German allies, vanished into the night sky. The ground, devoid of the lights of modern civilization, floated below. When altimeters on their wrists read 3,000 feet, they pulled their ripcords. The sliders deployed, slowing and silencing the pop of the ram-air elliptical chutes that provided maximum guidance. The four men drifted about each other in the light of a quarter moon, aiming for the same few square meters of desert at the base of a mountain.

On the ground, they suppressed the air billowing their chutes, made their way to the team leader and huddled in silence. Intel indicated that no enemy would be near this spot, but caution prevailed in making their entry as silent and invisible as possible. Hand signals sufficed.

They were a team of experienced specialists, one that Central Command could direct to capture a key enemy mullah. With the chutes disposed of behind a clump of rocks, they made their way up the mountain. In the chill of morning air, the team waited in a secluded place. As dawn broke, they realized, too late, that the enemy knew they were coming.

In war, leaders make precise plans with well-thought-out contingencies. During the heat of battle, these plans go to hell. So it was with this team as the enemy surrounded them and they were hit by fire from all sides. A young Afghan boy who shouldn't have been there stumbled into the line of fire. No contingency plan for this moment.

A man makes a snap decision that sets in motion events beyond his imagination.

New Mexico – Two Years Later

EXPERIENCED CAVERS FORMED THE TEAM. The moniker 'spelunker' did not apply. Spelunkers once were scientists erudite in geology, but now the term is used for the general unwashed cave explorers. Cavers bring sophisticated equipment to navigate through challenges created by nature. "Cavers rescue spelunkers," say the experts. Tom Littleton, an experienced caver with chambers in the Pyrenees named after him, led the team. Carlsbad Cavern was well explored and tamed to facilitate the paying public. Winding trails bordered by chrome rails lead through limestone openings. Tourists usually were unaware of nearby cave systems much too dangerous for the novice. One, called Lechuguilla, resembled a child's ant farm enlarged a hundred times. It offered long drops where only rappelling experts could descend. Open chambers and lakes were connected by passages barely wide enough to crawl through. Littleton had already explored Lechuguilla's furthest known reaches but believed more remained to discover.

Tom had studied reports of a partially explored area. Cavers rumored the possibility of an undiscovered connection to Carlsbad. Littleton had heard of some half-hearted attempts. A suggestion by a stranger, and Tom's own ego, egged him on. *He could do better.*

The team winched into the shaft, one-by-one. Previous cavers had hammered and chiseled outcroppings, so that the trip down would be unobstructed. Yet it was laborious to lower equipment for a four-day exploration by means of rope and harness, piece by piece. Littleton and his two teammates worked for hours to get themselves and their gear down and set up a base camp.

The shaft's floor consisted of powdered limestone trampled by cavers before them. The sides of the shaft, jagged layers like rings of a tree, depicted years of sediment from prehistoric seas. It was a rough chimney through which a man could see the last vestiges of daylight. The air inside was cool and still.

Their bodies remained in tune with the sun. They took advantage of fading daylight seeping into the chamber to rest. After tonight, they would move into the depths of the cave where darkness became perpetual. Littleton shared a simple fare of beef jerky and tea with his teammates, Josh Peabody and Jeremy Miller.

Josh served as tactician for the group. He carried maps of previously explored areas and constantly referred to them. He was the man who assembled the gear for this trip and who checked each item to be sure nothing was omitted. In his early thirties and slight of build, Josh had blue eyes seldom seen. They were usually looking down, focused on a map or book, even as he walked along cave paths. It was no mystery why his helmet bore the most dings.

Jeremy was the contrast to Josh. Redheaded, sporting an inch-long matching beard, his fiery hair matching his lively personality. A mid-twenties man with a quick wit and a smart mouth, he was the teammate who constantly looked above and around.

Littleton was not a tall man. Growing up, the boys picked on him since his name fit his stature. But no boy ever picked on him twice. Quick to use his fists from an early age, he pelted his tormentors in an undisciplined series of punches, but they did the job. He had wanted to be an athlete. Baseball or track presented the only way forward for a small, but quick, boy. So, he became a pitcher from little league through high school. Then he discovered caving in his junior year.

Exploring caves was perfect for a man who could squeeze through tight spots. Yet something more made caving right for Littleton. Caves were another world, hidden from the one above. There, in that world, Littleton felt at home.

Littleton possessed a trait he took for granted, but one which his caving teammates assured him was rare. He had a well-developed 'proximity sense.' Many people experience that sense when they feel some unseen person is looking at them. Scientists suspect when we were prehistoric hunters, we had a well-developed proximity sense necessary for our survival. Even today, the blind demonstrate a sense for unseen objects in their path. For Littleton, that sense allowed him to know where the walls of caves were, even in the dark when he couldn't see anything. He sensed his teammates' positions without looking.

"You got everything?" Littleton asked Josh going through the checklist. Of course, Josh had everything. When did he not? Yet Josh, always the self-doubter, hedged with "I believe so." For Josh, 99% signaled failure.

"Well, that was easy," Jeremy quipped at the end of his descent. "This place looks like crowds have been here. Tell me again, why are we here?" He directed the question to Littleton who had convinced the team to come along. "Remind me."

Littleton took time to formulate an answer. How do you rationalize following a random rumor passed along by someone you don't know, mixed with a portion of gut feeling?

"It's all about the proximity to Carlsbad. No expert team's been here," Littleton explained, "Until now, that is." A modest boast.

Josh and Jeremy grinned. They were experts, and knew it, even the doubting Josh.

"I suspect there's a connection to Carlsbad," said Tom.

"And no one has found it because…?" Jeremy asked leaving Littleton to complete the statement.

"Because they looked in obvious places," Littleton

responded. "Look, most cavers have tried to connect through the shortest distance between two points. That makes sense sometimes, but not always. I think we should try the path less traveled."

"Which means?" Jeremy asked.

"Which means, Carlsbad is to the east," said Littleton, pointing over Josh's shoulder. "So we go west." He smiled as he leaned back, pointing a thumb in the opposite direction.

Josh had done his homework. "Well, it's true the teams before us went east. Few went in the other direction. But in that direction, it peters out. I imagine most thought it was a dead end."

"How far has anyone gone?" Littleton asked Josh, already knowing the answer.

"About 3,000 feet."

"We can do that in a day, maybe two."

"Yeah," sneered Jeremy, "If we have to crawl all the way."

Littleton laughed. "Some deep knee bends may be necessary."

The exertion of lowering gear and setting up camp made sleep come easily; each man cocooned in his sleeping bag to ward off the coolness of the cave.

The next day, Littleton led the team into the "path less traveled." The first 3,000 feet were mapped as Josh pointed out the previous day. The team maneuvered over fallen rock and pits dropping hundreds of feet. It resembled a roadway crumbled by a major earthquake. As they continued, they descended 500 feet below the surface, still short of the 750 feet to the floor of Carlsbad. If successful in connecting to Carlsbad, they would have to find a passage that dropped further.

After hours of arduous climbing over rocks scattered along the way, the channel opened into a room the size of a small cottage. The team sat for a rest as they drank hot tea from their thermoses and considered their next move. Hot tea offered the antidote to both dehydration and the chill they would feel when the sweat evaporated after their climb. Above ground was the dry New Mexico air where perspiration disappeared as fast as it formed. But this was another world and another climate.

The walls of the room were made of limestone with its dusty white surfaces streaked with the browns and reds of iron oxide and occasional blues of carbon deposits. Although the path was cluttered with rock, the entrance to the room contained only a few that had rolled in eons ago. The rest of the room appeared clear. Josh and Jeremy sat on rocks the size of inverted kettledrums sipping tea. Littleton walked the perimeter of the room studying the walls. He examined each crack carefully.

Something is here.

"Well, so much for this idea. No way out," groused Jeremy.

Littleton stayed mute, focused on the cracks in the wall. Josh and Jeremy wondered if Littleton's rumored proximity sense was at work. Then, he announced "Here!"

Jeremy and Josh rushed over to Littleton. "What?" asked Jeremy.

"There's another channel behind this crack."

Littleton stood aside as Josh, then Jeremy, looked into the crack, shining their helmet lamps deep into the darkness. "There's nothing," Jeremy said.

Littleton smiled. "Look down."

Jeremy stood on his toes directing the light downward. Josh followed him, returning Littleton's smile at his discovery.

"I see it. There's something there," Josh confirmed.

"Yeah," said Jeremy. "We just need to shrink to ten inches wide to squeeze in."

"Not necessarily," said Littleton as he turned his back to the wall, took out his pick, and struck the wall at knee level near the crack. The soft limestone crumbled into the opening. He looked at his teammates and asked, "Shall we get busy?"

The men took turns hammering away. The first blows pushed through thin limestone at the edges of the crack, but later hammering worked against thicker layers and the progress slowed. Three hours of work provided a fissure just wide enough for each member to squeeze through. Though exhausted, adrenaline motivated each man to push on.

Littleton took a coil of rope and a large piton from his pack. He hammered the piton into the rock outside the fissure, snaked the rope through it and wrapped it under his arms, tying off with a bowline. Josh and Jeremy slipped on their rough cowhide gloves and grabbed the other end of the rope as Littleton lowered himself into the opening. He hammered another piton on the inside of the opening near the top and clicked his rope into it. His teammates would use that one to lower themselves down.

Littleton rappelled down the wall for seventy feet when he reached the floor. "Clear!" he yelled up to Josh and Jeremy as he unknotted the rope. The men each rappelled in turn.

Caves may be wet or dry. Under the surface of the arid New Mexico desert, Littleton had discovered a wet one. His helmet lamp illuminated stalactites and stalagmites surrounding him in a narrow passage, their sweating surfaces reflecting light brought into this chasm for the first time. A small stream flowed on the opposite side. The perfect clarity of the water allowed a view of the bottom only a few inches below. It was a narrow stream in a narrow cave. The water flowed deeper and swifter in another age. The floor of the cave offered a flat path carved by the much larger river parent. Small rocky rubble, falling every century or so, littered the path. Littleton felt like the first man on a secret moon. Josh and

Jeremy were soon the second and third man to step foot in this hidden place.

"Wow," the simple exclamation from Josh.

"Yes, wow," responded Littleton. "And look which way it leads. West that way and east this way," pointing behind them and then forward.

"And east leads to Carlsbad."

"So, we crawled 3,000 feet west to turn around and walk east?" questioned Jeremy.

Littleton grinned. "Well, at least it appears to be an easy walk."

"Yes, but for how long? And 3,000 feet just gets us back to where we started. Carlsbad is beyond that," stated tactician Josh.

"Guess we better rest," said Littleton. "And get our supplies closer."

"Which are up that way," Jeremy grimaced pointing back up the way they came.

"After you," Littleton responded with a wide wave of his hand.

Caving is hard work, but one never wants to be far from supplies. So, the team had no choice but make their way back to base camp. They returned over the same rocky path, exhausted by their efforts and immediately fell asleep. After eight hours of sleep and a dose of hot oatmeal washed down with tea, they returned to the same path, this time taking supplies to last the next extension of their exploration. They set up camp in the limestone room that once appeared to be the end of the line. Each man lowered himself through the crack and down to where they stood the previous day, now armed with food in their bellies and fresh batteries in their helmet lamps.

Once down to the stream bed, they made rapid progress over flat terrain. The team walked cautiously, but easily, along the path. The bright light from their helmet lamps enabled a view of their surroundings. As they walked upstream, seeking the source of the water, they calculated they had passed the 3,000-foot mark. That put them approximately where they started, only far lower.

Forward is Carlsbad!

Without speaking, each man's excitement grew at the prospect they might discover a new connection. They progressed well along the way for another 2,500 feet as the water flow increased. The stream generated a gurgling noise. But as they moved forward, it was joined gradually by the sound of a distant waterfall.

"Listen," said Littleton.

"I hear it," responded Josh, not hiding his exhilaration.

A hundred feet more revealed a shimmering waterfall cascading eighty feet from ceiling to floor. They stopped in silent wonder. Then reality took hold.

"Seems to be the end of the line," observed Jeremy.

No exit appeared. The waterfall covered the back of the chamber. Once again, Littleton refused to accept there was no way out, but back. He walked on a small ledge to the right of the waterfall. "It's not the end. Come on," he yelled over the roar of the water. Then he disappeared behind the fall. Josh and Jeremy rushed to follow.

Emerging from behind the waterfall, wet with a mixture of salty sweat and pristine water, they entered a small chamber. Just large enough to squeeze through, it led from behind the waterfall for a little more than sixty feet, and then opened into a larger area. It was much larger than the limestone room from which they started, and equally dry. As each man entered, their helmet lamps searched the wall surfaces. This time, no way out but back seemed evident. Even Littleton appeared less optimistic. Jeremy put his hand on Littleton's shoulder. "Not bad, my friend. I believe we've discovered a large arm of this cave. Looks like we have naming rights. What do you think? The Jeremy and Friends Cave?" He laughed.

"Wait!' Littleton said. "Look at the floor." Littleton walked across the room, pointing down as he neared a cascade of boulders on the opposite side.

"What about it?" asked Jeremy.

"The floor here is smooth, as if graded, and not by water.

There is a place in Carlsbad with the same surface." Littleton's smile expanded as he patted one of the boulders. "I bet Carlsbad is on the other side of these rocks!"

Littleton had walked to the rocks around the left edge of the room. He returned walking directly across the middle. When he took a few steps toward his teammates, the earth gave way beneath him. He fell into an opening and disappeared from sight with only a cloud of dust remaining. Josh and Jeremy rushed over to the hole shouting Tom's name. Then light shown up from the opening. It beamed from Littleton's helmet lamp and bounced in all directions as though reflected from a large mirror.

At last, Littleton spoke. In a slow cadence he reported, "You are not going to believe what I found."

Chapter 2

Washington, DC

SOME CALL WASHINGTON 'The most important city in the world.' Most who say it live there, implying their own importance. The nation's capital is where special interest groups bid for 'access,' the catchphrase for attempts to curry influence for writing special deals into law. It's a place where history lives only in stump-speech rhetoric and the future spans only the time remaining until the next election. However, a discovery in a cave in a western state would change the future. The discovery had no lobby representation, no votes in the next election, and no sway in public opinion. Not yet. So, it was assigned to the lower ranks of a senator's office, waiting for its importance to see the light of day.

Senator Peter Howard Morrison was serving his second term representing New Mexico, a sparsely populated state of just over two million. Morrison looked the PR version of a politician, slim and handsome, six-feet tall with thick sandy hair and a smile full of bright enamel. He came from a family of politicians. Both his uncle and father were congressmen from Arizona and served as cabinet members for different presidents. Morrison knew his late father would be proud that his son surpassed him by graduating from the House to the Senate. He smiled often at the photo of his dad he kept on his desk, assured in that knowledge.

Like many from western states, Morrison grew up as a Mormon. Depending on the situation, he either touted or skirted his religious beliefs in public. In his private life, he couldn't remember the last time he entered an LDS meetinghouse. While not considered devout by his Mormon friends, Morrison nevertheless led a straight-arrow life. He appeared to be the good Boy Scout, but he did not gain his power by earning merit badges. He made deals in back rooms with the best of them.

He married Denise Anderson when they were both twenty-one, and now they were approaching fifty. Although a faithful husband, Morrison had plenty of opportunities to stray.

Denise was a natural blonde, a clean-scrubbed western girl and anchor in their family for her two boys. Morrison spent most of his time in DC and Denise seldom traveled with him save for election time. She grew up on a cattle ranch and anything but wide-open skies vexed her. She wanted western values for her boys and was satisfied they lived in New

Mexico. Evidence proved her choice worked well for the family. One boy was in medical school and the older brother, an attorney in Albuquerque. Denise suspected her lawyer son would follow in the footsteps of her husband and run for office. Contemplating that kind of future provided an ambiguous emotion of pride and dismay. Denise loved being at home with her children and they played a central part in her life. But now, with the nest empty, she felt lonely. Always with something to do, but at the end of the day, she remained isolated.

Randy Wayland served as a congressional assistant to Senator Morrison. Randy graduated from law school, near the bottom of his class. But his parents were friends of the Morrisons. Often, the option available for a low-achieving graduate with well-connected parents was a low-status job in a high place. Randy started in the senator's office a year ago and performed duties somewhere above fetching coffee and way, way, below drafting bills.

The office in the Hart Senate Office Building, where the location of one's space is based on affiliation and seniority, spoke of prestige. Senator Morrison occupied a fine set of offices from which he had a stunning view of the Capitol. Randy, on the other hand, shared a desk crammed in an open area of a congested office – once again, low status in a high place. Regardless of Randy's desk assignment, his disposition continued to be upbeat. He was a five-foot ten, sandy-haired, late-twenties, country boy in a suit. He always wore a white shirt, de rigueur for the Mormon missionary he once was. The senator thought Randy epitomized the word eager. Politicians are born eager, eager to win, eager to advance. Randy was pure eagerness. It was this one attribute, and the senator regarded it as a positive one, that made this kid stand out.

Randy had a girlfriend in DC and a girlfriend in Santa Fe, a girl in every port, or the political equivalent. He adhered to his religious beliefs selectively when it came to women. He had sex with Miss DC, but not yet with Miss Santa Fe. Randy morally divided his life between the chaste back home and the Gomorrah that is Washington.

A chain of events made Randy a player in the cave discovery when the senator's chief of staff, Ed Granger, stopped by Randy's desk. Ed had been the senator's chief of staff ever since Morrison's first term as a congressman. Ed was a skilled politics wonk and trusted advisor to the senator. This was unusual for a man from Brooklyn, a far cry from New Mexico. An average-sized man with an oversized gut, Ed had a face molded like playdough by a child with no sense of proportion. Eyes too small and close together, a nose twisted by a punch long ago, and lips that curled to one side when he spoke. Ed's looks destined him to be the unseen man behind the man.

"Hey, Randy," he said as he poked his head into the junior aide's area.

Randy sat up straight. The chief of staff seldom came to see him. "Hi, Ed," he responded.

"Here's a file I want you to look at," Ed said handing a folder to Randy. "Seems the folks at Carlsbad Caverns discovered something of interest."

Randy's letdown showed.

What could possibly be of interest at a tourist site out in the desert?

Ed continued, "This guy from New York, a rich fellow, pulled some strings with the Park Service and set up shop in the cave. Seems some explorers found an artifact in the caverns and this guy has lights on it and other stuff working around it. He even poked a hole in the wall to gain easier access to it."

"Really?" puzzled Randy. "Who let him do that? Isn't it protected or something?"

"Or something, I'm guessing," quipped Ed. "Look, are you heading back home anytime soon?"

"Yes, sir. I plan to go back for the weekend."

"Why don't you extend that trip a few days. Head down to Carlsbad and see what's going on. The senator wants to know."

The senator! Randy could see himself standing before the senator making the report. "Sure thing," he beamed. "Who's the point of contact?"

"It's in the file," Ed responded. "The rich guy from New York is somebody named Nicholas Foxe."

Ed left as quickly as he came. Randy opened the file and thumbed through it. There were the expected sheets of permits and papers from the Park Service granting Foxe permission to 'conduct archeological exploration.' Randy was dismayed. He now imagined a dull visit after a five-hour drive from Santa Fe to Carlsbad, only to find a crusty old man bent over a small piece of soil brushing away dust from an Indian relic. The perpetually upbeat Randy Wayland felt depressed.

He decided to do a little on-line research on Foxe. His search surprised him.

Photos of Foxe were plentiful. Randy was at first confused by various shots of several men from a different time and place, one with a handlebar mustache. He discovered there was a series of Nicholas Foxes. The Foxe currently in the cave was number three, Nicholas Bradford Foxe III. There was an extensive bio on the first Nicholas Foxe. Seems he invented a drill bit named after him and used by oil wildcatting westerners that generated the family fortune. Not much existed on Foxe the Second, but the web was full of postings about number three.

The family came from old English lineage. The middle name Bradford came from William Bradford, the first Governor of Massachusetts colony, from whom the family tree sprang. The current Foxe married the New York socialite Nina Westervelt, no children, now divorced. Nicholas Foxe III was a scientist with degrees in both archaeology and cryptography. This fact gave Randy pause. He expected the archeology, but *what was the cryptography about? What did they find? Some old Indian hieroglyphics?*

The photos of Foxe were certainly far from that of the crusty old man Randy imagined. Many were of him in a tux, tall with patrician-straight posture, brown hair. There was one of him, again in formal wear, playing a piano with partygoers gathered around.

Interesting.

Randy, lifted from his funk, now wanted to meet this man. A contact number appeared on the permit. Seemed to be a New York City area code. He called.

"Mr. Foxe's office," officiously answered a woman. "How may I help you?"

"Hello, I'm Randy Wayland from Senator Morrison's office in Washington." Randy enjoyed announcing himself attached to the senator. He gained a more alert response from the party he called. Not this time.

"Yes, Mr. Wayland?"

"Is Mr. Foxe there?"

"No, I'm afraid not. May I take a message?"

"The senator asked me to visit Mr. Foxe on site at Carlsbad Caverns where I believe he's working. Is he there now?"

"Yes, he is, in fact."

"How may I reach him there?"

"I'm afraid that's not possible," the woman said expressing routine disappointment.

"Why not?"

"Well, Mr. Foxe is hardly within cell range in the bowels of the earth. However, I can take a message. He calls in from time to time. When would you like to visit?"

"This coming Monday, if that's OK." Randy felt like a kid asking permission.

"I will check with him. How may I reach you?"

Randy gave the woman his cell phone number. She agreed to call the moment she had confirmation.

As he sat back and reflected on what lay ahead, he received a text message from his DC girlfriend, Julie. "Hi," she texted.

"Hi back at ya," Randy responded.

"Up to c me 2nite?"

"Sure."

"8 my place."

No question mark from Julie. Just like her. States it, doesn't ask it.

That was a turn-on for Randy. He can fly out tomorrow. Tonight, he'll have Julie.

The Stranger lives in a cabin surrounded by forest in Wyoming, isolated. The few who encounter him, when he comes into Jackson Hole for supplies, call him simply 'The Stranger.' The town folk share suspicions. "He must have been a linebacker. Look at the way he's built," the owner of the hardware store tells customers. But for what team? No one knows. The Stranger doesn't say. He says little.

Now, The Stranger is standing in a yoga pose on a mat outside his cabin as the sun sets over the mountains. He inhales pristine, pine-tinged air, seeking the peace that continues to escape him. At night, he looks to the heavens, each star bright against a black sky. He puzzles over the Big Dipper, as he does most nights.

This night is different from all others.

They found it. It's time to act.

Chapter 3

New Mexico

THE TREK TO CARLSBAD ANNOYED RANDY. Over 500 miles roundtrip from Santa Fe, just to see a boring archeological dig. Little did he know that one day he'd gain prominence as one of the few people to see it in person.

He had a 270-mile drive south on US 285 through Roswell arriving in the town of Carlsbad, a community of 30,000 citizens surrounded by barren, dusty plains and oil rigs. From Carlsbad, he headed west on US 180 to the park entrance where the elevation increased, along with the green foliage. Thick sagebrush and pinyon pines lined the small canyon road, ending in a switchback climbing the mesa to the visitor center. The center was a long one-story putty-colored building with views in all directions of the desert below beneath a clear late-spring sky.

A scattering of cars and SUVs occupied the parking area. Randy found a space a short walk from the center. A Park Service ranger assigned to meet him stood smiling at the entrance. The ranger, a man not much older than Randy, wore the standard Smokey-Bear uniform. "Hi," said the park employee from beneath a hat outsized for his head. "I'm Ranger Smith. It's not every day we get someone from the Senate to visit us."

Randy understood special treatment would come his way. In DC, senate aides were commonplace, but not here. Smith's boss probably counseled him to make a good impression on one who controls the purse strings. If he only knew how far down Randy placed in the purse-strings-pecking-order.

Nevertheless, Randy assumed the bearing of a senior member of Congress. "Good to be here."

"They tell me you want to see what's going on in the cave. I mean the exploration being done."

"That's right.

"OK, I first have to give you this," said Smith as he reached into his breast pocket and pulled out a pass. The pass, encased in plastic with a clip at the top, bore 'Visitor' in large letters emblazoned across the front and a scan code below. Completely out of place for a national park, it resembled a pass used at top-secret military installations. Smith didn't wear any badge. Randy wondered why.

"I can take you to the site. It's not far from where public tours go through the cavern. But I can't take you in," said Smith. "I mean someone there will escort you. Put this badge on and walk with me." Randy detected disappointment when

Smith told him he couldn't go in.

The visitor center resembled many in the park system, with a gift shop to the left selling souvenirs and a small café beyond that. To the right were counters with tourists buying tickets for guided tours. The tourists had the choice of entering the cavern from the opening outside, originally the only way in, or taking an elevator to the bottom. Smith didn't offer Randy a choice since he assumed the man had little time for a leisurely walk, but rather led him to a small hallway with two elevators on each side.

"So, what's this all about?" Randy asked. "What have they found?"

"I wish I knew. I've never seen so much secrecy. I thought you could tell me."

Randy didn't want to seem uninformed. After all, he was from Washington, right? He should be in the know. So, he told Smith what he did know.

"Well, a cave team led by a man named Littleton made the discovery; but, I understand the scientist Foxe is working on it now."

"You mean Nick?" asked Smith.

"Excuse me?"

"Mr. Foxe's name is Nick," smiled Smith, seeing he knew more than this guy from DC.

"You call him Nick?"

"Sure, everyone does."

A New York socialite-scientist that's buddy-buddy with the locals on a first-name basis is a twist. This wealthy scientist Foxe is intriguing.

Randy hadn't been to Carlsbad since he was a kid. He remembered the paved switchback descending into the large opening of the cavern. It led visitors over an asphalt path winding back and forth as it descended into the depths, a more leisurely way down the 750 feet to the bottom. Randy appreciated the elevator ride.

Randy followed Smith into an open elevator cab with gray steel sides and doors. Windows allowed visitors to see the stone walls of the shaft slide by on the way down. There were only two button choices: 'V' for visitor center, where they were now, and 'C' for cave. Smith pushed 'C,' the doors closed, and they began their descent. The indicator above the door, which in an office building would display the floor number, showed the number of feet from the surface, changing every fifty feet. Randy didn't recall the elevator from years ago.

Did he climb those paths back up?

Few do. It's not a climb for the faint of heart. But he was young then. He probably did. Now he enjoyed the rapid descent as the stone walls rushed by. After a minute and a half ride, the indicator read '750' and the doors opened.

They exited into a subterranean visitor center, complete

with a snack bar and seating under a massive natural dome. A hallway carved into the stone, off to one side, connected to restrooms. The subdued lighting, cool air, and silence implied a place deep in the earth.

A tour walked ahead of them, a group of retirees with cameras at the ready. Smith exchanged a nod with the other ranger who was providing a pitch about what the tour would see.

They continued their way along a paved path between stalactites and stalagmites. Randy tried to remember what he learned in high school science.

Which go up and which go down?

He noticed a bundle of black cables running along the edge of the path. The cables resembled rock-concert wiring connecting equipment for the stage. Randy assumed they brought electricity from the outside to the work site. The cables seemed fresh and clean as though they were just laid. The visitors' path turned to the right, but the cables continued straight ahead along a makeshift path of gripper plastic tacked to the cave floor.

"This is where the tour folks turn, but we go this way," said Smith as he led the way along the new path. The light from the public area diminished as they walked, and the walls closed in to where the two of them were within an arm's reach of either side.

They turned a corner and ahead of them a man stood guard, dressed in black head to toe, black turtleneck, black pants. His shaved head resembled a bowling ball perched on broad shoulders without the aid of a neck. He was large, in all dimensions. Mr. Big Guy stood by an opening in the cave wall draped with opaque plastic strips, the kind used to divide the cool meat department from the rest of the supermarket.

As they approached, Mr. Big Guy appraised Randy. He'd seen that look many times in DC. Secret Service agents wore it, club bouncers, too. Mr. Big Guy seemed teleported a moment ago from a joint in a bad part of town.

Smith, brandishing a smile, approached the man. "Drake, this is Randy Wayland. He has an appointment to see Nick."

Randy considered this man Drake. Smith seemed friendly with him. And there's that 'Nick' again.

Are they all pals here?

If so, Drake didn't provide much warmth.

Drake examined the badge Randy wore and, without further acknowledgment, held the plastic apart in a gesture for Randy to enter.

Randy stepped through, leaving Smith behind. He looked back to say something to Smith, but Drake dropped the plastic like a door closed in his face.

Looking forward again, Randy assumed he'd find Foxe in a solitary pose on his knees studying some relic. Instead, the scene before him looked like a space launch. Large LED crane-lights lit the room as bright as a nighttime construction site along an interstate highway. In the middle of the floor was a square opening fifty feet on each side, with an aluminum ladder peeking out the opposite side. Across the way from the opening were banks of computers and an array of instruments flickering a random combination of colored lights. A man stood in front of the instruments, holding a clipboard. His back was turned to Randy and he didn't notice him. So Randy called out to him, "Mr. Foxe?"

The man turned, spotted Randy, and looked over the edge into the opening. "Nick, your guest is here," he said. Although it appeared to be an active work area, the man didn't yell. It was quiet here. If tools were in use, they were silent at this moment.

"Be right up," came a voice from the opening.

The man at the instruments walked over to meet Randy. "Hi," he said as he shook Randy's hand. "I'm Tom Littleton."

"Littleton." repeated Randy. "You're the man who made this discovery."

"You've done your homework," Tom smiled.

"And you're a caver," stated Randy.

"Caving is my avocation. Computer science is my vocation. I've worked for Nick on IT projects over the years."

"I see."

"When I made this discovery, I knew Nick was the one to work on it."

"The senator is very interested in what you've found. What can you tell me about it?"

"You'll soon see for yourself," said a voice from the ladder. Foxe was just coming out of the opening and walked over to Randy.

Foxe was a tall man. The internet photos didn't indicate height. He must have stood six-foot four. Dressed in khaki pants and shirt, he looked the part of an explorer.

"Nick Foxe, at your service," he said with a broad grin and hearty handshake. His accent was New England WASP.

"It's good to meet you, Mr. Foxe," returned Randy.

"No, no, it's Nick. There are way too many Foxes. Need some differentiation, you know."

"Well, OK." Randy, uneasy with informality, did not repeat 'Nick' back to him.

"So, you're our representative from the Senate."

"Well, that would be Senator Morrison, I'm..."

"Yes, yes, I know. You're at the service of the senator."

"Well..."

"That's not important," Nick said, patting Randy on the shoulder as though they were old friends. "The important thing is that you're here and you'll see what we've got."

"About that..."

Foxe continued to interrupt. "I must tell you to keep this all very hush, hush, you see?"

"But…"

"We can't let everyone know what we've got. Would be bad. Couldn't solve the mystery with all the distraction."

"Mystery?"

"Yes, yes. Mystery. Quite a mystery. But, we'll get to the bottom of it."

"I'm afraid I don't…"

"Don't understand? Of course, you don't. But you'll see. Let's take a look, why don't we?" Foxe said as he released Randy and walked to the ladder.

Randy followed Foxe around the edge of the open pit to the ladder. "Follow me," Foxe instructed as he turned and climbed down the ladder with his back to the pit. Randy followed suit.

Foxe reached the bottom and turned with his hands on his hips to admire the discovery. Randy reached the bottom, turned, and gaped with astonishment.

Three sides of the pit were stone much like the white limestone above the pit, but here, the walls were carved as smooth as marble on a monument. The floor, covered with a fine stone powder, displayed footprints of those now working, at this moment, just Foxe and Littleton. Two cameras on tripods, one on each side of the pit, and a bright array of lights were focused on the fourth wall. That wall was not stone. It was metal, the whole wall. The metal had no rust. It appeared to be chrome, or aluminum or some other silver surface.

Randy tried to make sense of it. "Who put this here?" he asked.

"A more interesting question is 'when did they put it here?'" said Tom. Randy hadn't noticed that Tom had joined them. The two men looked at each other.

"What do you mean?"

"Until I fell into it, this pit was undisturbed, the ceiling untouched, and with no opening other than the one I made crashing through. The best we can tell, nothing touched this area for thousands of years, maybe 10,000 years."

"Right," responded Randy. "You've got to be putting me on."

"No, my friend," said Foxe. "Indeed, we're not. And if you find that hard to believe, come closer."

Randy walked with Foxe toward the metallic glistening wall. As he did, he could see small black dots arranged across its facade. Randy stopped, but Foxe motioned him to join him close to the wall. As he did, the dots and spaces seemed familiar, like something he'd seen before.

"What do these look like to you?" asked Foxe.

"I don't know," said Randy as he reached out to touch the surface, "But it does seem familiar."

Foxe grabbed Randy's outstretched arm. "No, no," he said, "No touching!"

Randy quickly withdrew his arm as though a snake had appeared. Foxe sensed Randy's fear and said, "Nothing dangerous - we think. Just don't want to disturb the markings."

"What is it?" Randy asked.

"We're not sure. But, at first, we thought it was binary code, you know, bits and bytes."

"I thought this looked familiar. The computer department at college had a piece of artwork at their computer lab that looked like this."

"But, alas," Foxe said with a shrug, "Nothing seems to jell. We've tried all sorts of combinations and computer modeling. There is something we're missing, and we can't quite put our finger on it."

"We can help. I bet the NSA has people who can break this code!"

Foxe squelched Randy's enthusiastic suggestion regarding government help. He put up his hands pushing Randy's idea away. "What?" responded Randy to Nick's gesture.

"Randy, the last thing we need is government 'help.'"

Randy's deportment cooled. "You're right. I mean, what if it turns out to be a hoax?"

"Hoax? Hoax? You mean someone put a metal slab,

weighing tons, 700 feet underground, as a party trick?"

Tom stepped forward as an intermediary between Randy and Foxe.

"Look," he said to Randy. "We appreciate the offer. We really do. Your office contacted us. We let you see what we're up to. But we need to keep this under wraps, at least for now. I hope you understand. Media attention would not help."

"Gentlemen," Randy stated, "You invited a man from Senator Morrison's office to see this. I'm hardly going to hide what I've seen from the senator.

"Well, actually, you invited yourself," Foxe said.

"Nevertheless, I've seen it and I must report what I've seen."

"Of course, you do," said Foxe. "Just expose as little as possible. Something on the order of 'they've found metal in the cave with markings they're trying to figure out.' You really think the senator would want to pursue this further, with all that must be on his plate?"

"No," admitted Randy. He understood the senator would have sent someone more senior if he considered it important.

"Good man!" said Foxe. "When things change, I promise you'll be the first to know."

The Stranger packed his equipment case. To the casual eye, it appeared to be a tool chest, one not drawing any suspicion, sitting in the back of his Suburban SUV. But once opened, one would see his tools included an AK-47, an automatic pistol with a silencer, and night-vision goggles.

Tools he was born to use.

Chapter 4

RANDY HIT THE ROAD AGAIN, taking an unplanned detour to the senator's office in Albuquerque. He received a text message from the senator's operations manager to pick up a package and take it to the senator's wife on his way back to Santa Fe. The glow of excitement from witnessing the mystery within the cavern had not yet diminished over the hours. Being relegated to delivery boy insulted a man in possession of a great secret. He remained conflicted.

Why would he minimize the discovery as Foxe requested?

He stopped by the office in Albuquerque and ventured no further than the front desk where a manila envelope awaited him. He didn't know the people who staffed that office. He saw them only at campaign events. The receptionist was busy but looked up long enough to hand Randy the envelope before a call interrupted and her attention left him. He turned with a "Thanks" directed at her. She offered a smile and a wave as she returned to the call.

Santa Fe, an hour north of Albuquerque and several degrees cooler, was the locale of choice by artists and retirees. As the state capital, it also contained people running the government. Buildings retained the look of a place founded by the Spanish long before the pilgrims of Plymouth Rock crossed the ocean. Adobe structures were the norm. The Eldorado Hotel in the town center appeared built by ancient Pueblo Indians who had come into possession of modern construction equipment.

The senator's ranch, set among rolling hills on route to ski slopes, could be reached in thirty minutes from downtown Santa Fe. Randy had been there before working events hosted by the senator as the background guy checking people into the party. This would be the first time without a crowd.

The senator maintained a working ranch, or more to the point, his wife operated a working ranch. She trained horses. Randy recalled the senator remarking about his wife and shaking his head. "I've lost track of the number of times we've taken her to the hospital, a horse throwing her and breaking something. She likes to tame wild things. Guess that's why she married me." A pat story in his oral arsenal, deployed often. Randy had heard it more than once.

The area was high desert, dotted by squat pinyon pines. Randy entered a drive bordered by brown wood fences enclosing the range where horses grazed. As Randy drove his rented Honda along the drive, a stallion with a shimmering brown coat appraised him, and trotted alongside as though he might race the car, but stopped, reconsidering the effort.

The end of the drive opened to a ranch house built in adobe style, but much larger than most homes in the area. To the right, sat whitewashed stables and a groom nearby combing the coat of a speckled appaloosa. In a corral beside the stables, a woman jumped a speckled mare over steeplechase hurdles. The woman was the senator's wife, Denise. No mistaking her, although Randy had only seen her before in more formal attire. He parked and walked to the corral to watch.

Randy had seen the horse farms in Middleburg, Virginia where the wealthy of Washington, DC had large tracts of land, but somehow her riding style seemed out of place here.

Steeplechase is more what the rich do back East.

Yet he enjoyed seeing the senator's wife ride, raising herself above the English saddle and bouncing with an up and down rhythm.

The senator's wife noticed Randy, rode over to him, and dismounted. "Hello," she greeted him over the fence.

"Hello," returned Randy. "I'm..."

"You're Randy Wayland, aren't you?"

She knows who I am!

She flattered him by knowing his name, although it's part of the job as a senator's wife to remember names. Randy knew she and the senator were about the same age, but she looked much younger, more like forty than pushing fifty. She was Randy's height, five-foot ten, blonde hair in a ponytail, her face bearing the weathered tan common to outdoor people in this parched climate.

Randy smiled. "So nice of you to remember, Mrs. Morrison."

"Please," she said as she opened the gate and walked her horse out, "call me Denise. May I call you Randy?"

"Sure, Mrs.... I mean, Denise." The cool, sophisticated manner, so natural to her, flustered Randy. He walked beside her as she led the horse to the barn.

"So, what brings you here?"

"I have a package for you."

"A package?" she asked as she handed the reins of her horse to the groom.

"Yes, well, actually it's an envelope."

"So, where is this package, or envelope?"

"I have it, in the car. Just a moment," Randy replied as he stepped over to the car, reached in to the passenger seat, and produced his delivery.

Denise glanced at the envelope, reacting as one who receives frequent items of no consequence, and tucked it under her arm. Randy wondered why it required his personal delivery. She asked, "Would you join me for a glass of lemonade?"

"Sure, that would be nice."

Denise continued, as they walked toward the ranch house, "So, Randy, you work in Pete's Washington office, don't you?"

"That's right."

"What brings you here? I'm sure it wasn't to deliver an envelope."

"Well, I live here. I mean when I'm not in Washington. I'm just visiting." He wanted to add, *And I've seen something amazing!*

"Visiting?" Denise paused turning the idea over once and then looked at Randy with a smile, "You have a girlfriend here?"

Randy answered, "Yes, I do."

"What's her name?"

"Doris."

"Doris," considered Denise. "What a nice, old fashioned name."

"It was her grandmother's name."

"How nice."

They reached the ramada of the ranch house and, as if on cue, a short, young maid in uniform brought a tray with lemonade and glasses and set it on an iron-legged table. They took their seats beside it.

"Thank you, Eva," Denise said to the maid.

The shade of the ramada cooled the warm day as Randy enjoyed the scene and the company. Randy felt flattered, yet uncomfortable. Flattered that he was having a personal conversation with the wife of the man he served, a man who had never afforded the same one-on-one with him.

Uncomfortable speaking to the person who had the ear of the man he served, an extra filter of conversation he was uncertain how to manage. He attempted small talk.

"I noticed you rode steeplechase. We don't see much of that here."

Denise smiled, "Well, you see, I grew up on a cattle ranch. I could cut off the balls of a bull with the best of 'em. Even before I started dating. Don't think that didn't intimidate the boys."

Randy winced at the thought, surprised by Denise's refined speech taking a right turn into cowgirl. Denise enjoyed Randy's reaction to her steer-production experience.

She continued, "Daddy saw his little daughter becoming more of a cowgirl than he liked. When I was coming of age, they discovered the ranch sat on top of a large reserve of shale oil. It put a pretty penny in Daddy's pocket and provided money to send me to school in the East where they turn out ladies."

She turned to Randy and winked, "But some of that cowgirl's still inside."

Randy allowed a chuckle. Denise disarmed and charmed, putting him at ease. Perfect for a politician's wife.

"Tell me about your girl," she said.

For a moment, Randy thought she meant the girl whose bed he just left in DC.

How did she know?

"Doris, isn't that her name?"

'*Doris.*' Randy realized they had just talked about her.

Why did he think it was his girl in DC?

"Yes, that's right."

"How long have you known each other?"

"We grew up together. She lived next door and we went to the same grade school. Then she moved away."

"Must have broken your young heart," teased Denise.

"Well, we were friends, but I think we were a little young to be friends that way."

"And then…" coached Denise.

"We met again in college. We both went to Brigham Young."

"And sparks flew!" said Denise.

"Not sparks, but we became good friends."

"And now?"

Randy blushed. "Much better friends."

"And when do you see her again?"

"We'll have dinner tonight."

"How long have you been here?"

"Three days."

"Three days, and you haven't seen, your 'special friend'?" asked Denise. "What have you been up to?"

Randy hesitated, unsure how to manage his first

opportunity to spill his guts. It resulted in a palpable pause noticed by Denise.

"Well…?" she smiled as though Randy had been up to no good.

"The senator asked me to visit Carlsbad Caverns."

"Why on earth would he do that?"

"Well, it seems a fellow found something there, and he's trying to figure out what it is and where it came from."

"What fellow?"

Randy sensed a tone of questioning familiar to a congressional hearing and he was on the receiving end.

"The guy who found it is Tom Littleton and the man working the site with him is an archeologist named Nicholas Foxe."

"Nick Foxe of New York?" asked Denise.

Randy witnessed a certain recognition of the name in her eyes. "Why yes, do you know him?"

"I don't know him as an archeologist, but I know him as a major donor."

Randy thought this explained things.

Major Donor? That explains how he got Park Service cooperation.

"Did he contribute to the senator's campaign?" Randy asked.

"I believe he did," said Denise, "but you would have to ask

someone on Pete's finance committee. I don't keep up with those things. But I've met Nick. I can't remember which event. There are so many. But I remember him." Randy detected something faraway in the way she expressed her remembrance of Nick. "Is he working at Carlsbad?"

"Yes, he is."

Denise drifted away from their conversation toward thoughts of fond memories. An uncomfortable amount of time passed before she continued with a simple, "Interesting."

Denise focused once again on Randy and asked, "So, what's he working on?"

"Well," Randy started, as he began the prepared statement he'd formulated. "A caver, Tom Littleton, found a relic when he was exploring the cave. He knew Mr. Foxe and brought him in to take a look at it."

"What sort of relic?"

Randy squirmed. "They've found strange metal in the cave with markings they're trying to figure out."

"What markings?"

"I'm sorry, Mrs. Morrison…"

"Denise," she corrected.

"Denise. The senator asked me to report this back to him. I just sent an email with a full report. I don't feel comfortable discussing it," he stammered.

Denise saved him.

"Of course," she interrupted. "I understand. I'm sorry. I know there are things I shouldn't poke around in."

"I didn't mean to be rude," Randy said, humbled.

"No, no," she reassured. "Think nothing of it."

Randy's cell phone beeped. Thankful for the timely interruption, he told Denise, "I'm sorry" as he pulled the phone from his pocket and looked at a warning message. "Darn," he said. "I'm about out of power. I need a charge."

Although Randy was talking to himself, Denise acted.

Plucking the phone from Randy's hand, she said "No problem, I'll plug it into my charger in the kitchen."

Randy began to rise out of his seat with a polite protest, "But…"

She cut him off. "No, no. You just keep your seat. I'll be right back."

Randy, uncomfortable letting his phone out of his sight, saw nothing short of wrestling Denise to the ground to get it back. She was a strong-willed woman with velvet boxing gloves.

Denise carried the phone to the kitchen near the charger, but stopped before plugging it in. The phone was still unlocked, and Denise immediately opened the email app. She found the message sent to her husband's chief of staff and read Randy's report.

Well, well. Nicholas, you really have found something here.

She had to know more.

Chapter 5

TWO DAYS LATER, Denise heard the helicopter before it crested the hills to the east of the ranch. Another beautiful afternoon in Santa Fe, the sky clear and stark blue, silence all around interrupted by her guest's arrival. A well-scrubbed, natural beauty who seldom wore makeup at the ranch, for this guest, she applied a little lipstick and eyeliner.

Was he as she remembered him?

The helicopter design was familiar, a sleek white fuselage with a set of doors for the pilot, separate from the doors and compartment in back for the passengers. She had ridden in them several times before, when people who put a value on their time paid the hefty price to avoid traffic. Nick's transportation in this helicopter seemed out of place here in New Mexico.

The helicopter stirred the powdery gray soil in a clearing some distance from Denise. The pilot cut the engine after touching down and Nick stepped out. Nick waved to Denise and she returned a raised hand.

Yes, except for his outfit, he was just as she remembered him.

The years had been kind. Dressed in khaki cargo pants and a shirt with twin button breast pockets, he looked every bit the world explorer. His confident smile had not faded.

Nick walked over to Denise and greeted her with a hardy, "Dee Dee!" Nick was the only person who ever called her that. He made up nicknames for people he fancied. That's the one he made for her, and it charmed Denise. He gave her a hug and a kiss on the cheek. It was a greeting suitable for public consumption, but the unexpected warmth Denise felt remained private.

"Nick, how have you been?" she asked.

"Busy, quite busy." He smiled.

"So, I understand. Let's go have a seat."

She walked beside him the short distance to the same ramada where she had entertained Randy. Eva came from the house to serve them. She had brought lemonade for Randy, sensitive to his religious customs. But for Nick, Denise announced, "I'm having a glass of wine, how about you?"

Nick turned to Eva. "Beer, please. Any IPA would be fine."

"My usual," Denise told Eva.

"Dee Dee, how good it is to see you again," grinned Nick. "How long has it been?"

"Oh, years, hasn't it? Where? New York?"

Many years had passed since their last encounter, but Denise often thought of Nick and wondered how things might have been different, *if only*.

"Yes, New York, a long time ago. I've never known you here," Nick said, taking in the horses running through the field near the barn and the corral where she trained them. He remembered her talking about all of this, but dismissed it as hyperbole uttered in a society setting. "You really are a cowgirl, aren't you?"

"You know me too well. Daddy tried to make me a lady, but it didn't take."

"Maybe it's a city-thing/country-thing. You outshone the society ladies at the party where we met. The jealousy was tangible. Even Nina."

Before Denise could respond, Eva returned with beer and wine on a tray. She placed it on the table between them as Denise waited for her to leave. Nick took the beer and quaffed a third of it.

"Did Nina know?" Denise asked.

Nick understood. He stopped drinking, smiled and said, "As a guy, I say no. But guys are dumb. Women know, don't they always?"

"You credit us with powers you shouldn't."

"Oh, you have powers!" he emphasized.

Nick expressed a confidence bordering on cockiness that might offend a woman, but he wore it like a comfortable old jacket and, on him, it was dashing.

"How's Pete?"

"Pete gives me everything I need. He's warm and generous," she responded with a pat answer.

Why was her knee-jerk reaction such a lukewarm commentary on her husband?

"Whoa, I meant 'how's he doing?'"

"Wow," she laughed. "I guess I've memorized that answer about our relationship."

"Easy, Dee Dee. We're not on Meet the Press. I didn't mean to grill you. Take it easy."

Although years separated Nick from the last time they were together, she realized 'taking it easy' would be difficult around him. She paused to sip her wine and changed the subject.

"It's nice that you were able to come when I contacted you."

"Well, I want to see if we're sharing a secret."

"A secret? Nick, that was so long ago."

"Not that. Something our friend Randy knows."

"You know that I know?" she ventured.

"Of course, I do. Randy visited, didn't he?"

Denise didn't expect Nick to know the comings and goings of people in Pete's office.

Did he have spies everywhere?

"Yes, he did," She replied.

"So, tell me what you know."

"The short version or the long version?"

"Indulge me."

"Well, I know you discovered something amazing. It looks like it's from the future, but it was buried in the cave thousands of years ago. Bright and shiny, has markings on it you're trying to decode."

Nick broke into a large smile and laughed.

"What?" she asked.

"Tom won."

"Won what?"

Nick took a moment to compose himself. He couldn't stop laughing, much to Denise's noticeable chagrin.

"Tom and I had a bet," he continued. "I bet Tom that Randy would spill his guts within a week. Tom said it wouldn't last more than twenty-four hours.

Denise frowned. "Well, Randy didn't spill his guts, at least not to me."

Nick raised an eyebrow. "Then how did you know?"

"I have my ways," she said with a sly smile.

Nick grinned. "Oh, I know you do. Have you told anybody?"

"You."

Nick knew Denise could twist a question to the answer she wanted to give, a political instinct.

"I mean anyone else?"

"Of course not."

Nick held his beer glass up as though to toast her. "Of

course not, you're a senator's wife. You're used to keeping secrets."

Denise threw her red cloth napkin at him. "You bastard," she said, but his laughing was contagious, and she joined in.

"Look," Nick said as he set his glass on the table and leaned in to Denise. "We knew we couldn't keep this a secret. It would leak out. You're just the tip of the iceberg. In fact, we wanted it to leak, in a controlled way."

"You did?" Denise was puzzled.

"Dee Dee, if a guy comes along, gets on TV, and tells the tale you now know, what would you think?"

"Well, if it was you, there would be something to it."

Nick waved that answer away. "No, no. Just imagine it was some guy you've never heard of before."

She thought for a moment and saw his point. "I would think the guy was a crackpot."

"Right you are. Now imagine if rumors started to float around the media and a reporter asked the person to verify the discovery and that person vehemently denied the rumors and wouldn't allow anyone near the scene. What would you think?"

Denise smiled at the logic, although her political instincts said it was risky, and said, "I would think there's something to it."

Nick clapped his hands once in a by-George-she's-got-it

moment and sat back in his chair with a smug expression.

"But why do you want people to know?" she asked.

"It's not all people. That's ours to control as best we can. But Tom and I are, quite frankly, stumped. We shared our findings with top cryptographers. And believe me, I know the best. Nothing. We realized we have to cast the net wider. I just hope we haven't opened the gates too far."

"But I told you, your secret is safe with me." Then she thought a moment. "But… do you want it safe with me?"

Nick smiled. "Look, I didn't know where the 'secret' would land. I'm delighted it was with you. But I suspect it hasn't found its final resting place."

"I see," Denise said showing apparent disappointment.

"Look," said Nick, "Let's give it a little time. If nothing happens, why don't we talk again?"

"OK."

An uncomfortable silence settled as Nick drank his beer and Denise sipped her wine. Denise broke it by asking Nick, "Would you like to see the house?"

"Certainly," he said as he rose from his chair.

Denise led him to the sliding door, turned and said, "Forgive the mess. We're repainting the bedroom."

"I'm sure we can make do." Nick smiled.

Chapter 6

Norfolk, Virginia

THE PAST FEW WEEKS had not been kind to Josiah Jones. The televangelist had been riding high on the word of God. Millions, coast-to-coast, were tuning into his weekly broadcast.

Ten years ago, he opened the Temple of Power, a state-of-the-art facility unmatched in the soul-saving market with its own broadcast facilities and seating for over 2,000 of the faithful. In his office in The Temple, he designed a ten-foot-high window behind his desk with the cross of Calvary etched across it. On the wall next to the window hung an oil painting of himself with Jesus behind him, the Savior's hand resting on Jones' shoulder. Jones holds a Bible in one hand and the two stare straight ahead into the eyes of the beholder. In the painting, Jones appeared more attractive than in real life. In reality, Jones was an average height man in his fifties with an abundance of white hair making him look taller than he was. He appeared fit, but middle age was not serving his middle well and some newsmen began calling him 'paunchy,' *the devils.*

He was the pastor of choice for Congressman R. Scott

Everson. Everson had been a rising star in the US House of Representatives, a young man who represented traditional ways, with a nose for evil like Joseph McCarthy and the ideology of Strom Thurmond. Jones was at Everson's side when he declared himself a candidate for president. He had Everson on his weekly show frequently. Everson helped make him, and now, Everson was his undoing.

"I can't see it. I just can't," bemoaned Jones to his wife.

"See what, honey?" asked Gloria, Jones' wife and closest counselor since they opened their first Church of Jesus, LLP in a poor section of Norfolk, Virginia.

"Why is everyone turning away? Attendance last Sunday was miserable. Viewership is down. Sponsors are dropping their contracts."

"Now honey, we lost just a few."

"Gloria, Liberty University just cancelled."

"Lord help us!" This was news to her. "They supported Everson, too."

"Not any more. They've pulled out. They said something about Everson 'getting soft on Second Amendment rights,' but I know that's not it."

"Honey, we both know what it is."

"But he didn't rape that girl."

"I know, sweetie."

"Besides, we all know she looked older than sixteen."

"That she did."

"And he's always been loving to his wife. I don't care what those women say. So, what if he had a mistress."

"Ah, two, sweetheart."

"Two?" Jones asked.

"Yes, he was a busy boy."

"But Solomon had a thousand concubines. No one doubted his wisdom."

"True, true. But that's not it."

"Oh, I know what you're thinking. He didn't mean to shoot that boy. Besides, it was self-defense, if he did. This is a stand-your-ground state after all."

"Honey, he was the paper boy."

"How did he know that? The man's usually not home. He's always in Washington doing God's work. He never saw the paper boy before."

"I know, and you defended him brilliantly!" praised his wife. "But you know what it really was."

Not able to bring himself to say it, Jones finally admitted, "It was the dog, wasn't it?"

"Yes sweetheart, it was the dog."

"That was unforgivable, treating that poor animal like that," admitted the minister of forgiveness.

"And, let's be honest here, we're late in the game. Everyone else has already abandoned Everson."

"Even Liberty University," Jones admitted with dismay.

"Even them."

"Lord help us," said Jones. "We're screwed."

Gloria, her dyed blond hair puffed fresh from the parlor, her fire-engine red lipstick perfectly applied, walked over to Jones in the three-inch heels she chose for today (she had over a hundred pairs to choose from), sat on the edge of the desk beside Jones and said, "Look at me."

Jones looked up from his stupor of self-pity.

"You've made it from nothing to this," Gloria said as she held her arms out to encompass the glory of the Temple of Power. "You will recover."

"You're right," said Jones. Gloria was always the spark he needed. "I just need to latch on to something to turn things around." Jones stood and began to pace the room, his ego restored. "The faithful need a model, something to believe in. The power of faith is mighty," he said, slipping into his tent-revival persona. "Anything is possible with it. Anything! People just need to have something to pin their hopes on."

"Uh, the good book?" Gloria said as she picked up the Bible from the desk.

"Yes, yes, of course," he said, clearly not what he was thinking. "That's always a good starting point. For everything! But," he said as he pounded his fist into his hand as though to beat out the answer. "There's got to be something more.

Something new! Something dazzling! But what would it be? What would it be?"

Chris settled into the nightclub couch, with Julie's arm resting along the edge, behind his neck. The dark room, a notch above a strip joint, offered metal music and overpriced shots of your choice of booze. Chris took a long drag from a joint and held the smoke deep in his lungs. It was the blissful high he needed to take his mind to another place, far removed from thoughts of his father's 'temple.'

He studied the joint as he exhaled. The fine trimming appeared to be an industrially manufactured cigarette and not the crudely rolled model he used to make in high school. He admired the workmanship of the Colorado import.

These guys have their shit together.

He passed it to Julie for a hit.

Chris was a slight man of twenty with dark hair and the complexion of someone who didn't get much sun. He couldn't attract a girl on looks, but succeeded by providing the things money can buy.

Julie was his latest girl. There were many. This one, Julie, bordered on gothic with dark eye shadow and black lipstick, but her dress was dark red, not black, and she wore heels, not boots. She was just enough of the devil's own to please Chris.

"Hey, Christ, what's up?" It was Jeff, another loser Chris attracted. Chris didn't have friends. He thought he had a bunch of clowns hanging around him.

"It's Chris, you bozo! You know how I hate that."

"Just messing with you, man," smiled Jeff, an overweight young man perpetually garbed in knee-length shorts and a tee shirt bearing a different message each day. Today's special: 'Yeah? And so are YOU!'

"Christopher," he said formally. "Man, your momma was cruel, naming you that. Kinda putting the family brand on you, huh?"

"Don't bring it up!" snapped Chris.

Jeff put his hands up in surrender. "OK, OK. I get it."

Chris succeeded in hiding his sinful life from his parents. Rather than acting the morose young man he was, he joined the family for dinner every night, dressed in a shirt and tie, echoing a loud 'amen' after this father's droning supplication. He knew his dad liked to hear himself speak and his excessive grace at meals probably taxed God's infinite attention span.

As time passed, Chris matured, which, in the case of the sociopath he was, meant skill in pandering to his parents to get what he wanted. The new Corvette outside was proof. He attended a Christian college where he found the professors amenable to providing passing grades to the son of a leading evangelist. Class attendance became optional.

His father wanted him to take over the family business one day. The thought was so depressing that Chris needed to import more of Colorado's finest pot for his expanding personal use. He wished the 'business' would simply evaporate. The latest ratings and attendance figures pointed in that direction, to which Chris would take another toke and smile. Daddy had accounts in Cayman Island banks and Chris knew the access numbers. His future looked bright. The temple could be retired, as far as Chris was concerned.

The waitress placed shots of Maker's Mark on the table. Chris gave her a wink and a C-note. There were a half dozen shots, enough for all. As Jeff and Julie joined Chris in picking up a shot glass, Jeff asked, "You're going to the concert tomorrow night, aren't you?"

"What concert?" asked Chris.

"Man, Distorted Vision, who else?"

"I don't know." Chris smiled. "What would Jesus do?"

"Oh, man!" Jeff groaned. "It's the same shit."

"Yes," Chris said, "It is."

Nothing more needed to be said. Jeff and Julie knew Chris had to be aware of his public exposure. This club had been 'sanitized,' as Chris put it. The bouncer was on his payroll and made sure no one took a photo of Chris. It wouldn't be smart to leave evidence of his visiting a den of sin. Unfortunately, rock concerts were too wide open for Chris to control. A small price to pay, he thought, for an otherwise open door to the life of Don Giovanni. Yes, Chris knew opera. He wasn't stupid.

How could a dimwit pull off the duplicity he lived?

"OK. I get it," surrendered Jeff.

"No problem. It's a good life," smiled Chris as he raised his glass in a toast. "To the good life!"

They all tossed down their shots.

"Let's dance," he told Julie.

Chapter 7

THE PARK SERVICE expects crowds, especially on holiday weekends, but nothing like this melee. Two cable news networks had positioned their trucks with satellite antennae prominent. Reporters facing portable lights, spoke into cameras, mikes in hand, and provided commentary. Day-trippers were blocked from entering the cavern by the mass of news people standing in front of the opening. The Park Service had cancelled tours, but the media event entertained the tourists.

How did this happen?

Like a huge snowball forming from a small pebble rolling down a mountain, the media frenzy escalated. But what was the pebble? What started all of this?

Had the senator's wife spilled the beans? Randy told his girlfriend over dinner in Santa Fe. Did someone overhear the conversation? Was it the girlfriend? Was she the source of the article in the online edition of a Santa Fe paper about 'a mysterious metal object being found at Carlsbad Caverns?'

That article caught the attention of a cable network reporter with a flair for making the mundane spectacular. The piece went viral.

Nick Foxe's vague description of his discovery piqued public interest, just as he and Tom intended. But the resulting media maelstrom exceeded expectations. To help cope, Nick brought in Barbara Monroe, a press relations woman he'd employed in the past. She would be his spokeswoman to the mob of reporters. Miss Monroe, a forty-something woman, worked political campaigns. Her short, dark hair, tall stature, and welcoming visage combined the reserve of a corporate CEO with the complicity of a confidant. To those who knew her well, she was Barbara, but to Nick, with his penchant for quirky nicknaming, she was BeeBe.

A large event tent housed the press office. When she emerged from the tent, a chorus of 'Barbara' and 'Miss Monroe' greeted her. She stopped and motioned to the dozen or so to quiet down. "I'll answer all your questions, one-by-one. I promise." She pointed to raised hands in the crowd as a light wind blew the flaps of the tent behind her.

The first reporter, a young blonde woman in a light blue suit, ready for on-air presentation, represented the cable news giant CBN. "What can you tell us about the discovery? What does it look like? When can we see photos? When can we go in and see it for ourselves?"

"Well," responded Barbara, "I didn't expect all the questions to come from one person."

The reporters laughed as Barbara's calm style settled them down.

"It seems you all have heard a lot about the discovery

already. I can confirm much of what you may already know. It is a metal object. It's inscribed with code the team is investigating. We believe it was left here a long time ago."

"How long ago?" echoed separate reporters.

"We don't know," she answered. "I know you've heard it's been there for 10,000 years. We don't know that to be true. Geologists believe the cave system was formed long before that time, but we don't know if the slab dates back that far."

"What does it look like?"

"It's a flat metal surface made of a metal similar to titanium, twenty-four feet wide and twenty-four feet high. It's sealed in place along the edges by rock. Tests show the slab to be eight inches thick with nothing behind it other than stone. Regarding photos, we'll have some for you before the end of the day."

"Why not now?" interrupted an older man with gray temples. Barbara recognized him from an investigative series on cable.

"We're taking special care in making them," answered Barbara. "We have requests from several universities that need the photos in a specific format. For example, a Stanford professor requested ultrasound analysis."

"Can't we send someone in?" asked another dressed in jeans and sweatshirt, a Rolling Stone correspondent.

"I'm afraid not," Barbara replied with feigned regret. "You

must understand this is a very delicate archeological site. We don't know what we have and we must preserve the site until we get some answers. Let's take another question," she said as she pointed to an evening news anchor she knew well. She didn't expect someone who covered major world events would be among the pool. She was surprised this story had that weight in the nightly news.

"Barbara, what can you tell us about the code written on the slab?"

"We have top cryptologists working on it. I believe we'll have answers soon."

"Some say it's digital code. Is that true?"

"Well, at first, it appeared to be like digital code," she cautioned. "But it follows no code we can determine."

"My question is this: How could some person or persons place such a thing, deep underground, thousands of years ago, something that appears modern?"

"We don't know," she said shrugging her shoulders. "We just don't know."

The reporter continued, "And why did they do it?"

The news conference lasted a few minutes more. As the questions grew redundant, Barbara called it to an end and entered the tent.

Nick sat in front of five monitors which provided the news on different channels. On a sixth screen, he viewed a two-way feed to the work site where Tom was setting up cameras for filming. Drake was out of sight, standing guard at the entrance to keep anyone away who may have slipped through the barriers outside.

"BeeBe," he said with a smile. "Excellent job!"

Tom saw her from his side of the feed and chimed in, "Yes, great job."

"Thanks," she said, looking worn out. No matter how many times she performed this routine, a letdown followed the adrenaline rush of the moment. "You see…"

Tom put his finger to his lips to hush Barbara as he drew her attention to a talking head on one monitor. It was Judy Thorpe, the fiery conservative commentator. Her steel gray eyes pierced the camera from under her brown, stiffly sprayed coiffure. The tag line superimposed below her read, 'Cave Find: Hoax of the Century?' Thorpe, known for vicious commentary, always used her signature line, 'Give me a break.' Nick didn't want to miss a word.

"The press is having a field day, ladies and gentlemen. They've taken off to the desert to cover a discovery being worked by playboy archeologist Nicholas Foxe."

"Playboy?" Nick grinned. "No one has called me that before. Kind of like it."

"What have we learned? It's a big slab of 'mystery metal' buried in a cave and it has markings on it that look like a computer punch card."

"That's Hollerith code, you ninny," Nick yelled at the screen, offended by the misrepresentation of the binary-like code they found.

"Shush," said Barbara who was now focused on the commentary.

"And get this," continued Thorpe, "This modern slab is not modern at all. It was buried thousands of years ago. Give me a break!

"Folks, those of you out there who believe in aliens must know Roswell, New Mexico, is just up the road. You know, the place where a spaceship from another galaxy crashed years ago. Maybe those little green men made a stopover at Carlsbad Caverns for a picnic and left this slab behind. Give me a break!

"Are we to believe people thousands of years ago had the wherewithal to create titanium, and that they used, not hieroglyphics like the Egyptians did, but some computer code; and also, they could bury something like this deep in a cave without a trace around it? Really? What's going on? Is Foxe planning to open a new tourist trap? Why? He's got more money than God."

Nick breathed a sigh of relief. He didn't want exaggerated publicity enveloping this event. The news generated the interest he needed. He was working with the best universities in the world and had an established lifeline to each of them.

Thorpe calling this a hoax was pitch perfect. The learned people he now worked with had seen enough to understand this was not a hoax. He was on to something. Then Thorpe continued.

"But," she said with a serious gaze into the camera, "What if this is real? Wouldn't that shake the world?"

"Damn," said Nick.

Senator Morrison kept news channels going on three screens in his Capitol Hill office, all muted. When Thorpe appeared, he turned the sound up. He always got a kick from what she had to say, but wasn't so sure today.

The senator summoned his chief of staff, Ed Granger.

"You saw Thorpe?"

"Yes," confirmed Ed.

"What do you think?"

"With all due respect, Pete, I think we might have a shit storm."

Denise watched as well from the living room of her Santa Fe ranch. As a politician's wife, she sensed the public pulse. Without being in the same room and far across the country, she shared Ed Granger's appraisal.

What was not on Ed's radar was her relationship with Nicholas Foxe. Would the publicity surrounding Nick expose that?

Should I take preventive action?

The Reverend Josiah Jones was a Thorpe fan as well. She skewered the same unholy liberal targets he did. He watched the whole thing, alone, from the comfort of his office in the Temple of Power. At the end of the segment, Jones turned off the TV, picked up the Bible from his desk, and, holding it in both hands, looked to the heavens with a smile and said, "Thank you, Lord!"

The Stranger followed the news on the Suburban's radio as he drove south from Wyoming. Listening to the events unfold at Carlsbad, his well-honed instincts were working overtime.

I need to get there.

They're in for a world of hurt!

Chapter 8

Cambridge, Massachusetts

HER WARM BREATH fogged the frosty air of an unusually cool May morning as she jogged along the Charles River. The run by the river, with Boston's skyline across the way, cleared her head as she prepared for another day on campus in Cambridge.

Rachael Friedman was a twenty-six-year-old assistant physics professor at MIT specializing in string theory. Standing five-foot seven with a boyish build, but at second glance, she had a figure too shapely to fit that description. She wore black thermal knits with grey stretch athletic pants in the winter, changing only to black tee shirts in warm weather. She moved like a gymnast heading across a mat at the Olympics, ready to display her moves before a panel of judges. Her foot-long ponytail (her auburn hair was always in a ponytail) swung like a pendulum as she darted to her destination. She exuded intensity in everything. Anyone on whom her deep green eyes focused felt it. This included her partners in the bedroom. Rachael was a woman who selected whom to bed, the dominant force in the encounter, never letting emotions interfere.

Rachael burned her excess intensity by running, four miles a day, never marathons. With nothing to prove, she did not need to compete. She expressed passion at the keyboard of a piano and played. Very well. Invited to enter Curtis Institute, an honor few receive from the prestigious Philadelphia conservatory, she chose Harvard instead, to major in physics. But a Steinway occupied a central portion of her apartment in Cambridge. That possession and a Harvard education spoke of privileged wealth, which she had through a family trust fund.

Daddy was an investment banker who left Rachael money when he died a few years ago. Dad was the much older husband of her mother, a violinist for the New York Symphony. Mother joked that Rachael's father made an odd choice for a trophy wife. She thought all the ballerinas and models must have been taken. Rachael grew up in New York, educated in the best private schools, skipping grade levels. Rachael surpassed everyone in what seemed to be everything.

Rachael was content with her life. She entertained herself in the evenings, sometimes with a man, but always with her piano. Her only love interest was Chopin and his preludes.

She excelled in her professional career and papers she wrote in physics won praise. She needed no praise from her colleagues, no ovation for her private piano concerts, and lived comfortably in her own skin.

Rachael had many colleagues in her department with whom she spent time arguing theory, but she counted a man in another department as a friend, a father figure, although not much older than herself. Everyone was older than Rachael, young for her position.

Simon Greenwald, a professor of geology, was near forty, with a wife and two kids. He was average height, slim build, but with a belly that attested to many sedentary hours. He had thick sandy hair, randomly combed, and he displayed a warm smile. Rachael would drop in on Simon from time to time to take her away from her professional pursuits. His science was quite different from hers and discussions stretched her thinking. Most of all, she enjoyed his personal observations. Rachael considered him the reality check she needed from time to time.

Simon once shared what he called the 'only physics joke he'd ever heard' whose punch line became a code he used for oversimplifying the real world. The joke was that a large dairy started a research department. Besides hiring chemists and biologists, the research VP decided to hire a physicist. The head of the lab determined that each person should show what they'd been working on. For the physicist, he went to a blackboard, took the chalk, drew a circle and filled it in saying, "Assume a spherical cow containing a uniform density of milk." From then on, when Rachael began a simplistic explanation, Simon would say, "Assume a spherical cow…"

Rachael, one day, would recall when Simon changed her life, not by intent, but as in most life-altering events, purely by chance.

Why did she stop by his office that day? Why did the photos on his desk attract her attention?

All by chance.

"What's this?" she asked Simon as she picked up an eleven-by-fourteen photo on his desk.

"You know about the discovery in New Mexico," he said. "The one with the mysterious slab?"

"Sure, it's all over the news."

"Well, that's a shot of it."

Rachael felt a strong attraction to the photo, as though it taunted her.

"Why do you have it?" she asked.

"Oh, the department is looking at soil samples around the slab and the walls. I couldn't tell you the metallurgy, but it has the experts stumped. Nothing out of the ordinary about the soil, it's the same as the limestone in the rest of the cave. It's a mystery how the slab is sealed in place as it is. The people who did it knew something we don't."

"What do you mean?"

"The limestone's fused into the slab," responded Simon. "I couldn't tell you how to do that. It's as though the rock grew into the metal, clearly impossible."

Rachael was intrigued. "Mind if I borrow this?"

"Sure," replied Simon, surprised at her interest. "What do you see?"

"I don't know," she said gazing at the photo as though her intense focus would reveal its secret. "Maybe nothing."

Rachael returned to her office and set the photo on her desk, as she began the drudgery of reviewing student papers. As she worked, she couldn't ignore the photo. She picked it up, examined it, and put it in her messenger bag. Better to put it out of sight.

The sun began to set as she left the office. She walked onto the sidewalk with her bag snug across her chest, hanging under her left arm, keeping her hands free as she jogged back home. She admired the sunset lighting the sky in soft pink hues, but couldn't stop thinking about the photo.

It appeared to be code, perhaps binary, but Simon told her that top cryptographers had run it through thousands of algorithms and could not break it.

They had even looked into goofy ideas like standing at a distance to see if the dots formed a picture or laying the dot grid over a geographic map to see if it depicted locations on earth or in space.

Rachael lived on the top floor of a nineteenth-century stone and masonry mansion converted into apartments. It had room for her Steinway, always a priority.

As she entered her apartment, Rachael tossed the messenger bag in a corner, walked to the kitchen, a small space adequate for one who didn't cook, and poured a glass of merlot. She returned to the living room, kicked off her running shoes, and, as she sipped her wine, studied her bag as though she was bestowed with x-ray vision. Rachael set her glass down on the one clear spot of a coffee table otherwise covered by books, technical papers, and magazines, and picked up her bag. She took the photo from it and relaxed on the couch sipping wine and looking at the photo.

What did she see?

It was though a modern painting appeared before her, her subconscious aware of something abstract attempting to communicate.

Her cell phone dinged as a text message arrived. She put the photo on the coffee table and stepped over to her bag to retrieve the phone. David sent the message, asking what she was doing. David worked as a singer in a soft rock band in a neighborhood tavern. Hardly a band to fill a stadium, his group entertained a handful of drinkers with nothing better to do. But Rachael found him charming with his brown hair, parted in the middle, hanging over his ears, and his doleful expression during his stage performance. His personality changed to a wide-eyed optimist when he sat with her over a drink. He was no intellectual challenge for Rachael. However, that wasn't what she sought tonight.

She texted, 'Just hanging out. Like to come over?'

Rachael smiled, knowing the ultimate direction David's visit would take. The warmth she felt made her forget the photo, if just for the night.

Chapter 9

HOW A NEWS ITEM catches fire is hard to tell, but 'The Tablet,' as the media now called it, was hot. 'Slab,' an accurate metallurgical description, lacked flair. 'Tablet' spoke of messages, as those held by Moses with the word of God.

The internet buzzed with the news and did what the internet does best, distort reality like a house of mirrors. Conspiracy lunatics had a field day:

- The United Nations planted The Tablet with instructions for their takeover of the United States.
- Aliens left The Tablet behind to prepare for an invasion.
- The National Security Agency created The Tablet to record the names of each gun owner in the country.

However, the theory that took root did not spew from the internet, but from the mouth of Reverend Josiah Jones. His first Sunday sermon after the breaking news of the discovery signified the start of his career revival. His diminished flock heard it first, but word spread and the rebroadcast over the Christian Cable Network reached an all-time viewership.

"Folks, remember Moses?" he began. "The Lord God summoned Moses to climb way up high on Mount Sinai. He wanted a meeting. A meeting with God? Can you imagine such a thing? But when God calls, you do what God instructs.

"What happened when he got there? God says to Moses,

'Moses, my people are sinning, but they don't know it. They need guidance, Moses. They need their Lord God to tell them plain and simple what they can do to remain in His grace.'

"God's presence was mighty, and Moses had to look away or be blinded. But he shielded his eyes as he looked toward his Lord God and said, 'What is your will?'

"Now what did God do? He said, 'Moses, take up those two tablets of stone and let me write something for you,' and he did. What was it he wrote? Well, ladies and gentlemen, he wrote the words we can see up there on top of the Supreme Court, in many courts around the country where the heathen liberals haven't banned them, but they are right here in this Bible. I'm talking about the Ten Commandments!"

Jones held up a Bible and pronounced, "Can I hear a hallelujah?" The crowd joined in a hearty round of hallelujahs.

"And now, ladies and gentlemen, the Lord is once again speaking to us. He left us a tablet to discover. It's a new age and the Lord doesn't use stone these days. He uses space-age metals and computer code. He speaks to us in ways we can understand.

"Now they tell us the scientists are at work trying to figure out what the code means. Scientists! What good are atheist scientists when working with the word of God?

"But folks, God works in mysterious ways. When that tablet was uncovered, the light of God shone in my eyes. A vision as clear as all of you before me. He told me what it was, and for that I praise his name! Can we say 'Amen'?"

The congregation shouted, "Amen."

"Now, 'what did He say Reverend Jones?' you ask. What did He say?

"The Lord God said we are wicked. Yes, all of us. You and me, too. We are wicked and have to change our ways. He has a plan, and The Tablet shows the way."

The reverend spent another fifteen minutes repeating that the Lord says humans are on the road to hell, but the Lord seemed short on details. It left Jones the opportunity for his followers to tune in next Sunday for further revelations. And each week, his following grew.

Carlsbad was consuming more of Senator Morrison's attention than he liked. The national media's focus on a small corner of his state irritated him. He had battles to fight, and this drama was a distraction. The Bureau of Land Management owned property in the area where oil interests sought to drill. His friends in the oil lobby pressed Pete daily to do something to advance their agenda. The president represented the opposition party and had no reason to rein in the Bureau. On top of that, the show in Carlsbad starred

Nicholas Foxe. Pete counted Nick as a donor, but he didn't need the press nosing into the relationship between Nick and Denise. He believed if there had been anything serious, and he preferred to think there never was, it was long over. Pete was a trusting husband, but he followed Ronald Reagan's philosophy: Trust, but verify. Denise knew of her husband's trust but was in the dark as to his maneuvers to verify.

Randy swore that he told no one the details of what he saw in Carlsbad.

"Details," snorted Pete. "That boy will be a politician after all, hedging with a word like that." Pete knew Randy dropped by the ranch to deliver a package to Denise.

Did Denise have something to do with this?

He was not aware of Denise and Nick seeing each other again and would know if she took a trip way down to Carlsbad to visit. Pete didn't even like them being in the same state. He longed for the whole discovery brouhaha to go away.

The bomb maker worked from a backroom in Queens. He was a fat, bald man in his fifties who seldom saw the light of day. A mole of a man in overalls, he made a special product for a special clientele. He scoffed at the kids making homemade devices in pressure cookers.

Amateurs!

His were military grade plastic explosives, C-4 and Semtex.

Nothing but the best!

His customers could choose cell phone detonation or the always-reliable timer.

The man who walked in one day seemed to know his way around. The bomb maker's sources reported he could trust this new guy. He said he was buying for someone else, but that's what they all say. The bomb maker worked with some unsavory characters and this guy was as menacing as they came.

The customer bought three custom jobs, all with timers. "Why not cell phone models?" the bomb maker asked. "That's what everyone wants these days."

The man growled, "Cell phones don't work where these are going."

Chapter 10

SATURDAY, RACHAEL'S DAY TO SLEEP IN. The night before refreshed her. Lovemaking with David, now lying asleep beside her, helped. He proved to be a good lover, but Rachael seldom allowed her partners to stay the night.

Could she be getting soft?

She slipped out of bed and pulled on a large nightshirt. The white shirt, emblazoned with 'MIT' in large letters, came to her knees. It was a gift. She was proud of being on the faculty of a leading university, but disliked walking around with an ad across her chest. David mumbled and turned, but remained asleep.

She set a kettle of water on the gas stove to heat for coffee, took a bagel from the bag David brought, and placed it in the toaster.

Presumptuous of David to bring something for breakfast last night.

He gave her the bag with a wink, saying something about them being a day-old deal. Guess his idea of charm was a display of frugality combined with assumptions as to how the night would turn out.

Yet another reason not to get emotionally attached.

She looked out of the six-foot high, arched pane window

overlooking a residential street where few people stirred this weekend morning. A light frost painted the window. Spring refused to usher winter away and the chill of the morning competed with the radiator beneath. Rachael loved the warmth of old-fashioned steam heat, a charming, but costly anachronism for heating an old, drafty apartment. Her mind wandered to thermodynamics rather than romantic notions. If romantic notions lived within Rachael Friedman, they remained in undiscovered lands.

David rose from the bed, pulled on his white boxer shorts and stood behind Rachael holding her shoulders and kissing her neck. Though romance evaded her, tactile pleasure did not. She felt David's arousal against her back beckoning her to return to bed. The steam kettle whistled, ending the moment.

"Steady, fellow," she told him as she walked to the stove and extinguished the burner.

David stretched and then noticed the toaster where the bagel had popped up. "Got a bagel for me?"

Rachael scooped coffee into a French press, poured the hot water from the kettle, and responded to David, "Go ahead," relinquishing the bagel she had intended for herself.

He walked to the toaster, pulled the slices out and dropped them onto the counter, blowing on his fingers to quell the heat from the bagel. "Got butter?" he asked.

"What? No schmears? You shortchanged me," she grinned.

"The butter's in the fridge."

David's lack of grace the morning-after ought to annoy her, but she desired what occurred last night. Morning charm was optional. She put the top on the French press and squeezed coffee grounds from the water, poured a cup for herself and offered another to David who was slathering both halves of the bagel with butter.

"Thanks," he said, licking butter from his fingers and accepting the cup. "Got cream?"

Why doesn't this man think? He was just in the fridge. A quick check would have told him.

Rachael was reaffirmed in her refusal to maintain a man in her household. She remembered her mother's counsel with the adage, 'Why would a man buy a cow when he gets the milk for free?' She was not a cow, and it was she who gained the product without the price.

"Yep, in the fridge," she said, but David was already poking his head in the appliance's door without success. "Upper right in a red carton."

"Got it," he announced.

David poured a healthy dose of cream into his mug, fetched a spoon of questionable cleanliness from the sink, and stirred. He munched the bagel held in his left hand and washed it down with the coffee from the mug held in his right. Rachael beheld the metamorphosis of her Casanova of the night before into a morning slob and snickered.

"What?" said the perplexed David, as he chewed.

"Nothing," she said sipping her coffee. She put a bagel in the toaster for herself and waited with her coffee, amused watching David eat his.

David walked to the couch, about to sit, when he spotted the photo from the cave. "What's this?" he asked.

Rachael joined him and picked up the photo to save it from butter smears. "It's something I got from Simon, a geologist friend of mine."

"What is it? Looks like an airplane body with pit marks."

Out of the mouth of babes comes an interesting observation.

"You hear about the discovery in New Mexico?"

"Discovery? No, guess not."

David was cute, a great lover, but hardly in tune with world events.

"This is a picture of something found in a cave in New Mexico. They think it's coded information, but they can't figure out what it means."

"Who put it there?" he asked.

"That's the sixty-four-thousand-dollar question."

"The what?" he asked, doe-eyed.

David didn't seem in tune with old expressions either.

Why do I have him here?

David answered her unspoken question when he finished

his bagel, came close with the mix of garlic and butter on his breath, and kissed Rachael on her neck. She felt his moist lips with a few seeds mixed in as though she was the next item on his breakfast menu. She put the photo back onto the table and allowed David to feast.

After an abbreviated reprise of the night's lovemaking, David realized he was late for band practice, threw on his clothes and headed to the door with a quick kiss on the cheek for Rachael. Glad David left, she promised herself to limit his visits in the future. She had no desire for a live-in and feared the relationship was heading there.

Rachael slipped on her nightshirt again, walked over to the coffee table, picked up the photo, and puzzled over it.

What am I missing?

Needing to put it out of her mind, she sat at her Steinway, where she could always clear her head. Rachael knew music stimulated a different region of the brain and that part could use a little workout.

She started with Chopin's Prelude Number 20, short but strong and majestic. She loved to start with this piece but never played it for anyone else after a friend mistook it for the start of a Barry Manilow tune. The crooner borrowed this prelude for the introduction of a popular song time would forget long before the master's original work. She moved on to

Chopin's Number 4, *largo* with a rhythmic heartbeat in the bass, chords descending the scale. As she played, the image of the photo, burned in her memory, reappeared.

Why did the music bring it to light? Could there be a link?

She stopped and went over to the kitchen junk drawer to scrounge around until she found a magnifying glass. She remembered the man she entertained one evening who had used it as a prop in a local playhouse production of "Young Sherlock" and the sleuthing of another nature that occurred later that night. Only a passing thought, however, as she now needed it for its intended use. She walked over to the photo and, with magnifying glass in hand, put the photo on her desk and turned on the high-intensity desk lamp. She scrutinized the photo under magnification and soon laughed out loud.

I've got to go to Carlsbad!

Chapter 11

NICK AND TOM didn't spend their entire day in the cavern. Although the depths of earth where time of day didn't exist, seduced them into spending far more of their lives there than expected. Nick called it 'the casino effect' after gambling establishments where no windows or clocks existed. The pursuit of the next throw of the dice, or deal of the cards, promised a big win and made time vanish. However, this subterranean establishment provided no gambler's lucky streak. They continued to be stumped. Exhausted, Nick and Tom called it quits for the day and headed home. Due to the outside attention now paid to the site, Nick hired more guards and Drake stayed as one of the new shift workers. Nick said goodnight to a new man at the site portal and glanced at his watch. It was four a.m. He guessed 'goodnight' was the right acknowledgment in a place of perpetual night.

There were no tourists at this early hour. Nick and Tom rode the elevator alone the 750 feet to the surface. Nick pulled out his cell phone and summoned his driver. The number of reporters camped out had dwindled. The driver needed to take no evasive action to get Nick home, unlike the first week of the breaking news. Only three weeks later, the site was back-page news, except for a televangelist and conspiracy theorists.

Nick rented a house in Carlsbad. It was a classical Victorian built by an oil baron in the early twentieth century. It was on the market when Nick's agent struck a rental deal. It had been a B&B for a time and was furnished like one, making it an agreeable place to stay, although too lacy and quaint for Nick's taste. On the drive, Tom fell asleep, but Nick continued to be preoccupied. They had exhausted every bright idea the experts had thrown their way.

What were they overlooking?

The driver dropped them off at the house. Nick nudged Tom awake and they both headed to their rooms. Nick's fatigue overcame his pondering and, after taking off his boots, he fell fully clothed into bed and was asleep immediately.

It was mid-afternoon before Tom woke. He passed the closed door of Nick's room, the muted snores told him his cave buddy was still catching up on long neglected rest. Tom walked down the staircase into the kitchen, a place still equipped to feed a dozen overnight guests. The woman hired as a live-in housekeeper, Lizzy Rodriguez, greeted him. Lizzy was the offspring of a mother from Albany who followed the Grateful Dead and who fell for their roadie Ernest Rodriguez. Blue eyes and blithe disposition, she got from her mother. The dark complexion, from her father, or at least so she surmised from the photo Mom carried with her, the only link to the man she never met. Lizzy joked that she got the job sight-unseen because the employment agency thought the name Lucinda Rodriguez was a likely name for a housekeeper. The employment agency never laid eyes on the young woman in jeans and white tee who now stood before Tom.

"Good morning," her cheery greeting. "Coffee?"

"Yes, please," responded the somnolent Tom.

Lizzy popped a cartridge into the coffee-by-the-cup machine. She had told Nick and Tom when they first met that she made great coffee, but their odd hours and never knowing when they would be around, made this on-demand machine necessary.

"You boys out late last night? Partying it up, eh?"

"Yeah," Tom scoffed. "We're partying all the time."

Lizzy knew more details than most about their discovery since she lived with the men responsible for it. She had been in the cavern before. Everyone in these parts had. Yet, she never suspected there were so many lesser-known caves surrounding it. But then, she didn't think about caves much. Who does? But when she met Tom, a real caver, she felt compelled to know what drove him to spend so much time in such places.

"Why do you do it?"

"Pardon?" Tom said, as the first sips of coffee failed to lift the haze of sleep.

"Why do you like to spend time in caves? I mean, I've been in Carlsbad. It's beautiful and all, but I was walking on sidewalks, like through a park. You crawl around all those rocks, and some places are pretty tight."

"Yes," smiled Tom. "It's true."

"And you never know what's in front of you."

"Or sometimes, below you," Tom said.

Some people assumed Lizzy was an airhead. After all, she was the product of a mother following a rock band and lived in a trailer park. But it did not take long to find Lizzy was very bright. She knew Tom was referencing his fall into the chamber where The Tablet was found. That discovery fascinated her.

"Tell me about The Tablet," she asked.

"You too?"

"Me too, what?"

"You're calling it 'The Tablet,'" answered Tom. "That name seems to have caught on, hasn't it? 'The Tablet,' like the Ten Commandments. I think that preacher on TV started calling it that."

"You mean the Right Reverend Asshole?" Lizzy smiled at her gibe. She had little respect for preachers, especially the pompous brand. "I doubt aliens or the Lord God Almighty put it there. But if they didn't, who did?"

"We don't know," said Tom.

Lizzy wasn't buying it. "Come on, Tom. What do you really think?"

Tom set his coffee cup on the granite counter. Leaning back with his hands on the its edge, he gazed thoughtfully into space as Lizzy waited for an answer.

"One thing I'm certain about is that we're not the first men to enter caves, and I'm not talking about cavemen from some cheap movie. It's hard to imagine ancient people with little equipment, let alone reliable lights, getting as deep into the earth as they did.

"In France, I've been in caves where men drew animals using smoke and berry dyes. I've learned we humans want to leave something behind that says 'I was here.' Caves are perfect. No weather to wear away the message.

"Then there's this other thing." Tom looked at Lizzy as he asked, "Why do we believe our progress has been in a straight line from primitive to modern? Did you ever read the book *The World Without Us*?"

"They did a series on TV about it. I saw that."

Tom grinned.

"You remember that if humans disappeared from the earth, within a few hundred years, nature would reclaim all man had built. Even New York City would return to a swamp with every concrete structure crumbled and each steel beam rendered to rust. We'd like to think we build the way the

Romans did and we would leave structures like the Colosseum. Not so for modern man. We don't construct using stone. Mount Rushmore would survive to ponder like the rock figures on Easter Island. That's about it."

Lizzy knew where Tom was heading. She ventured, "So you think there were people a long time ago, who were super smart, and they left us The Tablet?"

"Deep in the earth," Tom continued, "Where it would remain protected."

"But what were they trying to tell us?"

Tom continued with a conjecture he felt in his gut, but his intellect thought improbable. "I think there were people on earth, before the civilizations we know of, that possessed knowledge far too advanced for modern man, until maybe now."

"Now?" asked Lizzy. "Why now?"

"I've been surprised to find how deep ancient man was able to venture into caves. This discovery was deeper than previously possible, until we had devised gear and equipment to get to it. It was only after I turned around and walked across a precise spot that the floor gave way. Even if a man had gotten there before, why didn't it give way then? Why me? Why that moment?"

"What do you mean?" Lizzy puzzled.

"I've had the ground give way beneath me before. This was

different. I don't know how to explain it, but this felt more like a trap door released. Like it was time to open."

"So, whoever put it there, wanted it to be discovered?" Lizzy asked. "And only when man had the equipment and brainpower to understand what they left?"

"That's what I thought, but they mis-timed it, because we are stumped," Tom said as he paused to take a long drink of coffee.

"You know," Lizzy began, "Don't get me wrong. You and Nick are plenty smart, and you have fancy degrees, but maybe that's getting in your way."

Tom focused on Lizzy. In just the few weeks he'd gotten to know her, he learned that her mind was like a diamond in the rough, not chiseled to fit a conventional design. "What do you mean?"

"What you see on The Tablet looks like something you recognize, digital code, right? But that's because you're trying to bend these ancient people's writing to what you know. You've got to start thinking like them."

"And that would be…?" said Tom wanting Lizzy to bring this thought to a conclusion.

Lizzy just smiled and said, "Different!" and turned to clean up the counter.

Before Tom could continue with the discussion, he sensed men staring at him through the window and stood with a start.

Lizzy noticed. “What's up?” she asked.

“Go to the window and tell me what you see.”

Lizzy walked to the kitchen window and parted the curtain. At the curb, was a black sedan. Inside were two men, in suits, looking toward the house. Tom may have a good perimeter sense, but Lizzy had a good cop sense and these guys activated it.

“Looks like we have members of the law checking us out.”

“They're in a police car?” asked Tom.

“No, a plain unmarked,” she said as she left the window and returned to Tom. “But trust me, they're cops.”

“Or feds?”

“Yeah, maybe,” she said. “But definitely something cop-like.”

Nick bounded into the kitchen with a boisterous, “Good day, all.” He had changed out of his clothes from last night and showered. His hair was wet and finger-combed. He wore a blue cotton bathrobe and slip-in leather sandals. Nick busied himself putting a cartridge in the coffee machine as Lizzy got a clean cup for him.

“We have company,” Tom said as he nodded toward the window.

Nick looked out at the men casing the house. “Members of the local welcome wagon, you think?” Nick quipped.

"Yeah, folks like that have welcomed people like me for years," said Lizzy as she handed Nick a cup of coffee. "but not rich white guys like you."

"What do you think they want?" asked Tom.

"Any number of ideas pop into my head," said Nick unconcerned, "but like my grandfather said, it's not the police cars I see that bother me. It's the ones I don't."

Tom learned that few things knocked Nick off stride.

Did a life of privilege breed that kind of confidence?

So, Nick dismissed the guys watching, or so it seemed.

"I've gotten an email from a woman at MIT named Rachael Friedman. Seems she's coming to visit us. Believes she has an angle on The Tablet we've overlooked, but she has to see the real thing to be sure."

"So, you invited her?" asked Tom.

"Invitation was not in the cards. She said she's coming. No 'may I, pretty please.' I had her checked out. She's a physicist. Not sure what she has to add, but my people tell me she's well respected, and a force of nature. She does things without asking. See any reason to stop her?"

"No," Tom said. "At this point, we need someone who thinks…," he paused, as he looked at Lizzy, "different."

Lizzy wore a pleased smile at Tom's validation.

Tom's cell phone rang. He took a quick look at the caller, excused himself, and walked to the living room.

"So, what was that about?" Nick asked regarding the look Tom gave in Lizzy's direction.

"Just some advice from one non-expert to an expert." She beamed.

"You're quite something, aren't you Lizzy Rodriguez?" laughed Nick.

"So, this is a woman from MIT coming to see you?" Lizzy asked.

"Yes, so expect another guest."

"When?"

"She's coming in tomorrow. I told her she could stay with us and we expect her to arrive here before we go to the cavern."

"I look forward to meeting her," said Lizzy.

"Me too," said Nick, as he sipped his coffee.

Tom returned with the phone still in his hand and wore a puzzled expression. Nick and Lizzy both knew something was amiss.

"What's up?" asked Nick.

"You remember my caving partners, Jeremy and Josh? You met them when we first started the dig."

"Of course."

"They're in a cave in Colorado and they've discovered something I've got to see."

Nick, confused as what could be more important, asked,

"Now?"

"Yes. Now."

Chapter 12

ALTHOUGH OVER 500 MILES AWAY in Colorado, the helicopter soon reached the remote site Tom's friends had specified. Nick stayed behind to meet the physicist from MIT. The only other person in the helicopter was the pilot, a man who Tom didn't know. "Your regular pilot couldn't make it," said the man with salt and pepper hair. He looked the part of a pilot from central casting. Tom noted that the pilot had been talking to a sickly-looking young man at the airfield before they took off and wondered who the guy was.

"Isn't Mr. Foxe joining us?" asked the pilot as he walked Tom to the helicopter.

"No, he had other business to take care of," responded Tom.

The flight took Tom to the base of the mountain range where his friends had directed him. He could see Pike's Peak in the distance as the helicopter descended to where Jeremy and Josh waited. No one else was around. The only vehicle in sight was the brown Jeep that had brought the cavers.

The helicopter landed and, as the blades slowed, Jeremy and Josh approached.

"Hey, Mr. Big Time Celebrity!" yelled Jeremy to Tom.

They shook hands. Jeremy's grip was firm and friendly.

"How's it going?" added Josh.

"Well, if you guys want to spend days and nights in a cave doing nothing but sitting in front of a computer screen, you're welcomed to join me."

"Boooring," said Jeremy, stretching out the word.

"So, what do you guys want to show me?" asked Tom. Looking around, he added, "Isn't this where the Indian paintings are?"

"Yup," smiled Jeremy. "And we want to show you one."

Josh led the way. "You've never been here?" he asked.

"No," said Tom. "I'm not much on cave art. Nick would probably be the one who would appreciate it more."

They entered an opening onto a flat walk, unchallenging for a caver.

Tom asked, "Why are you guys here? This isn't the usual type of cave for either of you."

"You remember Tony Viho?" asked Josh as he turned on the lamp he carried. The cave was an easy walk and none of the men had equipment other than their helmets.

"Sure," he joined our team in Switzerland a couple of years ago."

"Well, this is Tony's native land. He's an Ute Indian," Josh explained as they walked deeper into the cave. "He wanted us to see this."

Josh held the lamp high to illuminate drawings on the wall.

The drawings contained an odd combination of items. One might expect to see big game like buffalo with Indians, spears in hand, chasing them. Here, however, was a child-like outline of a man. Alongside were two snakes twirled around each other in a double helix. Next to the helix, a boot-shaped moccasin. Last of all, a long-necked bird in flight.

"Interesting," observed Tom. "But why did I fly up here to see this? What was so important?"

Jeremy took it from there. He smiled as he turned on his lantern, exposing another drawing. "Look at this," he said.

The drawing was clearly of bats flying out of a cave.

"According to Tony," said Jeremy, "This represents what we now call Carlsbad Cavern. Those bats have been flying out of there for years."

"Sure," replied Tom, his interest now piqued. "It's known for it. Tourists come to witness their nighttime flights."

"When Tony saw news of your discovery, he told us we had to check out this drawing," said Josh.

Tom puzzled over the drawing for a moment, then said, "Guys, I don't get the connection. We have a code that is way more sophisticated than cave drawings."

Jeremy frowned, frustrated. "Look," he said, "The Indians passed along stories generation to generation. Isn't it possible this is a story that was passed along by people who knew about The Tablet?"

"What people?"

Jeremy gave up trying to explain. "I don't know. But it must be something."

In the quiet that followed, as Tom pondered his friend's proposition, his peripheral sense tingled. Someone was in the cave behind them.

"Give me your lamp," he said to Jeremy. "There's something I need to check out."

Tom walked back toward the entrance as his friends stayed behind. They knew his special sense had kicked in, but had no idea what he was looking for.

Tom crept around a corner and saw the profile of a man lit by the light from the entrance. It was the pilot and he was placing something on the rock wall at the edge of the cave.

Tom relaxed, recognizing the pilot. "What're you doing?" He called out.

Instead of responding, the pilot pulled out a pistol from his belt and fired off a round, the bullet hitting the stone a foot away from Tom's head.

Tom moved quickly and ducked behind the corner as the pilot took another shot. Determined to catch the man, Tom channeled his baseball days. He picked up a ball-sized stone, peeked around the corner and threw it at the man, hitting him on the side of the head. The pilot wobbled, dazed as Tom darted toward the man, and slid into 'home plate.' The pilot fired another shot wildly as Tom knocked his feet out from under him. The pilot fell on his back with the gun falling from his hand.

As the pilot scrambled to his feet, Jeremy and Josh arrived. Jeremy took over, grabbed the pilot, and swung an uppercut, knocking the man further back into the cave. As Jeremy and Josh attempted to hold the man in place, the pilot's free arm struggled to reach something at the opening to the cave.

Tom suddenly realized what the pilot was reaching for. It was a bomb with a numerical ticker counting down and the pilot was attempting to turn it off, but Tom didn't think there was time for that.

"Get out of there!" he yelled to the men.

His command was punctuated by the explosion of the bomb.

Tom was blown back toward the entrance as fractured rock fell from the cave's ceiling.

It was hard for Tom to hold it together. He knew his friends were dead. Tom's first call was to Nick, who told him to sit tight. Nick would notify the authorities and have a pilot, the pilot he knew, come up and fly him back. The FBI arrived within the hour and cordoned off the crime scene. Turned out this was federal land and the FBI had jurisdiction.

As a medical tech cleaned the scrapes on his arms, Tom

answered an agent's questions. He described the pilot and the young man he'd been talking to at the airfield, just before they took off. More than once, he described the details of what happened.

While he waited, Tom tried to put the pieces together. He had scrapes and bruises. His friends were crushed to death. He would have liked to torture information out of the pilot, but that man lay buried in the same mound as his friends.

Tom held an image of the drawings burned into his head but had no idea what they meant. He doubted they had anything to do with their discovery, *but what if they did?*

Five hours passed, the FBI said he could go. Nick's regular pilot arrived to fly Tom back. As the helicopter lifted off, Tom saw a large man on a nearby hill standing beside a black SUV. Although he was too far away to see his face, the man somehow seemed familiar. The man got into the car and disappeared.

The Stranger knew men were buried in the cave. With the same certainty, he knew the caver he met in Wyoming, the man he set on this journey, barely escaped with his life. He might not be so lucky the next time. The Stranger returned to the SUV and continued south.

Chapter 13

"SO WHY DO YOU WANT to see the cave, and why is Nick letting you?"

Lizzy was nothing if not direct and was quick to probe Rachael when she arrived.

She was the only person to greet Rachael. Tom had gone to check out what his friends had found. Nick remained at Carlsbad Caverns, meeting with Park Service officials anxious about his progress. Nick told Lizzy about the MIT physicist coming, but was short on answers as to why. He'd seemed as mystified as Lizzy, but Lizzy knew Nick wouldn't have welcomed this woman unless he thought she had something to offer.

All Lizzy had was a name, a woman's name, and estimated time of arrival. The idea of a woman physicist fascinated Lizzy. The only physicist she could name was Albert Einstein and she imagined the female version as an old woman with wild, gray hair. So, when a woman close to her own age, with a trim, shapely figure arrived curbside by cab, her image shifted. Feminine animus at play, she evaluated a possible rival, a smart one. Lizzy enjoyed taking a reputed genius down a notch or two, a habit from high school where classmates thought she was stupid. Bad grades didn't mean flawed thinking. The girl who headed the debate team avoided contact with Lizzy after Lizzy demolished the smart girl's arguments over, of all things, the importance of the Roman Empire in shaping our government. How they got into that hallway debate, Lizzy didn't remember, but the history teacher who witnessed it never forgot. She encouraged Lizzy to do better in school, coaxing her to 'make something of herself.' Lizzy was pleased with herself, just as she was. No, Lizzy wouldn't let this woman with the fancy degree intimidate her.

Rachael struggled up the steps to the house carrying a large duffel bag. Dressed in her typical black stretch pants and gray wicking athletic shirt, ponytail bobbing, she looked like a marathon runner. Yet, she was much too lean to be a baggage handler, and Rachael swung the awkward, heavy bag with both hands, stumbling up the steps. Lizzy opened the door as Rachael made it to the porch. Rachael passed her with a quick, "Thanks," and a smile. She dropped the bag on the floor of the foyer and turned to Lizzy with her hand out and an introduction on her lips, "Hi, I'm Rachael."

Lizzy took her hand firmly. "I'm Lizzy," and uttered her questions before her hand had left Rachael's. Rachael didn't need an interpreter to understand this woman distrusted her, but thirst won the moment.

"We can talk, but first, you think I could have a glass of

water?"

"Sure," Lizzy said as she led Rachael into the kitchen. "Have a seat," as Lizzy pointed to the small, round kitchen table and the four wicker chairs around it. "Ice?" she asked.

"Yes, thanks."

Lizzy took a lead-crystal tumbler from the cabinet and filled it with ice and water from the refrigerator dispenser. She placed the glass before Rachael and evaluated this woman as she gulped half the glass.

She drinks like a guy, thought Lizzy, an observation Rachael further confirmed by wiping the residual liquid from her lips with the back of her hand.

"Thanks. Not used to the dry weather," said Rachael.

"Not Boston, is it?" Lizzy stated with stoic expression.

"Guess not. About your questions," Rachael continued. "Sorry, but I'm curious, how are you connected to this project?"

"Logistics," Lizzy responded.

Rachael displayed the puzzlement that Lizzy sought, the bad girl coming out in her. "Logistics?" Rachael repeated.

Lizzy could continue the charade, but realized she was back in high school, being difficult.

Why did Rachael put her there?

She seemed to be perfectly fine. In fact, there was something about her Lizzy liked. Lizzy mellowed as she smiled and said, "Look, I'm just yanking your chain. The logistics I'm responsible for is making sure everything's running smoothly here at the ranch. The men aren't exactly working regular hours."

"Speaking of which, where are Mr. Foxe and Mr. Littleton?"

Lizzy's brow wrinkled in puzzlement.

"Sorry," she said, "but I never hear those names. It's just Nick and Tom."

"So where are Nick and Tom?"

"Nick's at the caverns. He said he'll be here soon. Tom had to check something out with friends in Colorado, Josh Peabody and Jeremy Miller. They were the guys with Tom when they made the discovery in Carlsbad."

"Oh," Rachael said, "What did they find in Colorado?"

"His buddies said something they found pointed to the discovery here. But it didn't go well."

"What happened?"

"Not much information yet, but there was a cave-in," explained Lizzy. Tom's all right, but Josh and Jeremy may be dead."

Rachael didn't expect such news. "That's awful!"

"Sure is," said Lizzy. "We don't know everything yet, but it may have not been an accident."

Rachael's eyes narrowed as she said, "This discovery got a

lot of press. It's still talked about by wackos and that crazy preacher. Do you know if Mr. Foxe, I mean Nick, is safe? Is Tom?"

Lizzy relaxed, if only to allay this new woman's fears while her own continued. "Don't worry. They have round-the-clock protection. I haven't been to the site, but one of the guards, a guy named Drake, came by here once. He's one scary dude. I'm sure they're safe," she said with a smile meant to reassure her guest.

Lizzy changed the subject. "So, you told Nick something that interested him. What was it?"

"Oh, yes. Your original question," smiled Rachael, who under normal circumstances, would be inclined to tell this person she just met to mind her own business. Rachael had been cryptic with Nick. She was a scientist and her flimsy proof hinged on an observation from a photo. She had to see the discovery firsthand to validate that observation. In spite of the enmity Lizzy first displayed, something about her made Rachael speak freely.

"Let me show you something," Rachael said as she walked over to her duffel bag, reached in, and returned with a photo and magnifying glass in hand. She pulled up a chair beside Lizzy and laid the photo between them. "Here's a photo of a section of the discovery."

"I've seen several of these," said Lizzy. "Nick's been

sending them far and wide."

"A colleague loaned me this copy. Something intrigued me about it. I took it home and was clearing my head playing my piano..."

"You play?" Lizzy asked. Having grown up around musicians, Lizzy found this a potential bond with Rachael, although she knew this woman was more likely to play Rachmaninoff than rock.

"Yes, but then something struck me," continued Rachael. "Look closely at the pits in the discovery." Lizzy took the glass and examined the photo. "Apparently, the light source was from the left in this shot. What do you see?"

"Shadows," announced Lizzy.

"Yes, and different shadows. It appears the pits are different depths. The light illuminates some to the bottom, not others, and some part way down."

"Which means?" asked Lizzy, who had her own suspicion.

"The team may be blind to an important part of the code. I checked with the colleague who loaned me this photo and he asked around. It appears that everyone treats this as simple binary, zeros and ones, on and off. I suspect they're not considering the depths."

"And what would that add?" Lizzy queried.

"I'm not certain. Perhaps this is logarithmic," Rachael said as she stopped to consider her audience. "Logarithmic, I mean…" she started to explain.

"I know," said Lizzy. "Like a slide rule."

"Well, yes," responded Rachael.

"But I won't know until I get up close and run some diagnostics."

"Diagnostics," restated Lizzy as though a light bulb appeared above her head. "Look, could you wait here?"

"Yes, of course," Rachael responded, uncertain what Lizzy might be thinking.

As Lizzy stood, she asked, "You need more water?"

"No, I'm good."

Rachael watched as Lizzy bounded up the stairs off the foyer, taking two at a time. She could not size-up this woman. She wanted to know what Lizzy was thinking.

How unusual to care.

Lizzy soon returned, bounding down the stairs as she had going up, swinging off the end of the banister with one hand, holding something in the other, into the foyer and up to Rachael where she stood holding the object aloft. "Know what this is?" she asked Rachael. "This is something one of my mom's boyfriends gave me when I was little. Mom thought I would be interested in music and her boyfriend gave me this."

"It's a slide whistle, right?" guessed Rachael.

"Right you are, Madame Curie," joked Lizzy as Rachael acknowledged the playful jab at her science credentials. Lizzy put the slide whistle to her lips and blew as she took the slide up and down the scale of the simple gizmo.

"And so?" puzzled Rachael.

Lizzy took a seat at the table across from Rachael, leaned in, looked her in the eye, and said, "What if the depths are a musical scale, just like this thing," holding the slide whistle before her.

Rachael scoffed. "Well…"

"No. Think about it. Didn't your mother ever say, 'I don't like your tone'? You can say a simple word like 'what' a hundred different ways. It's the tone that changes the meaning. The Chinese are the prime example. Words have completely different meanings when the tone is different."

Lizzy searched Rachael's eyes for recognition of the idea. Rachael, in return, thought of several tonal languages with which she was familiar. Could it be the ancients who created this tablet had a tonal written language? Everyone was putting the code in today's context, not stretching in other directions.

"Rachael," Lizzy said as though leading a child. "Why do you suppose you thought of this angle while playing the piano?"

Rachael's reaction signaled to Lizzy that she doubted one had anything to do with the other. But that moment passed into careful consideration.

Music? Tones?

Rachael realized that she rejected such notions out of hand. There must be a more scientific answer.

Lizzy punctuated Rachael's silence by putting the slide whistle to her lips and playing a quick upward slide with a fluctuating ending used in cartoons to signal a question. Removing the instrument from her lips, her smile depicted confidence while recognizing Rachael's conundrum. Rachael smiled.

"Hello," Nick announced as he entered the rear door, scraping off the remaining cave dirt onto the mat. "Anyone home?"

"We're in here," Lizzy called out.

Nick entered the kitchen, wearing his explorer shirt and khakis, his hat in one hand, his hair and face smudged with dirt. Rachael rose to meet him as he put forward his hand and said, "You must be Dr. Friedman."

"Rachael," she said wanting to put formality aside as she returned Nick's firm grip.

How tall he is.

Rachael had seen photos of the man, but Nick possessed a commanding presence a photo failed to depict.

"Sorry I couldn't meet you," Nick said as he released Rachael's hand. "The Park Service is getting, what you might call, antsy. They would like this show to leave town."

He turned to Lizzy, who remained seated at the table. "You

know what they said? They asked when we plan to remove the discovery."

Lizzy returned the obligatory lowering of the eyebrows in a 'they can't be serious' gesture.

"It's not an exhibit of the Titanic moving from town to town!" exclaimed Nick.

As Nick shook his head reiterating disbelief, Lizzy announced, "Rachael has an interesting theory."

"So, I understand," said Nick as he turned his attention to Rachael. "Please tell me."

"Well," started Rachael, now unsure of what form the theory had taken after her discussion with Lizzy. "It's . . ."

Lizzy, seeing Rachael no longer knew where to start, rescued her by saying, "It's different."

Chapter 14

THE HELICOPTER LANDED, stirring a small cloud of dust near the tent where Nick and Rachael awaited Tom's arrival. When workmen erected the press tent, Nick quipped that the white pavilion resembled the staging for a wedding reception. Inside, rather than linen-covered tables, large monitors were scattered around the room on gray, metal tables. Each displayed different parts of the cavern. The press had stopped the daily hounding of the team and Nick's press contact, Barbara Monroe, now took calls from her office in Denver. The tent, with its array of monitors, assumed a new purpose. Nick placed additional security people inside and outside the discovery site.

The previous afternoon, Rachael explained her theory to Nick. Nick thought it 'different,' as Lizzy put it, but had not yet shared the idea with Tom. Not convinced Rachael's take on the discovery had much merit, Nick still itched to get into the cave to take another look. But he would wait for Tom.

As the helicopter blades slowed, Tom opened the side door and jumped out. Rachael had never seen executive transportation like Nick's Bell 407, painted in black with gold stripes and plush leather seating. Nick was wealthier than she had imagined, and she mistrusted his scientific qualifications.

How could a rich playboy appreciate the lucidity of her theories? Could coming here be a mistake?

Nick met Tom as he stepped away from the helicopter.

"I'm so sorry about what happened," said Nick.

"We've got to be careful, Nick," was Tom's simple reply.

As Tom approached the tent, Nick announced, "Tom, this is Dr. Rachael Friedman."

Tom shook Rachael's outstretched hand. "Hello, Doctor."

"It's just Rachael."

"OK. Rachael."

In Tom, Rachael saw a man at a funeral, somber and guarded, and she responded with, "I'm sorry for your loss."

"Thanks," was Tom's reply. After failing to crack the discovery's code and now grieving the death of his friends, he welcomed the distraction Rachael offered and asked, "I understand you have a theory for us?"

"Yes, I do," responded Rachael.

"Let's go inside and sit," directed Nick.

Inside the tent, Nick chose a table scattered with charts and maps and sat on one of the folding camp chairs beside it. He pointed to another like it beside him for Rachael. Tom pulled his chair up placing Rachael between the two of them. She extracted from her bag the photo she shared with Lizzy the day before and later, with Nick.

"Show Tom what you showed me," Nick said as he leaned

back in his chair. Instead of the photo, he studied Rachael as she retold her theory and Tom's reaction to it.

"If you look at the pits on The Tablet, you will note they are of different depths."

Tom shot a glance at Nick regarding this observation. Nick returned the look with a shoulders-up and palm-open gesture communicating, 'you've got me.' Neither of them had thought about variations in depth.

Rachael continued, "You've overlooked a constituent of code."

"Well, there is one way to find out," said Tom. "Let's go see."

"We need to locate special equipment to measure the variations," said Nick.

"I've got it right here," smiled Rachael, as she rummaged through her bag.

It impressed Nick that she had equipment at hand. He imagined a pricey piece of specialty gear and was dumbfounded when she came up with a can of compressed air and a palm-sized digital recorder.

"That's all?" he said, shooting a look at Tom whose turn it was to return the, 'you've got me' expression.

"Oh, no," she said as though she forgot something. She laid the two items on the table and fished out a silver laptop computer and set it beside the other items.

Nick returned a facetious, "Well, that's more like it."

Tom added, "How are you going to use them?" Unlike Nick, and genuinely curious, Tom sensed that there was more to this woman than he first had assumed.

"Let's go. I'll show you." Rachael stood, eager to proceed, as Nick sensed a shift in leadership. To most who knew Nick, his nonchalant manner disguised his need for control.

"OK," Nick said, "Follow me."

Was his statement courtesy or maintaining his leader status?

He wasn't sure himself, but he marched out of the tent toward the visitor center.

At mid-morning, a dozen tourists milled around the ticket counter waiting to join a trip through the cavern. In spite of a sign posted at the start of the queue stating that the discovery was in a restricted area and not on the tour, people were asking, "Will we see The Tablet?" The park rangers got that question eight or nine times a day, regardless of the posted sign.

As Nick walked by the line with Rachael and Tom, a woman in a straw hat poked her rotund husband in the side and pointed to Nick. His picture appeared frequently in newspapers and on TV and he was now a bit of a celebrity. A security guard held the tourists back so they could pass through. It rankled the Park Service employees having to do this extra duty and they couldn't wait for the spectacle to end.

Two of the four elevators had been out of service for months before Nick began his work. There were no funds in the Park Service budget for repairs. Nick paid for the repairs in return for having exclusive use of the two elevators while his work continued. The rangers were thankful for the repairs and thus had conflicted feelings about Nick's presence. He also revived the popularity of Carlsbad Caverns where the attendance had dropped over the years. Yet, in the eyes of park higher-ups and certain members of Congress, the site garnered too much attention.

Drake was the guard on duty at the private, roped off queue to the elevator. Dressed in his standard black, he looked the part of muscle working the line at a popular nightspot. He unlatched the rope cordoning off Nick's elevators and allowed the group to pass. Rachael stopped smiling as she considered Drake's enormous size, but Drake broke the tension by producing a flirtatious wink.

One elevator stayed at the top and one at the bottom, so Nick never had to wait the one-and-a-half minutes it took to traverse the depth of eighty stories. He pushed the button and the dull-blue metal door of the elevator opened. Nick pressed 'C' for cavern, the doors closed, and the cab dropped. The depth to which they descended impressed Rachael. As a physicist, an expert on time and velocity, she concluded this was the equivalent of the John Hancock Building, the prominent skyscraper in Boston, turned upside down.

How did anyone ever get here with The Tablet?

The indicator registered '750' and the doors parted. The diminished lighting, and breezeless cool temperature told Rachael she had entered another world.

They exited one-by-one through a revolving door to yet another surprise for Rachael. The expanse of a train terminal greeted her, carved from stone with a dome ceiling. Embedded in the ceiling were frozen undulations of gray rock pockmarked by air trapped beneath prehistoric seas. The floor consisted of man-made smooth cement. Other features of man were apparent, a lunchroom, a gift shop, and even a blue US Mail box for mailing post cards from beneath the earth. In the center, stood a round, cement and stone souvenir desk. A pillar at its center illuminated with fluorescent lights displayed an assortment of tee shirts and guidebooks for sale.

"I see that The Tablet was handily placed near a tourist stop," Rachael scoffed.

"This was not the way in, believe me," said Tom. "We were in an adjoining cave, one nobody knew about. I don't think the people who placed it here 10,000 years ago thought we would one day take an elevator to it."

"10,000 years ago," Rachael repeated. "Homo sapiens had only just discovered agriculture around that time. Who did this?"

"Let's move on," said Nick. "Conjecture does no good until we figure out what they were trying to tell us."

Nick led them to the far side of the room where they picked up one of the paved trails with stainless steel handrails. One such trail opened to a tunnel where the passageway was covered by grit plastic to form a more primitive path. A sign read 'Trail Closed,' but Nick pushed passed it with Rachael and Tom following.

The path rolled up and down with much lower clearance. Rachael took a cue from Nick as he ducked from time to time. Two minutes later they arrived at the entrance covered in vertical plastic louvers with another guard standing by. This man, with crew cut and military bearing was less massive than Drake, but nonetheless, imposing. "Hello, Jake," Nick said to the man as Jake pulled the plastic louvers back to allow them to enter.

"Lizzy told me I needed a badge to enter," Rachael told Nick.

"You're with me," he replied. The room was ablaze with lights. Rachael shielded her eyes with her hand as they adjusted to the contrast from the dark cave. Computers and other equipment lined the far side of the chamber. Rachael began to think twice about the simple tools she brought. She glimpsed The Tablet down below, but it was not until she followed Nick down the ladder that the magnitude of The

Tablet became apparent. It stood larger than expected and the metallic luster, so bright and flawless, betrayed its antiquity. She gasped an astonished, "Wow!"

Nick smiled. "Wow, indeed." Rachael froze in wonderment. "Now, how about it?" Nick prompted.

"About what?" stammered Rachael.

"The test," Nick reminded her.

Flustered by the distraction of her awe, she returned to reality. "Oh, yes."

She walked to a table near the computers where she deposited her bag. Spotting an empty beer bottle on the table, she picked it up and waved it at the men. "Late night party?"

Nick smiled, held his finger to his lips like a librarian hushing a child and said, "Careful, don't tell the Park Service."

"The bottle will do to demonstrate," she said.

"Demonstrate?" Tom asked.

"Yes, how do you measure the depth of this bottle?"

"A ruler?" Tom quipped.

"Sure, that's one way. But what if you had only the top exposed, and you knew the width of the bottle?"

The men returned blank looks.

Rachael put the top of the bottle to her lips and blew across it. The bottle emitted the deep tone any kid would recognize. Rachael put down the bottle and smiled as the men suddenly understood what she was after.

"So, I will blow air across each of the marks in The Tablet and record the tone. I will feed the recordings into a program on my laptop and see what frequencies we have. That will give us relative depths."

Nick and Tom exchanged a lukewarm acknowledgment of her scheme.

"It's a start," she admitted.

Without being asked, she walked over to The Tablet with the air can in her left hand and recorder in the right. She picked a row at eye level explaining, "It doesn't matter where I start. We're just testing."

She pressed the record button with her right hand and depressed the air nozzle release with her left. As she blew the air over each mark, everyone could hear the delicate tone from the flow. Not as deep and loud as the beer bottle, but slightly detectable like a faint breeze.

Rachael continued across two dozen marks and, satisfied this represented a suitable sample, walked to the table, put down her simple implements and flipped the laptop cover open. The screen came alive and Rachael entered a password to unlock the computer. Moving her finger across the touch pad, she clicked on an icon that opened a program for sound recording, with an editing line across the top and buttons for adjustments beneath.

She took a small black cable from her bag, inserted one end

into a computer port and the other into an opening on the recorder. In a few seconds, the waveform of the recordings appeared. They all could see that the waves were different as the recording captured the tones from each mark, but Rachael soon determined a pattern. Her mind replayed the silly tones of Lizzy's slide whistle, as she told Nick and Tom, "They're octaves!"

Chapter 15

SIMPLE TOOLS of compressed air and hand-held recorders weren't enough for a man who could afford anything. Nick flew in two technicians from California who worked for a Japanese company which produced precision measuring instruments. Twenty-four hours after Rachael noted the pit depths, two factory reps were erecting a robotic arm near The Tablet like one used to weld automobiles on an assembly line. Rather than holding a welding rod, this arm held a precision laser micrometer which rotated to stay perpendicular to the surface of The Tablet.

Rachael joined Nick and Tom where the technicians were working. Nick was pleased with himself, enjoying the sight of things he controlled. The project was now unstuck and moving ahead, although the end goal persisted to be undefined. "Now," he boasted, "We can scan the code, detect the depths, but not touch the metal. We'll record everything in the computer and analyze it with a program these men brought."

"Record how?" Rachael asked.

"What do you mean?"

"It seems you've been working on the code left to right as though it was binary."

Tom added, as he pointed to The Tablet, "Granted, but we've run it multiple ways. People write right to left, down and up. Maybe the people who wrote this, wrote from the inside out."

"Or they might have taken in the whole pattern at one time," added Rachael.

Nick winced at Rachael's remark. "Well, they must have thought we would be as bright as they were. I can't imagine the intellect needed to take in all of this at once."

"True," said Rachael. "And I suspect they were not trying to make it hard. I think they were trying to make it universal. They were probably trying to leave us something that, regardless the way our language evolved, we could understand."

"Well, a picture could help," added Nick. "Before we shot the Voyager spacecraft out of the solar system, we posted a simple picture of a man and a woman on the side."

"True," agreed Rachael. "But I suspect the people who left this were trying to tell us more."

"Rest assured," Nick said, "We add coding to the scans that tag each element. We use row and column numbers, but we can slice and dice in different ways to see what we come up with."

"That'll do," agreed Rachael.

Nick walked over to the two technicians. When Nick

approached, one bowed, and the other didn't. He would bet the man who bowed originated from Japan and the other, probably a native-born American. He pondered the culture and the people who created The Tablet and whether or not its social norms resembled any found today.

Might we be able to pick them out in a crowd as Nick felt he could identify the man born in Japan?

Could some of their descendants live among us today?

"Offerings are at an all-time high," gushed the Reverend Josiah Jones.

"Praise be," said loyal wife Gloria, who already knew the numbers. She made a point of keeping an eye on the books and always had ever since the early days of her husband's ministry.

"I've been preaching about The Tablet as the new word of God, and the faithful have responded. They hunger for it!" Adding an un-saintly aside to Gloria, "They can't get enough of it."

Gloria replied with her usual patronizing tone, "You've done well."

"But something's missing," Jones mused. "I can't continue

to go on TV with the same tired photos of The Tablet superimposed on the screen. We need the real thing!"

"Honey, you know how that Foxe man doesn't give us the time of day. That's why we sent Chris out there, to see if we can convince him to let us film."

"I haven't gotten a call from the boy lately," said Jones, as he took out his cell phone. "I think I'll call him."

Jones soon connected with Chris, who answered with a "Hi, Dad."

"Chris, my boy. Where are you?"

"Still in Denver."

"Denver?"

Jones was puzzled. The private jet he hired flew his son to Denver, but that was supposed to be just a refueling stop.

"Yeah, Dad, I'm trying to get a meeting with the PR woman who works for Foxe. She's here."

Jones, pleased his son sought to make inroads at a tactical level, continued to be anxious as time was running out. How long would he be able to make proclamations about The Tablet without more evidence? He signaled his anxiety, "That's a good idea, but we need to get moving on this."

"Don't worry, Dad. I plan to head down to Carlsbad, one way or the other, real soon."

"OK, son. Just keep me in the loop."

"Oh, Dad. I almost forgot. Did you hear what happened to

two men on the team that discovered The Tablet?"

"No. What about them?"

"They died in a cave-in near here."

"Oh, my God!" exclaimed the Reverend. "We must pray for them, and their families."

"You might do that at your next service."

"I most certainly will."

"OK, Dad. Got to go. Give my love to Mom."

"Will do, son."

"You're such a fine son. I'm sure your parents are proud," teased the woman lying nude in the hotel bed beside Chris. Chris reached over her to the side table and retrieved the joint he was smoking when the call came in.

"Yeah," sneered Chris, "I'm a saint."

The woman worked as an attendant at the private aviation terminal and had an eye for young rich men who passed by her station. A Vegas dancer before she blew a knee out, her vocation options were limited, but her choice of men, extensive.

"I thought Denver was a refueling stop for you," she said.

"You bet it is," smiled Chris as he held the smoking joint aloft. "I had to try the legal local fuel. It's the best!"

"What's this about two men who died in a cave-in?" she asked.

"You didn't know? Sad. I hope nothing happens to Foxe,

not until I get to him."

"Any luck with the PR woman you mentioned?"

"Honey, you're my PR woman."

"PR?" she questioned.

"Private Relations," grinned Chris as he pulled a deep toke.

Unsaid were his plans to destroy his father's ministry. The first effort was just a test, but needed improvement for the next time.

It was the first trip Senator Morrison made to his ranch since the discovery became public three weeks ago. It was far too long to be away from the ranch, away from his wife.

"Why didn't you tell me he had been here?" he fumed.

Pete found out about Nick's visit. Denise had few secrets from him, although she succeeded with a few critical ones.

"Pete," she said attempting to cool his fury, "Nothing happened."

"Nothing?"

She took his arm in a loving embrace and repeated softly, "Nothing."

"I don't like it. I don't like his being anywhere near here."

"Honey, that's all water under the bridge. It happened long ago."

It was nearing sunset and the last rays of evening light poured through the sliding glass door of the living room. Denise released Pete and he walked over to enjoy the pink hues cast over the yard and horse barn. He stared into the distance as he told Denise, "The men who were with Tom Littleton at the discovery are dead."

"I heard," said Denise.

"Caving is dangerous," said Pete as he continued to study the sunset. "Nick needs to be careful."

The technicians finished assembling the laser scanner. One of them returned home to California. The other technician, Benton, stayed behind to work with Rachael and Nick. He would help set up a computer to capture each element of the code, as Rachael had suggested. Tom prepared his computer system so it would take the indexed code and rearrange it in different patterns, right to left, left to right, top to bottom, however they desired.

As Benton worked, Rachael combined her tech talk with personal queries. Where did Benton grow up? San Francisco. Where did he go to school? Stanford. Benton's brown eyes darted between the keyboard and Rachael as the parallel discussions progressed. It was obvious to Nick that Benton and Rachael shared the commonality of age and social preferences of a certain generation. He felt sidelined and wondered why it made any difference to him. Accustomed to receiving women's interest without making an effort, Nick was surprised that he got no hint of it from Rachael. It bothered him more than he cared to admit. First, Rachael took the lead in his discovery, much as she was doing at this moment. Then, she related well to another man's intellect and company. Nick refused to believe he was jealous.

He was a man who didn't get jealous. Never had a reason to.

Yet?

Rachael looked up. "Done," she announced.

Nick looked to Benton for confirmation. "Yep," he said. "We're ready."

"How about you, Tom?" he asked looking over his way.

"Sure thing," replied Tom.

"OK," Nick announced, regaining control. "Let's give this a whirl."

Benton pushed a red button on the control console before him. The robot arm came alive and twisted the laser unit perpendicular to The Tablet. It moved smoothly to the upper left a foot away from The Tablet surface. A beam of blue laser light, made visible by dust floating in the air, measured the surface as numbers raced across the screen. Rachael concentrated on the numbers while Nick looked over her shoulder.

"Are we continuing to get octaves?" asked Nick.

"Yes," responded Rachael, calculating numbers in her head.

"How do you do that?" Nick asked.

"What can I say?" she grinned. "I'm good with numbers."

"You know, if the spaces are shift markers, we might be dealing with 16, 32, 64, or more character variables," surmised Nick.

"Enough for an alphabet?" asked Rachael.

"Perhaps enough for a simple lexicon."

Tom and Benton noticed the exchanges between the two and looked at each other with a smile. Tom interrupted them with, "Sounds like you two almost have this thing solved."

"Sounds?" Rachael repeated to Nick.

Nick liked the pun, and grinned.

"Hey, Benton," he said.

"Yes, sir?"

"Your company has sound amplifiers, don't they?"

"Sure, we use them to turn small vibrating surfaces into sounds."

"Did you happen to bring that equipment and a couple of good speakers?"

Chapter 16

THE BLUE LASER meticulously scanned each element of The Tablet, one pass taking over three hours. The team completed a scan the previous day and was completing another to ensure the validity of the data. Tom and Rachael analyzed the measurements collected from yesterday's scan. The going was slow as they focused on every one of the pit depths. The data gathered supported Rachael's initial observation that all pits were up to eight evenly-spaced depths or octaves.

Nick observed Benton as he worked with the sound equipment, and from time to time, watched Rachael and Tom at the computer. Nick's thoughts drifted to a conference he attended years ago in New York.

At a meeting of The Society of Cryptography, experts in ancient writing and language were in attendance, with one exception.

As a benefactor, Nick hosted a cocktail party at The Plaza Hotel. In the penthouse, a wall of windows overlooked Central Park. The large, open space contained plush gray couches facing each other in a living area where a dozen members sat talking. A long buffet table sat at one side of the room, loaded with an assortment of finger food. Wait staff in black shirts and pants wandered among the guests dispensing glasses of champagne. The members chatted with each other, animated by conversation that, outside this room, might bore most people.

One person was apart from the crowd, seated at a baby-grand piano. Nick guessed him to be in his sixties. His hair was curly and pure white, standing uncombed like a stereotypical, long-haired maestro. He had a large pockmarked nose and a slack neck falling out of his white collar from which a bolo tie hung. The man wore a threadbare gray suit, much too large, causing Nick to speculate the man had shrunk with age.

He plinked out notes, one at a time, from no particular tune. Nick walked over, holding his drink, and listened for a few moments, unacknowledged by the man. Nick opened, "You play?"

The man looked at Nick, startled, unaware that he had been standing there, but then grinned and responded in a strong Italian accent, "A little, but the *violino* is my instrument." Adding with pride as he put his hand to his chest, "My family makes them."

"Is that so?" asked Nick.

"Is so," he said as he stood. He was two heads shorter than Nick, who stepped back so as not to speak over the top of the man's head.

"I don't believe we've met. I'm Nick Foxe."

"Lorenzo Cristofori."

"As in Bartolomeo Cristofori? The inventor of the piano?"

"The same," the man smiled. "You know who he was then?"

"Yes," responded Nick "but I thought pianos would be your family business, not violins."

"Alas, my grandfather was, how you say, a black sheep?" he said with a mischievous grin. "He made *violini*, and we make *violini* to this day."

"What brings you to this conference?" asked Nick. "Seems cryptography is a long way from music."

The man's countenance turned serious as he lightly poked his finger at Nick's chest. "No, no. You are wrong. They have everything in common."

"Well, metaphorically, I get your point."

"No, is not metaphor, is real."

Nick's nutcase radar activated, as the man continued.

"There was a nation of people who used music as their language."

"You mean tonal language," Nick offered.

"No, music!" the man insisted, poking Nick one more time for emphasis.

Nick considered himself a scholar in ancient writing and

language. He had never heard of such a thing. He decided to disengage with grace.

"Well, I need to mingle. Being the host and all, you see."

The man grew agitated. "You must meet with me," he said. "Come to Italy. I have research. I will show you!"

"I will do that, next time I'm there," Nick said, backing away.

To Nick's back, the man continued his urging. "Come. You will see."

Nick moved on to his other guests and when he next turned toward the piano, the man had left. He never thought more about him.

Until now.

Benton announced that the second scan was complete and the sound equipment was ready to use. After thanking him, Nick joined Rachael and Tom.

"How's the data looking?" he asked.

Tom replied, "We've run a match on the two scans and they're within acceptable variance. We're measuring in micrometers and the confidence level is well within three percent."

"Let me take another look at the pattern," Rachael said. She was determined to find the elusive answer. "Tom, you can look at pattern redundancies with your analysis program, right?"

"Sure," replied Tom. Before him was a 45-inch monitor that replicated the pattern on The Tablet.

"OK. Show me all the pits that are more than eight levels deep."

Tom made a few entries on the keyboard and red dots topped each matching pit.

"Now the other pits."

Tom typed and green dots appeared on the remaining pits.

"Now," Rachael said, smiling, "Show me all the pits over eight levels that are beside each other."

All dots disappeared from the screen. None matched.

Benton joined the team studying the monitor.

"Benton," Rachael said. "I noticed you have a binder over there with your equipment. What's in it?"

"It's a collection of frequency ranges used for different applications."

"Could I see it?"

Benton walked to his worktable and returned with the binder. Rachael took the loose-leaf ring binder and scanned the pages. She turned to the page she suspected would be there and dropped it on the table for all to see.

"There!" she said, as the others gathered over a chart on the open page. "Eight down and twelve across."

"They're note frequencies," Nick announced reading the chart title aloud. "It's twelve note frequencies and octaves."

"Each octave doubling the frequency of the same note below it," added Rachael.

"So," said Tom. "The pits may represent notes and octaves? How?"

"The first pit determines the octave and the following pit, the note, or visa versa."

"What about the spaces between pits?"

Rachael, happy to have a 90% solution, remarked, "Perhaps they mark the number of times to repeat the notes that follow. We can try different things. At least, you now have an eight-times-twelve character alphabet to decode."

Tom didn't share Nick and Rachael's obvious excitement. He could understand Rachael's pride, but why was Nick so excited?

Something hooked Nick on this music idea, but what?

"So what, now?" Tom asked Nick.

Nick grinned. "Let's make some music."

Chapter 17

TOM CONTINUED TO DOUBT the value of Rachael and Nick's current pursuit. Thus far, they all agreed the code was comprised of an eight by twelve matrix. To Tom's thinking, that was enough. As a computer guy, Tom understood logic and the brain, not music and the ear. Sure, many scientists were musicians. Einstein played the violin. Tom was not one of them, but he let Nick play out his idea. He was the boss. Then, there was Benton. Tom squinted, evaluating the man as he chatted with Nick.

How could he not be enticed by this adventure just as Rachael and he were? Yet somehow, he remained aloof.

"I can set each pit to represent any tone. Which frequency would you like to start with?" Benton asked Nick.

"Hmm," Nick said scratching his head in consideration. "Let's play 440 hertz. That's the A note the lead violin plays to tune the orchestra.

"That would be the tenth one of the fourth octave," added Rachael as she examined the chart from Benton's manual.

"OK," replied Benton as he entered the frequency on a keyboard. A piercing sound, barely recognizable as a violin's A, flooded the work area.

"Whoa, too loud!" exclaimed Nick, as everyone grimaced

and Benton, embarrassed, turned down the volume. The steady frequency issued an artificial electronic sound, missing the timbre of a handcrafted instrument.

"That's better," said Nick. "Can we program in all the note frequencies?"

"Sure," replied Benton. "We have an entire music synthesizer if you want it."

Tom walked over to Nick, who was enjoying himself. Tom didn't share his friend's enthusiasm.

"Nick," he confided. "What's this about?"

"What do you mean?" Nick responded.

"Why music notes?" Tom asked. "OK, I get frequencies. I do. But the frequencies may be any set. Where are you going with this?"

Nick figured telling Tom he got the idea from a crazy Italian would not help his case, and left it at, "I have a hunch."

"Hunch?" Tom had come to appreciate Nick's dogged attempts to break the code, his investment of time and money, his reaching into the scientific community for answers. This was not like him. "That's hardly a scientific approach."

"Indulge me," responded Nick, cutting the argument short with a smile.

Rachael had doubts herself. Sure, the ancients had romantic notions about music and nature. The Greeks imagined the stars as fixed in harmonic spheres, one within the other. Could it be that the beings that made this code wrote in tones?

What if that was the genesis of music?

Whoa, girl. Don't get carried away.

"Let's try the octave and note arrangement," Nick told Tom.

"Give me a few minutes," Tom answered as he set about to adjust the program parameters to read the pits in the octave-note combinations.

Rachael studied Nick as he leaned against the equipment table near her. He was an interesting enigma: Social elite, aloof, yet childlike in his curiosity and, yes, handsome. She found herself on the defensive with him, didn't know why and didn't like it.

"What do you imagine you'll hear?" she asked Nick.

"What do you mean?"

"I doubt it will be Beethoven's Fifth."

Nick chuckled. "You know my family worked in the oil business, right?"

"The Foxe drill bit." Rachael chimed in.

Nick looked to Rachael with raised eyebrow. "I'm surprised you knew that."

"I've done my homework."

"Well, Granddad invented it. But, before that, he was a wildcatter in West Texas. He had success locating oil. The drill bit was the real key to his fortune, but he never lost his lust for hunting for oil. I barely knew him. He died when I was little. But I remember when he talked about working the field. He lit up. Even as a little kid, I sensed his passion.

"I'll never forget what he said. He told me he could smell the oil." Nick laughed. Turning to Rachael, "You believe that? Oil hundreds of feet underground?"

"Why not?" Rachael responded.

"Well, as a little kid, I believed it. Then again, I believed in the tooth fairy at that age."

Rachael smiled. In the little time she had known him, Nick's periodic warm manner often surprised her when she expected the aloofness of a blue blood. She found this sharing of a childhood story charming.

"I'll never forget that. 'Could smell the oil.' We tend to dismiss our other senses too quickly. Have you heard of synesthesia?"

"Isn't that when two senses link together?"

"Yes, it is. I met someone with that condition. She never thought it to be a detriment and couldn't think of living without it. When she read, individual letters were different colors. To anyone else, they appeared black and white. She thought herself lucky. Her mother had her tested and verified it. She had synesthesia. She told me she met others with the 'attribute.' That's what she called it, an attribute, not a condition. Some saw colors when they heard music. One boy could recite the value of pi to a ridiculously long number of digits. He envisioned each digit as the width of a path in the woods. That mental image was easier for him to remember than a string of unrelated numbers.

"So, why not music and language? Doesn't music bring out different feelings and thoughts?"

"Well," Rachael, the rational scientist, began, "Most assume associative connections between music and emotion are environmental. We learn them."

Nick smirked. "You think?"

"Come on, Nick, have you ever listened to a love song from India? It's not exactly a barbershop quartet singing *Let Me Call You Sweetheart*. To western ears, it's not about love at all."

"But to someone in their culture it is. It's just a matter of frame of reference." Nick shook his head realizing he was going far afield with the philosophical argument. "Look, let's just find out what happens."

"Ah, the 'throw the spaghetti on the wall and see what sticks' scientific method," Rachael mocked.

Nick couldn't miss Rachael's sarcasm, but he resisted, as he had with Tom, from invoking the crazy Italian's notion. He wasn't sure himself why he found that short encounter compelling. Yet the idea grew stronger for Nick as he considered the connection to music.

What would be the odds of that man appearing with his theory and Nick now facing the possible reality? Coincidence?

He had to push on.

Answering Rachael, Nick replied, "Sure why not?"

Tom walked over with Benton. "Benton and I've been talking," he announced. "We can play the pits as octaves and notes, but the spaces between remain a problem. What should we do with them?"

"Let's use them as blanks for now," Nick responded. "Set a tempo, say one per second to start, and let's see what we have."

"You mean, let's hear what we have," corrected Tom.

Nick smiled. "Yes, let's hear."

The screen before them showed the area being played with a red dot on the replica of The Tablet. The Tablet itself stood twenty feet beyond with a large speaker on each side. Tom typed in a command and the dot started at the top left proceeding left to right. The first three positions were blanks and no sound emitted. It was a long three seconds as the team stood in silence when the dot reached the first pit. The initial note sounded through the speakers as a pure electronic tone. With the position of the speakers beside The Tablet, it seemed as though the sound came from The Tablet itself.

As the scan progressed in one-second intervals, it became clear that this was not a flowing tune. The frequencies moved up and down octaves seemingly at random. At one-second intervals, it would take days to scan the entire tablet. Nick showed his disappointment as his grin vanished.

"How fast can we make this?" he asked Benton.

"One-tenth of a second would allow time to form a wave we might comprehend."

"OK, play it at one-tenth of a second. Ten times faster than we are doing now."

Tom moved the speed up ten times. The notes sounded in a random pattern, but too fast to pick out each note.

Rachael stepped behind Tom, seated at his computer console, and put her hands on his shoulders as she said, "We haven't addressed the blanks, have we?"

"No, we haven't. Got something in mind?"

"They must be signals as to how the following notes are to be played."

"But what signals?" he asked.

"I don't know," said Rachael as she released Tom and stood. "But the frequencies would make more sense if they were overlapping each to make new sounds."

Nick recalled a professor in grad school who studied the language of animals. He didn't appreciate attempts to train apes to sign in a human language rather than attempt to understand theirs. That was particularly true of whales and dolphins, who communicated in a series of clicks and tones. They're bright mammals, perhaps smarter than humans.

"What if the frequencies sounded like a whale's call?" He asked.

Tom and Rachael turned to him looking as though Nick had lost his mind.

"So, you think whales left this slab for us?" Tom said jokingly.

Yet, Benton, a bystander in these events up to now, took a visible interest in what Nick had to say.

"No," said Nick, "but many human languages use tones. So do animals. There's something fundamental about it."

Rachael considered what Nick said and it started to make sense to her. Just as we put letters together that denote certain sounds to make a whole word, this ancient writing could be placing tones together to make a sound that has a particular meaning.

"We're treating this as though each tone is played one after the other like each was a separate letter making a word. Perhaps the spaces are telling us how the frequencies are placed on top of each other and for how long."

Tom remained doubtful. "Great. So even if we can unscramble how the notes are to be played, assuming we even have the right frequencies identified, then what? We'll be hearing something that has no meaning to us."

"Tom," Rachael replied. "I don't understand a word of Chinese, but it sounds like a language to me. It has a cadence.

It has sentences. Let's see if we can produce something that even resembles a language."

"Well, there are a limited number of variations of the spaces. We can try different combinations, but it may take hours."

"Got a bus to catch?" joked Nick.

Tom shrugged his shoulders in resignation. It seemed there were now two to one wanting to go with this idea. Even Benton offered a rare smile in appreciation.

"OK. Let's get busy."

Benton and Tom began programming a series of code variations.

Nick walked over to Rachael. "I see you're getting into this," he said.

Rachael looked surprised. "Did you not believe I was 'into this'?"

"Well," Nick hesitated as he gathered the right way to express his feeling. "Let's say the music idea fell flat for you and Tom."

"Cute pun," she said, "But, no, I've thought there was merit to it. Maybe it's what Lizzy told me, about seeing things this way while I played the piano."

"Smart woman, that Lizzy."

"Nick, I learned a long time ago the difference between being educated and being smart."

Nick considered this woman before him. She had super smarts and confidence. Nick had met many men in his vocation with advanced degrees that wore their education as a shield against their insecurities. Rachael was so young, but so secure. The age difference between them was obvious, yet Nick couldn't discount the feelings developing for this woman.

Two hours passed.

"I'm ready," announced Tom.

Rachael walked over to Tom and said, "Let's do it."

Tom began the playing of the pits using Rachael's suggestion. Each person turned to the other in silence to see if they heard the same thing. The tones now composed faint voices. Although not human speech, it was as if a creature was making a muffled attempt to speak.

Thinking he noticed something, Nick walked over to The Tablet as the sounds continued. He looked at the edges where the mysterious metal met the limestone.

He yelled back to Tom, "Faster!"

Tom moved the speed up. The utterance sounded like ghostlike pronouncements of an unknown language.

Nick noticed the limestone crumbing along the edges of The Tablet.

"Louder!" He yelled.

Tom turned up the volume level to match an outdoor rock

concert and everyone could now see the limestone crumble. The room began to shake, but it was not from the loud methodical language echoing through the cave.

The sounds were unlocking The Tablet from the rock.

The ground beneath Nick vibrated. He stepped back.

"Louder!" he yelled, his voice almost lost in the sounds.

Tom turned the volume as high as it would go. Rachael put her hands over her ears. The soil before Nick collapsed as though a hinged door had released. The sound abruptly stopped. Tom, confused, examined his computer equipment and monitors, all of which had gone dark. He looked to Benton who, as mystified as Tom, could only shrug his shoulders.

Dust filled the air where the ground had collapsed. As it settled, the rest of the team cautiously joined Nick at The Tablet. Through the dusty fog, under what was previously exposed, was an extension of The Tablet no one had suspected was there. This extension did not contain more code, but rather drawings etched into the metal. To the left, were simple outlines of humans, two figures, male and female, side-by-side. In the center were two double-helix drawings, much like scientists use to represent DNA. Dots like a constellation in the sky resembling a bird in flight.

Tom's mouth was agape. "The drawings in Colorado. They make sense now. It's as if an ancient people saw these pictures thousands of years ago and passed them along for future generations to see. They are similar, but not exactly the same. Look here. The Indians had a bird in flight, but these are stars. The constellation Cynus I think. The Indians had intertwined snakes, but this is clearly a DNA double helix. Then, a boot, but what is this? An outline of Italy? Why Italy?"

Everyone was puzzled, except Nick.

"We're going on a trip," he said.

Chapter 18

DUST DISTURBED from the exposed part of the slab floated in the strong work lights. A musty smell filled the air as though someone had opened an old chest forgotten for years. The Tablet revealed new clues, human figures, helixes, a constellation, the Italian peninsula. These pictures were easier to interpret than the code through its various tones. That code continued to be unwavering in withholding its meaning.

What were these etchings? Did they point to missing pieces of the code?

The loud crash when the floor gave way caused Drake to leave his post and peer over the edge of the dig to see if everything was all right. Nick assured him everyone was safe, and Drake returned to his post outside the entrance.

This new discovery made Nick eager to share the crazy Italian's theory with the team.

Tom's eyes sparkled with excitement matching the time when he first discovered The Tablet. Now he understood Nick's interest in pursuing what he had earlier thought to be crazy. "But where is this guy now? Italy? It's a big place."

"I have his name. That's enough," Nick winked. "We'll find him."

When Nick and Rachael first presented Tom their theory

about the code having a relationship to music, he was skeptical. But seeing how music was the key to exposing new clues, his view changed. He was all-in and wanted to go wherever necessary to find answers held by The Tablet.

Rachael hesitated. "I have a job," she said.

"So, grading papers takes precedent," Nick said in a patronizing tone. "Of course, I understand how that would be more important than the world's greatest discovery."

Rachael pushed back. "No, continuing to educate the best minds in the country and pursuing my work in physics seem more important than following a jerk who got excited when I blew air over holes in a tablet."

Tom and Benton studied Rachael wondering what caused her outburst. Each thought better of getting in the middle and returned to their work.

Jerk? Nick thought. It had been awhile since a woman called him that, but he was no stranger to the term.

"Rachael," he said taking her aside. "I value your contribution to this work. You held the key to getting us to where we are now."

Still steaming from Nick's condescension, Rachael waited to hear what he had to say. She never before felt such mixed emotions as she had with Nick. He was smart and charming one moment and an intolerable egotist the next. She asked herself how she could turn down the opportunity to be a part of history. But there was more than logic at play, a sensation about this man she couldn't quite explain.

"Look," Nick said. "I understand your work is important. So is this. Isn't there someone I could talk to about your taking time off to follow this project?"

Rachael flashed a smug grin. "You mean someone you could wave money at?"

"Rachael! I'm shocked. I prefer to call it 'patronage.'"

Rachael knew it was not a simple matter to replace someone like her.

But then again, just how far did Nick's connections reach?

As she considered what Nick said, Benton walked up. "I have to go. I'm way overdue to return to my office."

That Benton wanted to leave surprised Nick. He had gotten involved in the work here as a factory rep, hauling in specialty equipment for a job. But as the work progressed, Nick saw Benton's interest rise. A man of few words, Benton focused on each and everything they did.

Now, with this amazing revelation before them, he wants to go?

"You're not sticking around?"

"I know it's crazy," Benton admitted. "This is fantastic stuff! But I can come back tomorrow. Everything is set up and you don't need me. I have equipment my boss wants for another job."

"OK," Nick said. "I guess that's OK." He wondered why

anyone would leave, for even a minute; but, Nick had no reason to keep him.

"Great. See you tomorrow," Benton picked up a large aluminum equipment case, climbed the ladder out of the dig and exited through the opening above. Nick was puzzled as his eyes followed Benton out.

"I see," said Rachael. "So, some people can come and go as they please without question."

Nick showed his exasperation as he reassured Rachael, "You're not Benton. There're lots of Bentons. There's only one you." Nick stayed focused, looking Rachael in the eye.

Rachael thought she never blushed, but her face felt warm. Logic told her 'faint praise.'

Something in Nick's eyes said more.

As Nick and Rachael spoke, Tom sensed activity outside the dig's opening. The light, random stirring of the louvers meant something, or someone, had disturbed the air. Benton had already passed through the plastic louvers a few minutes earlier on his way out. Nick assumed Drake was standing guard outside, but another movement was evident.

Did he hear something? A faint pop?

Tom returned to work as the motion subsided, but continued to glance toward the opening. Something was not quite right. He had to check it out. As Rachael and Nick discussed getting her released from MIT, Tom climbed the ladder and out of the dig. Around the dig was a ten-foot ledge. Tom crept along the ledge as though he might encounter an intruder at any moment.

Tom was half way around the opening when The Stranger burst through.

"You!" Tom yelled. This man was a stranger to most, but not to Tom.

He's the man in Wyoming who mentioned this cave to me months ago.

Was it him I sighted on the hill in Colorado at the cave-in? Has he been following me?

No one would forget the bulk of this man with broad shoulders and body-builder arms, steel blue eyes piercing Tom's. He dressed like a soldier with khaki shirt, camouflage pants, and army boots. Tom eyed the semi-automatic pistol holstered to his side.

Tom had no time to consider the man further. The Stranger yelled into the dig to Rachael and Nick, "You've got to get out of there!"

"But," stammered Tom.

The man cut him off. "*Bomb!*" he yelled.

Nick and Rachael began to grab notebooks and gear.

"No time for that! Get up here. *Now!*"

Nick and Rachael scrambled up the ladder and joined Tom. The man now waved the three through the plastic louvers as though he could propel them through with the might of his swinging arm.

Outside the door, Drake lay unconscious, a trickle of blood dripping from a gash on the side of his head. The Stranger followed them out. "He's alive," he said. "The bullet just grazed him. I'll get him. It's *that* we have to worry about." The man pointed to a brown package attached to the rock just above their heads. It resembled a rectangular box wrapped in craft paper. The top of the package contained a small black box with a digital counter. The counter read '1:20' with the twenty becoming nineteen in a second. Everyone understood what it meant without the man having to explain.

Even though Drake had the same massive build, The Stranger picked him up like a sack of potatoes and placed him in a dead man's carry across his back. "Follow me!" He yelled, and follow they did, Nick right behind The Stranger pulling Rachael by the hand, and Tom close behind.

Rachael engaged her sense of time as she counted down in her head. The underground visitor center was half the length of a football field away with twists, turns, and overhead obstructions. They ran down the pathway. The bomb timer must read forty seconds and she believed they were only a third of the way down the channel to the underground visitor center. She released Nick's hand. She didn't need it and could run better without it. Thirty seconds and they were only halfway back, but why did she believe the visitor area was safe?

The whole cavern might come down around their heads. Couldn't Nick move faster?

Five seconds and they reached the high ceiling center.

"Hit the deck!" yelled The Stranger as he dropped prone to the floor with Drake's unconscious body beside him. Tom, Rachael, and Nick were facedown a few feet away. Nick covered Rachael with his arm.

Events separated by fractions of a second played out as though time crawled. The center was awash with a strobe flash of yellow light. A moment later a rush of air passed by and a thunderclap echoed throughout the cave. Then there came the sound of stone falling as pieces held for millennia were loosened by the explosion. Had the team been in the tunnel at the dig, the force of the explosion would have ejected them like fodder from a canon. The huge cavern of the underground visitor center absorbed the compression and saved them.

Echoing sounds of falling rock took long seconds to subside. The Stranger turned and sat up. The others took it to be an all-clear signal as they joined him sitting on the rock floor. They were at the edge of the area occupied by the cement kiosk. The limestone ceiling of the cavern groaned as the team remained still, not knowing which way to move. Before anyone could act, a large section of stone dropped onto the top of the kiosk, smashing the display below. Tee shirts flew everywhere from the force of the impact, with several landing at their feet.

Nick broke the tension with "The Park Service isn't going to like that," as though the busted tee shirt desk was the worst of it. But then he sounded defeated as he groaned, "Well, I guess we've lost everything."

Rachael smiled as she held out her palm for all to see. In it was a thumb drive. Nick knew it must contain a backup of all the data they collected.

Nick beamed, "I love you."

Rachael, taking the statement as only a passing compliment, made a response from an old Star Wars movie, "I know."

Chapter 19

"WE'VE GOT TO MOVE!" commanded The Stranger, as he improvised a bandage from one of the tee shirts and wrapped it around Drake's bleeding head.

Dazed by the explosion, Nick, Rachael, and Tom stayed on the floor of the visitor center, not moving. They all had the same thoughts.

The Stranger saved their lives, but who planted the bomb? Who shot Drake? What happened to Benton?

The Stranger focused on bandaging Drake's head. No doubt the man had done it before.

Was he a soldier, a medic…? Why was he here?

"Who are you?" asked Nick.

"Name's Walter Tanner," said The Stranger.

"Walter Tanner?" said Nick, "Not Rambo?" Nick was surprised by the mild name for this man who he cast as an action hero.

The Stranger had heard that one before. "Cute," he said as he finished bandaging Drake. "Whoever did this is armed and may still be around. I suggest we move. We've got to get your man to a hospital and we've got to get the rest of you to safety."

Nick wondered whether Benton might be involved in this.

His unexpected hasty departure seemed odd, or was it only coincidental?

"Did you notice anyone leaving the site?" Nick asked.

"I saw no one," Tanner replied. "Look, we've got to move."

No one questioned Tanner's orders. Maybe it was his commanding presence or maybe no one knew what to do next. In either case, each member of the team responded. They stood up while Tanner got Drake to his feet, put his arm under his shoulder and stumbled toward the elevators.

Inside the elevator, Tanner, with Drake propped up beside him, occupied half the cab as the rest squeezed in. Nick punched the button for the top and they began their minute-and-a-half ascent. Time to ask the questions everyone had on their minds.

"I'm confused," said Tom. "You and I met in Wyoming. You mentioned this cavern. I could tell you weren't a caver, but you got me thinking about it. Now, here you are. And weren't you the man standing on the ridge at the cave-in in Colorado?"

"Yeah," said Tanner. "That was me. I was too late to save your friends. I'm sorry about that."

Rachael chimed in. "Save his friends? Walter, who are you?"

Tanner shot a sharp look at Rachael. "Only my mother calls me Walter, and you're not my mother."

Undeterred, Rachael asked, "So what do we call you, Mr. Tanner?"

Looking at no one in particular, he said, "Tanner's fine."

Only the whir of the elevator speeding up through the rock broke the silence as Nick, Tom, and Rachael wondered if they had just inherited a new member of the team.

They reached the aboveground visitor center after ten in the evening. At that hour, the tourists were gone and only a member of Nick's security team was present. This guard was young, in his twenties, tall at six-foot four, but not muscular like Tanner or Drake. The guard pulled his service revolver when he spotted Tanner carrying the wounded Drake, unsure of a possible threat. Nick told him to put it away, that everything was under control.

"What happened?" the guard asked. "I was in the tent monitoring the cameras when they all went dark."

"Did you see Benton walk out before the cameras went dark?" asked Nick.

"No."

"Did you see him leave from aboveground?"

"No. But his van's gone."

"Did you see this guy walk in?" Nick said pointing to Tanner.

"No."

"Dammit," said the frustrated Nick. "What the hell *did* you see?"

"Like I said, the cameras went out. I buzzed Drake on the intercom. He started to respond to me and then was yelling at someone. Then the line went dead. A few minutes later, I felt a rumble in the ground and I headed down here to check things out."

"What did Drake say?"

"He told me everything was OK there, then he called out to someone, 'Hey, can I help you?' After which, the line went dead."

"Look," Nick directed the security guard, "Get Drake to a hospital. We're going somewhere else."

The security guard, confused by events, kept a wary eye on Tanner. "Do you want me to call your driver?" he asked.

"Yes, use him to get Drake to a hospital." Turning to Tanner, Nick asked, "Do you have a vehicle?"

"Sure," said Tanner.

Then to the guard, Nick said, "We're going with him."

Outside, the desert night provided cool, crisp air allowing a million stars to shine against the black sky. Had someone not just attempted to kill each of them, the team would have stopped to appreciate the sight.

As the guard summoned Nick's driver on his cell phone, Tanner started to walk Drake out of the visitor center. Nick joined them seeking any sign of recognition in Drake's eyes.

"Drake, are you all right?" asked Nick. Drake didn't answer. Nick was eager to find out what Drake knew, who he might have seen, how this all happened; but those answers were not forthcoming.

The bullet wound was superficial. He must have hit his head when he fell.

As Nick studied Drake, Nick's driver pulled up in a green Land Rover. The driver stopped and walked around the car to Drake and Tanner.

Tanner helped lay Drake across the backseat of the car. Nick instructed his driver to get him to the nearest hospital right away. The driver, a short, old man was local, knew the area, and told Nick the name of the nearest hospital. Nick instructed the driver to stay there, at the hospital with Drake. He would call later to find how he was doing. The driver drove off with his patient in back.

As they watched the taillights of the car disappear down the winding road from the visitor center, Tanner waved his arm like an usher and said, "This way to my truck." The team followed.

Nick would have called Tanner's GMC Suburban an SUV, but he heard men call such vehicles 'trucks' before as though 'truck' was masculine and 'SUV' was too feminine.

An SUV is what soccer moms drive. Tanner was far from being a soccer mom.

As Tanner took the wheel, Nick joined him up front with Tom and Rachael in back.

"Where to?" asked Tanner.

"Do you know the house where we're staying?" asked Nick.

"Yes."

"Somehow, I thought you would. Take us there."

Tanner backed out of the parking space and headed down the road. Nick pulled out his cell phone and selected a frequently-dialed contact.

"Lizzy, we need to leave on a trip," Nick said as he looked in back for a nod from Tom and Rachael. Both knew where they were going. It was on The Tablet. "Can you pull together our things? We might be in a hurry."

"I haven't even unpacked," added Rachael to be helpful.

Nick concluded the call to Lizzy with, "Great, we'll be there in forty-five minutes."

Nick began texting someone who he did not want to share with Tanner. In the meantime, Tom questioned Tanner from the backseat.

"Of course, we appreciate your saving our lives, and all," Tom began.

Tanner smiled. "My pleasure."

"But why?"

"Why I saved you?"

"Why are you here at all?"

The lights from a passing car lit Tanner's chiseled profile. Tom sensed uncertainty, a man pondering how to express himself. The Suburban was about to pass a rest area on the right when Tanner did a quick turn onto the short access ramp to the deserted parking area.

"Whoa," said Nick in surprise at the quick turn. "What are you doing?"

Tanner didn't answer. He stopped in the center of the empty parking area, not taking the time to pull into a space. "We've got to talk," he said, as he killed the engine. He opened the door, climbed out, left the door open, headlights on, and headed to a nearby picnic table illuminated by the beams from the truck. He took a seat on the tabletop with his feet on the connected bench, lost in concentration, waiting for the others.

Nick, Tom, and Rachael didn't say a word. In a day in which one unusual event followed another, this was yet one more. The headlights on the truck timed out and left Tanner sitting in darkness save for the same thick canopy of stars seen at the visitor center. The noise of an occasional car speeding by broke the silence.

Not saying anything, first Nick, and then the others, opened their doors and stepped out of the truck. Rachael closed the door Tanner had left open as she walked by. They walked over to Tanner and each took a seat on the picnic table bench facing him as though they were students attending an outdoor lecture.

"I was in the Army for eighteen years, in the Rangers for twelve of those eighteen," Tanner began. "I saw a lot of action, but it was my last mission that not only ended my Army career, but almost cost me my life. It was also when I discovered The Tablet."

"You discovered what?" exclaimed Nick.

"There's more than one."

Tanner had the team's undivided attention

Chapter 20

Tanner's Tale

THERE WERE FIVE OF US. I'd worked with these men many times before in Iraq and Afghanistan. I was their sergeant and leader for this mission. A C-160 airdropped us into a northern valley, in the center of Taliban-controlled territory. We planned to capture a leader, Mohammad Mansour. Intel said he could be turned, that he might work with the government, that he wanted peace. To the Taliban, their leader would seem to be captured and not seen as a traitor. If he worked with the government, he would be released, maybe under some prisoner exchange deal. Others could work that out. We only had to get the guy.

"A crescent moon lit the night, just enough for us to see our jump site. Intel placed Mansour in a valley at the foot of the mountains in the Hindukush. We did a HALO drop from 20,000 feet into that area."

Tanner noticed puzzled looks and explained, "HALO, 'high altitude, low opening.' We flew like birds until the last moment to pull ripcords. It's a rush. The moon lit the snow covering the peaks as we headed into the valley.

"We dropped within sight of each other on the dusty plain and regrouped. I carried a radio with a GPS beacon, but we were on radio silence as we began phase two, along the side of a mountain, three klicks to our north. We made good time and reached our target area at 0600. We positioned ourselves in a rest-and-watch area from where we could see any movement. The sun rose behind the slope to our east, casting long shadows. We took positions out of sight behind a row of large rocks on the hillside with a walking path just over the other side. If we got lucky, we would find Mansour taking his daily walk described by Intel. We were not lucky. We were far from lucky."

Tanner paused, wearing the expression of a man reliving events he would rather forget.

"They must have known we were coming. We took automatic fire from high above and to our left. Two of my guys got hit right away. We pulled them from incoming fire, but I could tell they were dead. The team formed a semicircle, returning the fire. Then, out of nowhere, there's this kid. He must have been walking along the path when all hell broke loose. Maybe eight years old, he wore a long tunic and sandals like all those boys wore. The firefight frightened him, and he panicked. He ran along the path right between the shooting. I don't know what got into me. It went against my training. But I stood and ran the few steps between him and me, leaving myself open. Two shots hit my helmet, but didn't penetrate. I felt a sting in my calf and then in my right side. But I dove on top of the boy, covering him. The shooting stopped. The shot in my leg must have hit an artery. I began bleeding out. Just before I lost consciousness, I turned to see all my guys down. No movement. All dead. I thought I would be joining them. Everything went blank.

"I don't know how much time passed. I was in and out of it for what they told me lasted two weeks. A group of men with dark beards and turbans stood guard near me as veiled women attended, putting water-soaked towels on my head, rubbing who-knows-what on my wounds. A man walked in I recognized from photos, Mansour, our target for capture. He was a big, beefy man around forty years old with a large black beard. "Rather than put a bullet in my head as I expected, he looked at me with concern. Turning to the other men he said something in Pashto. I'm trained in the language and knew he asked if I would live. The men assured him I would. I wasn't looking forward to what they might have in mind, but I was so sick, I didn't care.

"In another day or two, I could sit up. My side hurt like a son of a bitch, but I was alive. They fed me and took care of me. There was this one man, about twenty, too young to have more than a scruffy beard. He appeared to be keeping guard and stayed with me all the time in the small hillside room. He hesitated to talk, even though I threw a few greetings his way in Pashto, the equivalent of 'hey, how are you?' Then, one day, I asked him why they took care of me. Why wasn't I dead? He told me I saved the life of their leader's son. I hadn't figured it out until that moment. The boy I jumped on top of was Mansour's boy.

"Soon, I could walk around using a crude homemade crutch they gave me. I wore the clothes they wore, a one-piece shirt to my ankles. It surprised me to see everyone getting used to having me around. Not much to do but admire the hillsides and talk to the goats. There was no doubt in my mind I wasn't spending the rest of my life here, but I wasn't in any condition to do something about it.

"Then one day, while I was sitting on a rock overlooking the valley, Mansour came with two of his bodyguards. He chatted in Pashto. Simple stuff: How was I doing? Allah had blessed me. Then he said in English, 'Come with me. I want to show you something.'

"He motioned to his bodyguards to stay behind and we walked together. Slow going since I still used a crutch. It took about an hour over a little used, rocky path to get to what he wanted to show me. I learned about him as we walked. I told him his English was good. He told me it was better than my Pashto and grinned, the first and last time a member of the Taliban would ever smile at me. He told me he'd attended school in England, which surprised me. I thought most of these men were ignorant goat herders. He understood my surprise and informed me we Americans knew nothing about them. But he thought me different. He said Allah had sent me to save his son. I didn't consider Allah had much to do with it, but I didn't argue. I was alive because he believed it.

"He asked me if I knew about the Buddhas of Bamiyan. I did. They were huge images of Buddha carved from a rock cliff two thousand years ago. They stood not far from where we were. When the Taliban controlled this country, they dynamited them."

"You considered them false idols," I said.

"He shot me a sharp look and corrected me. 'The amount of money you westerners put into maintaining those relics infuriated us when our country had much more important needs. It blew away some of your influence as much as anything.'

"He admitted with a look of disappointment, 'And yes, the less informed of my people considered them false idols.'

"Then he continued, 'But the destruction uncovered something, an object they brought to me as their leader. This was special. It needed protection. But I will show it to you.'

"I wondered why me, but I wasn't in a position to argue.

"We turned a corner to a deep cleft in the rocks. The smooth stone made a natural wall on each side, rising from the ground level up to fifty feet on either side. We walked toward the end of the wall a hundred feet away. It seemed to be a dead end with large stones scattered about. He told me to help him as he put both hands atop a stone to the left and began to roll it away. I put my crutch aside and helped roll the stone. Behind it appeared an opening five-feet high and three-feet wide. Inside, to the right lay a torch. Mansour stepped inside, pulled matches from his pocket, lit the torch and motioned for me to follow him. I grabbed my crutch and walked in behind him.

"The cave enlarged after a few steps to where I could stand. After walking a minute, it opened into a small room twenty-feet across and ten-feet high. I thought this cave was meant to be a tomb with this room the final resting place for a body. The far wall had a shelf carved into the stone about the right size to lay a body. But there was no body. Mansour held the torch high and pointed to the tablet on the shelf. Although it was far smaller than the one you discovered, it lit the room with its reflection.

"'This is what they brought to me,' he said. 'They thought it was an item westerners hid there, maybe the Russians when they occupied us. They knew it was something from a modern country. But how could that be? Someone had buried this tablet deep behind a monument thousands of years old.'

"I looked at the tablet. The dots and spaces looked like

binary code. I didn't understand what they meant, but the symbols below were clear. They showed humans, two lines intertwined, a constellation, then a basic map of Italy. Yes, I know, it's what you found at the bottom of your tablet. Your guard above ground wasn't the only one looking at the monitor of your site, although he never saw me. When the media reported your find, I suspected your tablet and mine had a link. When I looked at the etchings on the monitor, I knew it without a doubt. That's when I decided to pay you a visit, but seems a bomb got in the way.

"The story doesn't end in that cave in Afghanistan. For me, it just began. I asked Mansour why he showed me this relic. He told me a story passed down from generation to generation going back to when the silk route ran through that area. Traders traveling from East to West told stories of angels that came to earth and married women. Their offspring were gifted in many ways. He told me, 'Your own Bible talks of such things.'

"I knew the tale. Came from Genesis. I thought it was a way to explain why some of us are smarter or more talented than others. But Mansour had a twist in his version. He said his people told of a tablet of gold that showed where the angels lived. Perhaps this was it?

"Mansour was educated in the West. He didn't believe such a tablet pointed to real angels, but rather it told of powers only angels had. And 'gold' may have been an attempt to describe a metal no one had ever seen before. Yet, he made it clear he was a devout man. He told me that Allah had sent me. Saving his son was proof. And he shared this secret with me because Allah destined me to solve its clues.

"Yet, he wasn't about to give me the tablet. He told me it would remain safe in the cave where only he knew the location. He walked me out of the cave and expressed concern for my safety. His people may seem to ignore my presence, but there was talk. He would have something done. He made me swear I would never attempt to come back to this place. I asked him how I could solve the clues without the tablet. He said Allah would provide.

"I thought of the tablet and what danger I might face, but I didn't have to think long. The next morning, three men roused me from my sleep, grabbed me, tied my hands behind my back, and threw a hood over my head. Leaving my crutch behind, and holding my shoulder for support, one of them walked me out to a vehicle parked alongside the road. They threw me in the back seat. We traveled for two hours before we stopped, and they hoisted me out of the vehicle and pulled off the hood. We were in a valley, but not the one where I first landed.

"One of them cut my bindings loose. Another shoved the radio I first used when I arrived onto my chest and I grabbed it. They demonstrated their anger toward me with muted growls and spitting at my feet. They seemed to be following Mansour's orders against their own desire to cut my throat. Then they disappeared. The radio was in working order. I called in for rescue and the GPS beacon led the copters to my spot. I sat on the ground waiting for the Army to find me when I felt something poking me in the waist. I reached down inside my shirt and found a photo inside my waistband. It was a photo of the tablet. It wasn't Allah that provided. It was Mansour.

"I spent the next week at Ramstein in a hospital, still sore, but alive. My leg healed OK. Over the next year, I had a limp that slowly improved. Still bothers me in wet weather. But my lungs were shot, literally. A bullet pierced my right one. The home remedies the mountain women provided kept infections at bay, but the doctors at Ramstein had to put me under the knife to remove a section. My Army career was over.

"I didn't think God destined me to solve the mystery of the tablet, but now discharged with a pension, what better use of my time did I have? I showed the photo around. It was not a great shot and didn't capture the luster of the metal. Most people thought it interesting, but that was about it. I took a train to Florence to an academy that dealt with antiquities. A professor there took one look at the photo and his eyes brightened. He wrote the name of a man for me to visit at the

Vatican library in Rome. The professor said the Vatican allowed few people into that library, but he would make arrangements to be sure they allowed me in. He asked, 'You are an American, are you not?' He said they had a book there I would have a particular interest in.

"Another train ride and I arrived in Rome. Pushing through throngs of people at the Vatican, I showed a Swiss Guard the name of the man the professor recommended, a Monsignor Alonso Alberti. He knew him and, after a call, showed me the way to the entrance of the library. The library was huge, modern, and amazing. I realized it contained documents as old as writing itself. Monsignor Alberti turned out to be a young, tall academic with a perpetual smile as though he knew secrets he wasn't sharing. Although my Italian improved as I traveled around the country, he spoke flawless English, one of seven languages he spoke, as he told me about himself.

"He led me down through stacks of books into a room with an airlock. The filtered air inside was set at the perfect humidity level to protect ancient manuscripts. Alberti remarked that the air handling system was a necessary precaution, although the book he would show me was only four hundred years old. They have a different sense of what's old at the Vatican. He slid on latex gloves and handed me a pair. The man cautiously brought over a large volume, the size of an altar bible, with an ornate embossed design for its cover, and laid it on a tall reading table. He told me this was the journal of the first Spanish governor of Santa Fe, Juan de Ornate, written in 1610. Alberti asked me if he could see the photo I'd shown his friend in Florence. His perpetual smile broadened as he eyed the photo and opened the book. He turned the pages with care and he told me the text, in Old Spanish, described local Indian lore in which spirits married women of the tribe and their children were special. Some were the best warriors, others destined to be chiefs. They called these spirits the snake men with feet. In one region, far north of Santa Fe, Juan de Ornate himself found a cave drawing that represented the story and he reproduced it. He pointed to a page in which appeared a drawing of a man, two snakes entwined, a bird in flight and the outline of what looked like a boot. We both looked again at my photograph. If an Indian, hundreds of years ago, was able to glimpse this photo, he would have interpreted the entwined lines as snakes and the map of Italy, a country they would never know existed, a boot. They would remember a man, two snakes, and a boot. The only thing different was the picture had a bird and my photo had the Big Dipper. Don't know why.

"On another page, de Ornate drew a map depicting the location of the cave drawing. His topography was precise. It identified the area where Tom's buddies had found the cave drawings and it showed Carlsbad. Those would be my next stops.

"I spent four months in Carlsbad and visited the caverns multiple times. I couldn't find anyone who knew anything about the legend, or the old drawing de Ornate found. Nothing. Wasn't sure what I was searching for. The distraction this hunt had provided started to wear off and I began waking up in cold sweats from dreams about my dead buddies. I'd lost friends before, but those guys… I guess it was the fact they were mowed down and I wasn't. Just for doing a stupid thing, I lived.

"An uncle of mine left me a plot of land in Wyoming years ago. I moved there, built a place to be alone and think things through. Then you came along, Tom. You explored places no one had ever been. I heard about some of the other caves in the Carlsbad area. I'm no caver and suggested you check them out. It would be a shot in the dark, but it looks like you found it, what I've been looking for. Only thing is, now what?

"Before you answer, I need to tell you something the Indians believed about the snake men. Juan de Ornate reported the Indians believed the snake men were mighty spirits and they guarded powerful secrets. If you tried to find the secrets, they could make you die a horrible death in the blink of an eye.

"Any questions?"

Chapter 21

THE TEAM, NOW INCLUDING TANNER, arrived in his Suburban at Nick's rented house. Rachael, Tom, and Nick, were still in wrinkled, soiled clothing, sweat mixed with dust from the explosion. Tanner was in a similar condition, with the addition of a smear of blood from Drake's wound. They made a curious, bedraggled group checking into this Victorian B&B.

Nick directed Tanner to park in the rear out of sight of the black sedan stationed in front. That car had become a constant fixture with two men keeping watch. Tanner had already turned off the headlights a block away, killed the engine upon arrival, and let the Suburban coast into the rear driveway.

"You guys are a mess!" said Lizzy as she opened the rear screen door for the team. "Well, *hello*," she exclaimed as Tanner approached, pleased by his roughhewn appearance.

"Lizzy, this is Walt . . ." Nick started and then, remembering Tanner's reaction to using his first name, reverted to, "This is Tanner."

Tanner put out his hand, enveloped Lizzy's in a rock-solid shake, and smiled. "Hi."

Lizzy, captivated by the large man, tried not to show how she felt and responded, "Well, hi yourself, Tanner."

Rachael noticed Lizzy's interest in Tanner and fueled it

further as she passed by whispering, "And he saved our lives."

"Do tell," said Lizzy, with added sparkle in her voice.

Tanner, a man who chose the loneliness of Wyoming, didn't mind a lively, good-looking woman showing him some interest.

He had been the first to the door, but each member passed by as Lizzy continued to stand in his way. "Ah . . . I better get inside," he said.

After the team concurred that Tanner would be a member of their group, Nick asked if he would join them on the trip he planned. "That's what I'm here for," said Tanner.

Nick revealed that he had already texted his pilot to get the jet ready for a trip to Rome. That would not be their final destination, but it was one he felt safe listing on a flight plan. He confirmed earlier that Tom and Rachael had their passports. He asked Tanner if he had a passport with him.

"Which one?" asked Tanner with a grin. Nick paused a moment before he realized this man, equipped for dark missions, might have a selection.

Tanner confirmed that Nick's jet was a private plane. "Then I can take my gear." He said it as a statement, not a question. Nick understood Tanner packed toys over which TSA might have a conniption.

Inside the kitchen, the scent of a fresh pot of coffee filled the air. Lizzy, not only made sure she packed for everyone, but thought all might need a cup of coffee and bypassed the single cup brewer for a larger carafe. Nick would rather have a scotch, but there would be time for that on the plane.

"Look, Nick, I know we've got to get moving," said Rachael with Tanner nodding in agreement. "But I've got to get a quick shower."

"Sure," responded Nick. "Let's meet back here in fifteen minutes with our stuff and head out. The pilot sent me a text. He's ready to go. We have baths in each of our rooms." Turning to Lizzy, "Would you show Tanner a shower he can use?"

The image of this hunk of a man in a shower inspired Lizzy. "Sure," she beamed. "This way."

She danced up the staircase with Tanner lumbering behind carrying his duffel bag. The old steps groaned under his weight and further excited Lizzy. Her imagination couldn't settle on one scenario with this man before another, more outlandish, took its place. She showed him through the door of an unoccupied guest room, made up with fresh linens should Nick bring home a stray guest. Lizzy realized the fifteen-minute limit Nick announced meant the linens would remain undisturbed though she fantasized otherwise.

Lizzy could see from Tanner's dour expression that the clutter of ceramics adorning the room was hardly his style.

"The shower is there," she said pointing toward the bathroom door. "Sorry, but I only have those little, tiny soaps in there."

"No problem, I have my own soap," he assured.

Lizzy imagined his choice as a large chunk of rough lye soap like people made in a kettle in the olden days. Tanner said, "I'll be right out," walked into the bathroom with his duffel bag, closed the door, and soon the sound of the shower filled the room. Lizzy sat on the edge of the bed imagining the lathered body in the next room, but she had little time for that dream. The shower stopped after two minutes. She heard him drying off, the towel making audible slaps across his body. The door opened and Tanner stepped out with the towel wrapped around his waist, exposing the best-developed pectorals Lizzy had ever laid eyes on.

"Do you happen to have any underarm deodorant? Mine's used up," he asked, but the words passed Lizzy without adhering.

"Huh?" was her numb response.

Tanner chuckled at the obvious effect he had on Lizzy and repeated, "Deodorant?"

"Oh, sure, sure," she said as she went to the drawer of a side table. She always kept spare toiletries stored away in each room and pulled out a stick deodorant. "Here," she said as she handed it to him.

"Thanks," he replied, and, with a wink, he returned to the

bathroom and closed the door.

Lizzy stood by the closed door. She wanted to understand more and started a conversation as the unseen guest dressed.

"They said you saved them. What happened?"

"There was a cave-in and I got them out of there before anyone got hurt."

"A cave-in? Tom just lost two buddies from a cave-in."

"I know."

"So, you just happened to be there when a cave-in was about to happen. How did you know?"

The bathroom door Lizzy now leaned against jerked open and she fell into the fully dressed Tanner. He wore a clean set of the same camouflaged shirt and pants as before.

How many identical outfits did he have?

Undeterred by Lizzy, now attached to his shirt but trying to rebalance herself, Tanner looked down at her and continued. "There was a bomb."

Lizzy pushed away from Tanner with alarm. "Jesus! A bomb? First, we have guys casing our house and then bombs? What's going on?"

"What guys?" he asked.

"A couple of cops in a plain sedan out front on the street," Lizzy answered as she pointed to the window.

Tanner walked to the window, stood to its side, and pulled back the curtain to see the black sedan. "So, those are the guys

Nick wanted me to avoid." He closed the curtain and walked back.

"They don't know anyone's here," Lizzy said.

"Too late. There're lights on all over the house. How do you know they're cops?"

Lizzy gave Tanner a know-it-all look as though the answer was obvious.

"OK," Tanner said in response. "Let's say for now they are. We've got a plane to catch and I imagine they want to know all about that."

He looked at Lizzy evaluating this woman to see if she was up to the next task he had in mind. He surmised she had what it took.

"I want you to help. Think you're up to it?"

Lizzy beamed. It was time she got in on the action circling around her. "Sure," she answered.

"Here's what I want you to do."

Nick was first to return to the kitchen with Tom and Rachael joining him a moment later. Tom had two large, well-worn, hard-side suitcases and Rachael, a black, wheeled carryon. Looking at the small amount Rachael packed, Nick asked, "Will that be enough?"

"It'll do. Besides, they have clothes in Italy," Rachael responded.

"I don't think we'll be stopping in Milan."

Rachael, perturbed by Nick's reference to the fashion capital and that he didn't yet understand the latest style meant nothing to her, summarized her feeling with a caustic, "Please."

Lizzy walked in with Tanner, both smiling as conspirators.

"What's up with you two?" Nick asked seeking the reason behind the grins.

"I'm guessing you don't want that car in front following us," said Tanner.

Nick, who hadn't planned that far ahead yet, answered, "I would prefer not."

"Lizzy's going to help," he said.

"How?"

Tanner didn't answer, but rather moved his new troops out on their mission. "Let's load up," he said as he slung his duffel bag over his shoulder. He winked at Lizzy and she disappeared into the hallway.

Nick wanted to understand what was going on, but before he could call out after her, Tanner said, "You'll see soon enough. Ready?"

Tom and Rachael were already moving out the door. Nick, once again following rather than leading, begrudgingly tagged along behind his teammates out the screen door held open by Tanner.

Tanner opened the rear door of the Suburban. The team loaded their luggage to join the large equipment case Tanner transported. Each member imagined the tools of the trade Tanner might have in that case.

They assumed the same positions in the Suburban as before with Tanner at the wheel, Nick beside him, Tom and Rachael in the back seat. Tanner started the truck, this time with no regard to engine noise and revving the engine as though he wanted to attract attention. He backed out the short driveway, onto the street, put the truck in drive, and gunned it with a squall of tires. The Suburban raced through the intersection near where the sedan was parked. The sedan's engine roared to life, the headlights flashed on. There was another squall of tires as the car raced to follow the Suburban.

As the sedan reached the intersection, a dusty, red, ten-year-old Honda Civic passed directly in front of it. The sedan's left front crashed into the rear of the Honda spinning it sideways and stopping it ten feet away from the sedan. The driver of the sedan killed the engine and he and his partner stepped out. Both were dressed in wrinkled, ill-fitting suits with loosened ties, two middle-aged white men who looked as though they slept in their clothes. The driver of the Honda pushed her newly-warped door open with effort and the men in wrinkled suits were faced with a young redhead launching a rant of invectives in a mix of Spanish and English.

After sufficiently haranguing the two men, Lizzy asked, "OK. You two. Who's going to pay for this?"

Chapter 22

THE DANK DAY IN WASHINGTON, DC, matched Senator Morrison's mood. The discovery at Carlsbad had become a spectacle. Now came reports that exacerbated the frenzy.

A cave-in? Caused by a bomb?

The people trying to eliminate Nicholas Foxe had failed and caused massive damage in a federal park.

It was a clumsy attempt.

The senator received a call from his wife soon after the news hit TV. She asked about Foxe. Was he hurt? Her concern seemed neutral, not anxious, but knowing her history with the man, it bothered him for her to be asking about him. Yet, it was unclear whether she wished Foxe dead, or wished him well. Morrison assured his wife Foxe was safe. He had information the press did not. Foxe and three other people had boarded a private plane whose flight plan listed Rome as the destination. Other passengers included Tom Littleton, who made the discovery, Rachael Friedman, a visitor from MIT, plus an unidentified man traveling under the name of Raymond Ferguson, a suspected alias.

Who was that man?

The senator asked the US Embassy in Rome to question Foxe upon arrival, but by the time the embassy reps arrived at the Fiumicino general aviation area, Foxe and the others had vanished. No one knew where.

Randy reported to a conference room in the Senate Office Building as directed by the senator's chief of staff, Ed Granger. He didn't know why, but thought it had something to do with the explosion at Carlsbad. The small room had three blue swivel chairs positioned on each side of a well-worn wooden table. Oak paneling in need of refinishing covered the walls. The smell of cigarette smoke, absorbed by the fabric of the chairs and the American flag at one end of the room, lingered in the air. DC was a smoke-free city, but as in other things, House and Senate office buildings were exempt from the rules. Senator Morrison didn't allow smoking in his offices, but this room was not a part of his offices.

The door opened and the chief of staff walked in followed by a man Randy had never seen before. Randy was directed to take a seat. The man was lean, in his thirties, his hair closely cropped. He appeared freshly barbered with a neat part on the left. He dressed in a navy suit, white shirt, and blue tie. Randy wore a white shirt each day, but this man's shirt, tailored and crisp, made Randy's wrinkled one seem shabby.

The two men said nothing and took seats opposite Randy. Following them was the senator himself, who grabbed the third chair on the opposite side and rolled it to the head of the table. He wore a pinstripe suit with a light blue shirt, red tie, and his ever-present flag lapel pin. Randy regretted not grabbing his sport coat when he left his desk and felt exposed wearing an old tie.

"Thank you for joining us," said the senator breaking an uncomfortable silence with a greeting that didn't fit the occasion. Randy had no choice but to join them.

"This is Agent Wells," the senator said pointing toward the new man who acknowledged the intro with a slight, expressionless nod to Randy. "He's with the FBI and he's investigating the incident at Carlsbad."

This didn't bode well, Randy thought. When you're introduced to 'someone from the FBI,' your guard better be up.

"He wants to ask you some questions," the senator continued.

Randy hoped his panic didn't show. When told by the senator 'he wants to ask you some questions,' a host of private indiscretions flashed through his head.

"Just relax. Your answers remain secret. Ed and I are leaving the two of you alone."

Randy wondered why the senator and Ed took the time, albeit just a few minutes, to introduce the agent. Was it to emphasize the importance of the interview, to let Randy know they knew what was going on? There was no time to get answers, because, with those few words of introduction, the senator and Ed stood. Randy did, as well, out of respect, but Agent Wells remained seated watching Randy, sizing him up. The two men left the room and closed the door.

Agent Wells said nothing, took out a small spiral notebook, thumbed through several pages of notes until he arrived at a clean page. He set the notebook on the desk, reached into his coat, pulled out a ballpoint pen and clicked the point in place. He took his time, saying nothing. Randy wanted to break the silence, but managed to wait.

Wells opened with a series of standard questions to which the agent already knew the answers: Confirm his full name and spelling, the number of years he worked for the senator, what he did before coming to Capitol Hill. These questions made Randy relax as if taking an easy exam. Then Wells looked Randy in the eye and asked a series of more pointed questions.

"When you visited the site, did Foxe mention a plan to travel elsewhere?" Wells asked.

"What do you mean?"

"Did he indicate there was somewhere else he and the members of his team were going?"

"Team?" asked Randy. "There were only two of them, Foxe and Littleton."

Wells didn't enlighten Randy about the other people who later joined the two men. He could see by Randy's expression he had not kept tabs on what was going on at the site. Randy might not know about a Mr. Raymond Ferguson, but would know about Rachael Friedman if he were up to date. Wells moved the questions in another direction.

"You saw the slab up close, did you not?"

"Yes."

"What did you make of it?"

Randy needed little prompting to share his impressions. He gushed how it looked too new and the metal too advanced to be as old as they said it was. Yet, there it was, sealed into the edges of the stone wall surrounding it.

"What did the markings mean to you?"

Randy's expression depicted his uncertainty about how to answer the simple question. "Do you mean, what did they say? I have no idea."

"Did Foxe or Littleton indicate the nature of the code?"

"What do you mean?"

Agent Wells became annoyed. "Did they think it was a Greek play, a scientific formula, or some ancient civilization's grocery list?"

Randy suddenly realized this FBI agent had yet to ask him a single question regarding the bombing.

The agent didn't ask whether Foxe thought himself in danger. Had he seen suspicious people hanging around? Nothing. It was all about the slab itself.

Wasn't questioning always done by two agents. That much he knew from TV. Why only one this time?

The gray day turned to a light sprinkle by late evening when Senator Morrison left the Senate office complex. A Lincoln Town Car pulled up to the curb as he exited the building. The senator dashed down the steps, the rain too light to bother with an umbrella, but enough to hustle to the car, where the driver waited with an open door. The senator climbed in the rear and sat on the slightly damp, black leather seat. The smell of the other passenger's cologne permeated the car. It smelled like English Leather. He thought the same thing all the other times he met this man: *Why does he wear that stuff?*

"So, the FBI paid you a visit today," said the man.

"He paid my aide Randy a visit," corrected Morrison.

"What did Randy say?"

"That's something only the FBI knows."

"Cut the bullshit, Pete! What did he say?"

"Nothing useful."

The man smiled. "That's not bad. Not bad. Your man Randy is likely to know less than we do."

"You mean what we *think* we know," corrected Morrison.

The man seldom used his native Texas accent save for occasions like this where he thought it added to the point he was making. So, he drawled "Pete, my hunches are seldom wrong. And I've got a good feeling about this one."

The Reverend Jones sat in his office at the Temple of Power befuddled. He just saw the news of the cave-in at Carlsbad on TV. There was talk of a bomb causing it. His wife's first thought was for the safety of their son, Christopher. He was working on getting a meeting with Foxe.

Did he make it to the cave? Could he have been there when it happened?

Calls to Chris' cell phone went unanswered, and his mother left a dozen messages. The Reverend's first thought concerned the effect of these events on his ministry and not his son. He knew Chris to be a survivor, which turned out later in the day to be true. Chris eventually returned his mom's frantic calls to tell her he was unsuccessful in arranging a meeting and hadn't been in the cave.

Content his son was safe, but not terribly concerned, Jones ruminated on the next steps he needed to take in order to use the discovery in his preaching. His television flock had swelled to record numbers after Jones' sermon on the meaning of The Tablet.

Had The Tablet been destroyed? Would he lose this opportunity to build his television followers with The Tablet gone?

Gloria focused on her husband's concern and suggested they turn to prayer.

"Of course," replied the Reverend, forgetting for a moment that he worked in the prayer business.

The Reverend got down on his knees with Gloria, a position getting harder on his arthritic bones. "Oh Lord," he said, "I pray for Your guidance. I pray You guide me as I lead Your people through these events, seeking Your meaning."

Missing from the prayer was mention of the safety of those who were in the cave. Rather than a prayer for the souls of those affected, it became more of a supplication to God for a new business plan.

The news media did not yet have the same information as those in Washington. The public did not know that everyone in the cave had survived, that a guard was in a hospital in an induced coma, or that a group of cavers was on a flight out of the country. There was no information about The Tablet and its status.

The day passed with no response from the Lord God and the Reverend told his publicist to tell everyone that he was in prayer, seeking an answer.

The next morning started out a glorious day and the Reverend spent the early hours walking in the rose garden outside of the Temple of Power. The garden was more of Gloria's domain. She had the green thumb. He stopped to observe a spiderweb built across the rose bushes, the early morning dew highlighting it. A large spider posed on one side, waiting.

Gloria looked out the window, puzzled to see her husband in the garden since he seldom ventured there. She joined him as he studied the spiderweb and saw a look come across his face she recognized. He had an answer. She could tell by just looking at him. The Reverend didn't notice her until she spoke, "Honey, what is it?"

The Reverend turned to his wife, a big smile on his face. "I have it."

"Have what?"

"What caused the cave-in."

"What was it, Honey?"

"Terrorists!"

Chapter 23

Locorotondo, Italy

THEY SAT AT A SMALL TABLE outside the *Braceria Ristorante* under the brilliant Apulia sun. The bleached white walls of the town were a far cry from the depths of the earth from which the team had come.

Tanner smirked at the bicycle the restaurant hung on a wall near their table. It bore a sign announcing the establishment's name and was festooned with red flowers to enliven the contrast against the white wall. "Cute," was his sarcastic remark.

Tanner's rudimentary Italian came back to him the moment the private jet touched down at the terminal in Rome, and he took the lead as translator for the team. Nick had a Volkswagen Caravelle van waiting, large enough to hold the four of them and Tanner's gear, but small enough to navigate the medieval streets of small Italian towns. Tanner spoke his first Italian to the car rental agent when he asked if the van was the best he had. The Italian, with no frame of reference regarding Tanner's usual ride, appeared confused, and said it was a fine *macchina.*

"It's going to be OK," said Nick, as he walked up with Tom and Rachael.

"If you say so, chief," responded Tanner.

"Chief? Where'd you get that?"

"Don't like it?"

"Nick's fine."

"Whatever you say, chief," replied Tanner, ignoring Nick's request.

Nick studied Tanner. He hadn't said much during the eight-hour flight to Rome, mostly snoozing, as did Rachael and Tom. But Nick spent most of his time awake, thinking about Tanner.

Was it just a coincidence that Tanner showed up at the same time the bomb went off?

Wasn't it Tanner who planted the seed with Tom to explore Carlsbad Caverns for a new passage into the caves? It never was a tablet Tom was searching for. It was another passage to Carlsbad. And Tanner suspected The Tablet was there, but how could he have known Tom would stumble across it when he planted that idea?

Tanner had been on the trail of The Tablet ever since Afghanistan. Nick was sure he had to see this search through to the end.

But why?

What Nick did know for sure was someone was trying to kill all of them and Tanner was their protection.

Nick contacted Lorenzo Cristofori, the odd, old man he had met at the reception in New York. Cristofori had expounded on the crazy idea that a language of music once existed. It was Cristofori Nick thought of now that the nature of the code had become clear. During the plane ride over, Nick instructed a detective who worked for him to locate Cristofori. As a well-known maker of violins in southern Italy, he had been easy to find. Nick phoned him from the plane, explained what they had found, and asked for a meeting. Cristofori insisted Nick come at once to his home in Locorotondo. Cristofori suggested they meet first at the *Braceria Ristorante* as it would be difficult to explain where his home was located within the small town. The restaurant was easy to find, and he would meet him there.

Nick informed Cristofori he would be with three members of his team. "No problem," reported the old violin maker.

"More of you, the merry, eh?"

Tanner cased his surroundings as Tom, Rachael, and Nick studied their leather-bound menus. Most of the team had spent sufficient periods underground, away from the sun, screwing up their circadian cycle. Add to that an overnight trip to Rome and a car trip to Locorotondo, they hadn't adjusted to the time of day. They knew one thing: they were starving.

"What looks good?" Tanner asked the team members with menus before them.

"Seafood," responded Rachael.

"Well, doesn't surprise me, the Mediterranean is right over there," Nick pointed in the general direction of the coastline.

"You mean the Adriatic," corrected Tanner.

"Yes, to be exact," Nick admitted. He studied the sullen Tanner, who was drumming his fingers on the table, looking around as though he was waiting for something other than a waiter.

Was it a mistake having him here?

The waiter, a young man with a black apron covering his white shirt and blue jeans, came to the table. "Do you have any questions?" he asked in smooth English with a charming touch of Italian accent.

"Yes," said Rachael, pointing to an item on the menu, all written in Italian. "I believe this is what we would call a seafood sampler.

"*Si,*" grinned the waiter. "It is a selection of *frutti di mare,* our specialty.

"I'll have that."

"Me too," added Tom.

Then turning to Tanner, the waiter asked, "And you, sir?"

"You have veal, right?"

"Yes, sir."

"I'll have a quarter kilo, grilled rare, with a side of green beans, and a Peroni to drink."

The waiter, taken aback, meekly stated, "You know, sir, that is quite a large portion. It is about a half pound."

Tanner smiled for the first time and said with a wink, "I know."

"And you, sir?" the waiter asked Nick.

Nick, distracted by Tanner's order, took a moment to turn his focus from the big guy to the young man patiently waiting.

"I'll take the veal, but your *piccata*, regular size, please. And some house white wine for the table," he added as he got nods from Tom and Rachael. Tanner would have his beer, but Nick's experience was that Italians offered agreeable wine in a carafe as their house special.

On the way to the Carlsbad airfield, Nick explained to the team why they were headed to Italy. He related the whole story about meeting Lorenzo Cristofori in New York and his claim. The fact that the tablets exposed an outline of the Italian peninsula, added to the reason they were headed there.

Nick was optimistic that Cristofori had the key to unlocking the puzzle. The rest of the team was not so sure. Each face displayed silent opposition to Nick's cheery one.

Tom was the first to speak.

"Nick, I'm enjoying the bright Italian sun, but don't you think you're putting too much stock in this one man? I mean Tanner has scoured the country. Why didn't he find the answer? Why didn't he find out about this guy?"

Tanner made a raised eyelid, open palm expression to Nick that endorsed Tom's query. Rachael studied Tom and Tanner, thinking, always thinking, but listening for more information. Nick studied Tanner.

Is that what's bothering him? He thinks he's been down this path before?

Nick said, "Look, I didn't believe in fate, but I'm rethinking my position on that. Think about all the things that had to align to bring us here.

"Tanner got things rolling, although none of us knew it at the time. A decision he made, seemingly having nothing to do with anything other than saving a young boy, exposed him to the tablet.

"He found one key, the book the Spaniard wrote centuries ago that pointed to Carlsbad. Tanner wasn't a caver, but he got one involved. You, Tom.

"You found The Tablet. You said it yourself. It seemed that something unlocked and dropped you into that pit.

"Then Rachael added something we missed, the depths of the pits on the slab, and how that may be music. Heck, Lizzy saw that connection.

"And then me, I met Cristofori, and, as far as I'm concerned, he validated the music connection."

Nick paused as each member considered the premise.

"So, what are the odds?"

Finally, Rachael spoke. "Nick, you're familiar with the birthday paradox?"

"No."

"How many people need to be in a room to make the odds fifty/fifty that two of them have the same birthday?"

Nick shrugged.

"Twenty-two."

"Really? That few?"

"Yes, and the odds are almost certain when there are seventy-five in a room."

"Which means…?"

"The odds of four people coming together who share something is not in the realm of fate or a higher power."

Nick made a face.

"Thank you, *Professor* Friedman."

Rachael smiled.

"But, another thing," Nick continued. "Look at who's come together on this team."

Nick paused to allow each member to consider as they stole quick glances at each other.

"Rachael, you're the scientist. Tom, you're the explorer.

Tanner," Nick smiled, "You're certainly the soldier."

"And you?" asked Tanner.

"I don't know. Guess I like to think I'm the leader. Maybe I get bent out of shape if someone takes the lead."

Immediately, team members nodded agreement.

"Hey," responded Nick. "You don't have to agree so quickly."

Everyone laughed, including Nick.

Rachael cut Nick some slack.

"Look, Nick," she said. "You are the sponsor at the very least. Hey, this is Italy. Think of yourself as a Medici, a patron."

Nick smiled.

Last time, she called me a jerk. I guess this is an improvement.

The waiter brought the meals. Tom and Rachael had matching platters of an assortment of broiled selections, the prawns much larger than shrimp back home and served in their shells, eyes intact. Nick's veal *piccata* was layered with a light lemon sauce and sprinkled with capers. Large slices of veal weighed down Tanner's plate with a mountain of green beans beside them as though the cook believed the vegetables must be in proportion to the meat.

Rachael picked up one of the smaller prawns, looking for a clue from Tom whether to eat shell and all. Tom demonstrated by popping the body into his mouth and crunching down on the soft-shelled crustacean. Rachael did likewise, both smiling at each other over their acceptance of local culinary customs.

Tanner dug into the pile of meat, slicing off large mouthfuls and washing it down with gulps of beer.

Nick felt he was the only traditionalist at the table eating a meal that could have easily been set before him at a number of restaurants near his New York apartment.

The talk at the table diminished as eating became paramount. Nick looked around as he ate, taking in Locorotondo. The architecture of Apulia reflected the Greek influence of the area. A town, like this one, could be mistaken for one on Santorini or Mykonos. The clean white plaster walls of all the buildings, the random lay of travertine-paved streets undulated between curved buildings, each only wide enough for two people to pass each other. Citizens positioned pots of red flowers at doorways and on steps as accents against the white. Stone staircases rose to apartment doors on second or third levels. No street names were posted and only lines of sight to a church or clock tower provided a clue as to where you might be.

Lunch was soon devoured. Tanner lingered over his second beer as the others finished the carafe of wine. Nick looked down the narrow street as a man turned the corner and walked toward them. Cristofori was dressed just as he had been at their first encounter. He wore a gray ill-fitting suit, a bolo tie, and a mound of fluffy white hair. He walked with a jaunt. Nick rose from his chair as Cristofori neared and extended his hand. The diminutive old man grabbed Nick's hand with a firm grip. Nick was struck by the softness of this man's palm with its wrinkled fingers.

"Signor Foxe! So good to see you!" he said with an Italian accent, pronouncing the name as two syllables, 'Fox-a.'

"Same here, Mr. Cristofori."

"You had second thoughts about what I said at our last meeting, no?"

"You could say that."

Releasing Cristofori's hand, Nick placed his on the man's shoulder and turned toward the table. "I would like to introduce my team."

"Your team?" Cristofori smiled. "You play *futball*?"

"No," Nick seeing the twinkle of a joke in the man's eye. "But, you'll see."

Each person at the table stood as Nick began.

"This is Tom Littleton. He's the man who made the discovery."

"The discovery? The Tablet in the cave, no?"

"That's right," Tom said as he shook the man's hand.

"I see you know about it," said Nick.

"How could I not?" shrugged Cristofori. "It is big news everywhere. I know about Mr. Littleton and I know about you.

But I do not know about this young lady," as he smiled toward Rachael.

"This is Professor Rachael Friedman," explained Nick as Cristofori held Rachael's hand palm down between his. "She is responsible for unlocking the mystery of the code, and one of the reasons we're here."

"Ah, a beautiful young woman," Cristofori said and kissed her hand, "and so smart, too?" Rachael, unaccustomed to such old-world charm, offered no response but a blush, a very rare facial effect for her.

"And this is Tanner."

Cristofori stayed focused on Rachael as Nick turned to the fourth member of the team.

Tanner towered over the little man, but Cristofori took no notice as he shook his hand. Tanner had a firm grasp, but tried not to break what seemed delicate digits.

"Tanner is the newest member of our team and our security lead," Nick announced. Tanner shot Nick a questioning look at the new title coming out of the blue.

Security lead?

Nick responded to Tanner sphinxlike, offering no reason.

"It is a pleasure, Mr. Tanner," said Cristofori.

"It's just Tanner. No mister."

"Very well. Tanner," said Cristofori.

"Can I get you something?" Nick asked as he pointed to

the table now cleared of plates and only beer and wine remaining.

Cristofori shook his head. "No. *Grazie*. I want to take you to my home. You must see something. It is something you have been looking for."

Nick responded, "Please. Lead on."

Chapter 24

"TERRORISTS!" exclaimed Reverend Josiah Jones, as he gazed across his congregation allowing the dreadful term to penetrate the souls of the faithful. "That is who they are, demons who dare defile the word of God with the only pitiful tool they have: the bomb!

"They tried to execute the fine men who worked on the Lord's tablet, but God was with them! They were saved by His mercy. Can I hear a hallelujah?"

The congregation responded to the Reverend's call, a pavlovian reaction.

Jones' description of events had shifted as needed. First, God had come to him and let him in on what the code meant. However, Jones' interpretation lacked substance and was severely over-simplified. The details of The Tablet were secondary. That terrorists had attempted to destroy God's gift was everything. As he had hoped, however, the basic message of sinning and salvation worked to elevate his standing with his flock. It played to a mix of xenophobia and prejudice Jones' followers bore at their core.

Jones didn't have the details right. Mentioning that 'fine *men*' were saved showed lack of awareness that Rachael Friedman was there as well. Few people besides the security guards on Nick's Carlsbad house and their boss knew about Rachael. Even fewer knew about Tanner, the man who saved the team and was now a part of it. The news reported that the team had left the site, but were still unaware that they had left the country for Rome.

Details didn't matter. Jones was skilled in working up a furor with only a few facts. Fading from collective memory was Jones' support for the lecherous congressman, his paperboy shooting and the dog.

"What is our government doing to keep these godless demon terrorists out of our country?" Jones asked, followed by another trademark pause, "Nothing!"

His financial pitch followed.

"That is why God has directed me to do something."

A smattering of applause was heard.

"I've set up a collection to support antiterrorist action. When you give, you will support members of Congress who pledge to lock the door on these demons flooding our country. Give, and give generously. Our country depends on it."

Judy Thorpe picked up the terrorist drumbeat on her cable talk show. Having a bomb go off now made The Tablet sacred, at least within the temple of TV ratings.

Terrorists? Thorpe salivated.

"Folks, how about the latest from New Mexico? If we had any doubts The Tablet was the real deal, at least a band of terrorists thought it was. Why else did they want to destroy it? There must be something on that thing they don't want exposed. What would that be?

"And what is our government saying? Not much. Where's Nick Foxe? In hiding? Gimme a break! That guy doesn't hide. He's probably on the trail of whoever did this. Our sources say he and others working with him took his private jet out of the country. You can bet it's not for a vacation.

"Go get'em Nick!"

After Thorpe's piece, the Texan punched the remote to turn off the television in his paneled den. He drank a Jack Daniels straight. The teetotaler senator from New Mexico declined, although tempted now that the situation in Carlsbad was getting worse.

"Thorpe seems to be a dog with a new bone," drawled the Texan.

"It's just white noise. They don't know as much as we do," said the senator.

"And just what do we know?"

"We know that Foxe, Littleton, and a professor from MIT landed in Rome."

"Wasn't there someone else?"

"Yes, but we're tracking that guy down. The FBI thinks he has an army record."

"Thinks?"

"Yes, but they don't have many people who've seen him. One who has was the guard at the site, but he's in an induced coma. Another guard saw him, gave us a description. He's the one that said he must have been in the army."

"Now why did he say that?" asked the Texan.

"Takes one to know one. The guard was in the army, probably special forces."

"Wasn't there a woman at the house where Foxe stayed who saw him?"

"She's gone."

"Gone?"

"Yes, after hitting a car in an intersection, and giving the men inside a hard time, she vanished. No one knows where."

"Who were the men in the car?"

"Weren't they your guys?" the senator asked puzzled.

"Hardly, I'm not in the spook business."

The Texan took a long draw from his drink. "And we don't know where Foxe, Littleton, Miss MIT, and the mysterious soldier are now?" he asked.

"No," admitted the senator.

"Looks like it is time for me to be in the spook business."

"What do you mean?"

"I have people. People who can do the job."

The senator remained silent as the Texan thought and sipped.

Do they have any clue what they have?

Dr. Fezile Nodada worried over the recent events in America that now led to Italy. From his office in Geneva, the restful sight of lush lawns surrounding the World Health Organization failed to calm him.

Nodada was born in Durban, South Africa, a member of the Xhosa tribe, whose people, along with the Zulu, were prominent in the area. His mother moved the two of them to Cape Town where she worked as a secretary in the post-apartheid era. Cape Town provided Nodada the opportunity to develop his keen intellect.

His mother told her son that their family, a member of the Bhele clan, came from a long line of *igqirha,* or healers, and that he was destined to be a great healer one day. The clan boasted the great Nelson Mandela. Nodada even resembled Mandela, adding horn-rimmed glasses.

Nodada excelled in school and the headmaster took notice. He won a scholarship to attend the University of South Africa and medical school in Switzerland. His field was immunology, but his passion was genetics. He spent five years at the National Institutes of Health investigating how genetics determined why some humans succumbed to disease while others didn't. He imagined that answers to fighting diseases lay within our DNA.

Funding ran out for his work at NIH. He regretted having to leave, but he was welcomed at WHO where he was placed in charge of helping countries prevent the next pandemic.

Nodada was a practical man. However, a certain tale told by an odd little man absorbed him as an intern and pointed to something amazing. What precious spare time he had back then was absorbed pursuing the truth of the tale. He found many things to support it, but always ended short of a definitive answer. His day job suffered and his mentor snapped him back to reality. But faint remembrances of the tale would creep into his dreams at night.

Now, thinking about the Americans in Italy, the memories played at full volume.

Do they know what they have?

Chapter 25

CRISTOFORI LED THE TEAM through the narrow streets of Locorotondo. Nick and Cristofori took the lead with Tom and Rachael behind them. Tanner brought up the rear. Nick, Tom and Rachael were focused on the old man as he chatted away. Tanner continued to scan the surroundings, still cautious after the near-death experience in the cave. His gaze frightened an old lady sweeping her steps, but her young, shapely daughter smiled with a warm appraisal of what she saw. Tanner allowed himself a slight grin at the fetching woman.

The streets were almost empty. Most of the walk took them through quiet, curving streets, the buildings resembling plaster snow melted and smoothed into walls and roofs. A random set of steps appeared here and there to upper levels, no two alike.

"I have to ask," said Nick to Cristofori. "Why here?"

"What do you mean?" asked the old man with a twinkle in his eye.

"Why would you have your violin shop here?"

"You mean beside the obvious beauty of the place?"

"Well, yes," Nick admitted.

"I find the climate just right for the violin. It is not so dry, not so wet. The wood is sweet in this air. It curves well. And the finished product… Ah, it sounds right. Do you understand?"

Nick smiled at the man's expressions as he gesticulated with the tap to his ear to emphasize the 'sounds right.'

The narrow street opened into a small plaza fronting a church. The church appeared to be covered with white stucco, but on closer inspection, it was made of stone blending into the surrounding neutral color scheme. Stone columns hugged the large wooden entrance door. The entire front of the structure appeared to be one solid piece of stone lifted from a mold. In another plaza, just beyond, was a large red apartment building unlike the other white buildings surrounding it. Cristofori noticed Nick's attention to the color.

"The builder, we think, was colorblind," stated Cristofori eliciting a laugh by all but Tanner who didn't respond.

Just beyond the plaza, they entered another narrow street, and, within another block, Cristofori announced, "Here we are."

They stood before a narrow white house twenty-feet wide and three-stories high. Wooden double doors with large beveled glass windows graced the entrance with stone planters on either side. The second level sported a door matching the one below, but with a small ledge and iron railing before it. The third level contained the only window on the front of the building save for those on the doors. A small double window sat in the eaves of a pitched roof. Standing before the building, you could see both the left and right walls of the structure since the building widened from front to back. Although hidden away in this village, it was unique. Each member of the team had the same thought.

How could a workshop be in such a tiny building?

The answer became obvious as Cristofori led the team through the door and into the foyer. Visible at the end of the room, the hallway opened into a larger workshop in a connected building. Before they ventured further, Cristofori stopped by a desk in the foyer where a plump middle-aged woman with short, wavy salt-and-pepper hair busied herself with a stack of forms. Other similar papers and forms were stacked beside her on an ancient oak desk. She looked up at Cristofori.

She was upset. "*Lorenzo, il signor Alonso ha chiamato per il suo ordine. Sono passati due mesi. Ha chiesto quando sarebbe pronto.*"

Cristofori continued an exchange with the woman. Tanner could not follow all of the Italian. It had something to do with a customer order. The exchange was too rapid, but the woman's exasperation was clear. She ended the conversation with a shrug.

Cristofori turned to the team and reported, "Customer matter. A violin lives on beyond its first owner. It lives generations. And yet," he said with a small slap to the mouth making a pop, "they want its birth to be in an instant." He hung his head shaking in disbelief that someone could not understand.

"Please," Cristofori said as he motioned the team forward. Let me show you my workshop."

Tanner took Nick aside as Tom and Rachael followed Cristofori down the hallway.

"Look," he told Nick. "I think I'll wait outside."

"Don't you want to find how violins are made?" Nick asked acknowledging it was a courtesy to Cristofori, but not at the top of their agenda.

"I think it'd be better if I enjoyed the scenery on the street."

"You don't think we were followed, do you?" Nick asked.

"Let's be sure."

"OK," conceded Nick. "Do what you think best."

With that, Tanner opened the door and stepped outside. The woman at the desk looked up from her paperwork as he left and then at Nick with an expression of 'what's-up?' To which Nick shrugged and turned to catch up with the others.

Nick came to a work area where Cristofori had gathered with Tom and Rachael. The room smelled of fresh cut wood and glue. Cristofori was talking to a young man with a ponytail sitting on a tall chair positioned at a workbench. The simple workbench was surrounded by special hand tools.

Four violins in different stages of production hung high on the wall to the right. Further to the right on the wall stood a metal cabinet, the doors open, displaying a variety of liquids in bottles and other supplies.

Behind the group was a long table at which another man worked, shaping a flat piece into the familiar shape of a violin.

Nick stepped to the bench where the man held a finished violin.

"Ah, Nick," said Cristofori as Nick approached. "This is Marcello."

Marcello held the violin in his left hand and extended his right to Nick as he said in lightly accented English, "Pleased to meet you."

"Marcello just told us about the making of the violin," explained Cristofori.

Marcello continued as he pointed to parts of the violin he held. "You see, the violin is made of two arched plates we fasten to what we call a garland of ribs. We use a special glue made from cow hides."

"Ferragamo gets the hides. We get the glue," smiled Cristofori.

"The rib garland includes a top block," Marcello said as he pointed to the location. "and four corner blocks."

"Which cheap mass-made violins do not have," interrupted Cristofori, his pride clear.

Marcello smiled at the master and continued. "Do you know why the violin has its distinctive hourglass shape?"

Nick quipped, "To honor the shape of a woman?"

Rachael moaned. "To allow free passage of the bow," she said.

"That is right," said Marcello, appreciating Rachael's response.

"I liked Nick's explanation," added Tom.

Rachael frowned.

Are these grown men or little boys?

Cristofori turned to the other bench and placed his hand on the man's shoulder. "This is my brother Luigi," he said.

"Younger brother," Luigi added.

Cristofori smiled at his brother's clarification and continued. "Luigi is shaping one piece. He has great hands. You need to be steady to do this job."

"And you need to put up with this one," Luigi teased, pointing to his brother.

"I introduced these people to Marcello, Luigi. This is Miss Rachael Friedman."

Luigi took Rachael's hand in old-world style and kissed it. Rachael was charmed by the gesture yet uncomfortable being treated as a lady.

"This is Mr. Tom Littleton, he is the man who made the discovery in the cave we have all heard about."

Luigi took Tom's hand. "It is an honor," he said.

"And this is Mr. Nicholas Foxe the Third. He is the boss."

Nick, embarrassed by both the tag of *the third* and the title *the boss*, shook hands with Luigi.

"*Il capo*? Eh?" Luigi said with a smile as he studied Nick.

"Your brother is being very generous. We're a team."

"Yes, yes, of course," said Cristofori. "Where is Mr. Tanner?"

"He's outside. Can't beat the habit of standing watch," explained Nick.

"We all heard of your trouble," said Cristofori. "We told no one of your visit. Just as you asked when we spoke."

"I'm sure everything's OK," reassured Nick.

"You are so 'cloak and dagger'," said Luigi to his brother.

"Do not go into that again," responded Cristofori.

Marcello stayed in the background, uninvolved in the exchange. The brothers' bickering was not uncommon.

"My brother is not supportive of what I believe," explained Cristofori to Nick.

Luigi grunted with an expression signaling understatement. "I am sorry. My brother is wasting your time. He has these ideas of fancy."

Cristofori ignored him and spoke to Nick *sotto voce*, "If my ideas were not so good, then why are you here?"

"I am sorry," said Luigi. "I should have said nothing."

Nick told Luigi, "I know how you feel."

Luigi looked at Nick puzzled, as he continued, "When I first met your brother, I thought he was a crazy man. But since that time, I have seen incredible things. So maybe crazy is no longer the right word."

Luigi turned smiling to Rachael, anointing her the arbiter. "Do you believe in my brother's theories?" he asked.

"Well, I must see. But from what I know now, there seems to be merit."

Luigi grinned, "You sure you are a scientist and not a politician?"

Rachael understood how she hedged her statement, but only smiled at him.

"Very well," said Luigi throwing his hands up in surrender. "Let's see."

"You know I love this man," Cristofori said hugging his brother. "Even if he is, what you say, hard-headed?"

Luigi said nothing, but the bond of brothers was evident.

"Well, enough of this," said Cristofori releasing his brother. "Let us look at what I've brought you to see."

Cristofori started down a hallway leading out of the workshop. As he did, the soft tones of a violin playing a sonata filled the air. The music came from an open door along the path Cristofori led them. As they passed the door, Cristofori paused to let the group appreciate the performance.

The room was small, perhaps once a bedroom, with an open window allowing in cool air from the valley below. A desk and a chair were under the window, three violins lay to the right of the desk on a small table. Otherwise, it was bare of any furnishings or adornments. In the middle of the room stood a young woman with long black wavy hair cascading down the back of her dark blue dress, swaying to the rhythm of the violin she played. She appeared dressed to go on stage and entertain an audience. She finished the final diminished notes of the sonata.

The woman stared straight ahead at no one and said "no" with a distinct finality.

"No?" asked Cristofori.

Still looking straight ahead, not at Cristofori, she said, *"le stringhe devono essere cambiate."*

Cristofori looked to his baffled guests and said, "Quality control. She reports the strings must be changed.

"Maria," he said to the girl. "These are our guests."

Maria turned toward the group but looked over their heads as she said with a monotone, "hello."

"Maria is my daughter. She tests the violins," explained Cristofori.

"And I guess that one didn't make the grade," said Tom.

Cristofori shrugged. "No. It did not."

"But it sounded beautiful," said Rachael, her comment

directed to Maria who was unresponsive.

"Thank you, Maria," Cristofori closing the discussion. "Now please follow me this way." He stretched his arm forward in the direction they were headed. Nick and Tom followed Cristofori, but Rachael stayed behind.

Maria stayed fixed in position and stared into nowhere. Rachael tried to meet her eyes as she smiled and said, "You play beautifully."

"Thank you," was Maria's perfunctory, expressionless response.

Rachael, in her field of science and mathematics, had seen Marias before.

She's autistic.

"Do you play other instruments?" asked Rachael.

"Yes."

"I play the piano," offered Rachael.

"I do, too," said Maria, this time smiling, but not toward Rachael. It seemed she smiled at the idea of playing a piano, her fingers flexing as though touching keys.

"Perhaps we could play together sometime."

Nothing from Maria.

"Would you like that?"

"Yes," answered Maria.

Rachael smiled, at a loss for what more to say, but intrigued by Maria, who appeared to be her age.

There is something more to this woman.

Rachael caught up to the group in the next room, a room with a different scent from the fresh wood and glue smell of the workshop. Books lined this room. The musty fragrance of valuable old tomes permeated the chamber. It was a small room, just large enough for a partner desk in the middle with chairs on opposite sides. There was no window to let damaging daylight onto a book. The only light came from two desk lamps. Four shelves of books lined each wall.

Tom and Nick looked up as Rachael entered. Cristofori, wearing latex gloves, was beaming as he turned the pages of a large leather-bound book on the desk before him. Nick told Rachael, "Mr. Cristofori was just showing us a book written by his great-great-grandfather."

"Great-great-*great*-grandfather," corrected Cristofori.

"The man who invented the piano?" guessed Rachael.

"Si!" responded Cristofori. "It contains diagrams and specifications for his invention."

The old man gazed fondly at each page as he turned it. Then he stopped.

"But this is not what I want to show you. I want to show you what you came for."

Cristofori took care in closing the book and lifting it up to the shelf to an empty spot. He walked to the shelves to his left where Tom stood.

"Pardon me," he told Tom as Cristofori pulled on the bookcase, which opened as a secret door.

"In here is what you've come for."

Chapter 26

TANNER SAT OUTSIDE Cristofori's place on a small folding chair he found leaning against a wall.

Standing guard, but for what?

The small plaza before him stood empty, no crowds to scan. If there were, at least he would feel useful. He took stock of the situation.

I've already spent a year in this country on a wild goose chase, and now I'm right back where I started.

But, then again, he realized this time was different. He had followed the trail to the States but ended taking a hiatus. He had never been sure what he was tracking anyhow.

I never give up. I'm not a quitter.

When he met Littleton, he saw something in Tom right off. Being a caver was part of it. It's a skill Tanner did not have. In fact, he hated small places. He didn't want to be inside Cristofori's place. Too small. He'd rather be out here. No, somehow, he thought Tom might solve the next piece of the puzzle. Just a hunch. Seems he's not the only one playing hunches here. Nick sure was in bringing them here.

A violin maker? Really?

Tanner couldn't see being buddies with Nick. Nick represented everything he hated. Spoiled brat given position because he was wealthy. Tanner saluted men who earned it. Always had. Sure, you salute the uniform, not the man or woman, but Tanner had officers he respected. All the rich boys like Nick hid in the National Guard, not where someone's shooting at them.

Rachael, he liked. She had spunk. A smart, no nonsense woman. Easy on the eyes too, but he wouldn't push it with her. That cat's got claws. She's put Nick in his place when she had to.

But now he's part of the team. Like it or not, it doesn't matter. The team matters. He'll protect the team, and it looks like they need protecting. This place is picture perfect, but he's not relaxing. Someone trying to blow you up in a cave does that to a person.

Around the corner came a little boy kicking a soccer ball. The boy looked about eight years old and wore a mustard-yellow rugby shirt over white shorts. His feet were tucked into a well-worn pair of Nikes. He was coming in Tanner's direction when he lost control of the ball and it rolled to Tanner's feet. Still seated, Tanner kicked the ball back to the boy. The boy smiled and kicked it back to Tanner.

I didn't mean to get into a game with this kid.

Tanner stood and stopped the ball by stepping on it. He reached down and picked it up, his long fingers wrapping around the ball like an NBA player. The boy looked at Tanner puzzled whether the ball was coming back to him. Tanner held it out to the boy. The boy smiled and ran over to retrieve it.

"*Grazie*," said the wavy-haired boy with brown eyes.

"You're welcome," said Tanner.

"You are *Americano*!" exclaimed the boy.

"Yep."

"You here on vacation?"

"Business."

"What is your business?" asked the boy.

"You're kinda nosey, aren't you?" said Tanner giving the kid the once over.

Tanner rose over the boy like a giant, but undaunted, the boy said, "My name is Giacomo. What's yours?"

Tanner thought of offering a smart response, but disarmed by the kid, he sat back down to be at his eye level and said, "Tanner."

"Mr. Tanner," the boy repeated.

"No. Just Tanner."

"Just Tanner," the boy repeated like a comic.

"No…" Tanner began when the boy interrupted.

"Just joking," said Giacomo with a wide grin.

"Humph."

"Say, Tanner," smiled the boy bouncing the ball up and down in his hand, "You want to play *calcio*?"

"No," Tanner said. "Thank you, but no."

Giacomo's grin turned devious. "Afraid you will lose?"

Tanner stood.

Cristofori pulled on the bookcase. It opened like a door on unseen hinges. Behind was a set of six small doors, three on either side. Each door had a lock at the top. Every member of the team had the same thought.

If he had a precious book like the one he showed us out here, what could possibly be locked away behind these doors?

Cristofori took a ring of keys from his pocket and held it for a moment.

"Behind these doors I keep what you might call histories. I have collected them over time. It is behind this middle door that you must see today."

He chose a key from the ring and placed it in the lock and opened it. Revealed were a set of four leather-bound books cracked and faded from the years. Each was of the same design and appeared to be part of a set. There was space for a fifth book to complete the set, but it was missing.

Cristofori took a fresh pair of latex gloves from a box and handed the box to the others who each took a pair. With gloves on, the old man carefully removed the six-inch thick first volume from the shelf and put it on one side of the partner desk as the others gathered around him.

"Here is a set of histories commissioned by Federico Secondo. You would know him as Frederick the Second, Holy Roman Emperor," he said, and then witnessed blank looks on each face. "That is, if you know of him at all."

"Of course," said Nick. "He was king of a sizable part of Europe in the thirteenth century."

"Emperor," corrected Cristofori.

"Emperor," repeated Nick sensing the pride Cristofori had in this long-dead monarch.

"But here, we like to think of him by the name he liked best."

"King of Sicily?" ventured Nick.

Cristofori smiled. "Yes, indeed. King of Sicily. But Sicily at that time was not just the island. It was also where we stand at this moment. He stayed in our region when he wasn't fighting in the Crusades." Then added with a twinkle in his eye, "Or fighting with *Papa,* the Pope."

"You read Latin, Mr. Foxe?" the old man asked.

"Yes. Badly," responded Nick.

"I do as well, although reading all of these books has made my ability pretty good.

"Federico was an amazing man," Cristofori continued. "He spoke six languages: Latin, Sicilian, German, French, Greek and Arabic. The Arabic he picked up from the Crusades no doubt. He made poetry and science a central part of his court. The Italian I speak today, they say, comes from his literature and poetry. Like so much of what you speak comes from Shakespeare. It is all here," he said spreading his hands over the open volume before him.

"You see, in 1227, Federico set sail for the Holy Land with an army. He sailed from Brindisi, not far down the coast from here. He had to turn back due to an epidemic in Jerusalem. It was that year Ugolino became Pope Gregory the Ninth. Ugolino was a spiteful old man and didn't like Federico. You see, Federico didn't care much for religion, but you couldn't say so in those days. He was a man of science. And science is truth, is it not Signorina Friedman?"

Rachael, pleased at being tagged the scientist in the room, replied, "We like to think so."

"Well, in those days, Signorina, you may have suffered the same fate as Federico. The Pope excommunicated him. *Il Papa* said Federico went back on his pledge to launch a crusade. The truth is here in this book. Ugolino just didn't like Federico and his ways, plus the emperor was getting too powerful. The Vatican wanted all power. And you know what?" Cristofori paused. "Federico could not care less what the Vatican wanted.

"Federico launched another set of ships and soldiers the

next year. It says here," Cristofori pointed to the book. "It was to honor his pledge. I suspect it was 'I will show you Mister Pope.'

"This was where Federico showed how smart he was. His army was big, but not big enough. Al-Kamil, the sultan of Egypt, controlled Jerusalem and his army was huge. Federico knew this. Federico marched his men down the coast in a show of force but did not fight. Didn't need to. He talked with the sultan and he talked and talked. The sultan had his hands full with a rebellion in Syria, and probably didn't want to fight over Jerusalem. Federico found a way out for the sultan. He found an agreement from a few years before that the sultan could honor.

"Now the book doesn't say it, but I believe the sultan thought 'What difference did it make? This king marches into the city. He has a crown ceremony. Nobody gets hurt.'

"This took several years. It didn't happen overnight. And… everyone knows what I told you. It is history. We do not need these old transcripts to tell that tale again. What is not well known is what the other volumes tell," he said as he straightened and gazed toward the remaining three books on the shelf. What is told there is how Federico spent his spare time in Jerusalem.

"Remember," he said as he looked at each of the team members, "He was a man of science. The Arabs in those days were protectors of science. They invented inoculations against disease. They performed eye surgery. They counted in a system based on ten, as we do today. But they also passed along the Egyptian counting system based on twelve and that gave us the twelve-hour day, five times twelve for sixty seconds, and three-hundred and sixty degree geometry, and," he smiled, "A dozen donuts.

"The sultan had a mathematician named al-Muazzam who entertained Federico with his knowledge. He showed him how number systems can be many. The one Federico knew used ten characters, others used twelve. He said there was one that used eight. When he told him of that one, the one al-Muazzam called octal, Federico asked who used it. Al-Muazzam became very serious. Federico reports in the journal that 'the darkness of mystery fell across his face.' He said it belonged to a people that lived long ago, before history. They counted in octal, and they spoke in octal. Here is where Federico's own notes appear in the volume. Do you know what al-Muazzam said?"

"They spoke in music?" ventured Rachael.

Cristofori smiled as awareness crossed the face of Tom and Nick.

"Yes," said the old man. "They spoke in music."

"But what?" interjected Tom and Nick at the same time. "How?"

"Ah," said Cristofori, delighted in capturing everyone's attention. "That is where it gets very interesting. Federico wrote that al-Muazzam was very guarded. He wanted the emperor to be the only one to see what he possessed and asked to see him alone. Federico suspected a trap. His guards always surrounded him, but he took a leap of faith to trust al-Muazzam.

"That night, near the temple wall in Jerusalem, Federico and his guards went to meet al-Muazzam. The emperor writes there was a full moon. He could not have, how do you Americans say, 'made this stuff up?' It reads like a Latin mystery book."

The small audience was engrossed like a bunch of scouts around a campfire, waiting to hear what happens next.

"Federico commands his guards to stay behind and he follows al-Muazzam down the narrow streets of the holy city and into the doorway of a small building standing right against the Temple Mount. Inside, al-Muazzam walks to a door and moves eight levers into a pattern that only he seems to know."

"Eight?" repeated Nick.

"Yes, eight. Federico makes that clear. It seems to be some combination lock because as soon as he finishes, the door opens. He asks al-Muazzam what the combination might be. Federico reports that al-Muazzam smiled and said simply, 'It is a golden number.'

"There is only one lamp in the room. But when the door opens, there is a glow from inside, a reflection. It is a bright tablet.

"Signor Littleton," he said looking to Tom. "Does that sound familiar?"

"Of course," replied Tom, struck by the coincidence, centuries removed from his experience at Carlsbad. "What was on the tablet?"

"Ah, yes, Volume Four," said Cristofori as he closed the volume before him and returned it to the shelf. He then took equal care to remove Volume Four from the shelf, place it on the desk and open it.

"This did not mean very much until you told me what you saw on your discovery," the old man said as he turned several pages at once scanning for something. "Ah," he said as he stood back and the others looked. "Here it is."

On the page before them was an illustration, drawn by quill pen, of four items: A double-helix, the peninsula of Italy, human outlines, and the Big Dipper constellation.

Nick could not believe it. "This is impossible," he said.

Cristofori scowled. "No, it is a fake. I made it up. I did not know about the symbols until you called. I rushed out and forged an eight-hundred-year-old book and slapped your drawing in it. That is what I did?"

"I'm sorry," Nick said backing off. "Of course not."

Tom intervened, "It's just a lot to get my head around. And our tablet did not have the Big Dipper, if that is what it is. It had other symbols."

"Well, if you have that to get your head around, let me tell you about Volume Five," he said pointing to the empty space on the shelf beside the other volumes.

Chapter 27

CRISTOFORI WALKED OVER TO THE BOOKSHELF and gazed at the space meant for Volume Five, as if he imagined it was there. "You see," he began, "Federico had four sets of these volumes transcribed, except for Volume Five. That one he kept for himself. But Volume Four tells us what's in Five."

"And that is?" asked Nick.

"Federico tells us he brought al-Muazzam as his guest to Italy to continue his work on decoding the tablet. Federico promised him any help he wanted and a place to work. It took years."

Tom remained incredulous. "You mean this man, this al-Muazzam, could solve the code without the latest technology we've been using?"

Cristofori grinned. "Have you heard the story of Einstein's wife and the observatory?"

Only Rachael displayed a look of recognition, having heard this tale before.

"Perhaps you can tell us the story, professor," Cristofori urged Rachael.

"Well," said Rachael, "Prominent astronomers built a new observatory and Einstein's wife Elsa was on hand for the opening. The astronomers were proud of their state-of-the-art equipment and showed Elsa the huge new telescope they had built. After she asked the simple question, 'What is it for?' the scientists cajoled the little lady with, 'It's to explore the universe.' She responded, 'You mean you need all of this equipment to do what my husband does on the back of an envelope?'"

Tom winced. "OK, I get it. But I'm not so sure."

Nick jumped in. "So, is Volume Five al-Muazzam's decoding?"

"Yes, Federico writes that it is."

"And where is Volume Five?"

"No one knows for sure. In fact, unless you have seen the tablet as you have, why would one care? Whoever owns the other copies of these volumes would think they are the writing of a man with, how do you say, a screw loose?"

"And that leaves us where?" shrugged Nick.

"Ah, that means we must put two and two together," Cristofori announced mischievously.

"You see, during the years al-Muazzam worked, Federico built a castle. He shows the plans in Volume Four, the last volume I have. The castle stands today, but no one has ever come up with why he built it. No one ever lived there. It is empty. Let me show you."

Cristofori turned the pages with care to those bearing architectural drawings of a castle.

"Look at this one," he said pointing to a cross-section. "See the words here beside a staircase."

Nick read aloud the Latin words, "*Libro Domus.*" He looked up at the team with an expression of realization. "Home of the book."

"Yes. Coincidence?" asked Cristofori. "I do not think so. Also, you see in the drawings how many sides the castle has?"

"Eight!" observed Tom.

"Again, a coincidence?"

"Wait a minute," said Nick. "Is this the Castel del Monte?"

"Yes," confirmed Cristofori.

"Isn't it near here?"

"Yes, it is."

"Signor Cristofori," said Rachael. "Surely you've been to Castel del Monte."

"Of course."

"And you have a map of the staircase's location?"

Rachael paused for Cristofori to answer with the next logical question.

"So, have I checked out the staircase? No, I have not."

"Why not?" asked Tom.

"Because, the staircase is behind a solid wall."

"Behind a solid wall?" exclaimed Nick. "Then how do you know it even exists?"

"I had my doubts, too. I talked to the man in charge of the

castle and asked him about the hidden staircase and the possibility of a room below it. He thought me crazy." Cristofori displayed a weary smile as if the excitement had exhausted the old man, "Seems many think the same thing."

But then he smiled as though a shot of adrenalin surged through his veins. "Then I reread Federico's book. How I missed it, I do not know. Please, Mr. Foxe," he said as he turned a page and pointed to a passage. "Would you read this?"

"*Cantus arcana prodit,*" read Nick as he looked up and smiled at the team. "Melody unlocks the secret."

"I puzzled all these years. What melody?" said Cristofori. "I once even played a compact disc of music in the castle. Played all sorts of things. They threw me out.

"Then," the old man's face brightened. "You called and told me what had happened when you played the music of The Tablet. What was it?"

"A door beneath The Tablet opened." Nick said.

"Then, that same music…" Cristofori started.

"It wasn't music," corrected Tom.

"It may not be music as we know it, but it was music," insisted Cristofori.

"This makes little sense," said Tom, the doubter. "Whoever put The Tablet in Carlsbad locked it so that only someone who had figured out that the code was sound, could open it. That was thousands of years ago. Now, just a few hundred years ago, some Arab used the same trick to open a hidden door? Not likely."

Cristofori was the same height as Tom, never more apparent than when the old man stepped over to him and put his face inches from Tom's. Cristofori lectured, "How do you know this? You still think you and your fancy computers are the only way? You think 'some Arab,' al-Muazzam was his name, could not figure out the code and, how you say, reverse the engineer?"

Rachael, smiling at Cristofori's spunk, corrected, "Reverse engineer."

"*Si*, reverse engineer how those people did this?"

Nick stepped in, "Look, it's worth a shot. We've come this far," he said to Tom, who shrugged.

"You told me you have a recording of how the code sounds," Cristofori asked Nick.

"Yes, I have all the code on a thumb drive I backed up to the cloud while we traveled to Rome. I have the first part of the sounds made on a disc."

"May I hear it?"

Nick reached into the small leather satchel he carried and pulled out a compact disc in a simple paper sleeve. "Got a player?"

"Of course," said Cristofori. "One moment."

He gently closed the open volume and returned it to its secret place, closed the cabinet door, pulled out a key and locked it, and then stepped back and closed the bookcase.

"Come this way," he said as he walked out of the room.

The team followed Cristofori to another small room back the way they had come. Sunlight through an open window lit the area. Their eyes needed to adjust moving from the dimness of the library to this sunny room. It was a break room for the workers with a table in the middle, a single-serving coffee maker near the window and espresso cups nearby. To one side of the coffee maker was a shelf with a radio, CD player and speakers to each side. Not a high-end Bose system, but it would do. Nick pushed buttons to power on and open the CD tray. He slipped the CD in, closed the door, and pressed play.

The odd concerto of up and down pitches began. For a moment, Tom thought he had returned to the cave as faint echoes from another room drifted in. What were those? Rachael heard them, too. She stepped from the room. They were coming from down the hall. Rachael and Tom left to find the source of the echoes. Nick and Cristofori watched from the doorway as the CD continued.

Rachael and Tom walked to the room where they had first seen Maria perform her violin quality-control exercises. There, in the room, stood Maria perfectly repeating the sounds she heard, but in the sweet lilt of a soprano. Nick stopped the music. Maria stopped singing and stared ahead to sights only she saw.

"Maria," said Rachael. "That was beautiful."

"Thank you," she responded, continuing to look away.

"Would you come with me?" Rachael asked.

Without hesitation, Maria said, "Yes" and followed Rachael and Tom.

Both Nick, who had just met Maria, and Cristofori, who knew her all her life, gaped at the woman, as Rachael led her into the break room. Rachael stood near the table acknowledging no one.

"Please sing for us again. Is that all right with you?" asked Rachael.

"Yes."

Rachael pressed play and started the CD where it had stopped. Maria repeated the sounds, again lending the beauty of the human voice, to the random sounds. It was as though she was running through an odd vocal exercise prior to performing a familiar song. Then Rachael stopped the music, but what happened next astounded each person gathered at this solo recital.

Maria continued to sing. It was only for three seconds, but it seemed to complete some unknown line.

Rachael, without turning the player on, asked, "Maria, could you please sing the last three seconds of that last piece again?"

"Yes."

Maria repeated what she had sung after the stop button was pressed. Rachael then pressed play. Everyone then heard the next three seconds from the CD. It was a perfect transcript of what Maria had just sung, only lacking in the finesse of the human voice. It was as though she could predict the next notes.

The team looked at each other, but Cristofori gazed at his daughter. A man who had seen many amazing things from this woman, witnessed yet one more.

Rachael asked, "Maria, why did you sing those notes after the music stopped?"

"To finish," was Maria's simple response.

"To finish what?"

"Just to finish. That part had not ended."

Nick theorized Maria had a general understanding of music and she recognized a pattern.

Did she understand the code itself?

"What did it mean?" asked Rachael.

"I don't know."

"Then how did you know it wasn't finished?"

"I just knew."

Cristofori came close to his daughter and took her hands in his. "Maria, I realize music has meaning. You understand this too, do you not?"

"Yes."

"Does this music have meaning to you?"

"Yes."

"What word would describe what you heard?"

"Secrets."

Everyone looked at each other. Maria knew nothing about the discovery and what they were looking for, yet this young woman had encapsulated their efforts in the single best word possible.

"Is there another word?"

"Yes."

"What other word would it be?"

"Danger."

Chapter 28

NICK STEPPED OUTSIDE to find Tanner kicking a soccer ball around with a young boy. Tanner, agile for a man his size seemed no match for the kid. The big man ran and kicked the ball between his feet toward the other side of the plaza at some imaginary goal. But the kid dashed around Tanner's legs like a pesky bee and snatched the ball away in a blur. Tanner smiled as he watched the kid run the ball to the opposite wall. It was the first time Nick had seen Tanner smile.

"Seems you've met your match," Nick said, after watching for a minute.

"He's OK," admitted Tanner as the kid approached with a grin from ear to ear, Tanner's meager praise not lost on him.

"Signor Tanner is good," said the kid. "Maybe I am better?"

"It's Tanner, kid. Just Tanner."

"Maybe *you* can call him Walter," teased Nick.

Expecting a growl from Tanner with the mention of his detested first name, Nick instead witnessed Tanner put a finger to his lips uttering a soft shush. It seemed the boy exposed the hidden softer side of this rugged combat soldier.

"Hi," said the boy as he put his hand out to Nick. "My name is Giacomo."

"Pleased to meet you, Giacomo."

Cristofori walked out of the shop followed by Rachael and Tom. "I see you've met my grandson."

"Grandson?" asked Nick.

"Yes, he is Maria's son."

"But . . ." Nick started as Rachael caught his eye with a warning frown and a slight headshake. She anticipated his asking how an autistic woman could have a child. Nick realized the mistake of his knee-jerk reaction and stopped.

Cristofori focused on the boy he adored and didn't notice the exchange.

"But, what?" Cristofori said.

"But, how will we get to the book at the castle?"

Tanner, now all business, shot an inquiring look at Nick when he mentioned a book and a castle.

Cristofori responded, "Let's walk over to the garden to discuss."

After a loving rub of young Giacomo's head, Cristofori led the group around the left side of the shop.

Turning a corner, the team came to a garden nestled in a nook of the building. A white stucco wall curved around it. The colors of the red and blue flowers in wooden planters stood out against the whitewashed walls. Green shrubs defined the border of the garden. A steel mesh table and six matching chairs sat amidst the greenery. A small opening between the walls of adjacent buildings provided space for a gentle breeze from the valley below, cooling the garden and bringing the fragrance of flowers to the visitor.

Cristofori sat himself at one end of the table and motioned his guests to take seats. Nick brought Tanner up to date. Tanner's interest perked up when the story mentioned the Arab's possession of a tablet in Jerusalem. It took no mind reader to see that he wondered if it was the same tablet he saw after it made its way to Afghanistan.

After Nick finished, Tanner asked, "So, all we have to do is stroll into a castle, knock down a wall, and waltz away with an old book. Is that right?"

Tom interjected. "Not knock down a wall."

Rachael added, "Remember, when we played the code in Carlsbad, a door dropped to expose more of The Tablet."

Tanner wasn't buying it. "So, you think this Federico guy used the same thing to release the door? How would he know? Someone left your tablet thousands of years ago, and some guy six-hundred years ago had the same 'open sesame'?"

Nick said, "The secret must be in the tablet al-Muazzam possessed and he used it when he engineered the castle."

"Must have?" Tanner scoffed. "You're sure taking a lot for granted."

Cristofori listened to the exchange, saying nothing. When unresolved silence settled over the gathering, he addressed

Tanner.

"My son," he said. "Do you believe in destiny?"

Tanner showed puzzlement mixed with respect for the man's age. Rank and age were equals for him.

"Sir?"

Cristofori continued. "How is it I met Signor Foxe years ago at a party in New York? Did I know he would one day witness this discovery?

"How is it you found the tablet? Not to mention fate directing you to save that boy?

"How is it you made the suggestion to Signor Littleton to hunt in that cave? How is it he was the one who made the discovery? He was friends with the man I spoke to in New York. Accident?

"How is it Signorina Friedman came to see that photo?" With this, Cristofori cast a grandfatherly smile toward Rachael.

"And how it is you came to save everyone?

"And how it is we find ourselves here, so close to the castle where the secret is? Destiny? What do you call it otherwise?"

Tanner paused a few seconds. "OK, when is the castle open?" he responded, unclear whether he bought into destiny or just wanted to move on.

Cristofori said, "It is open to the public from nine to eighteen and a half."

"I'm guessing we're not waltzing through during public hours to open magic doors. But we need to case the castle first while it's open," said Tanner

Tanner smiled again, a first since soccer with Giacomo. Being in charge agreed with him.

"Who wants to take a tour?" he said.

The flattop mountain rose in singular defiance above the plains of Apulia as though designed by nature to receive a crown like the Castel del Monte. The bronze van wound around the south edge of the peak, leaving thick olive groves behind and ascending into a stubby pine forest. Tanner drove the vehicle through the entrance to the national park and stopped in a small lot beside a single-story visitor center. The center was an Italian version of an American park center, built of wood and stucco and crowned with sienna tiles. It housed a restaurant, but the team riding with Tanner, now joined by Cristofori, was not hungry at this early morning hour.

Everyone posed as tourists with Cristofori as their tour guide. The fact they arrived in a van added to the deception, not to mention securing favorable parking. Nick and Tom each wore jeans and a golf shirt and looked very much like the stereotypical American tourists. Rachael wore her standard fare of black athletic stretch pants and blue top. It was Tanner that didn't get with the program and continued to wear camouflage pants and an army green tee. He appeared more like a part of the Italian police. Cristofori got into the act, wearing a loose tan vest sporting a nametag he received from some past conference. No doubt he was the guide. Cristofori bought tickets at the visitor center for the group. From the conversation in Italian Tanner heard between Cristofori and the ticket vendor, it seemed he was asking for a group discount. Tanner didn't know if it was an act or if the old man was frugal. He found it amusing.

Stepping away from the visitor center, the team gazed toward Federico's huge monument set upon the apex of the mountain. Situated another hundred feet up on a grassy hill over a series of stone steps along a winding path, massive towers dominated the structure. The stone blocks, at first appeared a light gray, but on closer inspection, they were a variety of random tones from tan to cream. The castle was strikingly different from a medieval castle. It was tight and bulky, shaped like the handle of a massive screwdriver.

"Step this way," instructed Cristofori to his unusual tour group as he began the walk up the path.

"Note that this is a castle with no moat, no drawbridge, no cellar nor dungeon. There is not even evidence of a kitchen." he said as they walked. "People said 'how could this be a castle?' No one ever lived here. There were royals held here for years as prisoners. That was all. Did Federico use it as a hunting lodge?" He stopped and turned to the group. "Nice hunting lodge, eh?"

Pointing to the front, "But how many towers does it have?"

Four towers were visible from their viewing angle, but everyone knew the answer.

"Eight" said Tom.

"Yes," smiled Cristofori. "And each tower has eight sides. They surround a building of eight sides. What do you call such a shape?"

"An octagon," offered Rachael.

"Ah, yes," replied Cristofori who was very familiar with the answer. He lived the answer. "Octal, octave, the magic number." He turned and continued toward the castle.

As he walked, he said, "There is one room in each of the sections. So there are eight rooms on the first floor and eight rooms on the second."

"That's sixteen," Nick said.

Cristofori frowned. "Yes. Or two times eight. That always bothered me. What does that mean? It cannot be an accident."

"Maybe the king wanted a breeze and added a second floor," quipped Tanner who had yet to accept the hocus pocus of the magical octal.

Cristofori continued to walk, but smiled. "Maybe so."

Soon they stood before the entrance. Twin staircases led to a twelve-foot high wooden door set in an archway the shape of an artillery shell. A proscenium of columns on both sides and triangular stone molding above, framed the doorway. The door was open. They walked in. Cristofori handed the tickets to a docent. A short walk took them to the open center of the structure. Everyone looked skyward to appreciate the octagonal shape against a flawless blue sky.

"Here is the center of the building, and the open courtyard," Cristofori, the tour guide, instructed.

"Federico was fond of hunting with falcons. Something else he learned during his years in the Middle East. Some think he built the castle to house falcons. Unfortunately, the king died just before it was complete."

"When did al-Muazzam die?" asked Nick.

Cristofori straightened his vest as though to prepare for an announcement. "One year later."

"Where is he buried?" added Tom.

"No one knows," said the old man.

Tom and Nick glanced at each other.

As though reading their minds, Cristofori said, "Remember, this castle has no basement." Then leaning in to whisper, "But we know better, do we not?"

Tanner walked apart from the group. He glanced behind the front door. The docent shot a questioning look and Tanner smiled back. He found no surveillance cameras inside. He already checked that there were none outside.

Guess stone fortresses have a different level of security.

"Let's continue," Cristofori said as he walked through a doorway from the courtyard. Tanner followed the group, still watchful.

They entered a room with smooth gray marble walls devoid of furnishings. Only museum display boards occupied the area. They held drawings made over the years with accompanying text in both Italian and English telling the story of the castle and the mystery of its purpose.

Rachael's eye had been drawn to one name mentioned in the display, Leonardo Fibonacci. Cristofori noticed. He walked over to her.

"Do you see something you like?"

"Leonardo Fibonacci. He created the Fibonacci Sequence."

"Or rather, he lent his name to the sequence. Nature created it."

"Touché," replied Rachael.

Tom and Nick joined them as Tanner continued to case the room.

"What's up?" asked Nick.

"Fibonacci Sequence," is all Rachael had to say as Nick and Tom examined the name and the drawing of a conch shell sliced in half.

"Of course," said Tom. "The sequence where two numbers in the sequence, added together, makes the next number in the sequence. The progression is found all through nature, just as in the progressive proportions of this conch shell."

"And of this castle," added Cristofori. "The sequence starts 1,1,2,3,5,*8*. Eight, *otto*, the symbol of infinity."

Rachael came close to an eye roll before stopping to say, "OK, Lorenzo. I get it. But don't take the numerology too far away from real science."

The gentle old man cast a scolding look at Rachael. "Was it not you who discovered the depths of the code went to eight?"

"Yes."

"And now you stand in a castle thousands of miles away celebrating eights?"

"Well . . ."

"My dear. I believe we have already taken numerology far away from what you call 'real science.'"

Rachael, the great debater, fell silent.

Lorenzo believes in fate. I do not. Yet...

Cristofori looked at his tour group and, casting an eye to Tanner who was examining the one window in the room, said, "Shall we move on?"

He led the group through the next room which contained similar displays and on to the third, identical to the first two, but containing no displays. The room was bare, save for a large chest beneath the only window. He walked over to a narrow winding staircase situated in the wall, a feature common to other castles to allow passage to a floor above. The group was alone.

"Here," said Cristofori, pointing to the wall next to the stairs. The drawing tells us is the passage to the room below, somewhere behind this wall." He patted the marble which offered no sign of an opening.

Nick appeared dubious. "That's a solid wall. The drawing you showed us was not that definitive in the location."

Tanner interrupted. "Where does that staircase lead?"

"To the room above," said Cristofori.

"Can I get to a tower from there?"

"I believe so."

Tanner turned to the rest of the team. "I'm going up. Wait here." And with that, he ran up the narrow staircase.

Nick returned his attention back to Cristofori.

"Perhaps the drawing was not precise," said Cristofori, returning his attention to Nick's doubt. "But I am sure that if you play your notes here as you did in the cave, the way will become clear."

Tom shared Nick's skepticism. "The sound system we used in the cave is not small enough to lug into here. Especially without being noticed. And you remember how loud we had to crank it up to unlock The Tablet." He turned to Nick.

"Perhaps you can work your magic with the Italian park authorities like you did back home."

Nick shook his head. "We don't have time. It's clear someone's after us. I don't want to duplicate the media event here that we had there."

"Well, I think Tanner is casing the place so we can come back when no one else is here. But how can we 'play our notes,' as Lorenzo says, if we cannot set up our equipment?"

Rachael, considering all Cristofori had said about fate but not yet giving in to the idea, said, "I know a way."

Chapter 29

THE VAN RETRACED the same route the next night to the Castel del Monte. A half-moon lit the way. Tanner passed the entrance to the park, pulled over to the opposite side of the road and into the pine trees, hiding the vehicle from passing cars. Tonight, a guest had joined the team.

Everyone opened their doors and stepped out. Nick and Tanner from the front and Rachael and Tom from the rear. Cristofori exited, this time without the pretense of a nametag. Tanner tried to talk the old man out of coming. He would have none of it. This was a moment he had lived for. He turned and held his daughter's hand as she left the vehicle. Maria stepped out into the crisp night air dressed in black jeans and tee shirt, her hair pulled back. Everyone wore black, even Tanner, a departure from his usual army green. Tanner stopped short of making everyone wear camouflage makeup on their faces. Although not a war zone by any stretch of the imagination, they needed stealth for this operation.

Tanner went to the rear of the van and opened the hatch. He removed a large canvas duffel bag and Tom followed, removing a smaller bag. Tanner closed the hatch with a click, not a slam. Tanner led the team across the road and through an opening in the trees behind the visitor center. Although he had detected no security cameras around the castle yesterday, he found two located at the front and back of the visitor center. He figured the building that handled money was a more likely target for a thief than a six-hundred-year-old stone fortress. This path was out of sight of those cameras.

Tanner set the pace as the line of unlikely raiders followed the path. In fifty yards, they left the trees for the open grassy knoll of the castle grounds. No one said anything. Tanner had gone over the plans on paper that day and each person knew their part.

Rachael had brought Maria into this plan, but worried about the wisdom of it. However, Cristofori knew his daughter best and had no issue. Hers would be a brilliant contribution from someone he loved very much.

Tanner laid out a drawing of the castle grounds. He drew circles around the spot where he would park the van and the path to the castle.

"The distance from the car to the path is..."

Maria interrupted with, "350 meters."

Tanner, struck by the woman who said so little, responded, "Yes, that's what I figure."

He drew a line around the castle mound to the entrance. "I figure this path is another..." he said, this time pausing and looking to Maria.

"550 meters."

"I figured about 500 meters."

"You must consider the rise in elevation," Maria responded.

"You know this place, don't you?"

"Yes, I have been there." All of this from Maria with no hint she realized the keen sense just displayed.

Maria followed the others up the hill on the left, avoiding the exposed, front path to the castle. When they reached the large stone structure, Tanner led them single file toward the front entrance near the tower to the left.

"Stay here," he instructed as he turned and walked with duffel bag in hand back the way they came. Tanner sat the bag down at the corner of the tower furthest from the entrance and unzipped it. He removed a device from the bag that resembled a short gun wrapped in black canvas with large prongs sticking out from the barrel. His buddies at Battelle invented it for the Navy SEALs and named it a Tactical Air Initiated Launch device, TAIL for short.

Tanner walked twenty feet from the tower, extended the stock of the device and placed it against his shoulder. He looked to the top of the tower and laid his head against the device to aim. Pulling the trigger, a rush of compressed air shot a grappling hook toward the top, the hooks spreading upon ejection. His aim was on target. He set the device down and pulled on the rope. The hook was in place.

Tanner disconnected the rope from the TAIL with a push of a button. He carried the taught rope toward the duffel bag at the wall where he reached in and pulled out a pair of grippers and attached them to his boots. He reached high and grasped the bottom of the rope with the grippers. Leaning back, the grippers grabbed the rope, allowing the big man to climb it as though he was placing a solid step under each foot sliding each boot up as he climbed. In a minute, he reached the top and lifted himself over the stone edge and onto the top of the tower.

The group waited near the entrance, trying to remain as far out of sight as possible. They positioned themselves at the bottom of the left set of stairs, twenty feet below the entrance door. If there had been anyone near the visitor center below, the rise of the hill would hide them from view.

Not speaking, they were left to look at each other with questioning expressions.

Did Tanner do it? It's taking so long. Where is he?

The front door creaked open and everyone looked up. Tanner stood half out of the door waving the rest of the team up. Everyone walked double-time up the steps and past him as he waved them in. Once Tom, bringing up the rear, was in, Tanner closed the door and bolted it. Turning to the team, he smiled and announced, "Phase One complete."

Cristofori could not hide his excitement and took the lead. "Let's go," he said as he rushed off in the direction they had taken yesterday on their faux tour. The moonlight into the courtyard and through the windows in each room provided sufficient light to find their way.

In the third room, the one in which Cristofori claimed the hidden entrance existed, the old man stood anxiously waiting against the wall near the steps up to the next floor. "Here we are," he exclaimed, breaking the silence of the group. Quiet was no longer called for.

Rachael and Tom sat with Maria the previous evening. Tom busied himself setting up the sound equipment and the computer holding the code Rachael saved from the Carlsbad cave-in.

"You don't have to do this," said Rachael.

"I know," she said, looking somewhere over Rachael's shoulder. "But it is important."

Rachael paused. "Maria, did you go to school, I mean a regular school. I mean…" Rachael stumbled over her words.

"I know what you mean. Yes, I went to regular school. I went to university as well."

"And?"

"It bored me. They wanted me in classes. Why? I could

read the books and take the tests. I never got answers wrong. What did I get from listening to a teacher?"

Tom interrupted. "I'm ready."

Rachael and Maria stood.

"I'm going to play just a short piece of the code, from the start," Tom said, handing a small wireless microphone to Maria, "Repeat back as best you can. I will then let the computer tell us how well the two segments match.

Tom played three seconds of the code with its odd ups and downs on the tonal scale. The quick cadence of the notes wasn't one a diva would attempt, let alone this young woman. Tom was dubious. Maria repeated, and it was a perfect playback. Tom sat open-mouthed and Rachael smiled. Tom read the computer's analysis. It measured a match within three percent, the margin of error.

Maria asked, "More?"

After two more perfect repeats of longer and longer sections, Tom played the ninety seconds that had opened the door beneath The Tablet at Carlsbad. Maria repeated it all perfectly.

He looked at the excited Rachael. "We're all set."

Cristofori stood by the wall in Castel del Monte looking toward his daughter.

"Are you ready?"

"Yes," Maria said, as she walked to the middle of the room. The team stood in a semicircle around her. Nick and Tom appeared hopeful; Rachael, confident. Tanner scanned the area, still the protector.

Without a further cue, Maria began her odd song, her voice strong as a virtuoso intending to fill a concert hall with unamplified vocal strength. Tom, Nick, and Rachael heard the sounds last heard in Carlsbad, bringing back the experience. A minute passed. Then another thirty seconds. Maria stopped. Nothing.

Disappointment settled over everyone, except Maria who stayed as stoic as ever and Tanner with his continued skepticism.

"Are you able to repeat it?" ventured Nick to Maria.

"Yes. I can repeat it," she replied and executed a perfect encore.

"Nothing," sighed Nick.

As quiet again settled over the group, Maria said, "Did you not hear?"

"Hear what?" asked Nick.

"Over there," she said, pointing to the stone floor.

Tom opened his duffel bag and pulled out a lamp, much like one used at a campsite, but specialized for caving. He turned it on and a bright fluorescence filled the room. Taking the lamp to the spot on the floor near Cristofori where Maria pointed, Tom knelt and inspected the mortar of the stone with his fingers.

"Can you sing again?"

"Should I sing more than the first ninety seconds?" she asked.

Tom looked up, surprised. "You know more?"

"Of course."

"Then by all means, please do."

Maria started again with Tom eyeing the floor. Kneeling, he felt slight vibrations.

These can't be from her singing.

Maria came to the ninety-second point and continued. The vibrations grew stronger. Everyone in the room could feel them. Even Tanner was distracted from his surveillance duty and looked toward Tom, who now stood, his eyes on the floor.

Maria, whose voice was strong, raised her volume even more. The floor rumbled as though hit by the shock of a small earthquake. The ceiling joined in the effects with small amounts of mortar crumbling like snow. Everyone looked around the room.

Should they run?

But no one budged. Tom remained focused on the spot on the floor.

Four stones before him began to sink as if an ancient machine designed for this moment clicked into gear. The stones began to part as though hinged below on some pivot device, the middle edges rising and the far edges slipping below the floor. Tom stepped away. The stones accelerated their opening as gravity took over. They slammed open, falling back, level to the floor. The stones came to rest with a loud report as though a huge drum had been struck. Maria stopped singing. No one moved.

Tom walked over to the opening now exposed and shined the lantern in. He saw a spiral stone staircase, hidden for six-hundred years.

Tom, all doubts erased, lifted his lamp and smiled to all in the room.

"Who's joining me?"

Chapter 30

TOM TOOK THE LEAD down the narrow winding steps descending beneath the castle. Cristofori followed. Rachael was behind him, concerned the steps might prove too narrow and steep for the old man. Cristofori insisted on going as did Maria who followed Rachael. Nick brought up the rear with a second lamp. Nick worried about what lay ahead and whether the area below could accommodate everyone. Tanner stood guard above, so at least the group occupied less space.

The steps circled in a deep descent, deeper than any of the team had imagined, except for Tom. His caving experience and spatial sense told him what they sought was deep below ground. He pushed aside a thick mass of spider webs as he entered the staircase, but found no traces of insects as they progressed further down. Tom was familiar with depths such as these, but, despite his excitement, he had other concerns.

I hope there's enough ventilation below or we'll have to make this a short visit.

After eight rotations around the staircase, a number not lost on Tom, he entered a brick-lined tunnel about thirty-feet long, with an arched ceiling. Tom imagined the tunnel would accommodate a tall person like Nick (*or perhaps Federico Secondo?)* standing upright and being able to stretch out his arms to touch each wall. The others followed Tom into the tunnel. As they walked, Tom noticed sections of the roof missing bricks suggesting the likelihood of ventilation pipes. With the air above in the castle now cooler and heavy, Tom could feel a slight flow of fresh air against his cheek.

At least that takes care of one concern.

They came to a dark oak door at the end of the tunnel which displayed the craftsmanship of a medieval carpenter, with a family crest carved on its face. "The crest of Federico Secondo," announced Cristofori.

Below the crest were eight wooden levers, each just far apart to allow a hand to grab and pull up. Below them, the Greek letter phi was carved.

Nick spoke over everyone's heads to Tom, "Shall we enter?"

Tom grabbed a thick iron, three-foot long handle on the left side of the door and pulled. The door was stuck in place. Nick made his way to the front and grabbed part of the handle. "On three," he said to Tom. "One, two…"

Nothing. The door stayed in place.

"How about these levers? Can they move?" asked Nick.

Tom pulled on the first lever on the left. With some effort, he moved a mechanism untouched for hundreds of years. The lever loosened, and Tom pulled it up. As he did, the pivot point clicked with a sound loud enough for all to hear.

"Ten clicks," Tom announced as he pulled the lever all the way to the top.

"Try the others," Nick asked.

Each lever took the same effort to loosen and each reported ten clicks."

"It's a combination," said Nick. "But what combination?"

"It is right there on the door," exclaimed Cristofori. "It is phi, the symbol for the golden ratio!"

Nick and Tom shared blank looks at Cristofori.

"Remember who put this room here, al-Muazzam. Remember, he had his tablet locked away with eight levers, just like this."

"And what did he tell Federico about his combination?" Nick asked Tom as Cristofori's reasoning became clear.

"It was 'golden'," smiled Tom.

"And just to be clear, he left the letter phi for us," said Cristofori.

"Anyone know that sequence?" asked Nick to no one in particular.

From the back of the line of people in the tunnel, Maria spoke.

"The first eight digits are 1,6,1,8,0,3,3,9."

Nick and Tom looked at each other with the same thought.

What more can this woman do?

"Try it!" Nick told Tom.

Tom pulled the first lever up one click; the second, six carefully counted clicks. He continued through the seventh digit, a three. As he did, the air in the tunnel stirred with light dust being drawn to the door.

Tom looked to Nick, who returned a nod, and said "Go for it!"

Tom pulled the lever up toward nine clicks and the air movement quickened. He paused a moment at eight clicks, and then lifted up one more.

The door frame was set in brickwork with the bricks set sideways. Upon the ninth click, every other brick, now loosened by some unseen mechanism, shot into the wall as air pressure pushed hard against them. Air poured into the chamber from the ventilation ducts and from the staircase. Maria steadied Cristofori against the torrent. Rachael huddled with Tom and Nick.

The stream of air quieted after a few, long seconds.

Tom tried the door once more. It popped loose like the lid on a jar of jam.

"The room was sealed!" exclaimed Tom.

"A vacuum? How?" Started Nick. "It made sense to preserve things in a vacuum. But how did they pull that off six-hundred years ago?"

Tom entered the room with Nick close behind. Cristofori pushed his way past Nick.

The lights of the two lamps lit the white marble walls of a chamber the size of a rich man's library. In the middle was a hefty table with a chair on either side. The table bore scrapes and ink marks. Someone had performed scribe work here. At the far end stood an altar. Instead of a crucifix, a set of five books rested. A freestanding stone sarcophagus stood below the altar. A reclining resemblance of its occupant was engraved in its side.

"Al-Muazzam?" asked Nick.

"It must be," responded Cristofori. "Federico is buried someplace else."

Rachael observed how Maria took in everything. The young woman moved about the table examining the marks as though some message lay there. She rubbed the marble walls taking in the black streaks embedded in the stone. It was a marble pattern no one had ever seen before. On the low ceiling hung a candelabra, a circle of brass in which eight partially consumed candles rested. Maria examined each. The marvel Rachael experienced by this amazing place was second only to the mystery of how it might appear to Maria.

The men focused on the books on the altar. Cristofori touched the middle of the volumes and smiled. "They are my books, only in much better condition."

"And," Nick said with a huge grin. "This set has Volume Five!"

"May I?" asked Cristofori of Tom and Nick as he reached for that volume.

Tom and Nick stood aside as Cristofori slid the old volume from its place and walked it over to the table where he positioned it for all to see.

The old man opened the leather cover, shiny and clean as the day it was bound. The parchment pages were crisp and bright. Rachael and Maria came close. On each page appeared rows and rows of code translations displaying numbers to the left and Latin words to the right. To the right may be one word, or a whole expression, all in Latin.

Cristofori turned more pages. The numbers were two digits, then three, but each digit was never beyond eight. "Of course," said Tom. "An octal counting system."

"Something else," said Cristofori. "The numbers that are low, they are simple words: at, on, around. It seems the longer numbers are more complicated words. Look here," he said pointing to a word. "*Creamen*. Creation."

Nick stood, beaming. "Ladies and gentlemen. I believe we have found the answer."

Tom, more conservative, reserved judgment. "We need to test this out first."

"Then test we shall," Nick said. "Let's go."

Anticipating the acquisition of the missing volume, Nick had brought a leather satchel the size of one of the other books in Cristofori's collection. He slid the volume with care into the felt-lined satchel, lifted it and slung it over his head and onto his right shoulder. Tom grabbed a lamp and again took the lead. Everyone filed out. Tom waited as Maria stayed in place examining the room.

"Maria," said Rachael taking the woman's hand. "We have to go."

Maria followed Rachael out. Nick took the second lamp and followed the women. When in the tunnel, he turned and pushed the door closed. It shut firmly in place, but with the vacuum gone, anyone could now open it with ease.

Tom sprinted up the steps, but soon realized he must take it slowly. Cristofori struggled to climb the steep incline of the old, narrow steps. Half way up, gasping, he stumbled on a step.

"Papa!" yelled Maria, showing what, for her, was an unusual expression of emotion.

Rachael followed behind Cristofori and just in front of Maria. She caught the old man before he fell. "Are you OK?" she asked.

Cristofori, gasping, provided a heroic grin and said "Certainly… I must just… catch my breath."

Waiting a minute, Tom asked "OK?"

"OK," replied Cristofori as he turned, ready to go ahead.

Tom continued, but at a slower pace, stopping along the

way. He reached the top of the staircase where Tanner waited. Tanner helped Tom steady Cristofori as he reached the top. Tom guided Cristofori over to the chest under the window where he helped him sit. Tanner continued to assist the others out of the staircase.

When Nick appeared with the satchel, Tanner asked, "Got it?"

"Got it," replied Nick.

Did he detect a satisfied expression on Tanner's face?

Nick walked over to Cristofori. "Are you OK?"

Cristofori, weary from his exploit, said, "I am good… I am very good." Standing, he added, "Now let's see what your tablet is trying to tell us!"

Nick smiled at Cristofori's fortitude. "I couldn't agree with you more."

Cristofori cast a worried look toward the new opening in the floor, no longer a secret. "What are we to do about that?"

"Excuse me," said Tanner as he pushed through the men and picked up the heavy chest under the window. He carried the chest over to the opening and lowered it in place, covering the new-found steps going down.

Standing beside the chest Tanner said, "Problem solved."

Nick smiled. "Well, that may buy us some time."

"Time to do what?" asked Tanner.

"Figure this out before the Italian authorities figure out

who ruined their antiquities."

"Ruined?" questioned an unbelieving Cristofori. "You have opened a new part of the castle. It is an historic find!"

"And stole a part of that find."

"We did not steal," said Cristofori with mischief in his voice. "We borrow."

"Well, let's take the book we 'borrowed' from this library and get out of here," replied Nick. "Tanner, lead the way."

"First, douse those lights," said Tanner pointing to the two lamps still on from the exploration below ground.

Tom grabbed both, turned them off, and returned the lamps to the bag he carried.

Tanner grabbed his duffel bag and led the group out of the room, into the courtyard, and to the front door. He motioned all to stop as he unlocked the door to look out. Tanner told everyone to walk down the steps and stop. He turned the lock on the door. Once pulled closed, it would appear no one had entered.

Everyone waited as Tanner closed the door and walked the steps down the front side of the castle wall. He paused, as if to count heads. "OK," he started to say, but a sharp 'ping' interrupted him. The stone of the castle, just behind Tanner's head, popped as though a lit firecracker hit it.

"Get down!" He yelled as another ping hit just above him.

Nick, huddled beside Cristofori, who he told, "I knew your

police might be pissed, but shooting at us?"

"This isn't the police," growled Tanner as he unzipped his duffel bag and pulled out a 9-mm pistol.

"What?" said Nick. "You brought a gun?"

"Always," said Tanner. "Stay here," he told everyone as he crouched down and walked away.

Nick put a hand on Tanner's shoulder to stop him. "I'm going with you."

"You're the boss. But stay behind me."

Tanner and Nick walked around the tower nearest them. They continued to the rear of the castle where Tanner led them down the side of the hill to the tree line fifty yards below. Stalking around the perimeter of the trees, Tanner led Nick toward the spot where he saw the muzzle flash of the second shot. He carried his pistol in both hands pointed down and to his right. As he approached the spot where the shooter must be, he motioned Nick to sit down among the trees and to stay there. Tanner raised his gun in a shooting position and edged forward in a silent walk.

Before him, ten yards away, a man, wearing black and in a prone position, aimed a long rifle atop a bipod toward the castle.

At the castle steps, the team stayed low, seated, and quiet. No one noticed the small red laser dot floating on the wall above them. Tom turned to the castle wall to see the dot as it made its way to Maria's temple. He jumped forward and took Maria to the dirt as another ping hit the castle wall.

"Are you OK?" he asked.

Maria nodded.

The shooter, focused on the rifle scope, didn't hear Tanner approaching. Tanner stopped and raised his gun, but before he could call out to the assassin, something unexpected happened.

The side of the man's head exploded as the bullet from another high-powered rifle tore through his skull. The assassin's rifle had a silencer on it, but the rifle that killed him did not. A loud crack echoed off the hillsides as Tanner dove behind a tree. The assassin lay lifeless. Tanner peeked from behind the tree toward the origin of the fatal shot. He heard a car start and race away.

Tanner tried to make sense of all this. Whoever killed this man was a good shot, but didn't use much stealth.

Tanner stood, and Nick joined him. Looking at the corpse before him, he said, "Who's this?"

Tanner responded, "Don't know, but it's going to be hard to make him out with what that bullet did. The more interesting question is, who shot him?"

Nick added, "And why?"

Chapter 31

BLUE LIGHTS atop cars of the *Polizia di Stato* flashed against the castle walls from the road below. *Ispettore Capo* Rossi was clearly displeased with Cristofori. Rossi, a tall man with salt and pepper gray hair and an impeccable, trim mustache, wore the authority of his rank with dignity. He had spent most of his thirty-two years in the state police, rising to his current rank of *Ispettore Capo,* senior detective, and suffered no fools.

Is he expected to believe his friend Cristofori and the foolish tale he tells?

As his men continued to stake out the crime scene and the photographer finished shots of the lifeless body, Rossi went over the story one more time. Nick and Cristofori told the truth, but omitted several important details.

"So," said Rossi in English to accommodate Nick. "You say you heard a shot and here you are. Tell me again why you were here at this time of night."

"Well," said Cristofori, "It was not the middle of the night as it is now. It was early evening."

"*Si, si,*" said the exasperated Rossi. "Go on."

"I took Signor Foxe and his friends on a tour yesterday. They were spellbound by the castle. It is mysterious is it not?"

"*Si, si*. Continue."

"Well, Signorina Friedman wanted to see it again this evening, by moonlight. You know how romantic women can be."

This elicited an eye-roll from Rossi.

"We pull into the parking area, get out, hear a gun shot, come here. And we find this poor man."

"So," said Rossi turning to Nick. "This is how it was?"

"Yes, officer," responded Nick omitting a few details between parking the van and hearing gun shots.

Tanner and the others stood near the police cars talking to another officer. Rossi pointed to them and said, "We have an officer talking with your friends. Will this be the same account they provide?"

Nick and Cristofori said in unison, "Of course."

Rossi frowned at the unified response.

Too rehearsed.

What was Cristofori doing in this? A gentle violin maker would hurt no one. It is unlikely an assassin would target him. These Americans. They come to examine old books Cristofori has? Maybe, but they are an odd mix of characters.

Rossi revealed he had additional information. It appeared the victim was aiming toward the castle. "We discovered bullet marks on the castle wall near the entrance. The shooter was targeting something or someone up there. Who was it? Was it you?"

Cristofori appeared shocked. "Why would a murderer target an old man like me?"

Rossi let the non-answer go. There was more to learn, but he understood those things would not be learned tonight.

"OK. You may go," said Rossi. He looked to Nick. "I want you and your friends to alert me to your whereabouts," he said handing his card to him. "And you are not to leave the country. Not yet."

"No problem," said Nick. "We plan to stay here, and will discuss it with you if we'd like permission to leave."

Nick walked over with Cristofori to where the others were standing. Cristofori gave Maria a hug and a kiss on the cheek. He told the interrogating officer that Rossi told them they could go. With a glance toward Rossi for affirmation, the officer touched the brim of his hat in a salute and said, "OK."

Saying nothing, everyone walked to the waiting van, got in and, with Tanner at the wheel, pulled out and onto the road. Driving down the hill for a kilometer, Tanner looked into the rearview mirror. He saw no one following and pulled to the side of the road. Tom hopped out of the van and disappeared in the dense pine woods. He returned with his duffel bag in one hand, Tanner's in the other, and a satchel slung over his shoulder containing the prized Volume Five. Tom opened the rear lid of the van, loaded the duffel bags and satchel, closed it, and returned. The whole operation was quick, and Tanner took off less than one minute after stopping.

Tanner complimented Tom, "Good work. The police searched the van as expected. I thought we should stash our tools and other things before we called them."

Turning to Nick beside him, Tanner grumbled, "We had to call them. Right?"

"My decision," said Nick, unapologetic and reaffirming the chain of command that rankled Tanner. "Opening undiscovered passages in a castle and 'borrowing' a book, as Mister Cristofori puts it, is one thing. Leaving the scene of a crime, a murder, is another."

From the back seat of the van, Rachael, had remained quiet, until now. "Look, I too recognized the danger. Remember, I was there when the bomb almost killed us before Tanner stepped in."

Tanner quipped, "You're welcome."

"But, now we're dragging in others. Maria was nearly killed."

"I am OK," said Maria from the seat beside her.

Turning to her, Rachael said, "Maria. You don't appreciate what we're involved in."

Maria, responded in the neutral manner everyone expected, "Rachael, I think the word is 'patronize,' is it not?"

"What do you mean?"

"What you are doing now. You are patronizing me."

Rachael stammered, at a loss for words.

"You need not. People make the mistake all the time. Just because I seem different doesn't mean that I don't understand. You cannot see the world as I see it. Perhaps I do not understand everything, but what I do is not cloudy. I see clearly. Maybe more clearly than others do."

"Maria, I just…"

"Do not worry. I know this discovery is important. More important than maybe you even understand."

Rachael studied Maria.

What does she know?

Maria finished with, "The answers will soon be known. The answers will be amazing."

Tom and Cristofori listened to this exchange as they leaned over the back of the middle seat. Tom was relieved he saved this woman from an assassin and Cristofori, proud of his special daughter.

The van continued down the road, leaving the mountain pines and entering the dense olive groves of the plains below. There are many more olive trees than people in this region, something clear from the mountaintop they left. Whoever fired the fatal shot had many places to hide.

Tanner drove up the hill to Locorotondo. It was past midnight, but the moon lit the way as it turned the white walls of the town steel blue. He parked the van on the edge of town and opened the back. Nick joined him and removed the satchel. They left the duffel bags in the van.

As the others gathered, Tanner asked, "Now what?"

Nick led the group back to Cristofori's. "Now, we decode."

"So, let's get going," Cristofori said with a weak smile as he and Maria led the group through the maze of streets to his workshop.

Tom followed behind Tanner and Nick. He commented, "That will take time. The book has thousands of entries."

Rachael, walking beside Tom, added, "This time, we have no way to speed it up. If the text had been in print, we could scan it. But what do we do with calligraphy?"

Nick was quiet. He felt like a dog who, after chasing cars, caught one.

Now what?

He'd been playing this by ear and now nothing came to him. The team had booked rooms in a small inn near Cristofori's shop when they first arrived, and Nick decided to sleep on the matter. From the looks of the team, everyone was pretty tired. But first, they would stop at the violin maker's place.

At the door to the shop, and with everyone gathered, the old man flipped old, large keys around a ring looking for the one for the front door. Before he could put the key in the lock, something happened that jerked the team out of their haze.

Something incongruous with this time and place.

The door swung open and out stepped Lizzy Rodriguez.

"Hello, everyone," she chirped. "Wow, you guys look awful!"

Chapter 32

THE SUDDEN APPEARANCE of the housekeeper from New Mexico dazed everyone. Nick stammered, "Lizzy. What are you doing here?"

Lizzy smiled, knowing the effect of her sudden appearance. "It's a long story," she said. "Come on in. I want you to meet someone."

Cristofori was confounded, never having met this lively young lady who everyone seemed to know. As the team followed her through the open door, he asked Rachael, "Who is this girl?"

"She kept house where we stayed in New Mexico. I met her before the others. She's quite a woman."

"So, she pops up like magic, thousands of miles away?" puzzled Cristofori. "I guess she is indeed quite a woman."

Lizzy led the group past the now idle workshop to the room in which they first played the CD. There sat a black man who rose to meet them.

Lizzy said, "Everyone, I would like you to meet Dr. Fezile Nodada."

Nodada was dressed like the stereotypic academic. He wore a stylish tweed jacket and a school tie. The doctor shook hands with everyone but Tanner, introducing himself around the room. Tanner stayed by the door, cautious. Unsure why he left his pistol in his duffel bag in the van.

Lizzy looked over to Tanner with a smile and a wink and said to the doctor, "And this is Tanner."

"Mr. Tanner," repeated the doctor.

"No," the soldier replied. "Just Tanner."

"I see," Nodada paused a moment to assess the big man. "Please, let's all sit down."

Everyone took a seat around the table except for Tanner, who stood by the door.

The doctor opened, "I recognize that the activity this evening was stimulating and exhausting. The important thing is that you have found the missing volume."

"Now wait a minute," Nick said, stopping Nodada. "I don't know who you are or why Lizzy is here." And turning to Lizzy, "Are you here by your own free will?"

Lizzy rolled her eyes and replied with sarcasm, "*Please*, do you really think someone could force me to come here?" All smiled at Lizzy's response, even Tanner.

Nick returned his focus to Nodada. "So, how is it you know all of this?"

Nodada said, "I guess I need to explain. First, let me tell you about myself. I am head of Pandemic Medicine at the World Health Organization."

Tom reacted first upon hearing the threatening word.

"Pandemic," he exclaimed. "Are we dealing with some disease?"

"No, no," reassured the doctor. "There are… other subjects I pursue. Genetics, for one, has been a lifelong passion. I head up a well-funded genetics project that gives me some latitude in what I can do. But, I believe something else will help you understand why I am here. Something I obtained in my native South Africa long ago."

He paused, ensuring he captured each person's reaction to what came next.

"I have something I believe Signor Cristofori has too. I have the first four volumes of Frederick's books."

Cristofori's eyes widened at the news of this man being a member of the small brotherhood who owned Federico Secondo's masterpiece. He jerked forward in surprise, knocking an empty coffee cup to the floor where it broke. Maria left her chair to pick up the pieces.

"You have a copy?" Cristofori exclaimed.

Nodada smiled and nodded.

"Of Federico Secondo's books? The ones about al-Muazzam?"

"Yes," said the doctor. "And I look forward to comparing notes."

"OK," said Nick. "That's fine. But why now? Didn't you know about Cristofori and his books long before now?"

"The short answer is *no*. I did not. It is you who led me here."

"What?" exclaimed Nick.

"When Mr. Littleton and you made your discovery, I knew it was just like the tablet al-Muazzam described. I had to know more."

"You could have called," said Nick.

Nodada leaned back in his chair. "I did."

"What?"

"Check your phone logs. I called many times to your press agent. It was in the midst of what you might call a 'media storm'?"

"Well, Rachael got through. She showed up."

"I showed up too," responded Nodada.

"You did?" This puzzled Nick, and he studied the doctor to try and trigger recognition.

"Not in person. I sent two men from my security office. I am not sure if you met them, but Miss Rodriguez did."

Tanner unfolded his arms and exchanged glances with Lizzy.

So, those were the men in the car Lizzy took out when we escaped.

"You see," Nodada continued. "I was concerned for your safety."

"So was Tanner," Nick countered. "And he was the one

who saved our lives."

If one were to study Tanner, one might have seen a slight expression of pride. Lizzy saw it.

"Yes, we missed that one, but we saved lives tonight."

"What?"

"That was my man who shot the assassin," said Nodada

"Hey, that was under control," Tanner insisted.

Tom had to say, "Tanner, he had Maria in his sights when he was shot."

This was the first Tanner heard this detail, and he checked his ego.

"What made you believe we were in danger?" asked Nick.

Nodada turned to Cristofori. "Signore, you have read the volumes, have you not?"

"*Si*," responded the old man, not sure in what direction the doctor was going.

"So, I may repeat things you already know." And turning to Nick, "But, Mister Foxe. Do you know what the code is all about?"

Nick realized he was so caught up in the chase, he had pursued no clues given by the first volumes of Frederick's books.

"You might ask, 'if al-Muazzam had broken the code, why didn't he decode the tablet he possessed?' The books do not say that he did, but they indicate it was so. You see, al-

Muazzam writes about a people who lived 10,000 years ago. Where they lived was not clear. He writes they lived among us. That's all. He said these people could change the *sangue* of men. Their children would be different as would their children and so on. *Sangue* is Latin for…"

"Blood," Nick said, finishing the sentence.

"Yes, blood. And in that context, rather than blood, what would people call it today?"

"DNA," added Rachael.

Nodada smiled at the young professor. "Yes, that is my belief. And Doctor Friedman, he also says these people could make machines operate from seawater. I may be wrong, but I believe our modern translation would be they could harness energy from seawater."

"Maybe," responded Rachael. She believed this might be a stretched interpretation. But the next thing Nodada said caught her attention.

The doctor leaned across the table. "Al-Muazzam writes that, for these people, *tempus vanum est*. Time is meaningless. And I do not believe he was talking about how they used time. I believe they meant time itself. Perhaps Dr. Einstein would have liked to talk to them, do you think?"

Rachael had no response, but her imagination went into overdrive.

Could ancients ten thousand years ago understand a modern

concept of time? That it is fluid? They were humans, weren't they?

Doctor Nodada overwhelmed everyone's imagination, and all were quiet for long moments before Nick broke the silence. "So, what became of these people?"

Nodada leaned back into his chair. "Al-Muazzam writes simply *profecti sunt*. They left."

"They left?" Tom repeated as a question. "How, where?"

Rachael replied, "Well, if time had no meaning. Perhaps space did not as well."

"Careful, Rachael," cautioned Tom. "Don't get carried away."

Rachael returned a smile of one lost in possibilities.

Nodada turned to Nick. "Mister Foxe, do you not see the opportunity and the danger? There are men who want to own this and others who want to destroy it."

"It's the same story forever," responded Nick. "The powerful fear enlightenment, unless it turns a buck."

Nodada continued. "I have talked more about this with you than anyone. Who would believe it?" Turning to Cristofori and putting his hand on the old man's arm. "Except for my new friend Cristofori."

"I have mentioned pieces of this story in lectures, mere scraps of the truth. More in the lines of 'we believe that ancients provided clues to human health that deserve revisiting.' I mentioned examples like Romans chewing willow bark to relieve pain and scientists of today discovering the bark has the active ingredient of aspirin. But I would hint that there are other discoveries that may be more powerful.

"Once, when I did this, a reception followed the talk. I dislike that sort of thing, but my position requires it. I remember a man who came up to me. He had a Texas accent. The man sounded like a cowboy from one of the Westerns I enjoyed as a boy. He told me 'Doctor, if you ever come up with one of those discoveries from the ancients, I want to know about it.' I will never forget him. How could a man sound so friendly and menacing at the same time? Is that the way they are in Texas?"

Everyone laughed at the remark.

"He seems to have left an impression," said Nick.

"Yes," said Nodada, his expression darkening. "Plus, what happened the next day."

"What was that?"

"I keep Frederick's books in a safe and secure place. However, in my office, I keep a copy of my notes about them in a drawer. I like to review them when I get a chance. The next day, they were missing."

"Missing?"

"Yes. I don't keep that drawer locked, but I always lock the door to the office. It was locked that morning. Nothing else was missing."

"Sounds like a professional job," added Tom.

"Later that day, I passed the Texan who had a hat in hand, a cowboy hat, and a top coat over his arm. He appeared to have met with one of my colleagues. He said he was leaving for the airport.

"Hello, doctor.' He said in passing. He shook my hand, looked me in the eye, and said, 'Now I mean it. You keep me up to date on what you find.' His smile was like his voice, both friendly and menacing. And I may have read more into it than I should, but he seemed to know more than he did before. It was like he was expressing 'I now know what you know.'"

"Doctor," said Nick, "I've met no Texan interested in what we're doing. And if it were so, I don't think they would try to kill us."

Nodada gazed at Nick as if he were a school kid and raised a finger as to make a point. "Remember, people throughout time want to destroy what they don't understand. Do you know anyone like that?"

"When we had the media all over us, there were crazies who latched onto the discovery with plot theories. But, no, I'm not aware of any personally."

After considering past contacts for a moment, Nick continued, "Look we have a lot of work ahead of us. We need to take the decoding from Volume Five and key it in. That's the only way we can use what's already in our computer and make sense of it.

Doctor Nodada beamed. "That, my friend, is something I can help with."

Chapter 33

NICK'S GULFSTREAM cruised high over southern Italy in the crisp, clear morning. They left from Bari, the nearest airport, and flew over the Adriatic Sea. The plane circled to the west. Rome was their destination, a trip of six hours by car, but just over an hour by air.

Last night, Nick and his team returned to their inn in Locorotondo to shower and catch a little sleep. It gave Nick time to contact his detective in the States to check out the man now sitting across from him in the jet. Yes, Doctor Nodada is what he says he is, the head of Pandemic Medicine at the World Health Organization. The picture Nick received on his cell phone was Nodada. The detective reported the man was well respected, although it surprised him to learn Nodada had a sharpshooter in his employ.

Is Nodada leading a clandestine operation?

Nick sat in a leather chair at the front of the plane, sipping a cup of coffee. He focused on the group at the other end where Nodada, still in his tweed jacket and school tie, led an animated discussion with Tom and Rachael. Showering and changing into a fresh turtleneck and blue jeans, revived Nick. He noticed that Tom and Rachael were similarly dressed, with Rachael's only difference being her trademark athletic pants.

Nick winced, wondering whether they had spent so much time together they now dressed alike.

With another sip from the cup, Nick assessed the situation. He thought it smart to be carrying a photocopy of Volume Five with them. The original now resided secure in Cristofori's library. Tanner stayed behind to guard it. Lizzy volunteered to stay behind to help Tanner. Her attraction to Tanner was obvious.

Cristofori had wanted to come with them, but Maria kept him at home. The old man was showing signs of exhaustion, and it was best he stayed behind. Nick was worried about Rossi, who was stationed nearby,

How soon would he tire of Nick's omissions and stretching the truth?

The inspector was smart and likely doubted the assassin was shot by anyone he questioned that night. The man responsible for that killing was here on the plane, or more to the point, the man who hired the killer was here. But Rossi would eventually discover the raid on the unknown chamber under the Castel del Monte. Pieces would fall in place and Nick and his team arrested. Time was precious. They had to bring all this to a conclusion.

Nodada told Nick he sent his security team ahead to Rome. They would be ready to protect them. That news gave Nick little assurance, nor did Nodada's pledge to clear things up with the Italian authorities. Yet, the doctor promised something Nick needed. A workforce. Nodada claimed he had people who would take the code book and enter it into a computer within twenty-four hours. His people would allow Tom to run the effort. With the code matched against the information Rachael had recorded from the cave tablet and then from Latin to English, they would at last find what the ancient people had to say.

Nick frowned, pondering the multiple translations ahead. Bits to Latin. Latin to English.

It won't be literature, but I hope we can understand it.

Doctor Nodada enjoyed regaling Tom and Rachael with tales of his boyhood in South Africa, his beloved mother, and the breaks he'd had in his career. But Rachael became impatient, drumming her fingers on the table. She finally interrupted to ask the doctor about a missing piece in his tale.

"But what got you interested in all of this?" she asked.

"All of this? You mean the people who lived long ago and spoke music?"

"Well, we don't know they spoke it," added Tom. "But it appears they wrote it."

"True. In fact, I was not aware of that aspect of these people until I acquired Frederick's books."

"And you said you found the books in a rare book store in Cape Town?" said Rachael reaffirming a previous part of the doctor's tale.

"Yes," said the doctor. "No one knew what they were until I came along."

"And why did you know?" asked Rachael.

Nodada pulled at his ear lobe, considering how to tell these adventurers the odd reason.

"It happened when I was a young intern. We treated a man for a tumor in his abdomen. It proved not to be malignant and easy to remove, but considering the man's age and frailty, he spent a few days in the hospital recovering."

Nodada looked away as though he could visualize the man. "Now that I think of it, Mr. Cristofori reminds me of the man." Then turning back to Tom and Rachael, "But that was many years ago.

"This man always had a smile for me. It seemed he wanted to talk. Why, I do not know. But when he was well enough to sit up, we had a long conversation. He asked about my interest in genetics. I told him it was a passion. How magical it was that we are who we are because of a strand of nucleic acid.

"He enjoyed my passion. He asked if genes could be changed by man. I told him I believed it possible. This happened years before advances in that direction. Then he told me something that changed my life."

The doctor looked down and shook his head, not believing it himself.

"He said, 'What if I told you that genes have already been changed?'

"He continued by telling me what we already know about early man. For thousands of years, homo sapiens were hunters and gatherers. Then we changed. We specialized. Some became farmers. Others became soldiers, scholars, and leaders. I always held the belief that the discovery of agriculture propelled the difference. When man raised more food than he consumed, he fed others to defend him, to rule him. And with more advances, to entertain and to think great thoughts for him. I told the man this.

"The old man frowned. He insisted that people existed thousands of years ago who could affect a man's destiny for each one of those roles. The man told me about a set of books that told this tale. He described them in detail."

"Frederick's books?" asked Rachael.

"Yes, the same. I asked to see them. The old man's face turned dour. He said when he was poor and could not support himself, he sold them to a book merchant. I asked him which one and he told me. But that merchant sold them to another.

"This set me on a quest. Although I thought the story might be the fanciful rumination of an old man, I stopped in old book shops wherever I travelled, looking for these books."

Nodada chuckled. "Who would guess that years later, I would find the books in my own Cape Town. They were in horrible condition. Much worse than Cristofori's. But what I read fascinated me."

The doctor stopped and looked away, seeing those years pass by.

"What happened to the old man?" asked Tom.

Still looking away. "He died. The cancer returned.

"Then I learned what appeared on the tablet you discovered, as well as the one your Mister Tanner saw. Both had the helix we now identify as DNA." He looked from Tom to Rachael and back. "Do you think the old man was right?"

The pilot interrupted with an announcement they would soon land.

"Well," said Tom. "I guess we'll soon find out."

The plane landed at Ciampino Airport, a small airfield south of Rome used by discount airlines and private aviation. Nick thought the international airport might have people looking for them, suspecting they may try to leave the country. No customs officers or police were likely to be at Ciampino.

Nodada's security people had a Suburban SUV with heavy tinted windows waiting for them. The crew took their meager luggage from the plane and loaded it in the back. Nick stood frowning at the vehicle.

Draws too much attention.

"We're riding in this?" asked Nick.

"Oh, no," said Nodada reading Nick's concern. "That's for

the security people. They will take your luggage to your hotel. We're taking this," pointing to a nondescript gray Fiat Multipla, a vehicle resembling a small minivan.

"I felt discretion is key," said the doctor.

A driver standing by the Fiat opened the right front and rear doors inviting the team to get in. The interior was wide with three bucket seats in front and three in back, an odd configuration. The front middle seat looked like it should be a copilot's seat with dash instruments before it. Nick took the right front one. Rachael, Nodada, and Tom took the rear seats. Tom motioned Nodada to take the center rear seat and Tom rode beside him on the outside seat. They were off, following the black SUV. Nick appreciated the motorcade where the SUV would draw the attention of anyone interested in them and away from the Fiat following.

"So, where are we going?" asked Nick as they entered the highway.

"To a food market," replied Nodada. "Are you hungry?"

Chapter 34

THE CAR ENTERED THE SOUTHERN PART OF ROME, crossed the Tiber, and stopped before an open-air market. Doctor Nodada announced, "We're here."

Nick looked from the window of the Fiat at a line of modern enclosures. "We're where?"

"Patience my friend. I will show you."

Nodada led the team through a crowd of tourists and locals surrounded by the smell of fresh meats and cheeses. On one side, cases displayed cuts of meat with a butcher in a crisp, white jacket, ready to weigh each selection. On the other side, appeared a shop of pesto and other sauces. Shops along the way sold oddities like single servings of wine in a pouch. Rachael paused at a vegetable stand displaying an explosion of colors. Large carrots in one crate, fresh strawberries in another, separated by rows of zucchini, endive, and scallions twice the size of any in the States.

"Hungry?" Tom asked Rachael.

"Guess I am. Haven't been paying much attention to eating."

"Distracted, are you?" asked Nick. Turning to Nodada, "Doctor, I'm confused. Can't we get to work and have lunch later?"

Nodada grinned. "Mister Foxe, I thought you would know where we are."

"What?" puzzled Nick.

"Look ahead."

Stepping into the aisle between the roofline of the stalls, Nick spotted a grassy mound peeking above a row of single-story buildings.

"Wait," he said. "Are we in Testaccio?

"Indeed, we are."

Nick wandered ahead with the others following. At the end of the last row of market enclosures, they arrived at the grassy mound.

"Monte Testaccio," said Nick.

"Yes," confirmed the doctor.

Nick stood in wonder as Tom asked, "What is this?" To him it appeared to be a large hill of no consequence.

Nick explained. "This mountain is made up of broken wine jugs."

"Wine jugs?" repeated Rachael.

"Well, to be more specific, clay jugs used by ancient Romans to ship oil and wine. The jugs were called *amphorae*. I know you've seen them in pictures and movies." Nick traced the shape in midair as he described them. "The jug was oblong, coming to a spout on top, with a handle on each side near the spout. Picture a nubile wine maiden carrying one on her shoulder."

Rachael made a face at the reference to a nubile wine maiden, but Nick didn't notice as he remained focused on the mound.

"Residual wine or oil soaked into the pottery and made the *amphorae* unsuitable for reuse. So, the Romans broke the *amphorae* into shards and disposed of them here. The shards were called *testae*; hence, the name Testaccio."

Nick looked at Tom and Rachael and said with a sly smile, "Before you, stands the largest landfill in the ancient world. I've always wanted to visit."

"Why are those buildings right against the hill?" asked Tom.

Doctor Nodada told Tom, "There is a characteristic of the hill you might appreciate as a man who spends time in caves."

"What would that be?"

"A pile of masonry, with air gaps in between, stacked high, was, for centuries, considered useless. Until they discovered how cool it was inside. A perfect wine cellar, if you will. Most of these buildings are restaurants with fine wine collections. Let me show you one," said the doctor as he led them forward.

Each person now suspected something at play other than lunch.

The doctor came to the *Ristorante Romano*, its generic name displayed on the window. Aged oak framed the window to one side and the door. When Nodada pushed it open, a little bell announced their entry. Five round tables with crisp, white table cloths dotted the small room. Two men ate at one table, glanced up, and returned to their meal of pasta Bolognese, crusty bread, and a carafe of Chianti. The proprietor, a rotund middle-aged man, with a mustache waxed in Dali style, greeted them. "Doctor! *Buongiorno*!"

"These are the guests I mentioned," he said.

"Ah! Everything is ready. As you requested."

"Thank you."

The doctor led the team to an adjacent room where a window cut into the hill displayed a wall of tan shards of equal sizes, stacked on each other. The air grew cooler although there was no evidence of air conditioning. Nodada led them to the right down a small hallway where a door labeled *bagno* appeared. To the left, an identical door with no name. The doctor took a plastic card from his coat jacket and held it near the unidentified door to the left. A click sounded and Nodada pushed the door open. "Follow me," he said.

They entered another small hallway where florescent lights flickered on. This hallway consisted of smooth plaster walls and hinted at something new, not ancient. Twenty feet ahead, they reached a plain stainless-steel door. The doctor used a different card to click open this entrance.

They entered to find themselves on a gray steel-mesh

balcony overlooking a work area below. Above was a domed ceiling made of *testae* held in place by panes of tempered glass between a grid of steel supports. Below, they looked down upon twenty computer workstations with twenty workers busy at the keyboards and screens, oblivious to the visitors. Beyond the workstations was an area cordoned off by glass walls and two doors forming an airlock. Behind that wall were lab tables with a small group of men and women working with test tubes. Everyone in the place wore white lab coats.

Doctor Nodada turned to the wide-eyed team and said, "Please, follow me."

The doctor descended the stairs with the team behind, their steps making metallic echoes off the walls. At the bottom, a tall woman, carrying a clip board, walked up to meet them. She wore her hair fashioned in a bun and a pair of large, tortoiseshell glasses resting on her aquiline nose.

"Everyone," said the doctor, "I would like you to meet Doctor Angelina Moretti."

A smile and firm handshake greeted each person as they exchanged names.

Nick led with the question on everyone's mind. "Doctor Moretti, what is this place?"

Moretti shot a puzzled look at Nodada before responding. "Did Doctor Nodada not tell you?"

"We were in a hurry," quipped Nodada.

"Well," began Moretti, "This lab is for the study of pandemic diseases."

"You have a lab full of viruses in the middle of a metropolitan area?" exclaimed Tom.

"Rest assured, Mr. Littleton. We do not breed viruses here. We capture what we find."

The statement drew three puzzled looks in return.

"Perhaps we can go to the conference room to discuss this further?" suggested Nodada.

"Certainly," responded Moretti. "Please come this way."

Doctor Moretti led the group to a glass enclosure with a modern, oak conference table with a complement of ten mesh chairs arranged around it. Doctors Moretti and Nodada sat on one side with the lab workers visible behind them. Nick, Tom, and Rachael sat on the other.

Moretti began.

"Rome is once again a crossroad. 'All roads lead to Rome' is quite true today. The city is a perfect site to study how humans travel in a modern world. And this location, with a mix of locals and tourists, plus meats and produce, is a perfect place to sample.

"What do we sample? You may know we carry many, many viruses that cause no harm to humans. Some come from other animals in exotic places. Bats near the Ebola River carried a virus we named after that river. That virus has a devastating effect on humans. But other viruses travel in the same way and do not.

"What we do here is sample those harmless viruses and trace how they travel. The more that we understand about the transmission of the harmless ones, the better equipped we are to deal with the deadly ones."

"But how do you sample?" asked Rachael.

"You may have noticed that we have a number of restaurants here. You entered one on your way here, did you not? We work with these restaurants to recover samples from the food left on the plate. Since most viruses live a very short time outside their carrier, we have additives the cook puts in dishes before serving to help preserve their lives. We have sample vials at the ready to use when the plates are returned."

"But how do you know anything about the donor?" asked Tom.

Moretti smiled. "Most everyone uses charge cards these days. We can trace the person from that information."

"And if they paid for two people?" asked Nick.

"There is another thing we capture. The DNA is paired with the virus sample. Often it is a man and a woman who dine. We identify the difference."

"DNA sampling is extreme just to find out the sex of a person," offered Tom.

"It is not just for that," explained Moretti. "We can tell

much about where the person came from by their DNA. Not only geographically, but culturally as well."

Nick observed, "I'm guessing your secret location is due to the fact your work has 'pandemic' in its name."

"That is true," said Moretti. "Plus, the location provides a naturally cool atmosphere, important in our laboratory."

"And one other thing," said Nodada toward Moretti as to remind her of something she would rather not lead with.

Moretti's easy manner turned serious as she said, "Yes, containment."

Tom, Rachael, and Nick shot glances at each other.

"As I said, we study harmless viruses. However, were we to discover we have captured one not so harmless, as a precaution, everyone would exit through a chemical bath and we could seal the room."

A moment of silence followed as the team considered this. Then Moretti broke the ice by returning to her cheerful self and stated, "But that is an unlikely scenario and the exit plan is only a precaution."

Nick spoke for the team when he said, "Look, Doctor Moretti, Doctor Nodada. This has all been very interesting, but what about the workforce you mentioned? One that can help us enter the decoding?"

Nodada rose from his seat and walked to the window, casting his arm toward the people outside busy on computers.

"Here you are," he said. "We have briefed everyone. We are ready to turn to your work."

"Briefed everyone?" Nick asked with a worried expression.

Nodada recognized Nick's concern. "Everyone knows about your discovery. We didn't have to tell them. The media storm I mentioned took care of that. They know we now have data that may decode The Tablet. Everyone is excited to help."

None of this calmed Nick. He welcomed the help to type in the contents of Volume Five. However, he would have preferred clerks who didn't realize what they had in hand. The number of people who knew just expanded from a handful to over twenty people; and none of them known to him, including Moretti. And, although his detective checked out Nodada, did he know much about him? Nick realized there was nothing much he could do now.

Nodada took the chair beside Nick, whose expression continued to display his concern. "Don't worry," he said. "These people have kept the secret of this place for years. They can keep your secret safe."

Nick took a deep breath, let it out, and said to everyone, "OK. Let's get this done. Doctor Nodada, what's next?"

Nodada joined Moretti in a relaxed smile as Moretti said, "I suggest that your computer expert, Mister Littleton, lead the work."

Tom sat up straight upon hearing this.

Addressing Tom, Moretti said, "I will have you work with my IT person to set up the database for input. You can work with him on the translation program as well. You'll be happy to learn that we have a multilingual system in place for our day-to-day work that can translate between many languages, including Latin."

"Latin? Really?" asked Tom.

Moretti smiled. "You forget that we are a medical operation. We can translate Greek too, but I doubt you will need that. English, perhaps?"

Tom relaxed. He wore the expression of a little boy on Christmas morning waiting to open presents.

Nick asked, "And what will Rachael and I do?"

"Wait," said Moretti. "That's all you can do."

Nodada spoke up. "I can have my driver take you to your hotel."

Nick said, "We need to talk. Do you mind if we have the room for a moment?"

"Certainly," said Nodada as he and Moretti moved toward the door. "Just come out when you're finished. We'll be in the office just across the way." He pointed toward an office on the other side of the computer stations.

When they left, Nick turned to Tom and Rachael. "What do you think?"

Tom's enthusiasm continued to be high, "Nick, this is

great. Who would think these resources would appear?"

"Yes, said Rachael," caution in her tone. "It's just a little too easy."

Nick concurred with Rachael. "I'm with you."

"Hey," said Tom. "Cristofori told us about fate. Fate's been with us so far."

"And fate almost made us dead," added Rachael.

"And it kept us from being dead," argued Tom. "Look, Nick. You know how we're limited on time. Someone is after us, and it's not these people. Aren't you ready to see what The Tablet has to say?" Turning to Rachael, "Aren't you?"

Both Nick and Rachael remained silent, lost in concern, until Nick said, "OK. There are no other options I can see."

This made Tom relieved.

"But," Nick continued, "I'm contacting Tanner. I'll send him backup to guard the original copy of Volume Five. Aside from the one here, there are no others."

Rachael smiled and pulled a thumb drive from her pants pocket and waved it before them. "You mean, besides this one?"

Nick, remembering the same precaution Rachael had taken in the cave bombing, returned the smile and said, "Damn, you're good!"

"I know. And don't worry about Tanner."

"I don't know," mused Nick. "With Lizzy there, he's

distracted."

Rachael's reaction was opposite to Nick's. "With Lizzy there, he has an able confederate. Remember, it was Lizzy that blocked the guys following us."

"Yes. Now we know they were Nodada's guys. Knowing who to trust is a changing landscape."

"You can trust us," Tom reminded.

"Absolutely. You guys are great," said Nick. Turning to Rachael, "Come on. Let's get out of here and let this man work."

With that, the team headed to the office where Nodada and Moretti waited.

The Texan sat in an overstuffed blood-red leather swivel chair behind a huge oak desk. The furniture fit the richly appointed paneled office, paintings of old west cowboys on the wall. You could almost smell crude oil in the air. He sipped his bourbon and branch with his back to the underling briefing him.

Turning to the man, he asked, "So, you are sure about this?"

"Yes, sir."

The Texan broke out in the smile some found menacing. "Good work. Thank you."

His 'thank-you' was the man's cue that the Texan was done with him and he left.

The Texan picked up his phone and his secretary answered.

"Nancy," he said. "Call the senator and tell him I can't meet with him tomorrow. Something's come up. Then book me on a flight to Rome. The sooner the better."

Chapter 35

THE DRIVER WAITED for them curbside at the market. He was an unsmiling man of medium height wearing sunglasses and a black suit matching the black SUV. He wasn't the driver who brought them there originally, but it was clear he knew the passengers he was waiting for as he opened the rear door for Rachael.

How many people work for Nodada? Nick wondered.

"To the hotel?" Nick asked.

"*Si,*" answered the man. "I am Marco. Please get in and I will take you there."

Rachael and Nick entered the vehicle, and they were off.

Though not the intent, the drive could not have provided a better tour of the eternal city. They drove along the *Lungotevere,* the street paralleling the Tiber River. On the left ran a high stone wall and along the right, a continuing row of Lombardy poplars and stately Roman architecture. Marco took a right on *Via Circo Massimo.* A long park appeared to the left bearing the outline of the Circus Maximus. Tall remnants of the stadium where chariots once raced stood at one end. It brought to mind movie images straight out of Ben Hur. Taking another street and heading north, they circled the monument defining Rome, the Colosseum.

Fatigue from non-stop travel and the visual delights of the eternal city kept Rachael and Nick silent. Rachael took in the sites passing on her side. Nick enjoyed watching Rachael's reactions. Everything was new to her and Nick appreciated her enthusiasm.

"Been to Rome before?" Nick asked.

"No," she replied and cast a glance at Nick. "Does it show?"

"I've been here many times, but I never tire of this city. And I still have parts to explore. Today was my first time in Testaccio."

Rachael continued to stare out the window as they moved slowly forward into smaller streets on Capitoline Hill, one of the seven hills that comprise Rome. They turned onto *Via Baccina,* a narrow, cobblestone street with sienna-colored buildings on each side and a few Vespas parked along the way. They pulled up in front of a narrow, townhouse-like hotel, sienna plaster on the first two levels and pink on the top two. A small sign in front stated in English, 'The Inn at the Roman Forum.'

Nick climbed out of the SUV as Marco opened the door on the other side for Rachael. Nick appraised the modest inn and said, "Well, it ain't the Ritz."

Marco walked around the SUV with Rachael and responded, "I promise you, it is very nice. And it is secure," reminding Nick of Nodada's primary concern. "Your things are already in your rooms. Please follow me."

They followed Marco into a small lobby where a young, blonde woman behind the counter greeted them in a crisp English accent, "Welcome, Mr. Foxe, Miss Friedman. Your rooms are ready." With two keys in hand, she turned to a bellman and said, "Will you show them to their rooms?"

Marco removed his sunglasses and snatched the keys from the woman's hand. "I'll take them."

The woman seemed unconcerned and used to guests arriving with handlers like him. "Very well," she responded.

Marco led them to a small lift big enough for just the three of them. They stopped on the third floor where he led Rachael to her room as Nick waited by the lift. Opening the door to her room, Marco did a quick scan and handed her the keys. Marco returned and continued with Nick to the floor above.

"Have you worked for Doctor Nodada long?" Nick asked, trying to start a conversation with the man.

"I've worked for many years at the security company the Doctor uses."

"What company is that?"

"You would not know them."

Nick abandoned that line of questioning and tried another.

"Will you be returning?"

"I will stay here in the hotel."

"And if I need you?"

"Call the front desk. They will get me."

Information came in small drips from Marco.

At the next floor, the lift opened to the outdoors. Nick accessed his room by a walkway with an iron railing bearing flower boxes overflowing with lavender blooms. Marco opened a pale blue door to the room and handed Nick the key.

"When Doctor Nodada calls me, I will come get you and Signorina Friedman, and then drive you back."

"Thank you," said Nick as Marco returned to the lift.

Why do I feel like a prisoner?

Nick entered, shut the door, and took stock of the room.

Although the rest of the hotel offered the flowery feel of a B&B, this room had a distinct masculine tone. In the center of the room stood a large bed with its headboard against a wall of steel-gray bricks. Above the bed hung a piece of art adorned with copper gears. Positioned at the foot of the bed was Nick's carry-on suitcase. He opened it, found everything that should be there, and closed it. Unpacking could wait. He didn't expect to be here long.

He opened a sliding glass door and walked onto the balcony. He had views over rooftops with church domes visible in all directions.

He heard movement on the balcony below. Taking a guess, he leaned over the edge and called, "Rachael?"

Rachael's head popped over the railing below looking up to him. She smiled. "I see you're on top."

"I'll not comment further," smiled Nick.

"Think you're up for a walk?"

"You bet," said Nick.

"Meet you in the lobby," responded Rachael before disappearing.

In the lobby, Marco rose from a chair and walked to Nick and Rachael.

"We're going for a walk," Nick told Marco.

"I will go with you."

"You don't have to do that."

"It is my job."

Nick appraised the situation.

What harm could it be? If he trusted Nodada and his people, he'd know it's for his own protection.

But trust was not yet complete.

"OK," surrendered Nick. "But please give us some distance."

"Certainly," responded Marco.

"Where to?" asked Rachael. "You know the city."

"I spotted the top of the Victor Emmanuel Monument from my balcony. Let's head there."

"Okay."

They left the hotel and strolled down the cobblestone street with Marco ten yards behind, scanning the area, every bit the bodyguard.

Rachael seemed relaxed for the first time. After discovering a key to the code, rushing to New Mexico to almost die in a bombing, escaping by jet to Italy, breaking into a castle and being caught in the crosshairs of an assassin, she'd had little time to relax. Now, walking down a street in Rome in the evening sun with a handsome man, she breathed easy for the first time since this journey began. She wanted to learn more about this man with her.

She turned to Nick. "You realize I know nothing about you, don't you?"

"I know little about you," Nick returned.

She looked skeptical. "You mean when I told you I was headed to New Mexico, you didn't have your people check me out?"

"Oh, that. Rachael Friedman, daughter of Joseph and Nina Friedman. The father a successful investment banker and the mother a violinist for the New York Symphony."

Rachael smiled. "I thought you must have found that out at least."

"You would be disappointed if I hadn't, right? Your mother must be the source of your musical talent."

Rachael laughed. "She was younger than Dad. Mom told me she was an odd choice for a trophy wife. 'All the ballerinas must have been taken.'" Then she realized something. "Wait, what do you mean 'my musical talent?'"

"You play the piano. Offered a scholarship at the Curtis Institute, but chose math at Harvard. You were only sixteen."

Rachael stopped and turned to Nick. "I'm not sure I like you poking around in my life like that."

Nick put his hand behind her shoulder, encouraging her to continue walking with him as he said, "Please. All of that I could read in the newspaper. In fact, my detective probably did. But," he grinned, "I want to learn what they didn't publish."

"Ahem! I started this by asking about you."

"You mean you didn't Google me?"

"Of course." She smiled. "Lots of interesting photos of you at parties, with your wife."

"Ex-wife."

"Ex-wife. What happened?"

"Long story," he said. "Save that for another time."

Rachael witnessed a fleeting grimace, but moved on.

"Your fortune came from Granddad who patented a drill bit for the oil industry."

"Yes, that, and Dad did his part, investing wisely."

"Any brothers or sisters?"

"No, just me. You?"

"Same, but we both already knew that about the other,

didn't we?"

They came to a narrow opening between the buildings onto a broad street where an enormous white structure erupted from a circular plaza.

"Wow," exclaimed Rachael.

"Let's walk down to the plaza in front where we can get a good look at it," said Nick. The two of them, with Marco behind, crossed the wide street and turned to their left toward a grassy area.

The building was wider than a football field and as high as the US Capitol, dome included. Blazing white with over a dozen columns on the top half, supported by a windowless base of white marble. Crowning each end were matching bronze statues of the winged Goddess of Victory on a chariot pulled by four horses. An equestrian statue topped a tall pedestal in front of the building.

"This monument goes by many names," said Nick. "It is the *Altare della Patria,* Altar of the Fatherland, also the *Monumento Nazionale a Vittorio Emanuele Due,* National Monument to Victor Emmanuel the Second."

"The unifier of modern Italy," added Rachael.

Nick cast an appreciative glance at Rachael. "That's right."

"I studied things other than math and science."

"I'm sure you did. But guess what the locals call this." said Nick.

"What?"

"The wedding cake."

Rachael laughed. "The name fits."

The walkway cutting across the grass before the monument featured a waist-high wall. Nick leaned against the wall as he told Rachael, "There're things I want to learn."

"Like what?"

"Got a boyfriend?"

"No. You got a girlfriend?" Then with a sly look, "Why do you ask?"

"I don't know. I guess I like to understand if you're tethered."

"Tethered? That's an odd way of putting it. Sounds like something a caver like Tom might say."

"Who, also, has no one in his life. I'm just wondering why a group of people like us, like you, me, Tom, and even Tanner seemed to find each other. I'm guessing we follow impulses, for good or bad, without consulting anyone."

Nick looked away toward the monument. "Impulse," he said, "Contributed to my no longer being married."

"I'm sorry," said Rachael.

Nick looked back at Rachael with the smile of one who claims all is fine when it isn't. "No problem."

Rachael said no more but continued to study Nick.

He'd nailed it. An impulse took her to New Mexico. She never took time to consider who she would meet there, and she continued to have mixed feelings about this man in particular. She found him smug, but could that also be described as self-confident? When he talked about women, it seemed old fashioned and patronizing, but could that be respect for them as well? When he mentioned his ex-wife, it exposed a wide chink in the man's armor, one worn by someone she wanted to know better.

Rachael thought of the men she dated.

They seemed lightweight compared to Nick.

Was it simply that he was older and more mature? Was it Rome? Perhaps an intoxicating mixture of both?

Nick broke the silence. "Hungry?" he asked.

"Famished," she answered.

"I saw a rooftop dining area where we're staying. Let's check it out."

They returned the way they came. As they passed Marco, Nick told him, "We're headed back."

In another part of Rome, Nodada looked across a crowded restaurant. He recognized the man alone in the corner booth who beckoned him with a raised hand. Although they had met before for just a moment, the man had left an indelible imprint. As Nodada approached him, he saw he was drinking an amber liquid, probably bourbon, in a short glass. The man greeted him with a 'howdy' in the Texas accent he remembered.

"Doctor Nodada," the Texan exclaimed rising to offer a large pudgy hand. "It's so good to see you again. Thank you for accepting my invitation. Please sit down."

Nodada returned little of the relish the Texan displayed. The man had been cryptic in his call inviting him to this place. He sat while the Texan continued the look of an animal with his prey in sight.

"Would you like something to eat?" asked the Texan as the waiter approached with menus.

"No, thank you. I've eaten."

The Texan waved the waiter away. "It's late. Guess I didn't call in time. Sorry about that."

Nodada wanted to get to the point. "You said you were interested in our latest discovery."

"Yes, I am."

"What discovery might that be?"

"You know, Doctor. When I attended that little talk of yours. You remember the one I mean, right?"

"Yes," acknowledged Nodada.

"Well, when I attended that presentation, I thought you were talking about some things that might be closer to the truth than you let on," searching Nodada's eyes for some glimmer of recognition. The Texan was a gambler and thought the Doctor did a good job wearing a poker face. "Maybe some things are becoming more real."

Nothing from Nodada. The Texan decided it was time for an incentive. "Doctor Nodada, are you well-funded?"

"Yes. The World Health Organization has been very generous."

The Texan scoffed. "Doctor. I know what your funding is. And it's rather amazing. You've done well. But I'm talking about large funding, the type major pharma needs to bring new discoveries to market. You are nowhere near that. Am I right?"

"But we are not in pharmaceuticals," protested the Doctor.

"May I be blunt, Doctor?"

"Yes," hesitated Nodada.

"Let's cut the crap. I've been following Nick Foxe."

"Who?"

The Texan's expression transformed from the look of the predator to the menace of the final kill as he put his face close to Nodada.

"I know what you're up to, Doctor. You have a choice. You can be a member of my team and see this discovery thrive, or you can ignore it and be crushed."

The Texan leaned back in his seat, his smile returning as he waved his empty glass at a waiter who grabbed it for a refill. "Nothing for you?" he asked his prey.

Nodada, meekly shook his head, and the Texan sent the waiter on his way. He waited, watching Nodada, now visibly shaken. "Life has choices. If we're lucky, things come our way and we've got to seize them. I grew up dirt poor. I believe you did, too. Look at us now! We're doing all right, in our own way."

The waiter returned with a fresh bourbon. The Texan took the glass and had a sip as the waiter left. He held the glass high in a toast. "Here's to the future."

Setting the glass down, he asked, "Well, Doctor. What's it going to be?"

Chapter 36

THE LAST GLIMMER of the evening sun gave way to the streetlights of the city. Strong monument lamps lit the bright white marble of the Victor Emmanuel, one corner peeking over the roofs. The Victory statue provided a striking vista for the rooftop dining patio. A cool summer breeze blew gently over Nick and Rachael as they dined. Only four tables occupied the space, and they were the only diners this evening. Nick reasoned they likely were the only guests at the inn.

Security.

Rachael felt intoxicated from her exposure to Rome as well as from the two glasses of Pino Grigio she'd consumed. The first course of pasta with pesto was not enough to balance the libation. *Slow down,* she told herself. *Stay in control.*

Nick smiled back, happy to see her relax. The wine loosened Rachael's tongue. Before the second course arrived, she pursued more answers about Nick's personal life.

"Tell me about yourself, Nick."

"What do you want to know?"

Not yet relaxed enough to pry into more personal things about Nick, Rachael asked, "How did you get into tomb raiding?"

Nick laughed. "It's not tomb raiding."

"The chamber under Castel del Monte sure seemed to be," she pointed out. "After all, it contained a body."

"That was an exception. Usually, I'm rummaging around for artifacts. Ancient civilizations fascinate me."

"How come?"

"I'm not sure."

"Something your parents wanted?"

"Hardly," scoffed Nick. "Dad was a financier. But he didn't want me to follow in his footsteps. He wanted me to run for office."

"Really?" exclaimed Rachael, but she reconsidered. "The more I think about it, that makes sense."

"It does?"

"Look at what you did. You led this exploration. You put the right people in place. You even managed the press. People follow you."

"Including you?" Nick asked of the woman he saw taking her own lead.

Rachael could not help but keep his ego in check. "Do I have a choice?"

"I guess you do. But I'm happy you're a part of the team. You're smart, inventive, a good team player," he said.

Spoken like a true politician. Can't you add that I look good?

Nick smiled, "But there is also . . ."

The waiter's arrival cut him off. "Your *secondi,*" he said as he set the plates of sliced white fish over greens before them. "Red Snapper *Crudo. Buon appetito!*"

Nick picked up a fork and took a bite, but Rachael wanted him to finish what he began to say. "But there is also?" she prompted.

Nick finished chewing and dabbed his lips with his napkin. He reached for his wine. "There are things I would say that might offend a professional such as yourself," he said with a wink.

"Like what?"

"Like," he paused. "You're cute."

"Cute?" she replied.

"You have a way of wrinkling your forehead when you're cross or puzzled. See, you're doing it now."

Rachael put her fork down and grabbed her wine glass. "Guess I must work on that."

Nick reached out to Rachael's free hand. She felt a warm and powerful touch. His clasp was gentle but unhesitant. She stopped the wine glass in midair.

"Don't you dare change that," he said. "I like it. Once we get through all of this, I hope we can spend more time together."

Rachael chose her men. She resisted having it the other way around. Nick's appeal was on the rise, but she resisted. "We'll see," she replied.

He released her hand and raised his glass as in a toast to say, "That is, when people stop trying to kill us."

With that reminder, Nick brought her back to their reality.

"What's going on with that?" she asked. "Who's trying to do us in? And why? Does it make any sense?"

"No, it doesn't," acknowledged Nick. "Knowing what we know so far about the discovery, I would expect someone might come to us with a wad of money. That's what I usually experience in my work. I've discovered artifacts private collectors would pay a king's ransom for."

"And you've sold them?"

"Hardly ever. I don't need the money. Most are in museums on permanent loan from me."

"But are we looking for an artifact? Seems we've already found them. The Tablet at Carlsbad. It's beneath a ton of rock, but it's still there. The volume from Frederick the Second. That's valuable, not to mention the chamber we found under the castle."

Nick leaned back in his chair, a man who was taking stock of where they were in all of this. "No, I think we're after information."

Rachael wrinkled her forehead. "Information?"

"Yes, information. Secrets if you will. Something advanced. I believe we're being tested to see if we're worthy of those secrets."

"Worthy? You mean if we are sufficiently advanced to do something with them?"

"Exactly. Somebody fears what we're doing. They may be the ones trying to kill us. I wouldn't be surprised if there is also someone who wants to buy it."

"Remember, there is one person who knows who's trying to kill us."

Nick understood who she meant. "Drake?"

"Yes. Have you been in touch? How's he doing?"

"I've been in touch. He's out of the induced coma and out of the hospital."

"And…"

"And the bullet and the coma trashed his short-term memory. He doesn't remember."

Rachael was lost in the thought of the danger they were facing. The wrinkled forehead was not lost on Nick.

"Wait," he said. "Let's forget all that, if just for one night. Look at where we are. Feel the evening breeze. And this *crudo* ain't bad."

Rachael smiled. She would like nothing better.

The meal continued with a small lamb shank in an incredible sauce. Nick ordered another bottle of wine and its consumption returned Rachael to enjoying the evening with a man who she found increasingly attractive. They chatted about New York and Boston and which city was better. What music they enjoyed. It pleased her that Nick played the classics she cherished. "We'll have a classical dueling piano event, you and I," he joked.

At the end of the meal, Rachael took the lead. She said, "I found a bottle of Courvoisier in my room. How about a night cap?"

"Sounds good."

Nick stood and walked to her chair to pull it out for her.

Rachael smiled.

So now we're the gentleman?

Just enjoy.

Nick held out his hand and she gave him hers to rise from the chair, but he continued to hold it as he led her from the patio. Then she walked in front, leading him to her room, one floor below.

She opened the door and walked around the bed to the sliding door to the balcony. She opened it and asked Nick to pull the two light metal chairs into the room facing out.

"Have a seat," she said. "I'll get a couple of glasses."

The same cool breeze greeted them, but here, the noise of a Vespa somewhere on the street below filtered through. There was no view of the Victor Emmanuel, but a quarter moon above the city smiled a Cheshire Cat grin.

"Here you go," said Rachael as she handed him a snifter of

cognac. She took the chair beside Nick, cognac in hand, and looked out at the moon.

"When I was a kid," said Nick. "I always thought that moon was smiling at me."

"Wasn't it hard to catch the moon on the streets of New York? So many buildings in the way."

"I would lie on the grass in Central Park at night and see it."

"That's a dangerous thing. Central Park at night. Guess you were fearless then, too."

"Or stupid. Then and now."

He took a sip of the cognac as she did. The fluid warmed her.

Or was it his company?

She may have been conflicted before, but she had no doubt now. She put her hand on his. "You're hardly stupid."

He lifted her hand to his lips. "You're too kind."

She leaned over and kissed his lips in return. Nick left his chair and continued to kiss her as she stood. Smiling, she led Nick to the nearby bed. Her head was swimming with a beautiful intoxication. She felt she was in a dream, a blissful slumber as Nick kissed her cheek.

"Rachael, wake up."

The bright light of morning sun from the open patio door blinded her as she woke to a pounding headache. Nick sat on the edge of the bed, dressed as he was last night. She wore nothing but the bed covers, her clothes neatly folded over the nearby chair.

Hardly ripped off me, she thought.

Yet last night was a blur and she could not yet sort out dream from reality.

"We've got to go," Nick said with some urgency.

"What? Why?" she forced herself to mumble.

"Marco called me. They've solved the code."

Chapter 37

MARCO WOVE HIS WAY THROUGH ROME'S STREETS on the return to Nodada's lab. Rachael and Nick sat in the back, silent, their minds lost in what they might soon find out. Rachael no longer gazed at the sights as they drove by. Instead, she shared Nick's obvious excitement over cracking the code and couldn't wait to get to the lab.

They had left the hotel in a rush and had said little to each other. Now, in the car, she turned to look at Nick, who returned a smile. She felt foolish having to ask if they made love. The miles slipped away as she debated whether to ask him or not.

I have to know.

"Nick," she ventured.

"Yes?" he responded as he turned to face her.

"There's something I'd like to know."

"Sure, what is it?"

Rachael wished he'd returned something other than a blank, questioning stare.

"About last night. Uh . . . When we were…"

The SUV came to a quick stop, Nick looked out the window and exclaimed, "We're here." He opened the door and jumped out, ending the conversation before it began.

Marco opened the door for her, but she hesitated, witnessing the excited little boy in Nick.

Guess the answer will have to wait.

Unlike the previous night, Marco took the lead, rushing them through the crowds at the market, across the street on the other side, and into the restaurant to which Nodada first introduced them. They arrived at the unmarked door to the lab where Marco took a card from his inside coat pocket and placed it beside the door. The door clicked open. They stood once again in the area overlooking the lab.

Tom held a clipboard and was involved in animated conversation with Nodada when he looked up. "You're here," he said. "Come on down."

Tom's excitement was clear, but Nodada stayed subdued. Nick thought it odd the Doctor was about to learn the answer to a lifelong search and yet seemed so calm.

Guess it's the nature of the man.

"Let's go into the conference room," Tom said as he led the way to the same room they had used before. Nick and Rachael took seats on the side overlooking the lab. Nodada took a seat on the opposite side. Tom stood beside him, too excited to sit. "These folks have been busy," said Tom turning to the view of workers on the other side of the glass.

"Are they aware of what the code says?" asked Nick.

"No," responded Tom. "Not yet. It's up to us to determine

what they should know and when. I've been piecing together the translation in another room and I was just sharing it with Doctor Nodada when you arrived."

"So, tell us," said Nick.

"Well, remember this is rough. The doctor's people entered the information from al-Muazzam's book. I think al-Muazzam got most of the translations right, but some are questionable. Just the fact that he translated into Latin and then we translated into English. We had to read between the lines a lot. You've seen those puzzles where you read text with only the consonants and all the vowels are missing? My translation is a lot like that."

"But does it make any sense?" asked Nick.

Tom beamed with pride. "Oh, yes. And what it has to tell us is amazing."

"Tom. Sit down. Tell us."

Tom sat in a chair, two away from Nodada and unclipped a long printout, its pages connected one to the other with sprocket feeds. Nick smiled. He couldn't remember when he last saw such a printout. Even the term 'printout' seemed antiquated.

Tom began. "The first lines seem to be an introduction. Those are the ones we played first at Carlsbad to unlock the drawings and again at Castel del Monte. It's all subject to interpretation."

Nick, impatient, cut Tom off, "Tom, forget the narrative. Just tell us your best translation. OK?"

Tom recognized he rambled on about the process more than the essence. "OK," he said.

"Well, in any case, the opening lines are along the lines of 'Secrets transcend time and space making gods of those who face the danger of understanding them.'

"Maria," exclaimed Rachael.

Both Nick and Tom turned to her with a "What?"

"Remember, Maria said she understood two words in what she heard. They were 'secrets' and 'danger.'"

Nonplused, Nick and Tom remained silent. Nodada heard about Maria for the first time. He knew who she was, but little else. It seemed to him she had a role to play.

Nick continued to be doubtful. "Gods? Really? Is that what the translation says?"

"Al-Muazzam states *Deus* for god and he uses it several times. Of course, 'god' can be flexible. We mean 'God' as the old guy in heaven with a beard. We also mean 'god' with special powers but otherwise human."

As everyone considered the implications, Tom asked, "May I continue?"

"Sure," Nick said as he rolled his hand like a stage manager for the performance to continue.

"The transcript becomes first person. The writer is a scribe or secretary or historian. It isn't clear."

Nick nodded to Tom that he understood. "Keep to your best translation and cut the process talk."

"OK. He's a scribe."

"He?" asked Rachael.

"Look, Rachael, let's remember that al-Muazzam lived in a male world. He uses male forms of Latin."

"OK," Rachael said with a smile that told Tom she was pulling his chain.

"I greet you. Much time measured in moons and the central star, uh, the sun," Tom said correcting his tendency to be literal rather than interpretive. "Much time measured in moons and the sun may have passed as you read this. We cannot know. We left this writing for you to find when you are ready. We have placed it where you must be advanced to find. The language may be unknown to you. Some might keep parts of our language in their own. Some will not."

Tom looked up. "He may be talking about the tonal languages of Asia when he says, 'some might keep parts.'"

Tom continued reading. "You are now reading this in your own language. This is possible since you learned the way to unlock the script. But for that to happen, another had to create a lock with the same code. We knew then you could understand what we offer to you."

Nick sat up. "Is this guy telling us we could not have

unlocked this code in Carlsbad as we did unless al-Muazzam created a lock at Castel del Monte in the same way?"

"It seems that way."

For the first time, Doctor Nodada showed emotion as he smiled and said, "I believe our friend Cristofori would call it 'destiny.'"

"Yeah, but I'm not so sure," responded Nick. "Read on."

"We walked among you. You did not recognize us as different. We were like you in body, but our minds were different. They were not different in form. You have the same minds with the same abilities. We were the ones who made certain of that. We developed more knowledge than you. You were hunters. We set you on a different path. You learned to grow your food. You could feed yourselves and others. You see the design of life. You may know it as the blood that makes us as we are."

"He's talking about the DNA helix," exclaimed Nick.

"Yes," smiled Tom. "I believe he is. But listen to this: 'We changed you.'"

Tom waited for the dramatic effect this passage would have and he wasn't disappointed. Nick and Rachael were wide-eyed, and the doctor sat on the edge of his chair.

"We changed your blood. At birth, you will be destined for a role. Some will tend to the source of food and feed others. Some will be protectors. We made it so that some will be fighters and others will not. Others will rule, and you will want these as your rulers. There will be those who create things that please the senses. Because of what we did, you have people who walk with you who can master the understanding of our secrets."

Tom paused as it soaked in to each person gathered that some ancient, 10,000 years ago, claimed responsibility for making us who we are today.

"We reined in the light of our star to operate our things. We made fire from water."

Rachael interrupted, "They must mean solar power for the first thing, but fire from water?"

"Perhaps they understood how to generate energy from seawater," surmised Tom. "Listen to the next part."

"These things were more than you could understand. We believe that will change in the future. Before we leave, we bestow a gift."

"Leave?" asked Nick. "To where."

Rachael chimed in. "Remember what we read from al-Muazzam. These people had a different sense of time and space."

"OK," sighed Nick. "That sounds hokey, but they're not around anymore."

"Now for the exciting climax!" Tom said with gusto. "It's about the gift. We left for you an *omnis scientia*."

"All knowledge?" asked Nick.

"Yes, but it's written as a noun, as if it's a thing. I left it in the Latin."

Tom continued.

"Use it with wisdom. Conquer danger."

He stopped.

"That's it?" Nick asked. "He signs out with 'conquer danger?' Whatever that means.

"Oh, there is one more thing," grinned Tom.

"What's that?"

"He tells us where it is!"

Chapter 38

ANOTHER DAY IN LOCOROTONDO kicking the ball around. Lizzy and Maria walked out into the courtyard where Tanner was playing soccer with little Giacomo. Cobblestone paving followed the contour of the hill and Giacomo knew the contour and used it against his large opponent. He would kick, bending like Beckham. Tanner was a quick learner, but he could never match the kid's speed. It didn't matter. He was fond of the boy and enjoyed their time together.

Lizzy was becoming friends with Maria, although easy, ordinary communication with Maria was elusive. But Lizzy was patient and Maria was smart. Her crisp responses were so often spot-on, that Lizzy delighted in them. Lizzy studied Maria's face as she watched her son with Tanner and thought she detected a smile on a face seldom offering emotion.

Lizzy had also made something of a friend in Tanner. She managed to keep her lustful thoughts under control, but barely. Lizzy's first evening was spent with him dining in a restaurant overlooking the valley. The sun lit the grove of olive trees stretching to the sea as the shadows cast by the hills behind them moved across the surface. Tanner had asked Cristofori where he could get a hearty meal and he had recommended this place. Lizzy asked if she could tag along and Tanner said 'sure' with a smile. He wasn't seeking a romantic setting. It was happenstance. The waiter lit the wick of the lamp on the table so it seemed they would be dining by candlelight, while the light of the setting sun turned the horizon pink. Lizzy wished Tanner would focus more on her than filling his stomach.

They dined on pasta and lamb. Tanner made it clear to the waiter he was too hungry for the typical seafood fare and the waiter assured him they had a lamb shank ready. He ordered for the two of them, with a double portion for himself. Lizzy got a kick out of the man's appetite and enjoyed the small talk between bites. How different this place was. The people so friendly. The climate so perfect. Tanner told her he spent months in Italy after the army, but not in this part of the country. He liked it.

He asked her about herself. Most of the men Lizzy knew were so much into themselves they never asked about her. Although already falling for Tanner, he charmed her further just by asking. She talked about her mother and the life of the band follower. She liked Mom, but she died, much too early. Drinking had been her end. Lizzy drank wine and a little Jack Daniels from time to time, but when she got a buzz, a warning bell went off summoning an image of Mom, and Lizzy stopped.

They stayed at the table after finishing the meal as dusk

turned to night. Sipping her wine and Tanner, beer, Lizzy asked him about Italy and why he had been there before. Tanner felt comfortable talking to her. He told her about the incident in Afghanistan where he lost his buddies in a fire fight and how he draped his body over a kid to keep him safe from the bullets. He also told her about the tablet he saw in Afghanistan and the quest afterwards. All of it.

"You know," said Lizzy. "You're meant to be here."

"Destiny? Like the old man says?" He scoffed.

"Maybe."

Tanner changed the subject. "You ready to get back?"

"Sure."

They walked along the narrow streets illuminated by lamps hung on the edges of the buildings they passed. He took her hand and said, "You know, Lizzy. You're OK."

Not the most romantic sentiment, but it was enough. They walked hand-in-hand.

They soon arrived at Cristofori's place. In front of the door, she turned to him and motioned with her finger for Tanner to lean over as though she had a secret to tell. When he did, she took his head in her hands and kissed him. His look of surprise was brief and turned to a smile as he lifted her off the street and kissed her with a deep, lingering kiss.

"Oh, here you are!" said Cristofori as he opened the door with Maria behind him. Tanner let Lizzy slide to her feet in a scene resembling daddy, daughter, and date.

Ignoring the interrupted display of passion, the old man went on. "It's late and I am going to bed. Maria, show Lizzy to her room. Mr. Tanner, I think you know where yours is." The old man betrayed no annoyance, but the message was clear. There would be no hanky-panky under his roof.

Tanner smiled at the circumstances and said, "Good night, Lizzy."

Ispettore Capo Rossi worked in a tidy office. The surface of his simple gun-metal-gray desk contained a spotless blotter, set of pens to the right, and his name plate on an oak prism before him. No in-basket. He handled each folder, each document, one at a time. No computer. He required of his reporting police the same spotless regimentation he demanded of himself. Bari, the next large town from Locorotondo, housed his station in a modern building with a glass front. The Capo scowled each morning as he entered the building. It irritated him how out of place it was against the classical architecture around him.

Two Americans sat before him. They showed their identification. FBI Agents Wells and Arnold. They looked the part, wearing dark suits, white shirts and blue ties, although wrinkled from their journey. They just flew in they said. It did not surprise Rossi to have the FBI come calling. What the Americans told him at Castel del Monte made him suspect there was more than they shared. The G-Men told him what it was. Something about a bombing in New Mexico.

"Were they suspected of doing it?" he asked.

"No. But they remain 'persons of interest.'"

Rossi scoffed at the term.

Why have Americans watered down the word 'suspect'?

They asked about the dead man found at the castle. Rossi had identified the man as someone known to the authorities. He had loose ties to the Mafia. Rossi refrained from his natural tendency to spit after uttering the word 'Mafia.' 'Loose ties' meant that he was probably a hitman the Mafia called when they needed 'a job' done. He added that they had identified the dead assassin as 'a person of interest' in the murder of an American in Bari earlier this year.

It amused him to see the agents caught unaware of that case. But, it also made him suspicious. Rossi had worked with FBI agents stationed in Italy. He knew them. He did not know these men. The case in Bari, he explained, involved a girlfriend who claimed a man in America orchestrated the hit. So, this assassin, may have had connections with Americans. The agents seemed to brush that tidbit off, furthering Rossi's suspicions.

They were extremely interested, however, in wanting to know the whereabouts of Mr. Foxe. Rossi told them he was in Rome, but didn't know where. Foxe didn't share his travel plans with Rossi, but he didn't have to. Rossi had eyes on him.

They thanked him and left. Rossi did not offer any information they did not ask for. He didn't tell them that one of the group's members remained behind in Locorotondo. He had no intention of letting these men invade the privacy of his friend Cristofori. But he would put one of his men on him. For his own protection.

"Morning, sleepy head," Tanner said to Lizzy who rose late. It was almost noon and Tanner was on his third mug of coffee. He insisted on a mug although in the kitchen there was only a single-serving espresso machine. Maria assisted by heating a kettle of water and diluting the shot into a *café americano* for him.

Lizzy wore a flannel nightgown, white with small blue flowers sprinkled over it. Maria lent it to her. Lizzy's usual nightwear was nothing at all, but that wouldn't do here, although she thought the gown made her look like someone's aunt. Her bed hair didn't help.

Tanner had gotten up early. Maria was getting Giacomo

ready for school, fixing his breakfast and hurrying him along so he wouldn't be late. Giacomo wanted a rematch with Tanner, but Tanner told him no and to listen to his mother or he would be late for school. He enjoyed the scene and realized he played the dad to Giacomo when he told him to listen to his mother. For a soldier who had no one else in his day-to-day, other than soldiers like him, it was nice. He enjoyed it.

Why had he sought the hermit life after the Army?

Now, there was Lizzy. He knew she was hot for him. How couldn't he? He wondered, after not being with a woman for so long, why he hadn't been more responsive. He knew, however, it was only a matter of time and for now, he got a kick out of teasing her. Then there was the call from Nick this morning. They'd solved The Tablet and were flying down today to share it all with him. At last, the search would be complete. That came first.

"I got a call from Nick this morning," he told Lizzy. Maria handed her a *café Americano,* and she sat across from Tanner at the small table dumping spoonfuls of sugar into her mug.

"Oh?" she said through her sleepy haze.

"Yep. They solved the code."

Lizzy perked up. "So, what does it say?"

"Nick didn't say much. It seems there were super smart people 10,000 years ago."

"Duh. I doubt Neanderthals left space-age metals behind."

"It seems they left something for us. Something not far away."

"All right. Now we're getting someplace."

"'We? Kemosabe," chided Tanner.

"Yes, we, Lone Ranger. I dusted an old house while Nick and the others got to see The Tablet. I'm not being left out this time."

"Guess Nick has the say on that."

"No problem," she said knowing she could persuade just about anyone.

After a few more sips, Lizzy pushed away from the table. "I'm going to get ready. Did Nick say when they would be here?"

"Later this afternoon. He wasn't sure."

"OK. What're you going to do?"

"I think I'll go for a walk."

The day was another typical one of blue skies and bright sunlight. Tanner wore his usual camouflage pants and tee, adding a tan baseball cap to shade his eyes. Entering the courtyard where Giacomo and he played soccer, he noticed an addition. In one corner stood a man wearing dark pants and a white open shirt. The man looked as though he had simply removed a coat and tie to dress down. The man was suspicious in his attempts not to look suspicious. Tanner glanced his way but kept moving. As Tanner entered a narrow street, he noticed the man started to follow him.

Tanner strolled down the street, and stopped to inspect a shop window. The man trailing him stopped to look at his watch.

Amateur!

Tanner looked for an opportunity to step around a blind corner. He did so just ahead, moving onto a set of steps leading to someone's apartment. The man following him didn't notice. He passed by and Tanner stepped out behind him. Tanner was light on his feet for a large man and made quiet steps. The man before him didn't hear him. He walked a few feet more before realizing he had lost Tanner, he stopped, and then turning to go back, ran right into the large man he sought.

"Looking for something?" Tanner asked as the man bounced off him, startled.

"*Scusi*," the man said as he tried to pass Tanner. No such luck.

Tanner held the man by his arms and asked, "Why are you following me?"

"*Mio Capo*, Rossi. He ask me to."

"And why would he do that?"

The man quaked as he responded, "It is not you. It is Signor Cristofori. He fears he is in danger."

"Then why follow me?"

"You maybe wish him harm?" the man offered meekly.

"What? I think your boss got this wrong."

"You want to talk to him?"

Tanner had talked enough with Rossi the other night at the castle. Tanner didn't favor talking more. He decided to take another tact.

Tanner released the man and smiled. "No need to do that. I know he only has his friend's best interest at heart. Go ahead and keep watch, but you have nothing to fear from me."

The man appeared unconvinced, but offered a *grazie* as he returned to Cristofori's house.

Tanner strolled on, running scenarios through his head. *Why did Rossi believe Cristofori was in danger? Did he believe he was the target of the assassin that night? Perhaps he was. But why?*

He would continue a close watch. On everyone.

Nick's plane landed at the Bari airport in the late afternoon carrying Nick, Rachael, Tom, Doctor Nodada, and a transcript of the decoded tablet.

Ten-thousand years ago, people who 'walked among us' planted a coded tablet in a cave in New Mexico. That tablet, through the help of a brilliant Arab six-hundred years ago, was now rendered into a thick printout in English. It promised an *Omnis Scientia* containing a vast trove of advanced knowledge, and now they knew where it was.

But getting their hands on it might not be easy.

Chapter 39

TANNER SPENT THE AFTERNOON at a spot on the lower part of Locorotondo overlooking the expanse of olive trees stretching to the ocean. On the way, he found a shop selling Montecristo cigars, rare for Italy, and getting rarer stateside. Tanner didn't smoke except for an occasional stogie. He bought a cigar and lit it with a wooden match from the shop and savored the tang. A snifter of brandy would enhance the experience, but the cigar alone would do.

Back at Cristofori's, instead of the usual tee shirt, Lizzy had put on a lacey white top and headed out for a stroll. She thought the warm southern region of Italy called for something special and hoped Tanner might think the look more feminine. Although Lizzy enjoyed the occasional glance of appreciation from the few young men she passed, her focus was on finding Tanner. It wasn't hard to spot him in a small town. Tanner was leaning forward, his arms crossed on top of the white balustrade, cigar in hand, cap pulled down, shading his eyes.

"What're you doing?" she asked as she approached him.

Tanner, still leaning, turned to her. "Just thinking."

"About what?"

"I like it here. I've been to Italy before. You know that."

"Yes."

"But this time is different. Don't know why. You know I settled in Montana for a while."

"No. I didn't know that," she said.

"Guess I needed to get away. You know I had found another tablet."

"That I did hear about, from Rachael."

"I should show you the photo I have. I showed it to Rachael, but she said it didn't have the resolution of the photo she saw of the New Mexico tablet. Not sure if it had any use at all. But, it got me searching for what it meant. Think it's the one that al-Muazzam had?"

"I bet it is. I mean, how many of those things could be around?"

Tanner laughed. "Not exactly a tourist shop item."

Lizzy joined in his laugh and stood beside him overlooking the valley.

"Tanner?" she asked.

"Yeah?"

"Where do you think this is all going to end?"

Tanner paused, took another puff on his cigar, exhaled and said, "I don't know. But I've heard from Nick. He said they know the location of the final thing they're looking for."

"But what is the final thing? That's always been a mystery."

"I don't know, but when they showed me that tablet in Afghanistan, I saw something bigger than me. Don't know how to say it, but I felt both an honor and an obligation. Somehow, that Taliban chieftain thought I was the one who needed to see it. I felt anointed."

Tanner, embarrassed, stopped.

Anointed? Really?

Lizzy noticed what passed for a blush on Tanner's face, put her hand on his shoulder, and said, "It's OK."

Tanner cleared his throat and continued. "In any case, I had to follow a trail. I knew this was something important. I tried to do it on my own, but that didn't work out. When I met Tom, something clicked. I thought this was the guy who could find what I was looking for. To this day, I don't know why. But I did."

"And he *was* the one."

"Yes, and so was Rachael and so was Nick."

Tanner looked Lizzy in the eye and said, "And so were you, young lady. You had a part to play."

Lizzy felt moved and delighted. She wasn't used to getting credit, for anything. "I did what I could."

Tanner turned to the open valley. "One reason I walked down here was to spot everyone as they came back from Rome. That's likely them," he said pointing to a SUV coming up the road.

Tanner and Lizzy watched as the vehicle made its way up the serpentine tarmac. As it neared, they walked over to a cobblestone parking area nearby. The SUV pulled into an open space and parked. Nick stepped out and greeted Tanner and Lizzy with a smile.

"Well," he said. "Looks like we have a welcoming committee. How're you doing, big guy? Lizzy?"

Nick put out his hand and Tanner shook it, realizing this was the first time they ever traded that simple acknowledgment.

Tom and Rachael climbed out of the SUV with the driver helping Doctor Nodada exit. Tom now carried the printout in a messenger bag slung across his chest. The driver stayed by the vehicle, arms crossed, scanning the area. Tanner noticed.

Looks like we have an extra guard.

"So, Tanner tells me you've found something," Lizzy exclaimed.

Nick's expression changed to one of caution as he put his hand on Lizzy's shoulder to walk her away from the parking area.

"Yes," he said. "But let's talk about it at Cristofori's place."

Nick walked with Lizzy, the others followed, and Tanner brought up the rear. Nodada's driver stayed by the car. Tanner had mixed feelings about that. He would rather keep the driver in sight.

"You and Tanner do OK while we were gone?" Nick asked Lizzy as they made their way through the white streets, the late evening sun playing deep shadows along the way.

"Sure," she said, adding with suspicion in her voice, "Why do you ask?"

The manner of the response was not lost on Nick. "No particular reason. Should there be?"

"No."

"Well, OK then," he said, casting a sly smile toward Lizzy she refused to acknowledge.

Tanner observed the scene in front of him as he followed. He overheard Lizzy and Nick, which made him grin. Rachael and Tom's discussion was brief, but excited, talking about next steps, something about getting a boat. Nodada was unusually quiet. Tanner wondered why the change from when he last saw the doctor. Before, Nodada displayed a reserved excitement. Now, just reserve, worried.

What happened in Rome?

They all soon reached Cristofori's place. The workmen, including Cristofori's brother, had gone for the day. Only Cristofori and Maria remained. Giacomo was out playing. The old man saw the team approaching and threw open the front door, Maria just behind him. "Welcome," he said. "You have news?"

"That we do," replied Nick. "Let's go inside and talk about it."

Cristofori and Maria led them through the work area and into the room where Maria first demonstrated her talent for singing the code. The table was clear, but with Nodada and Lizzy now joining them, there were too few seats around the table. Tom didn't hesitate to take a center seat. Eager to show what they had, he took the transcript from the messenger bag and put it before him. Maria pulled out a chair for her father across from Tom and took the chair beside the old man. Rachael sat at one end of the table and Nick at the other. Nodada stood in one corner of the room with Tanner in the opposite corner. Tom made Cristofori his principle audience, knowing that what he had to say would be the culmination of the man's lifelong search. Cristofori sat across from him anticipating his words as manna from heaven.

"This is the transcript of what The Tablet has to tell us," Tom said as he put his hand on the printout. "There are details here we can dive into later, but I want to give you the highlights."

"*Si, si,*" responded Cristofori. "Go on."

"The Tablet was left by people who populated the earth thousands of years ago. The writer is a scribe of those people, but he is vague as to where they came from and where they went. He indicates they originated on earth. Popular myths of the ancients would say they were gods. Twentieth century myths would make them aliens from outer space. Although the scribe does not say, it's clear he means they started here. How they outpaced the advances of people around them, he does not say. But what he does say is they are preparing to leave. 'Why' is not clear. What is clear is they had a different understanding of time and space than we do."

Turning to Cristofori, Rachael interrupted, "The scribe describes this section in a way that Einstein would appreciate. The scribe talks about the *spatii flexio*, the flexibility of space. They may have left by means we cannot yet imagine."

Tom resumed. "The scribe makes many claims, but the one I find most interesting is where he reports that they had the ability to change the people around them. Our interpretation is that their 'blood' was actually DNA as illustrated on The Tablet with the double helix. He tells that humans around them were, what we today call hunter-gatherers. Some had started cultivating and growing crops. In the beginning, every man, every woman had the same job. Every man hunted and fought. Every woman bore children, gathered and cooked. But once man and woman could grow their own food, they could feed others. Those others would function as warriors to protect them, rulers to keep order, artists to amuse them, thinkers to advance them.

"But the scribe claims that development was no random

accident. His people were able to change the code for humans, so they were almost programmed from birth to be a warrior, ruler, artist, thinker."

Cristofori's response was in his expression. He was thoughtful for a moment. Then he looked around the room and smiled. Tom remained focused on his printout. Others in the room did not know why the old man smiled. But Maria understood. Her father and she recognized how some of these 'changes' Tom described were represented by people in this very room.

"Now for the good part," Tom said. "The scribe finishes by telling us his people are leaving something before they depart. In Latin, the name is *Omnis Scientia*, which means 'all knowledge,' but I prefer to use the Latin name. The *Omnis Scientia* is hidden among the cliffs along the sea of the peninsula shown on The Tablet. We all recognized the drawing as modern-day Italy. It was the exact location, however, that continued to be a mystery. Until now.

"Al-Muazzam translated his tablet and left his translation in Volume Five, but he left something else. He left us what his tablet told him about the location of the Omni.

"Tanner, you remember what was drawn on your tablet in addition to the people, the helix, and a map of Italy?"

"Sure," said Tanner, "The Big Dipper."

"That's right," replied Tom, "Also known as *Ursa Major*. I

now am sure the tablet Tanner saw was al-Muazzam's because Volume Five contains an illustration of *Ursa Major* that al-Muazzam copied from his tablet. He even highlighted the star *Dubhe* with rays. You can find *Dubhe* at the corner of the dipper that points to *Polaris*, the North Star."

Tom turned to Tanner. "You remember what we found on our tablet?"

"You mean the long-neck bird?" Tanner replied.

"That was a swan, the constellation *Cygnus*, the Northern Cross. The part highlighted was *Deneb*, the star at the top of the cross."

"How do you know this?" asked Cristofori.

"Because the translation of The Tablet states the Omni is *sub tribus astris*, under three stars, *iuxta mare*, by the sea at *media nocte*, midnight. Just to make it clearer, they put a map of Italy on The Tablet."

"But The Tablet in New Mexico contained just one star, did it not?" asked Cristofori.

"That's right, and with that alone, it could have been anywhere along the coast. But The Tablet in New Mexico said *duo libri unam fabulam faciunt*, two books make one story. Al-Muazzam had the other book. And the other two stars. So now we have our three stars and the time, midnight. No matter how you tell time, midnight means only one thing."

"So, can we get this to a sea captain to plot the location?"

urged Cristofori.

"Already done."

"You found a sea captain in Rome?" asked the old man with a dubious expression.

"Something even better. I worked on a project for a couple of years where we wrote code for GPS satellite systems. One thing we had to take into account was the wobble of the earth."

"The wobble?"

"The earth spins on its axis like a top, but due to its mass, it spins much slower. Yet, like a top, it is not a perfect spin. It wobbles. One wobble takes 26,000 years to complete. That may seem slow, but to locate things on earth with precision, it has to be taken into account.

"The result means that, what we call the North Star, the star directly above the axis of the earth, changes over time. When the Egyptians built the pyramids, it was a completely different star. But the ancients who left The Tablet accounted for that.

"Not knowing what arbitrary system we would be using today to measure the passing of time, they left us one that has universal precision."

Rachael and Tom heard all of this yesterday in Rome, but Rachael appreciated the science of these ancients even more, hearing it a second time.

"What would it be?" asked the violin maker.

"The alignment of the planets."

"Is there such a thing?" asked Cristofori. "I thought it astrology hocus pocus."

"Well, the planets do not perfectly align, but even astronomers use the term. It is the point in time where each planet is as close in our sky as they can possibly be. You could see them in the night sky no more than thirty degrees apart."

"You mean all nine planets?"

Tom smiled, "Well, they appeared to discount Pluto being a real planet, just as we do today. They meant all eight planets."

"Eight?" Cristofori smiled.

"Yes. Seems that number keeps coming up, doesn't it?

"Nevertheless, the ancients state they left The Tablet during a planet alignment. Alignments of all eight planets take place every 3,052 years. The next one will be the year 2492. We figure The Tablet is around 10,000 years old. Four alignment intervals from the year 2492 puts the alignment the ancients talk about exactly 9,242 years ago. The program I used for GPS systems could account for the wobble variation from day to day. I accessed that program while in Rome, made the adjustments, and found precise longitude and latitude down to the second."

Tom paused, waiting for the next question, which

Cristofori provided.

"And?" Cristofori asked, anxious for Tom to finish.

"And, we need to go for a boat ride."

Chapter 40

SANTA MARIA DI LEUCA defines the geographic heel of the Italian boot. Doctor Nodada arranged for a yacht to take everyone from there, along the coast, to their final destination. He said he knew somebody who owned one and was glad to help. Tanner remained guarded. The doctor led the way in his SUV on the two-hour drive from Locorotondo with Cristofori and Maria riding with him. Tanner followed with the rest of the team plus a new member, the kid.

It made sense for Cristofori to come. It was only right that he be at the culmination of his lifelong search. Maria joined them as the only person able to, if needed, sing a lock open as she did at Castel del Monte. That left her son, Giacomo. The kid made a pest of himself until his mother agreed he could come. But he had to remain on the boat when the team went searching.

"I want to ride with Tanner in his *macchina*," the boy insisted. Tanner scowled but relented. Lizzy thought it touching, and when Tanner mouthed to her, "Help," she agreed to keep the boy under control.

Tanner drove while Nick rode shotgun. Tom and Rachael took the third row to allow Lizzy and Giacomo the second. Giacomo spent most of the time propped on the back of the driver seat jabbering about the country, the sea, and how much he liked boats. He wanted a boat one day, and on and on.

Tanner reflected on the past few nights, being on a dark op mission, scaling a tower and avoiding an assassin at the Castel del Monte. Now the adventure had degraded into a Sunday drive, *en famille,* in the country.

This doesn't feel right. Something is wrong with this picture.

He told Nick his concerns in private the night before and was glad to find Nick shared them. With Nick's devil-may-care attitude, it was hard to tell what he was really thinking. A bond of trust, however, held the whole team together. Not so much with the newcomer, Nodada. The doctor had made a difference in decoding, but having a yacht at his disposal seemed suspiciously convenient, along with his sudden change in demeanor. Nick noticed the change, too. Tom's enthusiasm blinded his perspective, but Nick cautioned him in private before they left Rome. He asked Tom to make a change in his findings.

The previous night, Tom had shown everyone on the team a map depicting their final destination. Except that it was not their real destination. Before leaving Rome, Nick asked Tom not to reveal the exact location to the others. The place Tom pointed to was ten miles beyond the real location. This would assure that the team would reach it without uninvited guests waiting for them. Although Nodada had arranged transportation for them, they were stopping short of where he believed they were going.

The drive proceeded from the Adriatic side of Italy near Brindisi and turned inland toward Gallipoli along the inside of the heel to Santa Maria di Leuca. High bluffs along the ocean descended down to sea-level, rocky beaches as they entered the town. No doubt this was a location for the well-to-do. Substantial villas behind well-tended gardens lined the street, each built in a different, whimsical style. They passed a cream limestone structure fashioned with Arabic windows, a sienna-colored castle with turrets, and a classic Roman villa. A yacht, docked nearby, blended well with the lavish neighborhood.

Nodada's SUV led them to a parking area near the water where a travertine sidewalk, lined with tall palm trees, bordered the ocean. In the distance, a slender white lighthouse set upon a cliff signaled the tip of the peninsula. The vehicles stopped and the passengers got out, with Giacomo darting to the stone balustrade on the edge of the water. He leaned over the railing eager to spot whatever the sea offered, with Maria an arm's length away. Tanner got a kick out of the explosive energy of the kid. Lizzy noticed his smile.

"Cute kid," she said.

"Yeah, I guess," was all the soldier offered in return.

Nick walked over to Nodada. "So, where's the boat?"

"It's a short walk from here, at that marina," the doctor said as he pointed down the sidewalk.

"Tell me again who it belongs to?"

As the doctor explained, Tom, Rachael, Cristofori, and Tanner joined them. Lizzy stayed with Maria and Giacomo.

"I guess I didn't give the name. It's a man named Laurens Sarkissian. He is a successful importer."

"Importer? Of what?"

"Dried fruit."

"Really?

Nodada smiled. "It's the little things that can be most rewarding."

"I guess," said Nick. "You told us he was more than happy to help. How do you know him?"

"When I was a doctor at NIH, his daughter was the subject of a clinical trial. She had a rare genetic defect. One in which white blood cells destroyed red blood cells as foreign objects."

"Sounds like leukemia."

"Not the same cause, but the same effect. That's why the symptoms were misread. We used an experimental gene replacement therapy, and it was successful. Mr. Sarkissian told us we saved his daughter's life."

"So, he's indebted to you."

"He is a very generous man. And I am indebted to him. The therapy we validated has great promise. In gratitude, he offered to take me for a trip on his yacht. Happy coincidence."

Each member of the team screened the 'coincidence' through their own filter. Tanner's being the most skeptical.

The driver of Nodada's SUV stayed behind with both vehicles, as everyone walked along side of Nodada. Cristofori waved at Maria, Lizzy, and Giacomo to join them.

A car show occupied the plaza between their parked vehicles and the docks. Owners displayed their classic Jaguars, Fiats, Porsches, and the like. A crowd milled around the cars appreciating how well kept they were. Tanner, always on the lookout, scanned the crowd. He spotted a man wearing sunglasses, dressed in light slacks with a sweater draped over his back. Very Euro. Tanner sensed he seemed more interested in Tanner than in the special cars before him. Tanner would return the favor and keep an eye on Mr. Euro.

"Ah, there is his boat," announced Nodada, as they approached the dock.

It was easy to spot, at over 200 feet long and the largest object around. It had three decks topped by a sundeck. Nick murmured to Rachael who walked beside him, "I got to get into dried fruit."

The yacht docked stern-in where a roll-out ramp met the dock and provided a terrace. A gentleman with olive skin, made darker by the sun, and black hair with a noble streak of gray, waited there. He wore a light gray polo shirt, white pants, and blue deck shoes. No doubt the owner of this vessel. A wide smile filled with perfect white teeth greeted them. Rachael said "Wow" and Lizzy exclaimed "All right!"

"Doctor Nodada!" exclaimed the man as he stretched out his hand to help the doctor on board. "At last. You have taken me up on my offer. I am delighted."

"I would like to introduce my friends," returned the doctor as the others stepped down onto the terrace. Giacomo couldn't take it all in fast enough and his mother held his hand to keep him from running away into the boat. Introductions were made all around as a young blonde woman and a redheaded man, both dressed in white uniforms with shorts, emerged from below carrying trays holding flutes of champagne.

"I must welcome you with refreshments," said Sarkissian. The adults each took a flute while Maria declined. Tanner asked the redhead in an aside, "Got a beer?" The man responded with a "certainly" and disappeared into the boat.

Nick took a sip and said, "Thank you, Mr. Sarkissian, but…"

"Please, call me Laurens."

"Laurens. But it will be a short trip."

"Yes. I understand. And Doctor Nodada tells me you will explore grottos along the way."

Nick glanced at Nodada, who returned a slight smile showing he must have provided minimal information to Sarkissian. Tanner noticed as well. The redhead brought Tanner his beer, and as he took a sip, he studied his host.

"Yes," Nick said, measuring his words. "There are several areas we want to explore."

"Let's go inside and talk about it, shall we?" Sarkissian motioned with a wave to follow him.

Following the owner through the open sliding glass doors, they entered a lavish, cream-colored environment. Positioned to the right, a bar with three tiger-print stools faced a curved couch built against the bulkhead. "Right this way," he said, as he led them up a flight of stairs to the next deck, which opened into a living room the size of a boutique hotel lobby. The living room continued the cream-color motif adding tan accents. At the opposite end, beside another bar, a wide opening led to a large deck containing an endless pool.

In the living room, a circular seating area in the middle was made up of three leather couches set next to each other at angles forming a semicircle. Three matching arm chairs formed the other half of the circle. Blue and gold pillows rested against the backs. A round coffee table marked the center.

Sarkissian walked to the seating area and, with a wave of his arm, asked, "Please, everyone take a seat."

Most had finished their champagne. The blonde in uniform took the flutes and returned them to her tray, along with Tanner's empty beer bottle. "Is there anything else I can get you?" she asked. A general shaking of heads and polite 'no-thank-you's' sent her on her way. Giacomo made a beeline to the deck with the pool with Maria and Lizzy following. Rachael, Nick, and Cristofori sat on the couches. Nodada, Sarkissian and Tom sat in the chairs with Tom in the center, so he could show Sarkissian what he had. Tom opened his leather messenger bag and pulled out a map from a computer printer folded in quarters. He leaned forward and opened the map on the coffee table. Sarkissian perched on the edge of his seat and showed great interest.

It was a detailed map of the section of coast Tom said they wanted to explore with no designation anywhere of an *Omnis Scientia.*

Pointing to what he and Nick designated as the bogus destination, he said, "This is where we would like to head. But," running his hand along the coast, including the real destination ten miles lower, "There are other grottos along the way we would like to explore. If that's OK with you."

Sarkissian smiled and stretched his arms as if to encompass his floating villa, "The boat is at your disposal. I will take you to the captain and you can discuss your map with him. Is that OK?"

"That's fine."

"From what you showed me, we should be at your destination in three or four hours, but you can verify that with the captain. We have small vessels stored below for your exploration. You're welcome to use them as you see fit."

"Thank you," Tom said as he refolded the map.

"Now, how about a tour of the boat?" Sarkissian suggested as he stood and turned to the young woman who stood on call in the corner. "Alexa, would you give our guests a tour?"

"Yes sir," she responded.

"Come-on," said Lizzy to Maria and Giacomo. "We're going on a tour." Giacomo, all for seeing more, led Lizzy and his mother back inside.

As everyone stood, Sarkissian added, "And we have wardrobes you are welcome to use, should you like to enjoy the sun or take a swim."

This was the host's graceful manner of appraising the group's attire, which was more suitable for hiking than boating. Everyone looked at each other understanding his meaning and took it under advisement. Tanner was just fine in his traditional khakis and tee.

"This way," said Alexa as she led the group out of the living room.

"Doctor Nodada," Sarkissian said. "Would you mind staying behind? I want to catch up." Then turning to the exiting group, "Do you mind if I borrow the doctor?"

"No," said Nick. "We'll see you later. Right?"

Nodada smiled. "Yes, I'll see you shortly."

Tanner squinted.

Don't like the two of them alone.

Sarkissian put his hand on Nodada's shoulder. "Let's go to my office."

As the group went forward, the boat's engines came to life. Tanner, bringing up the rear, decided to walk aft and watch the boat leave the dock. Below, the ramp retracted into the boat. Water roiled below as the props engaged. As the boat eased forward, a small crowd gathered to witness the elaborate yacht depart. Tanner spotted Mr. Euro in the crowd. He had a cell phone to his ear.

Who is he talking to?

Chapter 41

THE SUNDAY EXCURSION turned into a cruise on the Mediterranean amidst sumptuous surroundings. On the starboard side, the crystal blue of the ocean melded into the sky. Along the port side, gray precipices rose from the sea. These crags appeared rich in inlets and grottos. Tom was interested in only one. He held a precision GPS device in his hands as he stood against the rail scanning the cliffs, lost in the beauty of the moment. The others were scattered over different parts of this vast floating mansion as Nick joined Tom on deck.

"Where are we?" Nick asked.

"About an hour from our destination."

"Did you check out the landing craft?"

Tom snickered. "You mean the array of boats Sarkissian has below?"

"Impressive, isn't it?"

"Well, I don't think the jet skis are fit for the job, but the eighteen-foot runabout should work."

Nick and Tom experienced a high from the adventure, but now, coming close to the final prize, they appraised their situation in sober reflection.

"But we don't know, do we?" Nick asked.

Tom understood. "Will the boat work for us? Will it take us where we need to go? I don't know. We do know where the Omni is located. Or at least, we've convinced ourselves we do. But we know little more. Is it in a grotto? Is it underwater? I'm taking scuba gear Sarkissian lent me, in case I need it."

Nick raised an eyebrow. "You've scuba dived before?"

"I've done wet caving. Some guys love it. Not me. But I can do it."

Turning to Nick, Tom added, "But Nick, we don't know what the Omni looks like. We don't even understand if it's something we can remove, hold in our hand, or if it's a huge tablet like before."

Nick stayed focused on the shoreline. "I know," he admitted.

"And we're hoping Maria can perform the same trick and open some passage to the Omni. We're lining up a lot of improbable things."

Nick turned to Tom. "Why do you cave?"

"What do you mean?"

"Doesn't seem very logical. You don't know where you're going. You don't know what you'll find. Sure is dangerous. So why do it?"

"So, is this your way of making me feel better about what we're doing?"

"Maybe. Maybe it's my way of making *me* feel better."

Both laughed.

Nick continued. "We've been through too much to stop now, my friend. Don't you think?"

"Guess so."

Nick put his hand on Tom's shoulder and turned him away from the shoreline. "Come on. Let's find the others."

Tanner sat beside the pool with Maria and Cristofori watching Giacomo splash with delight. His mother had taken him to a bedroom where Alexa provided a small swimsuit for the boy. Appraising the simple sundress Maria wore, she asked her if she would like swim attire. "Thank you. I am OK," was Maria's simple answer. She asked Rachael and Lizzy the same thing. Rachael, considering what might lie ahead was not in vacation mode, and declined. Her tee and exercise pants would be fine. Lizzy, on the other hand, chirped "Sure. Whatcha got?"

Lizzy had not been in the cave at Carlsbad nor in the catacomb at the castle. Perhaps had she been, she would not have been so cavalier. Then again, Rachael thought, Lizzy might be cool, game, and playful no matter what.

"Come in the water," Giacomo begged of Tanner.

"Nah. Water makes me shrink," smiled the soldier still dressed in his khakis and tee, sipping on a beer.

"Ah. You are so crazy," said the boy as he splashed toward

the big man.

Only a few drops landed, but Tanner took a line from the Wizard of Oz and said with dramatic gestures, "Oh. I'm melting… I'm melting…," to Giacomo's delight.

Lizzy appeared, dressed in a white two-piece bathing suit designed like a little girl's sailor suit, complete with tiny white pleated skirt. The contrast to her red hair and vivacious personality made Tanner laugh. The firm curves of her body, exposed to him for the first time, provoked a different, unspoken reaction.

"Well aren't you the cute one," he said.

Lizzy put her hand on her hip and snooted her nose in the air with a 'ha' for dramatic effect, but turned to Giacomo and asked, "Room for one more?"

Giacomo replied, "*Si*. Come in."

Lizzy entered, churning up as much water as possible and the two began an unofficial splashing contest.

Tanner glanced at Giacomo's mother and thought he could detect a slight smile.

Tanner stood shaking an empty beer bottle at the group in the pool. "I need another beer. I think I'll rustle one up."

Lizzy and Giacomo, engaged in splashing, paid no attention as Tanner left. As he walked down the hallway, he heard voices coming from behind a closed door. It was Sarkissian and Nodada having an animated discussion. He paused with his ear to the door.

"My friend," Sarkissian said. "I owe you much and you are asking much on this trip."

"For which I am truly grateful," responded Nodada.

"I understand the pressure this man you described has placed on you. Are you sure this is the way to go? I mean, it seems he can do you harm."

"I'm certain this is the only way. I have no choice. Once our friends have what they've come for, I can make sure it's safe. And, they are safe as well."

"But do they know?"

"No. They cannot know."

"Well, the precautions you've taken seem reasonable. If they work."

"Yes, we can only hope."

"Let's get some sun and enjoy the day, shall we?"

Tanner realized the two men would open the door and find him eavesdropping. So, he trotted down the hallway a few feet before they opened it, turned a corner and climbed a flight of steps. He came to the second deck near a patio shaded by a tarp. Beneath the tarp, Nick, Rachael, and Tom sat in director chairs around a small table.

"There he is," said Nick. "Come join us."

Tanner walked over and plopped into a chair. His apprehension was apparent.

"What's up, big guy?" asked Nick.

"I overheard Sarkissian and Nodada talking in a room on the deck below. Couldn't tell exactly what they were discussing, but it was clear they are keeping things from us."

Rachael added, "There was a change in Nodada. Something happened in Rome."

"You noticed it, too?" asked Nick.

"Somebody's gotten to him," said Tanner.

Tom, whose recent enthusiasm blocked his usual suspicious nature, now shared the concern the rest of the team displayed. "Gotten to him how, for what reason?"

"Somebody wants what we're after," said Tanner. "You guys think this gizmo's got all the knowledge in the world. That's worth something."

"Then why are people trying to stop us?" asked Rachael. "Bombs, assassins. I'm not feeling the love."

Nick considered what he heard and said, "Why does it have to be just one person?"

Rachael, puzzled, asked, "Huh?"

Tanner anticipated where Nick was going.

"Look, what we're after is something people want to own or want to destroy. We said that before. We might have both types after us."

"Well, the more the merrier," Rachael quipped.

Nick smiled, "I should have told you this earlier. I didn't

have the chance." He leaned in to the group and lowered his voice. "The location Tom pointed out to Sarkissian is ten miles beyond where we want to go."

"What?" exclaimed Rachael.

Tom continued the explanation. "Nick and I created a red herring. If somebody is waiting for us at that spot, they'll never see us. I spoke to the captain and told him that was our destination, but I heard about some other grottos and would like to check them out. He told me he would hug the coast and we should let him know where we wish to stop. I will do just that before we reach the real spot."

"So," said Nick, "Our plan is to take the eighteen-foot runabout from the yacht. The four of us will go, along with Maria. Cristofori and Lizzy will stay behind with Giacomo."

"But what about their safety while we're gone?"

Tanner spoke up. "What I overheard was about the safety of what you find. It sounds more like they plan to steal it from you. But how, I don't know. I haven't seen any muscle on-board. Not the blonde nor the redhead, and that leaves the captain. Unless there is someone else hiding."

"There's no one hiding," said Tom with authority.

"How do you…" began Tanner before he remembered Tom's special sensing talent. "Ah, that's right. OK, then."

Nick added, "Look, we don't even know if the Omni is something we can remove, let alone someone else steal it."

Tom glanced at the GPS device. “Everyone, it’s time to go. We’re here.”

Chapter 42

SARKISSIAN LED EVERYONE to the yacht's lower deck and turned on a light in a large compartment. This area held two Yamaha wave runners and a Chris-Craft Carina 21 serving as an elegant tender and water ski boat.

"Boats within a boat," observed Nick.

Sarkissian smiled, proud of owning a yacht with this feature. Pointing to the left, he said, "That part of the yacht lifts and the boat slides out and down into the water, all with hydraulic devices. You are welcome to use our runabout to investigate the grotto."

"Thanks."

Nick had used boats like the Chris-Craft before when he owned a place on Long Island. Two seats three-quarters of the way up behind a windshield, the driver sat in the right seat. Three seats in the rear were situated in front of padding over the engine. Nick could remember the bikini-clad misses sunbathing on the one he had in New York. The windshield contained a cutout in the middle to allow two more guests to walk through and sit on facing couches in the bow. Beneath those bow seats were storage compartments. The boat offered plenty of room for Nick, Tom, Rachael, Maria, and Tanner.

Nodada said he would stay behind and asked Cristofori to

join him to discuss their final destination. The old man had looked warily at the boat. He was not so sure of his footing on a small boat. Staying behind with Nodada was fine with him. The team had not let him in on the intermediate excursion being their final destination. Had they done so, Cristofori would jump on board, putting any doubts aside. Since Maria might be needed to open locks, Rachael let her in on the secret. She agreed and told her father she wanted to go because she had never seen a grotto. Her father thought this odd, but agreed.

Maria's son Giacomo was another story. "I want to go, too!"

Lizzy held Giacomo's hand and said, "Sorry, kid." She held her hand a foot over the boy's head. "You must be this tall to go on this ride."

The theme park reference was lost on the boy. He pouted, "It's not fair."

"I'll challenge you to another splash match in the pool," she said.

The boy enjoyed Lizzy and the pool. He was torn.

"Have you ever played the game Marco Polo in the pool?"

Giacomo knew nothing about what the famous explorer might have to do with a swimming pool, but he was tempted. He had changed out of his wet bathing suit and would have to don another. That was no problem to the little boy.

"Come on," Lizzy said, taking him by the hand and leading him to the steps to the next deck. You get changed and we'll hit the pool."

Sarkissian told the team, "Please return to the deck where we first talked, and I'll have the boat placed in the water."

Everyone left as the redheaded steward came down to maneuver the boat to the sea.

Lizzy led Giacomo back to the cabin where his bathing suit was drying. Alexa approached. "We have another suit, a dry one for you."

"Of course, you do," Lizzy offered in a manner of 'don't-you-have-everything?'

"Just go into this cabin and I'll bring it to you."

Giacomo opened the cabin door and walked in with Lizzy behind him, but he stopped.

"Please. I cannot have you with me when I change, no?"

"OK, little man," replied Lizzy. "I'll wait out here in the living room while you change."

With that, Giacomo closed the door and Lizzy walked fifteen feet away, dropped into a chair, and picked up a magazine to pass the time.

The steward soon had the boat tied up along the yacht beside a floating platform and remained to help. Nick led the others down a short set of steps to the platform, stepped in the boat, and stood beside the wheel, adjusting to the gentle roll of the boat and directing seating arrangements.

"Maria, Rachael, please take the seats in the bow."

Tom entered the boat after Nick and offered his hand to the women. Rachael seemed unaccustomed to the roll of the boat, stumbling toward the bow and plopping into the left seat. Maria walked with steady grace.

Tanner hopped into the rear. "Tom, I'll sit behind you. With Nick over there, it'll balance the boat."

Although it was clear Tanner meant nothing, Tom didn't like being reminded of his small stature and light body weight.

Sarkissian watched from the top of the steps. "Take as long as you like. Note that cell phones seldom work in these grottos. So, if we do not see you in two hours, we will investigate."

"Sounds good," Nick replied. Sitting behind the wheel, he turned the ignition key and the 240-horsepower engine sprang to life. The steward removed the line, Nick pushed the throttle forward, and the boat sped toward the cliffs.

Sarkissian watched the boat bounce over the waves, cutting a wake, heading to the grotto. Out of sight of the team, they could not see Sarkissian's perpetual smile turn to a look of concern.

"Hey, Giacomo, are you ready yet?" Lizzy yelled from her seat, her magazine no longer amusing her. No answer came from the nearby cabin. She got up and walked to it and tapped on the door.

"Giacomo, are you ready?" she asked.

Again, no answer. Lizzy opened the door. No one was in the cabin; the boy's wet bathing suit was still on the drying rack. Alexa walked by.

"Hey, did you see the boy?"

"I brought his dry bathing suit to him. He thanked me and closed the door."

Lizzy noticed the chair beside the bed. "You mean the one lying on that chair?"

Tom sat in the seat beside Nick with his GPS in his hands. "You're headed straight to it," he said.

Nick scanned the rocky cliffs spotting a cleft in the rock and steered toward it. He slowed the boat as though he had entered a no-wake zone, turning to the right a hundred yards out.

"That's the place," Tom said pointing to the opening. Tom looked at each member on the boat as though he was counting heads. Something seemed out of place, but Tom's attention was distracted by what lay ahead.

As they passed, with the cliffs to portside, it soon was clear the opening went deep. Nick eased the boat into the opening. It became a cave in the water, a true grotto. Tom was in his element. Nick checked the depth finder on the console. Plenty of water. They weren't about to hit the bottom. Gray rocks formed a rough dome over the canal, curving to the left.

How far did it go?

Even though daylight found its way into the canal, bouncing off ripples, everyone's eyes had to adjust to the gradual loss of light. Tom brought his duffel bag with basic caving gear, including a lantern. The only other bag on board was Tanner's backpack with his customary tools of his trade. Before Tom could fetch his lantern, as the light grew dim, they came to a fork. The canal divided into equal channels, one to the right and one to the left.

"Take the left one," Tom assured Nick. This was Tom's realm, and Nick didn't question his instinct.

Tom removed the lantern and turned it on before things were completely dark. With limited visibility, Nick was tapping the throttle to ease the boat along as slowly as possible. After fifty feet, the lamp lit a solid wall ahead of them. Rachael ducked by reflex. Maria had no reaction. Nick reversed the throttle in time to avoid colliding with the wall and took the boat out of gear when it came to rest.

"Guess we should have gone the other way," quipped Nick.

Tom assessed the situation, stepping to the bow and holding the lamp so he could study the water. "It's open on the other side of this wall."

"Is that your peripheral sense at work?" asked Rachael.

"That and the fact the water is flowing past it. Look," Tom said as he set down the lamp, took a piece of paper from his pocket, and wadded it up. He picked up the lamp. Tanner walked forward to see better and Nick leaned over the windshield. Tom dropped the paper into the water. It floated toward the wall, accelerated, and then was sucked under by an unseen vacuum.

"OK, so is this wall locked like the castle and Carlsbad?" asked Rachael.

"Only one way to find out," said Nick. "Maria?"

Maria understood it was time for her virtuoso performance. Tom sat beside Rachael with the lamp poised toward the wall. Maria stood. She began the same series of rapid notes in the sequence she remembered from the castle. The chamber echoed her performance as though coming from a deep well, filling the rock interior with the ancient chant that worked for them in Carlsbad and again in Castel del Monte. Everyone was rapt by the sounds.

Would the stones crash into the water? Were we far enough away to avoid being hit?

But nothing happened. The wall stood as they had found it.

The disappointment was palpable.

Was there another way in?

After a few moments, Tanner broke the silence.

"Nick," he said.

Nick turned to Tanner, still seated at the rear.

"Kill the engine," Tanner told him.

Nick smiled with recognition.

There was no other noise in Carlsbad. Pure silence in Castel del Monte. Was that the problem?

Nick turned the key on the dash, the engine stopped, and he asked Maria, "Please try again."

The chamber filled with Maria's voice, echoing more as Maria reached even higher with all the power she could muster. Small rivulets of stone dust fell from the top of the wall. Everyone hoped it was only due to the sheer volume of Maria's voice. The wall uttered a low groan like the timbers of an old sailing ship in rough seas. Small rocks from the stack dropped, splashing into the water. Maria continued to sing, raising her voice as best she could over the rising bass notes from the wall itself and the splashing stones.

A stone near the top, the size of a bowling ball, crashed into the water splashing the bow of the boat. It was followed by a cascade of other stones falling and splashing. They all sank without piling above the water line. The bottom appeared to be deep enough to accommodate them all. As the final stones crumbled into the water, the flow strengthened, pulling the boat along.

Nick began to start the engine to control the boat's movement, but Tom stood and gestured to him to stop.

"No," he said. "Let the stream take us."

The final few rocks fell away as the boat crossed the threshold, pulled by a strong but gentle current. Tom held his lantern for guidance but he thought the tunnel illumination brightened on its own. He soon realized the walls were glowing. It was as if they had triggered a motion detector which made the lights come on. Tom turned off his lamp as everyone gazed at the miraculous light show. Rachael provided the only analysis, "Are the rocks coated with some kind of luminescent material?"

"But from where does it get its energy?" asked Tom. There's no sunlight here, ever."

"Look ahead guys," Nick said, drawing Tom and Rachael's attention forward. The tunnel grew larger and, up ahead, a stronger source of light shone from the left. The current drew the boat a few feet more, and the ceiling rose high as a cathedral. The walls and ceiling were brightly lit from an unseen source.

The boat glided to a sandy beach and stopped as if following a script written long ago.

Nick said, "I guess we're here."

Tanner jumped from the side of the boat and into the shallow water. He walked to the bow and steadied it to allow the women to sit on the edge and swing themselves over where they could step out. He pulled the boat up onto the tiny beach and Nick and Tom hopped out.

Nick pointed to the right of the boat where the stream narrowed to three feet wide against the edge of the cave, making the current much faster. It continued for twenty feet where it disappeared into a crevice in the furthest wall.

"Don't want to step in that," Nick said to Tom.

"No. Be careful there. I've seen streams like that in caving. We would throw a dye into it so that others outside could find which river it ran into. This would be a rough ride for anyone, and who knows where it ends up?"

To their left was a boulder the size of a bus blocking the other side from view. Nick led the way around the boulder and into a room lit by the mysterious luminescence. Everyone looked above to marvel at a dome the size of the Pantheon in Rome, its surface carved into the gray rock, but smooth as cream. Beneath them was a floor of rose marble unlike any they had seen before. Everyone had the same impression.

This is a temple.

The floor bore a design like the points of a compass with eight wedges emanating from a point on the right wall where the edge of a small alcove was visible. The light that filled the room was a blue white. But from the alcove, a green light shined.

Tom looked at Nick.

"The Omni?" he asked.

"Let's find out."

Chapter 43

SARKISSIAN AND NODADA stood on the deck of the yacht. Sarkissian watched through binoculars a small boat near the cliffs. It was a sixteen-foot outboard with a lone person on it.

"Can you make out who it is?" Nodada asked.

"No one I know. A young man."

"It's not the boat we expect?"

"No," replied Sarkissian. "That boat will be much larger, with several men on board. Perhaps this is someone out for a ride. I don't think your man would send a kid."

They watched as the boat slowed and turned into the opening in the cliff where the team had entered.

"I better call Foxe and let him know. I suspect this man is following them," Sarkissian said. He pulled out his cell phone and punched in a number.

"No connection. Just as I feared. No cell service. They must be deep inside."

Nodada wrinkled his brow considering the options and said, "Perhaps we should go in."

"And do what?" Sarkissian snapped. "No. They're on their own."

The team hesitated, each looking toward the green glow from the alcove. Tanner stayed behind, casing the perimeter of the temple. Maria stood at the edge with him. Nick, Tom, and Rachael moved toward the alcove.

As the group stepped closer, the source of the glow came into view. They continued until they were twenty feet in front of it. On a shoulder-high marble pedestal stood a device resembling a cylindrical bronze lamp emitting green light from an unknown source through hundreds of small openings. It was large, two feet in diameter and three feet tall, supported by a round base just a couple of feet tall and slightly wider than the device on it.

Nick looked at Tom, who looked at Rachael, exchanging silent expressions of astonishment.

"The Omni?" whispered Rachael.

"It must be," answered Nick.

They crept slowly toward the Omni as though it might explode.

Approaching the unknown device, they crossed some unseen threshold. The light grew brighter, creating a field of identical green stars across the dome like a planetarium. A low rumble started, and the device began to rotate around its axis, moving the star pattern above. All three backed up. The tripped rotation accelerated. The rumble transitioned into the language of music they all had heard before, with its odd, rapid variation of tones. The rhythm of the music accelerated and turned to a chorus of multiple voices. The volume grew uncomfortably loud as it spun madly spreading a dizzying array of lights around the room. Everyone closed their eyes, hypnotized by the Omni. Each person began to dream, different ones for each person.

In Rachael's, she floated in the dark reaches of outer space unassisted by a space suit. A beam of light passed by her as though it had slowed to the speed of an arrow. Then another, moving even slower. Rachael realized it was she who was accelerating, moving at the speed of light through the void. She witnessed how everything appeared as time slowed and distances shrank.

Tom found himself in blinding snow. He turned to see outlines of fellow explorers following him. Trudging further up the side of a mountain, he realized it was Mount Everest. He led the team into a cave, unknown until then. The men behind him smiled and shook each other's hands to have found shelter.

Nick walked marble steps up to a podium in some government monument. As he climbed the steps, a throng of cheering people came into view. He stood before them smiling and waving to the multitude. As the cheering abated, he began to speak. As in a dream, he could not remember what it was he said, but the people were enthralled.

The Omni also cast its spell over Tanner and Maria, who were standing at the edge of the temple.

Tanner found himself on a battlefield dressed in Roman legion attire. An enemy horde was visible in the distance over an open field. Tanner led a small band of soldiers using modern hand signals to command strategic moves. He could take in the whole layout of the fighting as though studying it on a battle board.

Maria fell under the spell of the Omni in a much different way. She felt a compendium of facts filling her head like a video on fast forward. All different aspects of knowledge came to her.

The wheel, the music, all came to a sudden stop as the light dimmed in the Omni. Each person opened their eyes, groggy from the experience.

Nick, gaining his composure, gasped, "Did you, ah, dream?"

Tom responded, "Yes, it was crazy. I was on Mt. Everest, entering a cave; but there are no caves on Mt. Everest."

Tanner walked over to the group with Maria. "Did that thing spray a drug into the room?"

"Why?" asked Nick.

"I felt like I got cold-cocked, dreaming like I was knocked out."

"And your dream was what?" asked Rachael.

"Military moves, like some war game. I've never had dreams like that."

"Nick," asked Rachael, "Did your dream have something to do with leading a group of people?"

"Kind of. I was speaking to a crowd."

"Mine was a dream Einstein said he had, about riding a beam of light," added Rachael, her eyes wide with discovery. "You see what it was doing?"

Everyone returned puzzled expressions.

"Somehow that thing was touching something deep in each of us. Tom, exploring. Tanner, military. Me, science. You, Nick, leading. Maria..." she stopped and smiled at Maria whose window into her character continued to be misty, "But we haven't heard from you. Did you dream?"

With a slight grin of acknowledgment, Maria added more verbiage than anyone thought possible. "It knows much. The music, it was what we have heard and read from the translations, but much more.

"I heard a listing like an encyclopedia of subjects. Energy: It draws its energy from seawater. The lights of the grotto, they do, too. It can tell you how. Genetics: It tells how we are made to be different. I believe we heard what is at our core and responded. Just like tuning forks. We responded to the one that matched us."

"Like tuning forks?" said Nick. "I had no idea you were so poetic."

"The Omni holds more knowledge than our greatest libraries, and it is knowledge we do not have today."

As though they had passed an unwritten exam, the end of their search announced itself with a low rumbling and shook the rock on which the temple stood. Everyone looked around to see if they were in danger, but the sound of grinding by ancient gears began and all focused on the pedestal as it sank into the floor. In a few seconds, the Omni reached floor level and stopped with a thud that echoed throughout the chamber.

"I think we've been presented with a gift," announced Nick. "Let's take a closer look," he said as he approached the Omni.

"Careful," cautioned Rachael.

Nick kneeled at the edge of the Omni, looking around to see if it was connected to any tripwires. It was folly to think that a people who could harness power from seawater would use something as primitive as a tripwire, but he instinctively looked anyway. He tapped the surface with his finger as though he was testing an iron to see if it was hot. It was not. Then he put both hands on the device. He lifted it, rocking backwards before steadying himself.

"It's light as a feather," he said. "Let's get it back to the boat."

"No, let's get it to my boat," came a new voice in the temple.

Standing near the large boulder at the edge of the temple was a slight young man with a pale complexion. He held a pistol pointed directly at the group. Tanner looked at his backpack a few feet away from the young man, regretting he'd stepped away from the weapon within it.

"Who the hell are you?" shouted Nick.

"Well, I guess we haven't been introduced. I'm Chris Jones."

"Who?"

The man stayed eerily calm, his recent dose of drugs smoothing off edges.

"I believe you may have heard of my dad, Josiah Jones."

"The televangelist?" asked Tom.

"The one and only. Gosh you guys are hard to get."

"What do you mean?" asked Nick.

"Let me rephrase that," Chris sneered. "You guys are hard to kill. A bomb in your cave didn't do it. And even after I practiced with Tom's buddies."

Tom realized he was talking about the cave-in. "You!" he said as he started toward Chris, only to have Nick move his arm to stop him. Chris waved his gun with a warning of "Ah, ah, ah."

"Was that your shooter at Castel del Monte?" asked Nick.

With his free hand, Chris made a short, mock salute. "Yep. Isn't good help hard to find? Of course, how could he know you had your own defense force? But I made sure they are not anywhere near here."

"Why?" asked Nick. "Why did you try to kill us?"

"You guys were spoiling everything. You know how hard it is to have a self-righteous prick for a father? All my life, I had to play his little game to get what I wanted. Dad played the suckers well. Put a lot of cash away off-shore and I knew how to get it. All I needed was for him to crash and burn. I relished the day that would happen. And it looked like it was coming soon. His little friend, Congressman Everson, was taking him down with him."

"Scott Everson, the guy who killed the dog?" asked Nick.

Chris scowled. "Yeah. That guy. Dad's flock could tolerate mistresses and shooting the paperboy as long as popular political positions were right. But when a neighbor's dog bothers you and a home surveillance camera catches you hammering the thing dead with a lead pipe, well, folks, that's just too much. And people think *I'm* twisted."

Clear to all in this brief exchange was that Chris was indeed twisted, unstable and dangerous.

"Everson was taking Dad down and I was preparing to

bail. Then, you came along, with your magical discovery. Dear old Dad found a way to make it a message from God and boost his ratings. Turned things around. I had to stop it. I couldn't let him ride this train."

Chris, already steeped in faulty logic, became maniacal.

"I had a man get three bombs. I tried the first one out on your friends. Worked as promised. Well, not exactly. The dumbass I hired to plant it died in the cave-in as well as your buddies. Then I tried Carlsbad. You got away. That complicated things. I wanted everyone who ever saw The Tablet dead.

"But that left me with a dilemma. I had an extra bomb. What to do? What to do? Well, before I left home, I placed it in the rafters of Daddy's Tower of Power, set to go off at next Sunday's eleven-o'clock service. And guess what? It's Sunday!"

Chris glanced at his watch. "What time is it back in Norfolk? I'm always bad on time zones. Anyhow, I won't be there to enjoy the final curtain. I have places to go. So, let's get this thing to my boat, why don't we? I think it would fetch a pretty penny. A side bonus, if you will."

Nick and Tom picked up the Omni. Tanner spotted something behind Chris that put the hardened soldier's heart in his throat. Peeking from the edge of the bolder stood Giacomo.

He hid in the boat's storage compartment! I thought I heard something.

As Chris looked to his right watching the efforts to bring the Omni to him, Tanner began creeping toward his backpack.

If I can just get my piece.

Giacomo moved and kicked a loose rock. Chris turned around, pointing his gun at the noise.

Tanner was in Afghanistan again. A boy who shouldn't be there was crossing into harm's way. The same reflex from Afghanistan engaged, the one that saved a life and started this whole adventure. Tanner took three rapid steps and hit Chris' gun arm, his pistol discharged to the ceiling, a loud report echoed throughout the chamber.

Maria, unaware until then that Giacomo was in the cave, raced to the boy and embraced him. Chris' gun fell from his hand and landed beside the rushing stream near the edge of the temple. Chris, backing away from Tanner, landed an expert kick into Tanner's solar plexus. Tanner was more surprised that Chris knew some judo than being hurt by the move. Tanner grabbed Chris' ankle and twisted, sending him sprawling.

Chris stumbled to his feet and swung at Tanner's jaw. Tanner stopped the punch with his left arm and delivered a hard jab with his right into Chris' jaw. Chris felt the bone snap. Tanner, infuriated by the punk pointing a gun at Giacomo, put another right into Chris' nose, splattering blood across his face.

Tanner's temper clouded his strategy. Chris fell to his knees, right beside his gun that lay near the stream. Chris picked it up and stood, pointing the gun at Tanner's head, but he was woozy and staggering. He stepped into the rapid stream and it pulled him down. Chris held the gun with his right hand and clawed at the earth as the stream sucked him toward its end point into the unseen depths of the cave.

Tanner rushed over, trying to save Chris and avoid getting shot at the same time.

"Drop the gun and take my hand," he yelled.

In response, Chris fired a wild shot barely missing Tanner. Tanner moved away as Chris lost his grip and the stream pulled him like a water slide to hell. Still holding the gun, he hit the small opening at the end of the cave, the strong current sucking his body like a broken window on a jet. His pale face turned bright red as the blood pushed up his torso. With a pop like a cork yanked from a bottle, he was gone. All that was left was his gun lying beside the rushing water.

Tanner walked over to Giacomo who grabbed onto the big man's leg. Maria, a true mother, once her son was safe, scolded him. "You were not to come here."

"But I wanted to see," he pleaded.

Nick, Tom and Rachael joined them. Nick grasped Tanner

by the shoulder.

"Well done," he said. "That's two times you've saved our lives."

"Let's not make it three," Tanner said.

"Are you all right?" Rachael asked Giacomo.

"*Si*. I am fine."

Nick led the group back to the beach and to their boat. It was now joined by the boat left behind by Chris.

"Nick, what time is it back home?" Rachael asked, and Nick knew why.

"Crap," he exclaimed. "It's twenty minutes 'til eleven on the east coast.

"If Chris really planted a bomb in his dad's church, it's going to go off in twenty minutes with a crowd of people inside. You guys load up in our boat. I'm taking that bastard's boat ahead until I get a cell phone signal. I have someone who can alert the police and they'll believe her."

Nick pushed off the second boat, turned the ignition key, fired up the outboard, whipped the boat around and gunned it. He held his cell phone in one hand, steering with the other, looking at the phone's screen begging for a dot or two of signal strength. He almost hit the side of the cave, turning straight with a second to spare.

"Distracted driving," he muttered.

A moment later, one dot appeared, then two. Nick killed

the engine and punched the frequently dialed number for his press relations woman, Barbara Monroe. She answered in two rings.

"BeeBe, it's Nick."

"Nick, what an unexpected pleasure. Where are you?"

"Can't get into that now, BeeBe. This is not a joke. I know that at eleven, in fifteen minutes, a bomb will go off in the Temple of Power in Norfolk."

"Josiah Jones' Church?"

"The same. Call the police there and get them to clear the place."

"I know the chief of police in Norfolk."

"Great. Call him, and then call me back."

Nick rang off with no pleasantries as the other boat came into view with all aboard. Nick waved them over and held the side of their boat against his.

"I called my PR woman. She knows the chief of police in Norfolk. She's calling him and will call me back."

A low rumble came from deep inside the cave. The water beneath them rippled from tremors below. Nick hopped over the side into the other boat. Tanner was at the wheel with Tom in the seat beside him.

Nick stood between them bracing himself with a hand on each seat.

"Let's get out of here."

Stones fell from overhead as Tanner pushed the throttle forward. Nick turned to see the boat he left behind, now fifty feet away, fold into two as a large rock fell from the ceiling and through the center of the boat.

Chapter 44

CHRIS JONES HAD BECOME ADEPT placing bombs by his third attempt. A domed roof crowned the Temple of Power making it appear like a sports arena with pews. Before Chris left for Italy to meet his final fate, he traversed a catwalk to reach a support beam one third up the curve of the dome and attached his last bomb. At precisely eleven on Sunday morning, it detonated. The bombed part of the dome looked as though an errant jet from the local naval air station put a missile through it. The dome blew a cloud of debris outward a moment before the dome turned to its side and collapsed. A young man took a video of the event on his phone. People who saw it on TV thought they were watching a planned demolition of the building which, in a morbid way, they were.

A swift current had pulled the boat into the cave when they arrived. Collapsing tunnels now pushed the boat out on a wave. Everyone on board held tight to their seats as the vessel careened through the tunnel. It scraped against the jagged sides and Tanner's control of the steering was hindered by the gushing water. At full throttle, it sped to the entrance to the cave. The boat flew out into open water. The bright sunlight blinded the passengers before their eyes could adjust.

They first heard the sirens. As their eyes adjusted to the light, they saw the outline of a large craft, an orange stripe down the side. A boat from the *Guardia Costiera* pulled alongside their small vessel. On deck was *Ispettore* Rossi. Joining him, in addition to three crew members, were Sarkissian, Doctor Nodada, Cristofori, and Lizzy. An odd team, but all seemed to be comfortable with each other. Nick noticed Nodada smiling for the first time since leaving Rome.

The crew attached a ladder to the side of the boat and Nick led the passengers off. After yet another attempt on their lives, each of them stayed guarded, in spite of the trusted faces smiling at them. They left the Omni under a tarp in their boat. After all were aboard, Lizzy stepped forward and kneeled to Giacomo's level as she berated him.

"Young man, you have some explaining to do."

The boy sought protection with his mother as he leaned into her, and Maria placed loving hands on his shoulders.

"I'm sorry. Am I not, Mama?"

Maria just smiled at Lizzy and Lizzy returned a wink.

Rossi spoke to the group.

"Signor Cristofori told us all about your adventures and straightened out what happened at the Castel. We were able to find who hired your shooter, a man by the name of

Christopher Jones. You know this man?"

Nick grinned. "We've recently met."

"I, myself, was visited by two men who had, what appeared to be, valid identification from your FBI. I know such agents but did not know these men. Something felt wrong. I checked them out and found they had connections with an American who may not have had your best interests at heart. Signor Cristofori confided in me your plans and I alerted the *Guardia Costiera.* We found these men in a boat waiting up the shore from here."

Rossi added with a meaningful smile, "You would not believe all of the regulations they violated. The *Guardia* had no choice but to take them in for further questioning."

Nodada continued the explanation. "*Ispettore* Rossi knows my role in taking out the assassin. I also asked for his help. You see, a man came to me threatening to harm me if I didn't bring the Omni to him. Perhaps I should have admitted this to you when it happened, but I felt responsible, and wanted to take action to protect you."

Nick looked at Sarkissian. "You knew about all of this?"

"Yes, I did. But we didn't know about this spot being your final destination. We got suspicious, especially after that young man followed you into the cave. I then redirected *Ispettore* Rossi to come to this location. Was that young man Christopher Jones?"

"It was, but I must follow-up on something immediately," said Nick as he opened his phone to check the time. Everyone who had been in the grotto had heard about the bomb Chris had planted in his father's church and knew what Nick was doing. Nick saw an unanswered call from Barbara Monroe. He punched the return-call option.

"Nick," Monroe answered without waiting for Nick to say anything. "I'm glad you called."

"Were we in time?" asked Nick.

Nick heard a lilt in Monroe's voice uncharacteristic of the calamity she faced. "No lives were lost."

"Great. That's a relief."

"Nick, there was no one in the building."

"What?"

"Turns out the Reverend Josiah Jones was arrested two days ago. Tax evasion and money laundering. The authorities took control of the Temple of Power and sealed it off. There was no one inside!"

Nick beamed, and the group shared his relief as he mouthed the words, "No one was hurt."

"But," Monroe continued, "The police chief called his men who were guarding the site, warned them about the bomb threat, and told them to back away. You may have saved their lives, because the bomb did go off and the whole place came down. Someone took video and it's all over the internet. Quite a show. Nick, shall I create a press release?"

"No!" Nick shouted. "Sorry to be so emphatic, but we need the opposite. Keep my name out of this. I'll explain later."

As a PR person, Monroe could not conceal her disappointment, but she was a professional and could coverup when called upon. "Understood. But you will let me know all about this sometime soon."

"You bet. Got to go," and Nick clicked off.

Nick explained the details to everyone. To those not in the cave, he explained why Christopher Jones would not be coming back.

Doctor Nodada asked, "You have the Omni?"

Nick looked to the others for any concerns they may have, ending with Tanner, who gave Nick a nod of consent.

"Yes," he said. "It's in the boat."

"With your permission, I would like you to join me in a secure location where a team of experts can help unlock its mysteries," requested Nodada

"Not Rome again? You must have had a mole there."

"That 'mole,' as you put it, has been dealt with," growled Nodada. Nick remembered this was a man with resources that put a bullet in the head of an assassin.

"No, we are going somewhere else. To a place that is known for keeping secrets."

Chapter 45

Basel, Switzerland

THE OMNI now hid in plain sight, or so it might seem. The public now knew of its existence and that a top team of scientists were investigating the Omni's secrets. They were using The Leibniz Supercomputing Centre in Munich. But that was not where the Omni itself resided. Nick and the team transported the device to a set of offices deep beneath a location owned by Credit Suisse. "What better place for something valuable than a Swiss Bank?" joked Nick, who had a banking relationship with Credit Suisse for his own funds. Such a valuable customer was Mr. Foxe that the bank director provided a secure location for the Omni along with offices for his team.

Tom took the lead in the work with the Omni. Working from an office deep below street level, he discovered that, unlike The Tablet that shrouded its meaning in mystery, the Omni was forthcoming with its data. The top computer scientists at Munich could not comprehend the advanced design of the thing. The Omni could adapt to whatever data interface was available to it, an amazing self-learning capability. Bluetooth, WiFi, cellular wireless, anything available. Through a series of data handshakes, Tom was able to choose the highest speed broadband offered to connect the Omni to the Munich computer. The Omni worked with the supercomputer to agree to a data compression algorithm. The data flow reached the theoretical limit scientist thought possible.

Nick and Rachael stood beside Tom as the Omni connected for the first time. The director of the Munich center watched from a video conference link beside the terminal Tom used. As the Omni connected and worked its magic, the expression of the director was a mixture of surprise tinged with fear. For a moment, everyone thought the same thing.

Was the Omni taking over the supercomputer?

Tom typed a few commands, and the Omni disconnected. With a few more commands, the Omni reconnected. Like an animal, the Omni obeyed its master.

Intense work settled in over the next two weeks.

Tom used the supercomputer to organize the data into comprehensible catalogs. One pertained to medicine, principally genetic science; another, physics; another, energy.

Rachael was all over the data for physics. She made one office her private cell, absorbed in what she was learning. She struggled to understand the mathematical formulas from the Omni since it used techniques unlike those accepted today.

But what she did understand from the associated narrative was the promise to solve, what Rachael knew as the unified field theory, a means to combine the forces of nature in one explanation. It was a problem that hounded Einstein to his dying day, but it might unlock mysteries of time and space.

Nick used Barbara Monroe's skills to manage the news about the discovery. The theoretical physics that inspired Rachael would be a big yawn to the public, but the science of DNA shared with Dr. Nodada was the talk of the town. Nodada, back in his offices in Geneva, announced that the findings from the Omni pointed the way to curing viral diseases by changing the DNA of the virus itself. A cure for Ebola, HIV, coronaviruses, and many other viral diseases might now be possible.

There was one area Nick kept secret – energy. The Omni detailed how to use seawater to generate electricity. Nick explained to the team that, when scientists proposed using nuclear power for generating electricity, pundits claimed 'electricity would be too cheap to meter.' Sadly, time proved this not to be the case. However, the Omni might hold the answer to fulfill that claim. Nick suggested, and the team agreed, this information would be too disruptive to announce. What would happen if seawater replaced oil and gas? A collapse in oil prices would cripple the economies of many countries.

The Omni had led the team to believe a machine that could perform this conversion existed.

How could something like that exist, undiscovered after 10,000 years? But then again, didn't the Omni, now in a vault next door, survive the same length of time?

Nick wanted to find the machine, validate it could work, and then release the news to the world.

Nick busied himself setting up the relationships with the Munich center, managing announcements with Nodada, and writing press releases with Barbara. He often passed Rachael's office, the glass wall allowing a view of a woman who was either heads down in printouts or writing formulas on a blackboard. Every time he asked if she wanted lunch, her response was "Thanks. I've ordered something brought in."

One day, he had something to share with Rachael that might bring her out of her self-imposed exile.

"Hi," he said as he poked his head in the door.

Rachael leaned back, taking a rare break to face Nick. She looked paler than he'd remembered. The circles under her eyes were new.

"How's it going?"

"You caught me at a good time," she smiled.

"Why's that?"

"I've brought some colleagues at MIT into this work. They're excited. There's a man from the Institute for Advanced

Studies at Princeton who's visiting them at MIT. They want to meet with me."

"When?"

"As soon as possible."

"Happy coincidence," smiled Nick.

"Why?"

"I have to fly back to the States. Can I give you a lift?"

"That would be great."

Rachael shared a special smile with Nick he had not seen since Rome.

"I know Tom's staying here, but where is Tanner and Lizzy?" Rachael asked.

Nick laughed. "You really have been heads down on this. Tanner stayed around until he decided the security here was adequate. Lizzy's with him, taking in the city. In fact, they told me where they'd be today. We might pass them on the way."

Rachael was puzzled. "On the way where?"

"To see Cristofori. He's here."

"That's great. I thought we had lost track of him."

"I know. He would have felt left out."

"Well then," Rachael said, standing and pushing her chair to her desk. "Let's go."

Tanner stood on the Wettsteinbrucke Bridge over the Rhine under a blue sky with a mixed fluff of clouds overhead. The heat of this late summer day stood in contrast to the cool weather normal for this time of year. Rachael had spent so much time underground, she'd forgotten that a city existed above her. Unusual warmth made an unusual local pastime more popular. Tanner spotted people carrying a tote for a change of clothes over their shoulder in something that resembled part bag, part inner-tube. Arriving at the bridge, he found the intended purpose as people floated down the river in the inflated gizmo while the outer clothes they shed remained dry.

Nick and Rachael strolled the city and met Tanner on the bridge. The large man leaned on the balustrade scanning the sea of humanity gliding wherever the current took them.

"Hey, big guy," Nick said, announcing their arrival.

Tanner turned, smiled, and raised his hand in a silent hello. Nick and Rachael could not help notice how relaxed Tanner looked for the first time since they had met him. It reflected the inner peace the man came to know after years of personal turmoil. The hand of fate that grabbed him years ago when saving a young boy in a hostile land led him here. No man could find a greater satisfaction than he did at this moment.

"Looking for something?" Rachael asked as she came close to Tanner who appeared to scan the river below.

"There she is!" he exclaimed.

Although Tanner pointed, he didn't need to. Lizzy, floating

among the river crowd in the only bright pink tube among the bunch, was waving and hooting a greeting to her friends on the bridge. Nick and Rachael waved back, and Tanner motioned her to the right bank just beyond the bridge.

"Let's go meet the bathing beauty," he said.

At the end of the bridge, the three descended steps along a stone wall, to a small grassy beach where Lizzy had just walked ashore, wet and sassy.

"Man, that's a hoot. I've got to take this home with me."

"And where are you going to use it?" Tanner teased. "The rivers in New Mexico are an inch deep."

"Hey, there's lots of world out there. Lots of rivers to explore."

"Lizzy, how about drying off and changing?"

"No problem," she said as she opened the tube and took out shorts, a tee, and sandals. She pulled out a towel, dried her hair, and tossed the towel to Tanner. "How about holding this up to give a girl a little privacy?"

With her back to the stone wall and Tanner holding the towel before him, Lizzy slipped out of her wet bottom and top and changed into the shorts and tee. Tanner had his head turned away being the gentleman, but took a peek, which earned him a slap from Lizzy with her wet swimsuit.

Changed and putting the wet suit in the tube, she asked Nick and Rachael, "So where are you guys going?"

"We're going to see Cristofori," Rachael responded.

"At that music place?"

Rachael turned to Nick. "I don't know. Is it that 'music place'?"

"Yes, it is."

"So, what's this music place like, Lizzy?" asked Rachael.

"We visited Mr. Cristofori there yesterday," said Lizzy. Then she smiled "It's different."

Rachael shared a laugh with Lizzy over one of the first things Lizzy ever told her.

Nick and Rachael walked on as Tanner and Lizzy stayed on the bridge, enjoying the day, and their time together.

Rachael made an aside to Nick, "I think those two have something going on."

Nick glanced back at the couple and responded, "Ya think?"

The Music Museum was located in a quiet part of Basel near a church and a square. It owed its remoteness to the fact it was once a small prison. Abandoned for years, ingenious curators found the individual cells to be the perfect size for displays of instruments and the thick walls between each to offer fine acoustics for demonstrations.

Nick and Rachael walked up to the second floor, which housed a harpsichord and early piano in the common area.

Each cell displayed, behind glass, instruments through the ages. Each instrument had a number beside it. At the end of the cell, under a small window, was a keypad. Punching in the associated number would start a recording of the instrument selected. In one cell, were flutes and other wind instruments. Another contained variations of stringed instruments. Music from violins filtered out of the cell containing that instrument. No surprise they found Cristofori sitting on a bench in the center of that cell.

Nick and Rachael stood, quiet, as Cristofori listened.

"You see the piano outside," he asked. "Just like the one my ancestor created. I like the piano, but this. This is my work, the violin."

"That and solving great mysteries of the ages," said Nick.

Cristofori laughed. "Yes, that too. But now that has come to an end," he added with a weary resignation.

"It's just the beginning," cheered on Rachael.

"Yes, for many. But not for me."

Nick and Rachael witnessed a lively man with the life in him ebbing. How could they cheer him up?

"You have so much to live for. A daughter. A little rascal of a grandson," said Rachael.

Cristofori nodded and a smile appeared as he realized the wisdom of their words.

"Perhaps I can give tours of the chamber at Castel del

Monte."

"Perhaps so," added Nick. "But the story has to be managed. Besides do you think you're up to those stairs?"

"You can manage such a story?" asked Cristofori.

"We are trying. The press now knows The Tablet led us to a chamber under the castle. We found an ancient book of code. Scholars are trying to figure it out. It ends there."

"And no one will ask for more?"

"After a few news cycles, they'll forget it."

Cristofori said, "You Americans. Nothing lasts long enough to get old. Look at all this," he said waving across the display of violins. "We love our history."

Rachael sat beside the old man.

"Maybe we only look to the future," she told him. "But the future has changed. You made that happen."

Cristofori smiled in appreciation.

"You will see new discoveries in the coming years. Fantastic advances. And you will know that what you did caused them to happen," she added, fueling the desire to live years longer.

The old man patted her hand and with a tone that showed renewed vigor, "And you will visit me over the years, no?"

"You can be sure of it."

Nick's jet was empty save for just the two of them in the passenger area. They were now headed to Boston for Rachael to meet with her colleagues on her work. One unresolved item remained.

"Nick?" asked Rachael

Nick looked up from a magazine he was skimming.

"There's something I need to know."

"What's that?"

"You remember the night in Rome? When we had dinner together?"

"Yes," Nick said, closing the magazine.

"I woke the next morning with, ah, nothing on. Did we do anything?"

Nick laughed. "You mean you don't remember?"

"Um, no."

"Well you did undress in front of me. You were reeling about as you did, laughing. That was a guilty pleasure for me; but, no, we didn't do anything. You were soon asleep. I don't take advantage of unconscious women. I tucked you in, took your things off the floor, put them in a chair, and left."

He opened the magazine again. Rachael considered what he said.

"Nick?"

"Yes, he said."

"How long before we arrive?"

"Six hours."

"Well, I'm fully conscious now."

Nick tossed the magazine away.

ACKNOWLEDGMENTS

I first want to thank Lucy Stauffer who helped me name my hero Nicholas Foxe. I had a better picture of Nick by talking with Lucy.

The early chapter-by-chapter development of *The Code Hunters* was made possible by regular meetings with fellow authors Bill Kennedy, Walt Curran, Frank Hopkins, and Jim McCormack.

Thanks go to my beta readers, Barbara Guzak, Brenda Shaw, Pat Soriano, Judith Hall, Susan Cleveland, Laura Maestro, Roger Schreiber, and John Walker. My special thanks to Susan, Laura and John for getting the details right.

One of my first readers was Phil Winkler, an expert caver who provided guidance about venturing underground.

The Latin phrases were reviewed by Valentina Asciutti. Thanks, Valentina, and thanks to Luigi DeLuca for putting us together.

The Code Hunters has a great look due to the cover design by Claudia Sperl at Label-Schmiede.

This book is dedicated to Ellen Coppley, my wife and partner in prose. We talked plot endlessly and Ellen was the first and last editor of the manuscript.

The Action Continues

The Ocean Raiders

A Nicholas Foxe Adventure

Chapter 1

The Ocean Raiders

Chapter 1

NICHOLAS FOXE waited by the canal while the Venetian police fished the corpse out of the water. The large body was laid in a peaceful repose as though asleep. The smashed rear of his skull remained hidden from view.

Nick sat on a crate borrowed from the nearby fish market. Separating him from a crowd of onlookers, the police strung yellow tape marking this as a crime scene. Nick pondered a question the dead man could no longer answer.

Why did you try to kill me?

The flight into Marco Polo airport was uneventful. Nick's private jet made great time in clear skies. He would not have accepted the offer from billionaire Nevin Dowd to come to Venice were it not for Christine Blake's involvement. It had been years since he'd last seen Christine and had fond memories of their time in Paris. He was pleased to hear from her, but surprised she now worked for Dowd. Nick had seen an interview of Nevin Dowd. The man displayed a remarkable public persona, yet there was something unsettling about him. Nick expected Christine would build a career in a blue-chip company. She had perfect business decorum, but Nick smiled, remembering the personal side he discovered in Paris.

Christine offered to have a car pick him up, but for Nick, there was only one way to enter the city of water. He contacted Guido Bartoli who ran a water taxi service from the airport. Guido, a tall Italian with a streak of gray emphasizing his dark hair and cinema-star looks, was Nick's go-to guy for getting around Venice. In a place where a street number has little meaning, he needed a man like Guido who knew the city well. Guido stood front and center among the limo drivers holding a sign reading 'Foxe.' Nick was surprised seeing Guido himself and not one of his people. It spoke to the value he placed on their friendship.

Nick walked over to him and exchanged a firm handshake.

"Guido! So, the boss is picking me up. Where's the boat driver?"

"I will be your driver for the day."

"Well..." started Nick.

"I would not have it any other way, my old friend. Let me have your luggage tickets."

Nick fished the stubs from the side pocket of his khaki travel vest and handed them to Guido, who handed them to the short, young man beside him.

At least he brought someone to do the heavy lifting.

"Let's walk this way," Guido said as he motioned to the right. "My man will see to it your bags reach your hotel."

The walk from the baggage area to the Darsena piers would take ten minutes through a covered promenade using moving walkways. Nick was particularly interested in the last flood and of course, the virus outbreak. Venice has its *acqua alta* several times a year when the tide washes over the banks of canals. Tourists wearing boots navigate through iconic Saint Mark's Square on elevated platforms. But this was no simple high tide. It was a devastating flood.

"I haven't been here since the last flood."

"You mean the big one?"

"Yes. Has Venice recovered?"

Guido smiled. "We have always recovered. But this one was big. You'll see signs of it still."

"And what about the virus?" Nick asked. "I saw photos in the news that made the city look deserted."

"You must remember, this city made it through the plague. We are resilient. Speaking of the news. I've seen reports about you lately. Seems you like caves." Guido smiled.

"Great places to visit," responded Nick. "If you like people making attempts on your life."

"I saw the news of the big find. Is it as dramatic as they say?"

"It was nothing to brag about."

Guido stopped and faced Nick as other passengers hurried by them.

"You are coy, are you not?"

Nick grinned but said nothing.

"I know, I know," said Guido, tossing his hands in the air. "You cannot say. It is my business to keep out of my client's affairs." Then he winked. "But maybe as friends?"

Nick just smiled.

Guido resumed their walk and changed the subject. "So, it is Signor Dowd you have business with, is it not?"

"That's right." Nick had told Guido why he was coming and the reason for it. "You know the man?"

"Only from the news. He's made a hit here. Wants to save the city from the rising sea level."

"You must feel the effects of that more than me, being a man of the water."

"How can anyone live in Venice and not be a man of the water?" responded Guido. "But yes, we appreciate his efforts. When I started as a young gondolier many years ago, water taxis like the ones I now own could move anywhere. Now, when the tide is high, most bridges are too low. It is the gondoliers who can squeeze beneath, but my taxis cannot. It means lost business."

"The government is doing something about it, isn't it?"

Nick's statement drew dramatic gesticulations from Guido, ones best delivered by an Italian, the culture that perfected them.

"The government!" Guido exclaimed. "You mean the project Mose? Gates to halt the rising tides? Behind schedule and over budget. Why am I not surprised?"

Stopping to look Nick in the eye, Guido asked, "This Dowd person is involved in that project. Is that why you are here?"

"No," responded Nick. "Dowd is dredging up artifacts he wanted me to examine."

"Is that so?" Guido asked, unconvinced.

"And it's a chance to reacquaint myself with an old friend."

Guido lifted an eyebrow. "A woman friend?"

"Well, yes."

Guido laughed. "Ah, Nicholas, my old friend. I knew it had to be a woman. Who is it? Is she someone I know?"

"Christine Blake. I don't think you would know her."

As they reached the pier where water taxis shuttled people to and from the airport, Guido turned to Nick, looking as though he was about to tell his friend something offensive.

"I am so sorry my friend, I must take other passengers with us. We are swamped with customers today. I hope you do not mind."

"Of course not."

Nick's simple response made Guido's pleasant demeanor

return as though the weight of the world had been lifted from his shoulders.

Water taxis filled all the slips at the pier, each a sleek, low-slung thirty-foot wooden vessel similar to those in Guido's fleet. Most riders of any height at all had to duck to enter the boat's enclosure where couch seating lined both sides. Tourists preferred to head to the rear of the boat where they could stand in the open. It was a clear, warm day and most passengers stood.

Guido walked Nick to his boat where they saw other passengers waiting. There was a couple of retirement age, clearly tourists from the camera around the man's neck to the map in the woman's hands. They were engaged in an excited discussion, pointing to sites on the map. Off to one side stood a large man dressed in a black suit with a white open shirt. If water taxis had bouncers, this man would be one. Nick hoped this wasn't the other passenger. He oozed malevolence.

The couple looked up expectantly as Guido approached them.

"*Scusate.* You are the Wagner couple, no?" he asked.

"Oh, yes, we are!" chirped the little woman.

The man shook hands with Guido. His wife provided enough enthusiasm for the two of them.

"We're so excited to be here!" she exclaimed.

"I understand you will be staying on Murano. Is that where

I am taking you today?"

"That's right," said the wife. "We were here before and visited the glass factories. I told my husband we had to come back and spend plenty of time to pick out a piece or two."

Nick observed this conversation thinking looks are deceiving. Since the couple said they've been to Murano before, they must realize the price of the least expensive hand-crafted piece is thousands of dollars. They didn't look the part of customers with that much money to burn.

The man asked, "What do we do with our luggage?"

Guido snapped his fingers, getting the attention of one of the porters standing nearby who responded by loading the bags on the boat. Guido directed the couple with a simple "please," and motioned them to climb aboard. The Wagners followed the porter, who helped them board the taxi. The porter left while Mr. Wagner caught up with his wife who had already darted to the open rear of the vessel and was looking around like a puppy dog in a car window.

Guido then addressed the dark-suited stranger. "Signor Smith?"

"Yeah. That's me."

Nick couldn't place the man's accent.

"Where is it you are going today?" Guido asked the man.

"Drop me off at the Rialto Bridge."

"As you wish. Please board and make yourself

comfortable."

The large man climbed into the water taxi. He appeared unaccustomed to a boat and the rocking caused by his appreciable weight.

Nick whispered to Guido, expressing doubt about the man's responses. "Smith? Rialto Bridge?"

"Yes," said Guido. "They were, how you say, generic answers."

"Let's keep an eye on this one," said Nick, watching the man who, by then, sat on the port-side couch near Guido.

"Why not join him and keep him company?"

Nick winked at Guido and got on board, moving past the man with a simple "excuse me" and he took a seat further back on the starboard couch near the Wagners.

Guido removed the ropes from the pier, took a seat behind the wheel, and backed out like a man who had done the maneuver a thousand times. He was well in tune with his boat. Heading forward, the water taxi soon darted across the lagoon toward Murano.

Nick entertained himself by talking to the Wagners, all the while keeping the large man in his peripheral vision. The Wagners introduced themselves and Nick responded, "Pleased to meet you. My name is Nickolas Foxe." Mr. Wagner replied, "Hey, aren't you the guy who found that tablet in a cave?" and turning to his wife, "You know honey, it was all over the news."

Nick nodded, noticing the large guy glanced toward him with a vague look of recognition. Now that Nick had revealed who he was, the large man knew he was tailing the right person. It was a moment defining the hunter and his intended prey.

Guido slowed the taxi to avoid creating a wake and slid dockside at Murano. A young man on the pier tied up the boat and assisted the Wagners. Once the luggage was placed on shore, Guido backed out with his two remaining passengers, heading toward Venice. The large man stared dead-eyed at Nick. Guido slipped into the canal that would take them from the North side of Venice to the Grand Canal. As the engine quieted, the man spoke for the first time.

"So, you're Nicholas Foxe," he said, looking at Nick from his seat in front.

"That's right."

Through a sneer, the man said, "That's good. I've been waiting for you. I'm taking you to a meeting."

"A meeting? With whom? Do I know you?"

"With whom?" the man repeated, mocking Nick's proper use of basic English. "The whom is someone who wants to see you in, let us say, 'the worst way.' That person has a proposition for you."

Nick understood 'the worst way' not to be in his best

interest. Guido shot a glance at Nick over the man's shoulder. Guido's expression indicated he knew the danger of the situation but didn't look worried. He had a plan.

Nick, looking as though he was thumbing through a mental calendar, replied, "I'm sorry, I don't have room in my schedule for unplanned meetings."

They passed under the bridge at Strada Nova. Nick looked up at the brick arch only a few feet away. He knew by the limited clearance they must be at high tide. Guido knew it as well.

The man pulled a 9mm Glock pistol from beneath his coat and pointed it at Nick.

"Perhaps this will help you make room in your calendar."

When he saw the pistol, Guido took action. He gunned the boat into the Grand Canal. The man lost his balance and dropped the gun. The acceleration threw both the gun and the man past Nick to the open rear of the craft. Nick leaped from his seat toward the gun, but the man reached for it at the same time. Now on a wide waterway, Guido jerked the boat back and forth, throwing the man away from the gun.

The Grand Canal became a raceway with Guido making erratic turns, much too fast, dodging a variety of watercraft. The boat's wake slammed against a vaporetto causing the water bus to rock violently, startling tourists waiting to board.

Out of a side canal, a police boat gave chase, its siren

blaring. Guido was well aware of the police behind him, but Nick and the large man were now wrestling on the floor of the boat. He decided his wild piloting was his best contribution to keeping Nick alive.

The man got to his feet. He tried to pull Nick up, but Nick, at six-foot four and two-hundred-ten pounds, was no small package to lift.

Guido, approaching the Accademia Bridge, swung into a wide arcing curve from one side of the canal to the other. The boat leaned to one side, toppling the man to the seat beside Nick. Nick swung his body to straddle the man. He braced his knees against the seat, in order to deliver a series of punches to the man's face. Nick pounded the man's jaw to the right, to the left, but the man seemed unfazed.

Nick's fists ached.

What is this guy made of?

In a canal-side café near the Accademia, a pair of young American newlyweds were enjoying a late breakfast. They had a destination wedding in the city the day before. Taking advantage of Daddy's wealth and her own pretension, she wouldn't have had it any other way. Her new husband, equally pretentious, was dressed in a Gucci jacket and black tee. She wore a blue silk garden dress complemented with matching hat to shade her from the morning sun.

They only had eyes for each other and were unaware of the

theatrics taking place until another tourist yelled, "Look out!"

Guido was finishing his arcing turn too close to the café. He turned the wheel of the boat sharply to the left only a few feet away. The couple saw what was happening only a second before the wave hit. Water rushed over them as though they had stepped into a wave pool. Drenched, her hat drooping to one side, this delicate flower of a bride erupted in a string of obscenities that would make a longshoreman blush.

The Fondaco dei Tedeschi is a palace turned into a shopping mall providing a rooftop view of the Grand Canal. The few morning sightseers there had an unmatched view of the entire event. Though no one had met before, the chaos below generated boisterous conversation among strangers trying to make sense of what they were witnessing.

One figure stood apart, silent, watching events unfold.

As Guido straightened the boat, the man being pummeled shoved Nick away. The gun slid toward them. As each man reached for it, Guido gunned the boat. The gun slid to the back of the boat with the men tumbling behind it.

Nick grabbed the Glock and stood. But before he could get a good grip on the gun, the man delivered a hard, backhand blow to Nick, knocking him to the couch at the rear of the boat. Nick lay on the couch, dazed. He thought he still held the gun until he saw it pointed at him. The man steadied himself against Guido's maneuvers by bracing himself against the corner of the boat's roof.

"Sorry, Foxe. I have orders. You might say this is a dead-or-alive situation. Looks like you made your choice."

Guido steered the boat straight across the canal toward the Rialto Market. He rocked the boat as the man tried to hold a steady bead on Nick. The man had his back turned and did not see what was coming. He should have.

Several small boats were tied up to slips on one side of the market. Between the market and the boats was a small canal. A water taxi could handle the canal bridge only at low tide, and then just barely. It was not low tide.

Guido's aim was perfect. The speeding water taxi entered the canal and passed under an ancient bridge. It all took a split second. The underside of the bridge scraped the top of the boat a moment before it struck the man in the back of the head. The impact's momentum lifted the man over Nick and into the water where he floated face down, unmoving.

Guido pulled back on the throttle and put it in reverse to stop the forward motion. He killed the engine and joined Nick at the rear of the boat. They looked back under the bridge where the body floated.

The police boat that entered the chase on the Grand Canal arrived. The policeman who first approached the scene recognized Guido, who began his explanation of events.

On top of the Fondaco dei Tedeschi the conversation

among strangers continued.

"What was that all about?"

"I think I saw a gun?"

"A gun? No way!"

"I think they must have been filming a movie."

The figure who stood apart from the others knew exactly what happened.

The fool. How clumsy. I trusted Bosch when he recommended this man. I'm glad I had a backup plan. Bosch better get that one right. I tried to play nice. No more.

ABOUT THE AUTHOR

In addition to *The Nicholas Foxe Adventures,* Jackson Coppley is author of the novel *Leaving Lisa.* His short stories appear in *Beach Life, The Apollo Project, Bay to Ocean,* and other publications. He writes a daily blog on his web site www.JacksonCoppley.com where the entry, *Steve Jobs and Me,* won an award by the Delaware Press Association. A graduate in physics, Coppley's resume includes a career with world communications and technology companies and the launching of what the press called "a revolutionary software program." Now a full-time writer, his work focuses on adventure.

BOOKS BY JACKSON COPPLEY

Nicholas Foxe Adventures

- The Code Hunters
- The Ocean Raiders

Leaving Lisa

Tales From Our Near Future

SHORT STORIES BY JACKSON COPPLEY

- Apollo Summer
- Funland
- Sam Shade
- The Bomber Jacket
- Three Boys and the Moving Pictures
- Women in Cities

For more information, go to www.JacksonCoppley.com

Printed in Great Britain
by Amazon

32443281R00258